Samuel Lover

He Would be a Gentleman

Treasure trove

Samuel Lover

He Would be a Gentleman
Treasure trove

ISBN/EAN: 9783337351076

Printed in Europe, USA, Canada, Australia, Japan

Cover: Foto ©Andreas Hilbeck / pixelio.de

More available books at **www.hansebooks.com**

HE WOULD BE A GENTLEMAN;

OR,

TREASURE TROVE.

A Romance.

BY

SAMUEL LOVER,

AUTHOR OF "RORY O'MORE," "HANDY ANDY," "IRISH LEGENDS
AND STORIES," ETC., ETC.

TWELFTH EDITION.

LONDON:
CHAPMAN AND HALL, 193, PICCADILLY.

TO THE READER.

———

MOST people have experienced the inconvenience in society, of not being made perfectly to understand who the person is to whom one is introduced; and as the title of "TREASURE TROVE" did not convey a distinct idea of the spirit of the following tale, it was deemed advisable to prefix another title that should: therefore, on this fresh presentation of my hero to the world, I say, "HE WOULD BE A GENTLEMAN."

SAMUEL LOVER.

HE WOULD BE A GENTLEMAN'

OR,

TREASURE TROVE.

———◆———

CHAPTER I.

MORE than a hundred years have passed since the hero of this story existed, and the wild and dangerous days of that period were more productive of romance than our tamer and safer times : we premise thus much, to account for some of the surprising adventures recorded in our story, and do not begin with our "hundred years ago," to induce the belief that our tale smacks of antiquarian profundity. By no means—we are not profound nor grand—even our HERO was of very humble origin; and, as far as the chances of his early position are concerned, had not the smallest right to be ever heard of out of the street he was born in, and certainly would have died unchronicled, but for his devouring passion for all that was genteel; in short— *He would be a gentleman.*

He was the son of one Denis Corkery, an honest, and humble, though wealthy trader, in the ancient town of Galway, and his wife, Mary, which sweet, poetic name, Denis *would* vulgarise into "Molly." This son of Denis, however, was christened Edward, in deference to his mother, who thought it more genteel than Denis. But Denis took his revenge, by never calling him anything but Ned.

Ned, however, inherited, in the female line, a desperate hankering after all that belonged to the upper ranks. Even when a child, his very name sounded unpleasantly in his ear; he would mumble over "Corkery" to himself in disgust, and wish he was called Burke, or Blake, or Fitzgerald, or Macnamara. As he grew up, he looked wistfully after every well-mounted cavalier who pranced gallantly up the street, and the full-toned rumble of some grand family coach was music to him, while the sharp rattle of a country car was a nuisance. He would run to the counter of his father's shop, and listen eagerly to the more refined accents of a lady or gentleman customer, but he showed no desire for that place of business when vulgarians were carrying on their traffic. These peculiarities of the boy (whose mother died while he was young) were unnoticed by his father, a plain pains-taking man, who, having scrambled his way upward from the lowest class, had the ambition, so general in Ireland, to see his son possess "school knowledge," the want of which he so much regretted,—and, perhaps, over-rated, as men do other things of which they are not possessed. Accordingly, he gave him all the advantages of the best school within his reach, whereby the boy profited so well, that the master soon bragged of his pupil, and the father looked forward to the cultivated mind of his son with a prospective pleasure never to be realised; for all this but stilted the boy more and more above his natural level, fed the mental disease with which he was infected,—in short, to speak antithetically, *strengthened* his *weakness*. The more Ned learned, the more he liked *gentility*; and when, having learned just enough to make him conceited, he retired finally from school, his father's friends and acquaint-ances, whom, with a profuse hospitality, the father gathered round him, were looked down upon for their ignorance and vulgarity; and the more the youth grew, the more repugnance he showed to engage in his father's trading, which could open to him no better company than the punch-drinking community amongst whom he was daily thrown. It may be questioned, how a boy should entertain a dislike to vulgar company, without ever having seen what was superior; many believing that we can only arrive at conclusions upon this subject by comparison. But the more observant may have had occasion to remark, that, in some minds, there is a natural dislike to everything coarse; and examples may be seen, even in the same family, of the wide difference often existing between children whose education has been equal, in their native adaptation to vulgar or refined habits. On a mind open to impressions, the slightest oppor-tunities will suffice to stamp the difference between vulgarity and good breeding. In his father's shop, the boy had observed the contrast between the superior orders of his father's cus-tomers, and his father's acquaintances. The stripling, further grown, on the neighbouring race-ground, was not insensible to the difference between the daughter of a farmer on her pillion, and the daughter of a squire on her side-saddle. The more refined accent of the one fell on his ear more graciously than the broad brogue of the other; and what produced a coarse laugh in the country girl awoke but the smile of the lady. Such things will always make their impressions on intelligent minds, let those who like say nay; for occasional glimpses of refinement may sometimes effect more results in a sensitive shopkeeper, than an academy of punctilio could produce upon an obtuse man of a higher grade. But, be this as it may, such an action was going forward in young Corkery's mind, however it got there, and soon began to produce unhappiness between the father and son; not that the latter ever openly expressed his feelings, but the former was shrewd enough to see, almost as soon as the other felt, this growing repugnance to the consequences of his station; and many was the accusation of "Puppy," and "Jackanapes," hurled at poor Ned by the indignant trader, who, occasionally, when moved overmuch, relieved his mind by indulging in sundry curses on the hour that "put it into his head to rear up his own child to be ashamed of the *father that bore him.*" Now this was not fair to the youth, for it was not true, and only aggravated the cause of disunion.

Did the stripling wish, in return, he had never been educated?—No. To whatever trials and troubles one may be exposed by education, however much it may render the feelings by cultivation more sensitive, and, consequently, more liable to be wounded, I believe none who ever possessed the prize would relinquish it. The utmost the young man ever ventured to retort, was the natural question—if his father could expect that education would not make some difference in him?

"To be sure, I think it should make a differ. It should make you more knowledgable; but, instead o' that, it's a fool it made o' you. And it should make you convarsible; but, instead o' that, it's the devil a word you'll say to anybody,—thinkin' no one good enough to spake to you. And it should make you more 'cute in thrade, by rayson of fractions, and algibera, and the cube root; and a betther marchant, by rayson of jogriphy, and a knowledge o' foreign parts, and the like o' that; but it's thinkin', I am, you turn up your nose at a marchant, my young masther; and its po'thry, and pagan hist'hry, and panthenions you have crammed your numskull wid, till there's no room in it for common since, at all, at all. What is it you'd like to do wid yourself, I'd like to know? I suppose you'd fancy an aisy life, and would like to be put 'prentice to a bishop—eh? Or, maybe, it's a jintleman all out, you'd like to be? Well becomes you, indeed!—owld Corkery's son a *jin'leman*, and his owld friends laughin' at him!"

If the son attempted to slip in an apologetic phrase, as "Indeed, sir!"—or, "Pon my word, father!"—he was silenced

directly with a " Whisht, whisht, I tell you!—howld your
tongue—did'nt I see you lookin' at Miss Macnamara the other
day? Bad luck to you—how dar you lift your eyes to a Macnamara—the owldest blood in the counthry? The dirt on her
shoes is too good for you, you puppy!"

"Indeed, sir——"

" Whist, I tell you!—shut your face, and give your red rag
a holiday—you're too fond o' waggin' it, so you are. The con-
sayted dhrop's in you, I tell you. What am I to do wid you?
Thrade's not good enough for you! How genteel we are, to
be sure!—your sarvant sir! I suppose you'll want *to turn
prodistint* next. You'll be of the *ginteel religion*, I go bail. I
wouldn't wonder! Faith, you'll go to the divil yit, Ned. Oh,
wirra! wirra!"

The end of these frequent bickerings was, that Ned, to
escape from his father's trade, his father's reproaches, and his
father's friends, requested permission to go a voyage with the
captain of a trading ship whom the old man chanced to know in
the course of his business. This was not quite to the taste of
either of the parties,—the father disliking it decidedly, the son
only looking forward to it as a step to something else. The
latter, by reading romantic scraps of sea voyages, got his
imagination inflamed with the charms of nautical adventure.
The former made a long calculation that a voyage in a trading
ship was at least a step towards commerce, and hoped that when
his son should be sufficiently tired of " sailoring," as he called
it, he might settle down into a mercantile man.

Under these circumstances it was agreed between the parties,
that three months should elapse before the decisive step should
be taken, after which time, if Ned found he could not settle
down to business at once, his father consented to let him try
the sea. During these three months, therefore, Ned had more
liberty and fewer reproaches than he had ever known in his
life,—the father hoping, by such indulgence on his part, to make
the shore more agreeable, and the sea less tempting; and Ned
was not slow to take advantage of this leave.

Among other amusements, Ned especially loved horse-racing;
and a forthcoming trial of strength between some of the best
horses and most dashing bloods in the country promised rare
sport, and set the pleasure-goers on the tip-toe of expectation.
At the approaching races, one match beyond all others excited
most interest, between two very celebrated horses to be ridden by their owners, both of sporting notoriety, but of very
different characters,—the one being rather conceited and stand-
off in his manners, the other familiar and frank; the former
being satisfied of his great attraction among the fair sex,—the

latter quite as anxious for, but not quite so sure of, their smiles; Mr. Daly being perfectly certain he had but to ask and have favours, while young Kirwan (or *Kierawaun*, as the admiring peasants called him) was grateful for as much as was granted. They were both handsome, only that the good looks of the latter were increased by the expression of gay good humour that played on his sportive countenance, while the *temper* of the former often militated against more than his good looks.

On the day of the race in question the neighbouring town poured forth the sport-loving portion of its inhabitants, and the peasant population were, as usual, in great force on the race ground. As the hour of trial drew near, so did the ponderous carriages-and-four of the gentry, with the gay cavalcade of the rank and *younger* beauty of the neighbourhood, whose heavy saddles, studded with silver nails and ornamented with gold fringe, marked a distinction in rank which the plainer equestrian appointments of our time do not indicate. Amongst *these* beauties was the identical Miss Macnamara, to whose pretty face Ned had been accused by his indignant father of lifting his eyes, and may-be Ned was not there in time to catch the first glimpse of the graceful Amazon as she cantered up the course towards the group of carriages and glittering cavalcade that clustered round the winning post.

But ah!—fleeting is the triumph of beauty!—even the triumph achieved over the hearts of despairing burghers. Before Miss Macnamara had arrived, a newer and more commanding *belle* had displaced her in the heart of the susceptible Ned, who stood transfixed as he gazed on the face of a young and lovely girl whose beauty attracted universal attention, as she took up her place beside a stern-looking man of middle age, whose costume of somewhat heavier cut than that of the gentry surrounding, and bronzed visage, imparted a foreign air to his appearance. A servant, mounted on a stout horse, was in attendance upon them, and many questions passed amongst the assembled throng touching "who they were;" but no one knew. Ned took up the closest position he could maintain near them, and while he feasted his eyes on the unknown beauty, little dreamt of the damage he was doing to his heart all the time.— It was that sort of entrancement which woman alone can achieve, and which tongue or pen cannot tell, and those can only know who have felt; therefore we shall say nothing about it, but leave it to the imagination or sympathy of the reader to guess or feel how Ned was suddenly enslaved.

A shout disturbed him from his trance;—it was the appearance of the racers, who paced before the assemblage of the *élite* as they passed onwards towards the starting post. The usual bustle of the moment prevailed,—the admiration of the horses, the expression of hopes for one, and doubts of another, the excitement of betting, the watchfulness of the start; and then, as the changes of the race round the plain were perceptible, the intenser interest of the brief struggle, till the last breathless moment of suspense, when the straining steeds, urged to their utmost energies, are seen coming up to the goal—the sod resounds beneath their rapid stroke—the thunder increases—the very earth trembles—they seem to fly!—they are past!!—a shout rends the sky!!!—the race is over.

Brief pleasure!—not so the pain for those who have lost their money. Such were races then—as they are now—*only they were somewhat honester.*

That race being over, the most interesting contest of the day was next in succession. The company had not long to wait;—a cheer announced the approach of Mr. Daly, who, mounted on a splendid horse and exquisitely dressed, approached the principal group of spectators. He paraded up and down for some time, manifestly pleased to exhibit himself and his horse, and a furtive glance cast into the principal carriages betrayed his desire to know how much he was admired.

While he was thus amusing himself, a thundering shout, mingled with roars of laughter, disturbed his serenity, which was soon overcast by an expression of the darkest anger as he saw the cause of the cheers and the merriment, which were provoked by the appearance of young Kirwan, cantering up towards the group of rank and beauty on a shaggy little pony without a saddle, while he himself was attired in a coarse frieze jacket, tied round his middle with a straw rope, while on his head, instead of a hunting cap, a peasant's *caubeen,* with a *gad* * for hatband, holding a *dhudeen,*† was rakishly stuck on one side. From under this hat Kirwan's sportive smiles displayed his white teeth, as he rode laughing up and down along the line of carriages, whence answering mirthful recognition was showered upon him, while his rival horseman could not conceal his rage at thus having his trim attire ridiculed as it were; he approached Kirwan, and said with as much calmness as he could command,

"Do you mean this for a joke or an affront, Mr. Kirwan?"

"A joke, to be sure."

"It is a very bad one, then, sir."

"Sure an affront would be worse?"

"It *may be so,*" said the other, putting spurs to his horse, intending to gallop to the starting post; but the horse, an ill-tempered animal, instead of obeying this summons as it was

* A peeled osier twisted.   † Stump of a pipe.

meant, plunged violently and engaged in an angry struggle with his rider, who finally conquered, however, and rode him to the post.

This was all Kirwan wanted ;—he knew the horse and rider were both ill-tempered, and his grotesque dress was assumed for the purpose of provoking the fury of the animal through the vanity of his master, and thus, with a horse of inferior power, but gentler nature, securing the winning of the race. After making a few jokes with the ladies, who were yet enjoying his absurd costume, he cantered his pony after his angry rival, and, on arriving at the starting post, alighted, and sprang into the saddle of the racer, which was there held in waiting for him. After some false starts, arising from the sulky horse of Mr. Daly, "Whip, spur, and away !" were successfully answered to, and off went the competitors. But the tussle between Daly and his steed were fatal to his hopes.—If there be a time when horse and man should, as the Mexicans imagined, be one animal, it is in the race ; if they go not together, they go not at all.—For a time the race was contested, but the temper of Daly's horse, once roused, was irretrievable, and the brute, bolting at the last turn, Kirwan won in a canter.

The shouts of *Kierawaun ! Kierawaun !!* were deafening, and Daly made the best of his way to the stables.

Immediately after this race, while Ned was bestowing his attention on the fair unknown, the gentleman with whom she rode addressed some words to her, and afterwards to their attendant, and she at once cantered off the course, followed by the servant, while he of the bronzed visage followed, in an opposite direction, in the wake of the crowd, which, as soon as the heat was over, rapidly cleared the course, and hurried to an adjoining field, where cock-fighting occupied the intervals between the races. The cock-pit was very simple in its construction—no regularly levelled platform for the combatants, nor inclined planes of seats for the spectators. The fairest portion of a pasture ground was taken for the field of battle—a circle, marked by fresh-cut twigs stuck in the earth, around which gentle and simple crowded and got a sight of the sport as best they might,—the gentle mostly mounted, it is true, who thus overtopped their neighbouring pedestrians ; but often, as a late arrival on horseback placed the new comer beyond the point of view, he would dismount, and leaving his horse to the care of some *gilly*, push amongst the mass of the peasants, who made ready way as his presence declared him to be of the upper class, while, if "the handlers" within the ring caught sight of such a personage, they urged the populace to give place by strong

representations of their unworthiness to see the sport before
their betters.

"Back out o' that, Dimpsy, I tell you!—Is it stoppin' his
honour o'Menlough you'd be?"

Dimpsy made himself as small as possible, and the Blake
came forward.

"Cock you up, Shaughnessy, and is it you 'ud see the cock-
fight afore the quality?—Make way for his honour, Misther
Lynch."

Shaughnessy squeezed back, and Mr. Lynch pressed forward,
while another handsomely dressed candidate for the front row
followed in his wake.

The handlers shouted, "Way for his honour the honourable
Misther Daly—hurra! for Dunsandle!—way I bid ye!"

While such exclamations were ringing on every side, and the
crowd swaying too and fro, Ned had obtained a foremost place
amidst the bystanders around the ring, and observed, conspicuous amongst the horsemen, him of the foreign aspect.

His attention, however, was more forcibly arrested by the
presence of a blind man, who struggled hard to keep a foremost
place in the ring, and whose endeavours for such accommodation every one of the peasantry seemed willing to aid, while
kindly expressions towards his pitiable state were mingled with
merry allusions to the utter uselessness of one deprived of sight
occupying a front rank to *see* the sport. But at the same time
that this mingled pity and merriment went forward, there seemed
to exist a degree of respect towards the man, quite at variance
with pity or jesting, and difficult to account for, but for the
leathern pouch at his side, whence some ivory-tipped tubes of
box-wood protruded, and showed cause for the affectionate
attention of the peasants.—He was a piper; and who, in the
Land of Song, would not stand well with the minstrel?—one,
ever prized in Ireland, through the most endearing associations,
either as the traditional transmitter of ancient bardic effusions at
the wake, the mirthful stimulator of nimble feet at the fair, the
contributor to love or fun in musical plaint or planxty; or, perchance, the exciter of sensations darker and more secret, by the
outpouring of some significant strain which had hidden meaning in its phrases, and bore hope and triumph in its wild ca-
dence.

All the influence arising from such causes *Phaidrig-na-pib**
held pre-eminently; and "Stand fast, Phaidrig," and "I'm with
you, Phaidrig," and "Hold by me, Phaidrig," were amongst the
ejaculations which greeted the piper, as offers of assistance were

* Patrick of the Pipes.

made to him on all sides. The "dark"* man was pitied, though the blind witness of cockfighting might make food for mirth. But though he could not see, he took deep interest in the savage sport, and would bet on the fate of the battles, inquiring only who was the owner of the birds, and what their colours; on knowing these, his knowledge of the various breeds of the cocks would decide him in backing the combatants, and mostly he was right in his selections.

The ring was now crowded to suffocation, and a movement between the handlers promised a commencement of the encounter, when a fresh commotion in the crowd indicated another struggler from the rear to the front. He was caught sight of by the officials within the ring, and "Room" was called for his honour Misther Bodkin; but the serried mass seemed too compact to admit of another being. "Arrah, boys, is it keeping out Misther Bodkin you'd be?"

"Faix, and if he was a needle instead of a bodkin, 'twould be hard for him to get in here," said Phaidrig.

"Sure, he's like a needle in one respect, any how," returned the handler—"he has an eye in him; and as you have not, you might give him your place, and stand behind."

"Sure, if I'm blind, that's a rayson I should have a front place," says Phaidrig, "as a man with eyes has a better chance of seeing."

The crowd paid the good natured tribute of a laugh to Phaidrig's pleasantry upon his own misfortune, and the handler sought another person to displace for his honour Misther Bodkin, who at length got into the front, and the battle began.

The usual hasty offers and acceptances of wagers on the contending birds rang in rapid succession among the mounted gentlemen in the crowd, and those who held the front standing-places in the circle. It was the first time Ned had ever seen a cockfight, and his attention was distracted for a time between the fierce conflict of the birds and the sounds of triumph or dismay which followed the blows or the falls of either, and the bets which were offered or doubled in consequence; but all these gave place at last to observation of the blind man, whose excitement surpassed that of all others as the fight proceeded, and who appeared by his exclamations to know, as well as those who could see, the vicissitudes of the battle; his sense of hearing seemed to give him the power of distinguishing between the strokes of the combatants, as an occasional exclamation of "Well done, red cock!" sufficiently proved; and the crow of each bird seemed as familiar to his ear as the voice of an acquaintance.

* A phrase applied to the blind.

The fignt between the first pair of cocks was over, and a fresh pair produced : as they were brought into the ring, one of them challenged, and on hearing his bold clarion-like defiance, Phaidrig's countenance brightened, as he exclaimed, "That's the cock for winning—I know his shout—'tis the Sarsfield breed."

"That is not the name I give the breed." said a handsome cavalier. of noble appearance, who was mounted on a splendid horse.

"But that *is* the breed, my lord," said Phaidrig, nowise daunted by the voice of the nobleman; "sure I know it, egg and bird, for long ago—and what better name could a bowld breed have ?"

Phaidrig's answer was relished by the crowd, who evinced their pleasure by a low, chuckling murmur, over which the voice of the nobleman was heard rather reprovingly to the piper, telling him "his chanter* was too loud."

"Sure the noble Clanrickarde should be the last to turn a deaf ear to the name," retorted Phaidrig, "when one of the fair daughters of De Burgo was wife to the bold Sarsfield."

"Put down the cocks," said Lord Clanrickarde, anxious to terminate the parley.

As the birds were set opposite to each other, the strange cavalier exclaimed, "Five guineas on the black bird."

As the Pretender was known to be often designated in Ireland under the *sobriquet* of the "black bird," every eye was turned towards the stranger as he uttered the words, and angry glances, as well as those of admiration, were bent on him,—the angry ones openly, from the consciousness that those who gave them were backed by authority,—the others, timidly and furtively, as indicating an unlawful desire.

A stern horseman beside the stranger, in answer to his offered bet, said, " The black *cock* you mean."

"The black bird !" returned the stranger.

"The cock !" repeated his neighbour.

"A cock is a bird, sir, I believe," the stranger returned, coldly, and then repeated his bet, "Five guineas on the black bird !"

"Done !" said his stern neighbour, more influenced by the spirit of political opposition than cockfighting.

This altercation had so far operated on the handlers, that they paused in their duties, and the battle did not begin until the word "Done" had been uttered; then the birds were let loose, and rushed eagerly on each other.

* The principal pipe of the set.

An interest was imparted to the contest, beyond that of the mere sport, from the words by which it was preluded; and the spectators saw in the two cocks the champions, as it were, of two parties; and hopes and fears, almost superstitious, were attached to each stroke of the combatants, whose blows were exchanged fiercely and rapidly, for both the birds were high game. At last the black received a double stroke of his adversary's spurs, which brought him to the ground, and a cheer of triumph rose from the surrounding gentry, as the handlers rushed forward to disengage the birds.

"Two to one on the red!" cried several gentlemen, and another cheer arose on their part, while a breathless silence reigned amid the crowd of peasants, foremost amongst whom Phaidrig-na-pib bent his head over the ring in the act of eager listening.

"'Twas only a body blow, you say," muttered Phaidrig to a neighbour.

"Yes," whispered the other.

"Then, no matter," said the piper; "he'll bide his time and hit his match in the head. I know the breed well—they always strike for the head."

The birds were again set in opposition. The black went in boldly, and made a vigorous dash at his enemy.

"Well done! he's strong yet!" muttered Phaidrig.

A bold bout now ensued between the birds; their wings flapped fiercely against each other, and some ugly blows were exchanged, but it was evident that the double stroke the black had received was telling against him; he bled profusely, and exhibited symptoms of weakness, yet still his courage failed not, and he continued to exchange blows, until another heavy stroke from the red brought him down, and a fresh shout of triumph rose from the gentlemen.

"Behold the fate of your 'black bird' now, sir!" said he of the stern visage to the stranger.

"A battle is not lost till it is won, sir!" was the answer.

A dead silence ensued, during which the handlers were counting time, for the victorious red cock, having disengaged himself, was left to tread the field in triumph, while his sable adversary lay drooping on the ground, which was stained with his life-blood.

For a few seconds, the red eyed his stricken foe, and stood as if on guard, in expectation of a fresh attack; but when he saw his head gradually droop, he seemed at once to understand that so bold an adversary must be beaten, or he would return to the assault, and with an air of conquest he stepped proudly towards him, and standing right over him, flapped his wings, and raising his head to its proudest height, he crowed his triumph over his fallen foe.

The sound acted like magic on the dying bird. The trumpet of victory could not more have stirred the heart of a vanquished hero. It was manifest the cock could not have struck another blow, if his enemy had not crowed over him; but the insult roused him at his last gasp, and the defenceless position of his foe placed him within the reach of vengeance. And vengeance was the work of an instant; he made one convulsive spring from the ground, and his spurs clashed together through the brain of his exulting adversary, who dropped dead under the expiring victor. A wild shout rose from the peasantry, and vexation was depicted in the countenances of the gentry.

"Is he dead?" asked the owner of the red cock.

"As a stone, your honour," answered the handler.

"And there goes the black now;" said the other handler, as the gallant bird stretched himself in death. "'Tis a pity such a bit of game should ever die!"

"Give him into my hands here, for one minute," cried Phaidrig-na-pib; whose request was granted by the handler.

Phaidrig pressed the bird to his heart, and in his native language vented a wild out-pouring of eloquent lament for the "*black bird*," in which many an allusion of an exciting character was caught up by the populace; and Lord Clanrickarde, not approving of the temper they exhibited, very judiciously put an end to the cock-fight, by saying it was time to run the last heat of the race.

He gave example to the gentry by his own act of galloping at once to the winning post, and was followed by a crowd of horsemen, most of whom cursed the unlucky chance of the fight. The peasantry drew off in another direction, in the train of Phaidrig-na-pib, who, "yoking" his pipes, poured forth the spirit-stirring strain of "*The Blackbird*," and the shrill chanter, as it rang across the plain, to such admirable music, but questionable loyalty, was—

"Unpleasing most to noble ears."

CHAPTER II.

AFTER this day of excitement, the night brought, with its darkness, silence, also, over the town of Galway; and, to judge from the quiet within its narrow streets, out of doors, one might think it brought peace likewise; but it was not so. Could the interior of many of its ancient domiciles be seen, the excitement of more than wine would have been apparent, and the turn the cock-fight assumed brought from its lurking-place many a feeling laid by, as the possessor thought, for ever. But such feelings, like our great grandmother's state suits, were too often laid by, only to be brought out on favourite occasions, and sometimes, more unfortunately, were left as heirlooms. And though it is long since we have laughed at this custom of our grandmothers, the other we have likened to it has, unfortunately, long survived it, and is only now left off because, thank Heaven, it is worn out. Party will lose its pattern as well as silk, and time crush the stiffness of creeds as well as brocades; hoops and wigs will flatten and lose their beauty in spite of buckram and powder, and other high things, as well as high-heeled shoes, be content to come down to a reasonable level.

But, to return to Galway; many a dinner and an after-bout of drinking the town saw that day, comprising the proudest names and the humblest. A sporting occasion, such as the one just mentioned, is sure to spread the board, even in our degenerate times, which are as nothing, if we may believe chronicles, to those of our fathers, when the "pottle-deep" potations were in vogue, and a more indiscriminate hospitality exercised. It will not be wondered at, therefore, that at a later hour of the night, many a hot-headed blade had to traverse the dark town, more ready to give than to take an affront, and the better-humoured ready, at least, for "sport," which, after dinner, in all times, meant giving somebody else annoyance, and bears the same definition to this day.

Ned Corkery was one of the out-of-door people, who was returning, after a dinner, to the parent roof, where he expected a reprimand for staying out so late, when his attention was attracted by a lantern borne by a gentleman, on whose arm a lady leaned; and, as Ned passed, the light of the lantern, flashing on her face, discovered the features of the beautiful girl who had so smitten him on the race-course. He paused as they passed; they were followed by a blind man and his dog, and Phaidrig-na-pib was easily recognised. Ned followed the light of the lantern with longing eyes, knowing it showed the fairy foot of the sweet girl where to pick her steps; and when a projecting abutment of one of the ponderous old edifices with which the town abounds to this day screened the lantern's gleam, he could not resist following. A thought of his father's additional anger for every additional minute came over him; but the desire to know where that matchless girl lodged was a superior consideration, and he pursued the *magic* lantern—to him a magic lantern indeed! for, strange and wild were the shapes which, through its agency, his future life assumed.

He had not followed far, when the party stopped, in consequence of a servant saying he had dropped some money, and begging of the gentleman to lend him his lantern to search for it. The request was granted, and, after a few seconds, the man joyfully exclaimed he had found the money, and, laying the lantern at the gentleman's feet, ran off. He, who had conferred the obligation, remarked, that he thought the man might have been civil enough to hand him the lantern he had lent: but how much greater was his surprise, when, as he stooped to take it, the lantern was pulled suddenly upwards, till it swung from a projecting beam above; and a loud laugh from a distant part of the street showed it was a practical joke which had been played off upon the unsuspecting stranger, the servant of this "sportive" party only having feigned the loss of the money, and, while he affected to look for it, tying to the ring of the lantern a string, which was pulled by the remote jokers! The gentleman was very indignant, and shouted loudly some opprobrious names, meant for the persons who had treated him so scurvily; and, at the same moment, Ned advanced, requesting him to be calm, as he would recover the light for him. The stranger thought this might be some fresh jest, and intimated as much; but Ned assured him that he would scorn conduct so "ungentlemanly," and requested immediately that Phaidrig would stand beside the heavy porch of an old doorway, and enable him thereby to clamber upwards. The suggestion was obeyed; the youth sprang upon the shoulders of the stout piper, laid hold of the projecting entablature of the ponderous masonry, and twining his legs round one of the pillars which supported it, thus climbed his way to the top of the pediment, whence he was enabled to reach the beam where the lantern swung. As he was about to lay hands on it, the string which the distant party held was relaxed, the lantern lowered, and Ned near tumbling. A fresh laugh was raised, and another curse uttered by the impatient gentleman; but when Phaidrig was told what had occurred, he called his dog, and placing him on his shoulders, and, stooping, that the animal might gain a spring from his back, cried, "Seize it, *Turlough*."* The dog obeyed the command, sprang at the lantern, and, laying hold with tooth and limb, clung to it; but the string was sufficiently powerful to haul up both dog and light to the beam, which fresh trick was accomplished; but Ned was enabled to catch the rope, and, seizing the dog, drew him, and with him the lantern, to the platform on which he stood, and, spite of the

* Anglicè, "Thunderer."

tugging of the party, who still bellowed forth their laughter held fast, till he was enabled to cut the cord, and regain the light. This he lowered to his friends beneath, and began to descend himself, when he heard the rush of the defeated jesters coming forward to make good the capture of the lantern by downright assault. He hastened his descent, therefore, and sprang to the ground, just as he heard a voice from the assaulting party exclaim, as the light flashed on the face of the stranger, "Tis he, by Heaven!—down with the traitor!"

"Misther Daly I know your voice," cried Phaidrig-na-pib, "take care what you're about!"

"Ha! you rebel rascal!" cried another voice, "you there too?"

"That's Misther Burke," said Phaidrig; "you'd better not brake the pace, gintlemin, or see what the mayor will be saying to you to-morrow morning!"

There was a momentary parley among the bloods; but an angry voice (it was Daly's) was heard above them all, saying, "By Heaven, I'll take him on my own responsibility!"

At the same moment, his sword flashed in the lamp-light, and the stranger, knowing the disadvantage in a fight a light is to him who holds it, extinguished it promptly, and drew his sword. His daughter clung to him.

"Nell, release me," he said, in a low voice, as he freed himself from the obedient girl, who now eagerly seized the arm of any other protector, and that arm was Ned's. He felt the might of giants, and the courage of heroes, at the touch.

"Seize him!" again shouted the enraged Daly.

"Beware, sir," returned the calm but determined voice of the stranger, who stood on his defence. It was only in time, for his blade encountered that of his assailant. The clashing of the swords was the signal for a general fight. That between Daly and the stranger was brief, for the latter was an able swordsman, and, in the dark, had the advantage, as being superior in *feeling* his adversary's blade. A few passes convinced Daly he had enough to do, and a few more made him quite sure the surgeon would have something to do next, for he received a severe thrust in the sword arm. His friends, on finding he was wounded, became savage, and rushed on more fiercely, but they were held at bay; for the blind man's keen sense of hearing enabled him to strike with his heavy stick with wondrous precision; and, as soon as the dog heard his voice engaged in the fray, the snappish whining which he had uttered on the top of the portico in his desire to get down, was changed for a fierce yell, and springing into the midst of the combatants, he gave the first on whom he alighted an unpleasant memento of the night's amusement. Then,

cheered by the voice of his master, he bit at their legs, and gave
such terrible annoyance, that the odds were lessened against the
little party which yet held the portico; but still numbers were
against them. Fortunately, however, they were enabled, from
their position, to keep a close front, the portico in the rear forming a defence for the lady, and leaving her protectors at ease
upon her account, certain she could receive no injury amid the
storm of blows which were falling thick and fast. Ned had
wrested a sword from the first assailant who had fallen foul of
him, and though his position in life debarred him from wearing
one, he nevertheless knew its use, his genteel propensities having
urged him to learn fencing from an old sergeant, who had seen
service in the Netherlands. Ned poked away fearlessly, and
pricked one of the party pretty smartly, so that the bloods, finding
themselves so stoutly resisted, and two of their set wounded,
were fain to beat a retreat, venting curses, and threatening vengeance. It may be imagined there was no desire to follow them;
the moment the road was free, the little party who held the portico hurried down the street in an opposite direction, when, to
their dismay, two men, bearing lanterns, led by a gentleman who
seemed hurrying to the scene of action, appeared coming round
an adjacent corner, the leader exclaiming—

"Peace in the king's name! keep the peace."

"By Jakers, that's the mayor!" said Phaidrig.

"Then strike out the lights, and let us force our way past
them," cried the stranger, with more of anxiety in his manner
than he had yet exhibited. "You take the right hand one,"
said he to Ned—"I'll manage the other."

With this determination they advanced, and the demand of
the mayor to "stand in the king's name," was answered by each
lantern-bearer being attacked. He who fell to the stranger's
share was overpowered instantly, and the heel of his heavy boot
went crash through the lantern; the other was yet tussling with
Ned, when the stranger turned to his assistance, but, in engaging
in this service, he himself was collared by the mayor; whereupon Ned, who had got disengaged, bestowed such a hearty
blow under the worthy mayor's ear, that the portly dignitary
measured his length beside the first lantern-bearer, over whom
he tumbled, as the other was in the act of rising; this left the
third quite helpless, and after laying him sprawling, and
extinguishing the light, the adventurous little party ran for it.
the blind man leading at a smart trot, his dog keeping close to
him, a little way in advance.

"Take care of yourself, Phaidrig," said the stranger, as he
hurried after with his daughter, beside whom Ned kept up his
guard at the other side.

"Never fear me," answered the piper; "with the help o' Turlough, I could thread the darkest lane in the town without spoiling my beauty—mind, a sharp turn to the left here—that's it," and they dived down a narrow alley, as he spoke. "It's no light we want as far as finding the way goes, only the young misthress will slop her purty little feet; but dirt rubs out aisier than the grip of the mayor's bailiffs——Whisht!"—and he paused a moment—"by the powers, they are afther us, hue and cry—hurry! hurry!" He quickened his pace, and after one or two more windings, which were executed in silence, the dog stopped before an entrance, aud began scraping at the door fiercely.

"Knock, Phaidrig,'" said the stranger.

"No, your honour—no—the knock might be heard by our pursuers, and the scratching can't—but will give *them within* notice."

The result proved Phaidrig right; a step was heard stirring inside the house, and soon after the drawing of a bolt and an open door admitted the fugitives to a timely sanctuary, for the shout of pursuit was heard at the entrance of the "close," and the portal was barely shut and barred, when the heavy tramp of men was heard rushing past, the hunters little suspecting that the thickness of a plank only was between them and the prey they sought.

The party within made no move till the tramp of the pursuers died away in the distance, then Phaidrig, with a low chuckle, spoke. "Close work," said he, "as the undher millstone said to the upper, when there was no corn."

"'Twould have been grinding work, sure enough, had we been taken," said the stranger.—"You tremble, Nell," said he in a gentler tone to the girl.

She only answered by a long-drawn breath.

"All safe now, my lady," said Phaidrig; "put your little hand on my arm, and I'll lead you—for we must have no light."

She obeyed his summons, and was led by the blind man into an apartment, where the low embers of a fire gave a faint glimmer, and where the sound of rushing waters was heard.

The rest of the party followed.

"Could you get the boat ready soon?" said Phaidrig.

He who had opened the door answered in the affirmative.

"Then we had better cross the river, your honour," said the piper; "for it might come into their heads, them haythens of bailiffs, to go searching the neighbourhood, and once we are over the wather into the Cladagh, we are safe, for it's more nor a mile round by the bridge, and they could never catch us, even if they got the scent.—Bad luck to the mayor, though he's a worthy man!

2

why did he come out at all? it was no harm pinking the bloods, for that's as common as bad luck, but knockin' down the mayer will make a stir, I tell you, in Galway, where they are so proud o' their privileges—there is no standin' the consait of the mayors of Galway, ever since Walther Lynch hanged his son. Get ready the boat, Mike."

The stranger now addressed Ned in terms of thankfulness for his first polite assistance, and for his gallant bearing in the riot, and concluded by expressing his regret that he should have been involved in such a serious brawl, with hopes it would be of no material injury to him.

"Faix, he's in throuble, I tell you," said Phaidrig. "Sure it was himself that gave the mayor the *polthoge* that upset him—faix, my young masther, you have a delicate taste, considering your youth and inexperience, that nothing less than a mayor would sarve you."

"'Twas in *my* defence," said the stranger; "and I regret, young sir," said he to Ned, "that my circumstances are not such as to offer you protection adequate to the risk you have encountered for my sake."

Ned made a flourishing speech here, declaring he never was so happy in his life—that to render service to a gentleman—and—a lady—and Ned stammered as he dared to allude to the lovely cause of his dilemma.

"Indeed, sir, I thank you," said the girl, in a sweet voice.

Ned felt more than rewarded, even if he fell into the power of the offended magistrate.

Phaidrig here quitted the chamber, to "hurry Mike with the boat," as he said; but as he left the room, another person entered, and approached the stranger and his daughter, with whom he conversed in an under tone; and even the glimmering light cast by the fire, enabled Edward to see that his bearing towards both indicated the most intimate familiarity between the parties. In a few minutes the father was silent, and the conversation was continued in low whispers between the lady and the young cavalier, while the father, as if lost in thought, threw himself into an old chair that stood before the fire-place, and as if unconsciously, began to stir the dying embers with the toe of his heavy riding boot. A bright flame flickered from the smouldering heap, and revealed to Edward the person of young Kirwan, whose attitude was expressive of the most devoted attention, as he still continued to converse, in whispers, with the attentive girl.

Edward felt anything but comfortable, as he witnessed the courtly address of the handsome Kirwan to the lady. The folly of such a feeling was apparent to himself, yet still he could not conquer it; the influence that had been cast over him by his admiration of the morning, and the adventure of the night, seemed to himself as extraordinary as it was unreasonable. Why should he be angry that the gay and gallant Kirwan should pay his court to a lady of his own rank, immeasurably above a trader's son, and to whom *he* might not address a phrase beyond that of the humblest courtesy? His heart could only answer with a sigh! This being, whom he had seen but twelve hours since, with whom he had not exchanged twelve words, and to whom he dared not aspire, nevertheless had filled his heart with passion; the pang of hopeless love was there, aggravated by the seeming favour in which another was held, and poor Ned became the prey of a jealousy as intense as it was absurd.

With a painful watchfulness he marked how closely they talked together, while Kirwan held the lady's hand all the time. He would gladly, at that moment, have engaged the favoured cavalier at the sword's point!

Phaidrig now returned, and announced the boat "ready." Ellen's father rose, and taking Kirwan by the hand, said, "Here we part for the present. You shall know where to find me— farewell!"

"Farewell!" returned the other, with an energy of manner, and hearty shaking of hands, denoting between the parties deep interest, and warm fellowship.

"Allow me," said the stranger, "to recommend to your care this youth, whose brave assistance makes me so much his debtor, and places him in some jeopardy for the present. You, I am sure, will give him shelter."

"Willingly," said Kirwan.

Ned recoiled from the thought of accepting safety a. such hands, and replied that he did not fear returning at once to his own home.

"*Baidershin!*" said Phaidrig, "how bowld we are!" Then, addressing the stranger, he added, "If your honour will be advised by me, you will take him over the river with you, for, 'pon my conscience, the sweet town of Galway is no place for my young masther to-night."

"Be it so," said the stranger; "and now for the boat." Kirwan offered his arm with courtly grace to Ellen, but her father drew her arm within his own, and said, "A truce to compliments now. You shall hand her to her carriage, when we see you at ———"

Ned could not catch the name of the place the stranger said. Ellen and her father hurried from the chamber, and Phaidrig, taking Ned by the arm, the party proceeded in silence and darkness along a passage, through which a current of cold air

was felt, and the roar of a rushing torrent heard ; a small door
was reached, which opened directly over the rapids that hurry
the foaming waters of Lough Corrib to the sea, below the ancient
bridge. The sheet of white foam was visible in the darkness,
and made the boat, some feet below the door, perceptible, as it
plunged on the eddying current.

"Let the heaviest go first," said Phaidrig ; "'twill steady the
boat." The stranger going on his knees, and laying hold of the
threshold of the door with his hands, let himself down till his
feet touched the gunwale of the boat, where, taking his seat, he
called out to the piper to take care of his daughter.

"Now, my lady, steady—don't be afeard," said the piper,—
"don't be angry with my rough fist for taking a sharp grip o'
you ; give your other hand to the young gentleman at the other
side."

Ellen silently obeyed the instruction, and a thrill of pleasure
shot through Ned's heart as he held firmly the delicate hand of
the girl, in assisting to lower her to the boat, where her father
received her and placed her in safety beside him.

"Now, young master, in with you," said Phaidrig.

"Had not you better go first?" said Ned ; "I may assist you
from above."

"My own grip is worth all the assistance in the world," said
Phaidrig,—"obliged to you all the same. I go bail I'll not leave
go of the threshold till I feel a good howlt with my foot in the
boat."

Edward lost no time in obeying, and the piper followed
in safety.—"Off with you now, Mike!" said he.

The boat swept down the current as he spoke.

"Where's the dog!" cried Ellen, anxiously.

A splash in the water followed her words.

"There he goes," said Phaidrig ; "his own bowld heart and
strong paws would put him over a wilder stream than this ; the
dog who can't swim is only fit for drowning."

The boat now plunged over the boiling waves of the rapid,
and Ellen instinctively held her father with a close embrace as
they hurried through the hissing foam, which soon, however,
became less and less as they swept onward, the waters gradually
darkening as they deepened, streaked only here and there with
long lines of surge, and the heavy gurgling of a strong current
succeeding the roar which had appalled the ear of Ellen.

They were soon enabled to pull the boat shoreward from out
of the current ; and, as they touched the strand, Turlough was
waiting, ready to receive the party, snorting, and shaking the
waters of Corrib from his brave sides ; a few minutes more
placed them all under the shelter of a fisherman's cottage, and,

while horses were being prepared for the stranger and his daughter, the former repeated his thanks to Ned, shaking him heartily by the hand, and commending him to the care of the fisherman. The latter promised safe keeping of him for the present, and undertook to communicate with Ned's friends in the town, on the morrow, swearing, "by the hand of his gossip," that he would have good care of the youth, for "*his honour's sake.*"

The nags were soon ready, and Ellen was lifted to her saddle by her father; but, before parting, the gentle girl presented her hand to Edward, and expressed a fervent hope he might incur no injury from his generous conduct.

Edward stammered an unintelligible reply, and ventured to press the little hand. The next instant the horses were in motion; the rapid clatter of their feet up the stony path died away in the distance, and Ned, with a sinking heart, retired to the fisher's hut. Burning with curiosity to know who these gentlefolks might be, he thought the fisherman would inform him, and asked a question with that view; but the fisherman, returning him a glance that had in it much of displeasure, replied :—" They did not tell me who they were, sir, and *I* asked no questions." Ned felt the reproof keenly ;—it seemed there was some mystery about the stranger, and then, for the first time, Ned began to consider in what an awkward adventure he had become involved.

CHAPTER III.

THE next morning the fisherman, at Edward's request, went into the town to communicate with worthy Mister Corkery, who already had heard an exaggerated account of his son's adventure, so that the real truth, though bad enough, lifted a weight of horrors from his civic heart, which had sunk to the lowest depths of despair at the thought of the city's peace being broken by a boy of his, and the daring hand of Corkery lifted against the mayor, and *that* the mayor of Galway. When he found, however, that Ned had not murdered six men, as was reported, and only *tripped up* the mayor, (though that was dreadful), he was more comfortable, but desired Ned to lie quiet, and he would write to him in the evening. All that day the trader worked hard at a letter, which was a mighty task to him, and at night the fisherman returned, and bore to Ned his father's epistle :—

"Deer Ned,

"Mi hart is Sore, and the mare's hed kut, and His Wig will nevr doo a Dais gud, the Barbr tells me, fur sartin—his blew and gool kote all gutthur. O Ned, to tutch a mare is a foalish bizniz,—i no foalish aut to bee spelt with a YEW, but I kan't make a YEW to know it from an EN. Yew must get out off this kounthry for sum tim—praps the sailorin bizniz is the best now til The storee is past and gone, and when yr. unfortnate tale is not tuk up by the foals, but let too dhrop, wh. is the prair of yr. offended but afekshint father,

"Denis Corkery.

"i send 5 ginnys by the barer, for the rod to Dublin, wher McGuffins ship iz—ax for the industhery, thatz hur nam—you will see hur on the blind K.

"lite gool duz for the rod, so the ginny's is lite.

"mi hart is hevvy, Ned.

"i wood go see yew ned, but Am afeerd they wd. watch and trak me, for ye. mares i iz on mee.

"Beewer ov bad Kumpiny.   "Yours, D. C."

Ned, in obedience to orders, prepared to start for Dublin; he wrote an obedient and repentant letter to his father, hoping forgiveness, and promising good behaviour for the future. In the dead of the night, when the slumbering majesty of Galway's civic dignity rendered it most convenient to make a start, Ned set out for the metroplis, and, before dawn, had put several miles between himself and danger. Dublin was reached in safety, and as swiftly as Ned could accomplish it; and on the Blind Quay, sure enough, he found the good brig, Industry, and the exemplary Captain McGuffin, who was to sail with the next tide for London.

Before Ned was over the bar, it was all over with him. Sea-sickness contributes much to feelings of repentance, and Ned began to entertain flattering notions of the susceptibility of his conscience, which his stomach was more entitled to; he wished for nothing so much as death, and hoped the Land's End would have made an end of him; but he survived the Channel, and, after doubling the North Foreland, found his appetite again. On passing the Nore, he was as fresh as a lark, and while tacking up the Thames nearly created a famine on board. After this, Ned liked the sea well enough; in short, it suited him perfectly.

In some respects, he felt that, under certain circumstances, he could love it; but the captain of the trader was a sober, steady man; and the monotonous life on board of a merchant-vessel, whose voyages were confined to the British waters, had not enough of excitement and interest for a spirit like his. Nevertheless, he served nearly eighteen months in this way, patiently looking forward, however, to better times some day, on board of a nobler craft, whose wings might be spread for longer flights. During all this time, many a fond thought reverted to the fair girl of the race-course, whose image was as fresh in his memory as though he had seen her yesterday. But, notwithstanding this youthful love-sickness, he employed himself diligently to become as good a sailor as circumstances could make him, and, for a mere coasting mariner, was a very smart fellow. Ever, on his return from sea to Dublin, which was the port whence the vessel traded, Ned found a letter from his father waiting for him, in which lamentations for his " foolish bit of consait " in the streets of Galway continued to be made, with recommendations to keep away for some time yet, as it was not " forgotten to him." Sobriety, industry, and frugality, were recommended, with this assurance, that

> " Early to bed, and early to rise,
> Make a man healthy, wealthy, and wise; "

and, furthermore, this solemn fact was put forward, that—

> " A pin a day, is a groat a year."

On the receipt of such letters, Ned generally muttered, that he wished his father would send him a little less advice, and a little more money.

But, in uttering this wish, Ned was unreasonable. The old man, though frugal, was not parsimonious; and allowed his son quite enough to enable him to enjoy himself reasonably on shore, when the duties of his ship did not demand his presence on board; for it was no part of his intention that Ned should be screwed down to *all* the hardships of a sailor's life, though he did not wish to make that life too fascinating to a young fellow of naturally an erratic turn. He remembered that Ned, when in port at Dublin, must see some friends there, and it would never do for a respectable citizen of Galway to let his son appear in the " slops " of a captain's mate. No, no; Ned was well supplied with the means of casting his marine attire, and assuming a landsman's garb befitting his station ashore; and, from his innate tendency towards gentility, his clothes were rather of a smarter cut than he had quite a right to indulge in, and certainly far finer than he would have dared to assume in Galway, where his father's eyes, to say nothing of neighbours', were as good as sumptuary laws. Considering the old man rather objected to the pursuit of the maritime profession for his son, it may be wondered at he did not make him feel as much privation as possible, in the hope of inducing a distaste for it; but, on the other hand, when it is remembered that an only son was forced to seek shelter on board ship, to save himself from the consequences of a mischance; that he was forced to fly his native town, and that without even the paternal embrace, who can blame a father for having yearnings of compassion for his absent boy, and seeking to make his exile as bearable as it might be?

Truth, however, compels us to say that Ned thought much more of the beauty of the race-course than of his father; and the decking of his person in something of a superior costume, was insensibly influenced by the desire to see himself look as well as possible for her sake, though, in all human probability, he should never see her again. But this is no reason why an ardent imagination is not to think of an object by which it has been excited; and, in truth, there was seldom a day in which Ned's heart did not wander to the recollection of the day he first saw her—that eventful day which brought love in the morning, pleasure at sundown, and jealousy before midnight.

He was not mad enough to suppose, in his wildest moments of dreaming, that the events of that day could ever " come to anything;" but still the recollection of them clung about his heart, and though he dared not hope, he could not forget.

How many a night, on his cold and dreary watch, did the memory of the parting pressure of the fair girl's hand return upon him! At such moments he would pace the deck, and, looking upwards at the stars, inwardly exclaim, "Oh, that I could see her once again!—Yet why indulge in these foolish yearnings?—As well might one of those stars be mine, as that lovely being!"

Perchance a shooting star darted across the heavens as he spoke, and as its brightness vanished, Ned, indulging the superstitious fancy of his country, would curse his stupidity for not wishing for her while the star was falling.*

At length it chanced his ship was ordered to Hamburgh, and Ned was delighted at the thoughts of making a foreign port, which, in good time, was achieved; and, after discharging cargo, he lost no opportunity, while lying in port, to see all he could of this far-famed city. The remarkable and picturesque costumes of the surrounding neighbourhood—the grotesque old houses which towered over its canals, which, like so many veins

---

* The superstitious say, that if you express a wish before a shooting star vanishes, it will be realised.

of wealth, carried commerce into the heart of the town—its ancient churches, its dancing-halls and theatre;—all these, and more, filled Ned with wonder, and fed that greedy desire which youth always has for novelty.

But exploring different quarters of the city was his principal pursuit; and, in doing this, he had occasion to remark the absurd custom of the Hamburghers in the profuse use of carriages in streets so narrow and so crooked, that their vehicles could scarcely get on, from the mutual impediments they presented. In one of these frequent "*jams*," just as one coach was passing another, he caught sight of a face that set his heart all in a flame: it seemed the face of the beautiful girl of the race-course, and he sprang forward, in hopes to assure himself it was so; but the coach became disentangled before he could look into it, and drove on;—he pursued it, but could not overtake it, and it soon turned into a gateway, which, when Ned reached, was closed. He lingered about the place for some time, provoked and disappointed; he could not be satisfied whether his notion was true or not; he could not even ask to whom the house belonged, for he was ignorant of the language; so he was forced to retire in a state of excited imagination, which not only deprived him of sleep that night, but kept him on the alert for several days, as he became possessed more and more with the idea, that the beautiful girl was in Hamburgh.

Full of this notion, he looked into every carriage he saw, frequented the theatre and other public places more, and made a point of going to "The Maiden's Walk," at the hour it was most frequented. Just as he was one day entering upon it, the truth of his surmise was realised; he saw the idol of his wild passion at the opposite side of the canal, going to church, as he thought, from the servant who followed her, with a prayer-book hanging upon one arm suspended by a silver chain, and a brass stove suspended from the other. The canal lay between them, and he looked out for a boat, and, perceiving one lying opportunely near a neighbouring stair, ran towards it, and springing into it, almost like one who was crazy, astonished the phlegmatic German by his urgent signs for speed, which the boatman, who was smoking his pipe, not being willing to obey, Ned seized the oars himself, and pulled vigorously across the canal, on whose opposite bank he sprang, without paying Mynherr, who was at once stimulated to activity; and a double chase ensued—Ned after the girl, and the boatman after Ned: it made quite a sensation on the Maiden's Walk to see a handsome young fellow hunted by a pursy boatman, hallooing after him a "thousand devils," and swearing for his *denier*. Ned heeded not; he had caught sight of the last fold of his fair one's skirt, as she went

round a corner, and for that corner Ned made all speed; but
when he reached it, out of breath, no lady was to be seen, but
the fat boatman was close at his heels, saying a great deal to
Ned, which it was well for the boatmen Ned did not understand: but guessing the cause of his pursuit, and remembering
he had forgotten to pay him, he threw him a *groot*, and continued his search.   The boatman caught the coin, and looked at
this increase of the sum demanded with wonder, (though it was
only a penny,) and, raising his eyes to heaven, ejaculated an
aspiration to the Deity, with the remark, "What extravagant
robbers are the English!"

Ned searched every church in the neighbourhood, in hopes
of finding the object of his wishes, but in vain; indeed, it was
useless, for the service was over in all.   So the lady had been
returning *from*, not *going to*, church, as her pursuer thought.—
Ah! lovers are very liable to make mistakes!

The theatre he now thought the most likely place to see her,
and here he constantly resorted.   It was the last place he would
have gone to otherwise, for, not knowing the language, the entertainment could not be very amusing, though indeed, for that
matter, any one might understand the greater part of it as well
as the Hamburghers, for it consisted, principally, of practical
witticism, such as cuffs and kicks, smart boxes on the ear, hearty
cudgellings, alternated with hugs and kisses.   Nevertheless, all
this buffoonery our hero sat out, night after night, in the hope
of seeing this phantom of beauty, which seemed to appear only
to elude him.   At last his perseverance was rewarded.   One
night, as he was talking to an obliging stranger, who could speak
English, and had been explaining some passage in the play, he
saw the lovely girl, listening to what appeared to be courtly
compliments paid to her, judging from the gracious manner
of the handsomely dressed person from whom they proceeded,
and the half diffident, yet smiling, manner in which they were
received.

Ned was breathless!—there was the beauty of the race-course!
—she, for whose sake he had engaged in a street riot, angered
his father, and was forced to fly his native town, and for whom
he would have made far greater sacrifices.

There is nothing, perhaps, so totally subversive of self-possession as the unexpected sight of one we love.   It paralyses by the
too great intensity of its nervous excitement.   It smites the heart
to its very core, and the stream of life is arrested in its course;—
we cease to breathe;—every function of life seems suspended, but
that of sight;—the eye usurps the power of every other sense,
and we can only gaze.

Ned was disturbed from this state of fascination by a tap on the shoulder from his obliging neighbour, who had acted interpreter.

"I say, sir, that's the star you sail by, I reckon," said the new acquaintance, with a knowing toss of his head towards the quarter where Ned was still gazing in admiring wonderment.

Ned could neither speak nor withdraw his eyes.

"Hillo!" added his friend, "dumb-foundered—eh? If you can't speak, you'll never win a woman."

Ned attempted a faint smile.

"Where did you see her before?"

"Before?" echoed Ned.

"Ay—before. No one ever looked at a woman for the first time as you did at her," said the other, sharply.

"I saw her in Ireland."

"Ireland?—ho, ho—shouldn't wonder!—but it's rather a hot place, I should say, for Count Nellinski."

"A count?" echoed Ned, in surprise.

"Oh—counts are common enough in *Ja-armany!*" returned his informant, with a laugh.

"She is going," said Ned, looking up at the box, and rising to follow her example.

"And you are going, too?" said the stranger.

"Yes."

"I don't care if I do the same—the play is dull work." Ned hurried to the entrance, and watched eagerly for the appearance of the beautiful girl, but in vain, and after some time perceived his new acquaintance standing near him.

"Can't see her, eh?" was the question he put, while a provoking smile played across his countenance.

Ned answered in the negative, with a chagrined air, upon which the other laughed outright, saying, he was watching at the wrong entrance, for that the game was flown by another.

Ned was half inclined to be angry at the seeming enjoyment the other took in his disappointment, till, with a voice of the most cheery kindness, the stranger slapped him on the shoulder, and said,

"Never fret, man!—I know the hotel she stops at, the *Kaiser-hoff;* see her there, if so be you want it. Come along and sup with me—the *Weinkeller* furnishes good tipple and victual—come!"

So saying, he drew the yielding arm of Ned within his, and they bent their course to a celebrated cellar, then of great repute in Hamburgh, where the best company in the city, both natives and strangers, resorted to drink Hock, of which wine this cellar contained the choicest store, whence the government drew a large revenue. On their entrance, Ned saw but a confused mass of people, for the dense tobacco-smoke in which they were enveloped rendered a clear perception of any distant object difficult; and, as soon as they could find a seat, he and his companion had a flask of right Johannesberg set before them, which Ned at that moment was most willing to enjoy, as he considered himself under the influence of the happiest fortune in having met, in the person of a stranger, one who gave him the means of once more seeing the lovely being who so enslaved him.

The stranger filled his glass, and spoke;—"My service to you, Mister——what's your name, if I may make bold to ask?—mine is Hudson Finch, at your service."

"Mine is Fitzgerald," said Ned, who was ashamed to give so vulgar a one as his own to so dashing a gentleman; but he blushed as he spoke, for the ghost of the departed name of "Corkery" rose up reprovingly before him. But he swallowed his shame and a glass of Rhenish together, to the health of Mr. Finch, who returned the like civility to Mr. Fitzgerald, with the remark, that it was a good name. Ned thought, at the moment, that good names, like other good things, had the greatest chance of being stolen.

Finch now pointed out to him several persons among the company worthy of note, with amusing anecdotes of almost every one he indicated.

"Do you see those two in yonder corner?"

"Smoking and drinking so hard?" asked Ned.

"The same. Now, I would wager a trifle those two poor devils are spending here to-night every stiver they are worth."

"Why do you guess so?"

"They are young graduates in law:—now, how do you think they live?"

"By their profession, I suppose," said Ned.

"No, but by their *processions*."

"How do you mean?"

"These young graduates, sir, have scarcely enough to keep life and soul together. There is not a *Häringsfrau* in all Hamburgh who does not know the whole tribe; for pickled herrings and beer are what they mostly live upon, and the "God-send" of a procession alone can enable them to show their noses in the *Weinkeller*.

"But you have not yet explained to me about these same processions."

"Why, sir, these proud citizens of Hamburgh love processions almost as well as beer and tobacco, and the smallest occasion is seized upon to get one up; sometimes to present an address to somebody, for nobody knows what; and as a procession is nothing without good company, these younger members of the learned profession are regularly engaged and paid to make the thing look respectable, and render the compliment greater."

"And is this well known?"

"As well known as the Bank?"

"Then how ridiculous to have recourse to it, when all the world can see through——"

"Through the '*humbug*,' you were going to say?—My good sir, is not the world itself one great humbug?"

"I confess that's new to me," said Ned, simply.

"Because you are new to the world," was the other's prompt reply. "How many forms, laws, customs, names, *et cetera, et cetera*, are bowed down to—how many things are in a flourishing existence round us, which are rank humbugs—which are known to be humbugs—admitted to be humbugs—and yet are not only permitted to exist, but respected? Oh, my dear young friend! *Monsieur* the WORLD has a very large nose; and whoever, whichever, or whatever, can lay hold of it, *Monsieur* the WORLD follows as tamely as a lamb."

This outpouring of contempt for the world made Ned think Mister Finch a very clever man. He remarked, however, that he thought the Germans more prudent than to spend their money on one expensive entertainment, when they were forced to live mostly, as Finch said, on pickled herrings and beer.

"My dear fellow, that is a part of their game," said Finch. "They must have good clothes, and be seen sometimes rubbing skirts with gentility, or they would lose their employment."

"Oh! I perceive," said Ned.

"For instance, those fellows who are so jolly over there, I saw this very day, in a funeral procession, looking as if their hearts would break. The deceased was a tailor, whose kith and kin prided themselves on having law students among the mourners. Very likely they got a new suit of clothes on the occasion;—but, hold—look over there!—do you not perceive?"

Ned looked in the desired direction, and was delighted to see his bronzed friend of the race-course—the Count Nellinski himself. Ned would have given the world to speak to him, but the count was engaged in earnest conversation with a military man, of iron aspect; so earnest, that Ned felt it would have been intrusion to attempt a word with him: therefore he continued to listen to Finch's lively raillery, though, truth to say, he did not comprehend much of it, so totally was his attention absorbed by the father of the lovely Ellen.

This distraction of mind, however, did not long continue, for the count soon after rose, with his companion, and retired. Ned looked hard at him, in hopes to catch his eyes as he passed out, but the count seemed too absorbed in his own thoughts to

heed external objects.   Ned consoled himself with the hope that
he should see him on the morrow, at the *Kaiser-hoff*.

As no object now intervened to disturb his present enjoyment, Ned did the duty of the hour like a man, and, after a jolly
supper and a merry drinking bout, the acquaintances separated,
Ned thanking fortune over and over again for the chance she
had cast in his way; but the slippery jade was laughing in secret
at Ned all the time, for she was at that moment but playing him
a scurvy trick; for when, after a night of feverish dreaming,
in which a German supper, strong Rhenish, and love, strove for
mastery, Ned rose with a hot head, and hotter heart, and, making
himself as smart as he could, set out for the *Kaiser-hoff* to
inquire after his enchantress, he heard, to his utter dismay, that
the Count Nellinski and his daughter had left Hamburgh that
morning.

<hr>

CHAPTER IV.

WHEN we have made up our mind to some great pleasure, and
feasted by anticipation on the sweets imagination spreads before
us—when thus hope forestalls reality, we purchase our joys in
a very dear market.   How bankrupt in heart we feel, after
thus drawing on the future, to find our cheque returned with
the answer, "No effects!"   It was thus with poor Ned when
he inquired with the most "galliard" air he could assume at
the *Kaiser-hoff* for his fair one and her father, and found they
were gone.   His look became so suddenly changed, so utterly
blank, that even the slow-going German could not help noticing
his disappointment.

Ned was transfixed with dismay for some seconds, and stood
in sorrowful silence before the door of the hotel, till catching the
cold eye of the German fixed upon him with something like a
smile upon his countenance, a sense of shame came over him,
and he walked down the street.   But he could not leave it;—
there he staid, looking at the house where she *had* been, while a
quick succession of fond imaginings whirled through his head,
and drove the blood rapidly through his heart.   The gentle
speeches he thought he should have made to her, and had almost
gotten by heart, (he went over them so often in anticipation of
the interview,) recurred to him, and seemed to mock at his fond
yearnings.   "Hard fate!" he muttered to himself; "cruel
disappointment! at the instant I thought I should address her

once more—once more touch that dear hand—at such a moment to have my hopes dashed, and made the very sport and mockery of circumstance. 'Tis hard! alas! 'tis doomed—doomed—I am never to see her again—never! Yet why should I seek it? the daughter of a count:—cursed infatuation!—No, not cursed; call it fatal, but nothing can be cursed that springs from such an angelic cause. O Ellen! Ellen!—I know my own unworthiness —I know the hopeless folly of my passion, but I cannot resist its fatal influence; the deadly, yet darling poison is in my heart, and nought but death or you can assuage the pain." With these and other such exclamations he wandered up and down the street, and after some time wished he could even enter the apartments she had last occupied. "Were it only to pace the room she trod," said he; "to see the table where she sat, to touch the chair she occupied, to look in the mirror which late reflected that lovely face, to stand in the deep recess of the window where she had stood—even this were a sad pleasure:—I will return to the hotel and try if I cannot accomplish it." Acting upon the words, he retraced his steps to the *Kaiser-hoff*, and by means of some few words of English, understood by an attendant of the house, and some pieces of silver on the part of the lover, he contrived to be shown the apartment whence the Count Nellinski and his daughter had so recently departed. It was yet in that state of litter which the room of a hotel always exhibits after the "parting guest" has retired, ere the order has been restored which may welcome the "coming" one. Edward's imagination occupied the deserted chamber with its recent lovely visitant, as he cast his eyes around;—she had reclined on that couch—that little quaint table of marquetry was for a lady's use—there was a pen upon it—*she* might have used it; he would have taken it, but the eyes of the attendant were upon him, and he felt ashamed of *exposing* a weakness which, nevertheless, he did not blame himself for entertaining. Oh! that *exposure*, how many love fooleries does its terror prevent! Peeping from behind the cushions of a large easy chair was a little glove, which Ned determined to have, but still the presence of the attendant was a check upon him; feigning extreme thirst, he asked for a glass of water, which the attendant retired to procure; and the instant Edward was free from observation, he pounced upon the glove with hawk-like avidity, and dragged from beneath the cushion a morsel of music-paper also, whereon a few notes were pricked down, to which a few words were attached. Ned paused not to read them, but thrust glove and music inside his waistcoat— seized on the pen, and perceiving in a far corner a few flowers which seemed a discarded bouquet, ran to secure them ere the attendant could return; and when he had sipped a mouthful of

the water which was presented to him, in an instant after hurried
from the house in the pride of his plunder; and it is a question if
he would have exchanged these trifles for all the plate in the
Kaiser-hoff. He did not feel quite secure of his booty till he had
turned the corner of the street, and then hastened to his quarters to deposit his treasure in safety. There he folded up his
flowers—not a leaf was permitted to be lost;—he dated the paper
with the purloined pen—he drew forth the glove and kissed it
passionately, between fond ejaculations,—kissed it on the *inside*
where the dear hand had been O Ned! Ned! how desperately,
irretrievably over head and ears in love wert thou! So intent
was he in his love-sick occupation, that he did not hear the
entrance of his hostess into his room, and the first notice he had
of her presence was an exclamation behind his chair, as he
imprinted one of his wild kisses on the little glove.

"*Mein Gott!*" exclaimed a fat, squashy sort of voice, which
when the words were uttered, went on with a guttural chuckle,
while Ned turned round startled, and looking as foolish as if he
had been caught robbing the good woman's cupboard. The
situation was absurd enough, (Ned thought it *disgusting,*) that
while his imagination was filled with the form of a sylph, and
wrapt in the secret idolatry of love, he should be startled by the
presence of a fat *frau,* and have his sweet visions broken by the
laugh of derision.

He thrust the glove into his breast, in the vain endeavour to
conceal it from the landlady; but she only laughed the louder,
pointing first inside his waistcoat, and then to her own fat fist,
on which she impressed a great smacking kiss, and shook with
laughter again, exclaiming in the intervals of her cachinnation,
"*Mein Gott!*"

On Ned desiring to know what this interruption meant, she
pointed to the door, and said, "Herr Finch;" at the same moment
ascending footsteps were heard on the stairs, and Ned's acquaintance of the *Weinkeller* soon made his appearance. As he entered
the room, the landlady, still laughing, repeated the piece of pan-
tomime towards Edward, and bestowing another smack on her
hand, and gurgling up "*Mein Gott!*" retired and shut the door.

"Hillo!" said Finch, "what insinuation is this, my friend?
have you been kissing your landlady?"

"Kiss *her?*" exclaimed Ned, with a curl on his lip as though
it were on the brink of a cup of rhubarb.

Finch laughed outright at the expression of nausea which this
insinuation of gallantry had produced, and asked if Ned thought
he had so poor an opinion of his taste.

"But did you prosper in the other affair?" continued he.
"Have you been to the *Kaiser-hoff?*"

"Yes," said Ned, with a sigh.

"What! sighing?" said Finch; "a sigh is the worst wind that blows,—'tis the very wind of the proverb that 'blows nobody good:'—was she denied? or was she cruel?"

"She is gone!" said Ned, with an air of despondency worthy of a criminal going to execution.

"Pho! is that all?" said Finch. "Can't you go after her?"

"I know not where they are gone to," said Ned.

"And what have you a tongue in your head for?" replied Finch.

"But even if I did," returned Ned, "I cannot follow them; and after all, if I could—what's the use?"

"What's the use?" cried his friend, in surprise; "what's the use of following the girl you love?—what a question!"

"Oh!" sighed Ned, "if you knew all;—were you but aware—" he paused, and looked wistfully into Finch's face, as though he would make him his confident. Young, inexperienced, and of an ardent nature, he longed to have some one to whom he might unburthen his heart, and this seemed the only chance for it. Extending his hand to Finch, who took it cordially, Ned exclaimed, "It seems to be my destiny that my love and friendship must be of the mushroom nature—both the growth of one night."

"But not so soon to perish, I hope," said Finch; shaking his hand warmly.

Ned returned the genial pressure, and continued, "I know not how it is, but I feel myself drawn towards you in a most unaccountable way, and if you will have patience to listen, I will tell you all about this romantic affair."

"I will listen willingly," said Finch; "but don't be so down in the mouth, man," he added, slapping Ned on the shoulder, "'Faint heart never won fair lady.'"

Taking a seat, after uttering this cheering exhortation, he threw himself back, and showed he was resigned to the operation Edward proposed.

Our hero made it as little painful as possible; passing over, for obvious reasons, much about himself and family, and banishing the name of "Corkery" beyond the pale of history, stating, however, that his rank in life, as the son of a trader, presented a barrier to the pursuit of a lady of condition—how that lady was first encountered, the street broil, his subsequent banishment and irrepressible love were recounted as briefly as they might be, and the listener seemed infected by the spirit of romance which appeared to have presided over the whole affair, for, when Ned concluded, Finch expressed not only admiration of his spirit, but even went so far as to encourage his hopes.

3

"You do not mean to say I have a chance?" exclaimed Ned, whose flashing eye betrayed that his feelings were at variance with the doubting nature of his question.

"And why not?" returned Finch. "You are young, full of courage, and fit for enterprise ; the world offers plenty to do for all such. Look at the Low Countries at this moment, for instance ; the theatre of daring achievements that lift bold men above the heads of ordinary mortals. Glorious graves or living laurels may be had there, and fortune, too, if you have luck on your side."

"I would dare a thousand deaths a day!" exclaimed Ned, "to win her ;—even to deserve her ;—but where could I get a commission?—I have not friends, and to serve as a volunteer requires more money than I can command."

"Money!" returned Finch—"ah!—you have said the very word that has more magic in it, lad, than all else besides—if you had money *enough*, you need care for nothing besides—the £. s. D.— the pounds shillings and pence reign triumphant over all else."

"True!" said Ned, with a sigh.

"Well," returned Finch, "money is to be made, and adventure found in other places than in Flanders. The sea offers reward as well as the land. The Indies, for example, afford scope to the enterprise of the navigator."

"Would to Heaven I had but the opportunity of engaging in such a venture!" cried Ned, enthusiastically.

"Well," said Finch, "there is no knowing how even *I* might help you in that particular ; I have sailed East and West myself." Here he launched forth at some length on the subject, embellishing his recital with some piquant bits of sea stories, which quite came up to all Ned fancied of nautical adventure, and set him quite agog to realise those dreams in which he had sometimes indulged, and which he found, from his friend's narrative, were not beyond reality. Finch spoke with contempt of *paddling* about, as he called it, in muddy channel seas. He talked of "the blue waters;" and certain lofty phrases of "Indian skies," "waving palm-trees," and "soft savannahs," quite fired Ned's brain. In truth, his new acquaintance was a dashing fellow—there was a fine free tone about him above the narrow prejudices of those to whom Ned had been accustomed ; there was that in him which approached nearer to the romantic than he had yet witnessed, and he began to hope the world was not such a hum-drum place as, of late, he began to fear it was. Under his present circumstances, he felt the companionship of his new friend the greatest relief; he diverted his thoughts from the absorbing theme which unmanned him, by his good spirits and the profusion of amusing anecdote with which his memory was stored, till Ned began to entertain a regard, as well as admiration for him, and every spare moment he could command was given up to his society.

All this time Captain M'Guffin was loading "The Industry" with her cargo, and Ned Corkery with reproaches; for his attention became quite alienated from the interests of the brig, for which the recitals of the dashing Finch had engendered a thorough contempt, and the worthy M'Guffin's displeasure might have assumed a harsher form, but that Ned was the son of a wealthy man. £. s. d. have their collateral as well as direct influence.

The moment approached, however, which was to separate Ned from the sober reproaches of the master. Meeting Finch by appointment, one day, an unusual brightness illumined the countenance of his friend, who, shaking him warmly by the hand, announced that he had some good news for him.

"I have heard of your charmer," said he.

Ned listened breathlessly.

"The Count has travelled south, and if I don't mistake much, is on his way to Dunkirk, or, perhaps, Courtrai; but I would venture a bet he is at either of the places, where it won't be hard to find him.

"Of what avail is that to me?" said Ned, sorrowfully. "To hear they, whom I wish to see, are hundreds of miles away, without the power of following."

"Wait, lad! don't jump to your conclusion so fast; suppose I put you in the way of following—of seeing your 'ladye love'— mayhap of winning her."

Ned could only gasp forth an amatory "oh!" and clasp his hands.

"Listen, then. *Imprimis*, as lawyers begin people's wills. *Imprimis*, you must leave that clumsy old brig, and the fusty M'Guffin. Who could do any good with such a name as M'Guffin?" cried Finch, contemptuously.

Ned was delighted; he had thought of changing his.

"I will give you a berth on board the prettiest craft that ever floated, and take you with me to Dunkirk; there you will be nearer your game than here, and you may have some days' leisure to play it too; and when, under my advice, you make the most of an interview with your charmer, return on board, and it will go hard with me if I don't show you the way to fortune.

At all times the promise held out to a young man of being put in the way of making the first step in the course Ned's friend pointed out, is most tempting; but, under the peculiar circumstances such promise was made, the temptation was irresistible. At that moment Ned would have followed Finch to the uttermost end of the world, and, with all the enthusiasm belonging to his country and his time of life, he made a wild outpouring of thanks to his friend, with a hearty acceptance of his offer.

"Then, to-morrow evening," said Finch, flinging forth his hand to our hero, in a fashion which says, "Trust me."

"An' 'twere this moment!" returned Ned, grasping the offered gage of friendship, and, in the warm pressure which his heart prompted, expressing more than he could have spoken.

"Enough!" cried Finch, and they parted.

What a tumult of thought and feeling passed through Ned's head and heart, after the separation! that which in the enthusiasm of an excited moment, seemed easy as volition of flight to a bird, had its difficulties and objections presented when about to be brought into action. He was going he knew not where—nor for how long:—nor of time or place could he tell his father, and though implicit obedience was not a virtue Ned exercised pre-eminently, yet the natural affections, which were strong in him, forbade he should take the step on which he had determined without writing to the old man. A letter was accordingly composed for the exigency of the moment, saying that, desirous of seeing the world and making his fortune, he was bound to foreign parts, hoped to be forgiven, and all that sort of thing, which irregular and erratic young gentlemen who have the use of their limbs, indite to men of slow habits who go upon crutches. This letter was entrusted to the care of the deserted M'Guffin, enclosed in one to himself; and Ned, seizing the occasion of the sober master's absence from the "Industry," transferred his chest from that simple brig to the knowing little craft, "Seagull," which, immediately after, weighed anchor, and a flowing sheet soon put leagues of water between Ned and his "*Industry*."

The breeze, at first so favourable, soon chopped about; but the adverse wind only served to make Ned more in love with the boat. Unlike the brig, that lifted her heavy head out of the sea, and flopped it in again, as if she were half asleep, the lively Seagull clove the waves, dashing the spray right and left aside of her graceful bows, answering her helm with the delicacy of a hair trigger, coming into the wind as fast as if the point whence it blew were a magnet, and she had a needle in her bow-sprit, and away again on the opposite tack, as though she were gifted with an animal instinct, and doubled, like a hare before greyhounds.

"Come down," said Finch, "we need not stay here; we'll **make ourselves comfortable below, and then turn in.**" The evening was spent agreeably, accordingly; Ned liked the skipper more and more, and wondered how his father could have had the barbarity to send him to sea in such a heavy tub as the " Industry," while such craft as the "Seagull" swam. He turned in, and dreamt of "blue waters, waving palms, and soft savannahs."   In the morning he partook of the nicest breakfast he ever saw on board a ship; the next day's sail was all that could be wished, and the next and the next day were more pleasantly passed by Ned than any other days of his life; they made Dunkirk, and fresh enjoyments were before Ned; he was happiest of the happy. He remembered the couplet of the song, which says—

> "—he talked of such things,
> As if sailors were kings;"

and Ned thought there was no *if* about it, but that no king could be happier than he, ever since he set his foot on board the " Seagull."

The port of Dunkirk, at that time, was a stirring scene of action; the fortifications, which by the treaty of Utrecht had been destroyed, and the extensive basins, capable of receiving forty sail of the line, which had been filled up, were now being rebuilt and cleared out; and already the docks were capable of affording accommodation to a considerable armament, preparing for a descent upon England, under the command of the renowned Marshal Saxe, and for the purpose of re-establishing the house of Stuart on the British throne.

The bustle of workmen, the shouts of sailors, the drum, the trumpet, and the cannon, all contributed to the martial din and tumult of the place, which perfectly astounded Ned, who, notwithstanding, was less influenced by the thought of the mighty game which was preparing to be played than by the hope he entertained of seeing his beloved one. Inquiry lay within so small a compass in Dunkirk, that Finch was soon enabled to ascertain what persons of note were in the place, and Count Nellenski was not amongst them. The Marshal had gone to Courtrai; and there Ned was recommended to repair, in search of his darling object. Finch stoutly avowing his belief the game would be found in that quarter, he gave Ned several hints as to his mode of proceeding, placing in strong array his own knowledge of the world in general, some little insight into the circumstances of the particular case, and, beyond all, his conviction that a *coup de main*, where a lady is in the case, does wonders. "Be bold," he said; "tell her at once you love her, the first moment you have an opportunity, and that you entertain hopes of being soon in a position to claim her hand; draw a little on futurity; and if the woman likes you, she will put it in bank in her heart, and then you'll have something to draw on. Remember my axiom —'tis that good old one I have often repeated to you—' Faint heart never won fair lady.'"

Along with such advice he furnished his friend with a passport and copious directions, and Ned set out on what he could not help confessing to himself was a wild-goose chase, spurred by the strongest stimulus that can inspire the heart—love ; and upborne by the most enduring power that can sustain human exertion—hope ; both the bright companions of life, but brightest in youth.

The time which fortune had thrown in our hero's way was not the most favourable for travelling ; the frequency of military posts, the scrupulous examination of passports, the suspicion with which the most trivial circumstances in connexion with a traveller was regarded, rendered the wayfarer liable to many discomforts, and not unfrequently to danger ; for sometimes straggling parties of soldiers roved up and down, who, taking advantage of the exigencies of the times, made the public cause but an excuse for private rapine, by vexatious and rude interruptions, which enabled them to raise pecuniary contributions from defenceless parties whose ill luck threw them into such unwelcome company, and whose only chance of permission to proceed on their journey was giving a bribe ; the loss of their money being, in most cases, preferred to the loss of their liberty, more particularly in the hands of such unceremonious captors.

It was Ned's evil fortune to fall in with one of these marauding parties, in company with some fellow-travellers with whom he had left Dunkirk. When stopped and questioned, and, at last, detained by the soldiery, one of the party, a sturdy burgher, protested loudly against the proceeding ; swearing lustily that it was not care for the public cause, but the mere desire to mulct the passengers, by which it was prompted ; and though he paid for leave to pass, he grumbled ominously, and some muttered words of making it a matter of debate in his town-council, and having it strongly represented at head-quarters, caught the ears of the soldiers ; while he further averred, that though scarcely a day passed without hundreds of such stoppages, he never heard of a single instance of their daring to take a prisoner before the authorities ; clearly proving that it was a piece of knavery, and nothing else.

This was so generally known, that the depredators lost no occasion of pulling up any really suspicious person, to give a colour to their proceedings ; and as it happened that Ned, speaking nothing but English, and his passport not being what they chose to consider satisfactory, was just the man for their purpose, they rebutted the accusation of the burgher by making a prisoner of Ned, whom they feigned to believe a spy; and he was, therefore, parted from his companions, and despatched to Courtrai under a guard. This was but an inauspicious commencement of his voyage of discovery; and the miles which he had yet to traverse towards the town, were passed by our hero in melancholy forebodings, which grew darker as he entered the strongly-guarded gate of the fortress, and saw the fierce looks which were cast upon him as he was pointed out for an English spy. He was forwarded directly, by the officer in command of the gate, under a special escort, to the provost-marshal; and, after a brief charge made by his captors, who made matters appear as bad as they could against him, the more to glorify their own vigilance, and one word of which Ned could not contradict, as he did not know what they were saying, he was thrust into a dingy cell lighted by one small window with a strong iron grating; and, as the guardian of the den was about to close the door, he cast back a significant look, and, putting his thumb under his ear, with an ominous twist of his mouth, and a smart click of the tongue at the same moment, he slammed the door on his prisoner, whom we must leave, for the present, to his hempen meditations.

CHAPTER V.

FRENCH Flanders, whose greater portion was won by the valour of the British arms, had been reconquered in subsequent campaigns.

The genius of Maurice, Count de Saxe, had retrieved the fallen fortunes of the French, and the victories of the illustrious Marlborough were remembered with impatience at home, as the recent successes of this later master of the art of war swept away the result of the British hero's conquests. With an inferior force, he now held in check the armies of the allies; and, though unable to maintain a pitched battle, the judicious distribution of his battalions prevented his adversaries from concentrating, and forcing him to a general engagement. Until his presence might be required, he had retired from Dunkirk to Courtrai, where he was better able to enjoy the pleasures he loved. Of these, the theatre was one; and though a dramatic company attended his camp, which he might command at all times, he preferred **Courtrai** to a mere seaport town, as in the former a more distinguished audience might do honour to the exalted efforts of the artists whom it was his pleasure to patronise. Amongst these, the exquisite Adrienne le Couvreur stood pre-eminent. It was she who first inspired the Count with his passion for the drama, which, in her hands, could enchain the imagination, and engage the passions. Her embodiment of the poet's conceptions, showed a power in the histrionic art which he did not conceive it possessed; and the fascination became the more potent from being unexpected, and was enduring as it was sudden. The admiration her talents excited, made him desire to have the acquaintance of one who so often charmed him in public, and in the society of this gifted actress he found new charms; her conversation was an enjoyment he constantly courted, and she obtained sufficient influence over the soldier to urge him to the study of elegant literature; his mind, hitherto absorbed by authors who could only extend his knowledge in the art of war, was thrown open to the contemplation of those who move our hearts to the better purposes of peace, and embellish social life with the adornments of poetry and the fine arts; and thus endowed, through her influence, with a new and more exalting power of enjoyment, he more and more esteemed his beautiful benefactress. Profuse in his expenditure, his patronage of Adrienne was munificent; and on one occasion she had the opportunity of proving that his liberality was not unworthily bestowed. When, under adverse circumstances, he was combatting for the duchy of Courland, Adrienne, then in Paris, pawned her jewels and plate, and sent a considerable sum to replenish the military chest of her patron.

Here was a fresh cause of admiration on the part of the Count, whose sense of such noble conduct raised her still higher in his opinion, and the fair Adrienne became such a favourite, that she was admitted to the freedom of friendship with the noble Marshal, and might venture to say or do what few would have dared to one in his exalted position.

Whenever the exigencies of war, on his part, or of the *Théâtre Français* on hers, permitted, her presence was always requested by the Count, to add the lustre of her dramatic art to the many other courtly pleasures with which he always sought to adorn his camp, thereby rendering an exile from the capital more bearable to the young nobles who followed his standard. One of these occasions had now arrived; hostilities, on a large scale, were laid by, and the Marshal awaited with impatience in Courtrai the arrival of the renowned Le Couvreur; for the pleasure of the theatre was held in dearer anticipation at that moment from his being debarred from active exercise, in consequence of a wound received in early life and neglected, and, often causing pain and inconvenience, now exhibiting some of its unpleasant symptoms. The Count, for the greater ease of his wounded limb, was in *dishabille:* habited in a *roquelaire,* and wearing on his head a silken cap, in which a small aigrette of heron's feathers was quaintly fastened with a jewel. He was surrounded by maps and books, plans of fortifications, and other evidences of an active commander, and poring over a projected movement, which he measured with hand and mind, balancing all in the scale of contingency, when the arrival of Mademoiselle Le Couvreur was announced. The compasses were flung aside, all thoughts of the campaign were abandoned, and joy at the sight of his lovely and welcome visitor, put "grim-visaged war" to flight. How the hours glided by—what amusing anecdotes the actress brought from Paris! The tittle-tattle of that brilliant place was served up to the Marshal with the piquant sauce of the fair Adrienne's manner; even court plots and state intrigues were at her fingers' end, and the king himself did not escape.

"There is one thing, however, he did that I love him for," said she; "he created *you* a Marshal; I need not tell you how *I* rejoiced at that well-deserved proof of his majesty's favour. I have not till now had the opportunity of making my congratulations; pray, Marshal, accept them!"

She then asked, in that womanly spirit which enjoys the outward signs of triumph, to see the *báton* which the king had presented.

Saxe smiled at the fond folly, and said, "Is it not enough to know that I *am* a Marshal, without looking at the bauble which represents the rank? it is not half so fine as many of the insignia you wear upon the stage."

"But more real," answered Adrienne; "and that makes all the difference——."

"Some of the dignities of real life are quite as unsubstantial as your pasteboard crowns," returned the Marshal. "What," for instance, is my coronet of Courland worth? It is dear to me for *one* reason, certainly; the struggle to win it proved there was yet a noble and disinterested friendship left in the world."

He fixed his bright eye significantly on Adrienne as he spoke; she only answered by a smile, and with an inclination of the head.

"But I repeat," continued the Count, "what are many of the dignities, the triumphs, and the honours of this world, more than a theatric pageant, only not so amusing, and a little longer sometimes; while the world applaud or hiss by turns, and on which the curtain falls at last, when Death 'rings down?'"

"Go on! go on!" said the actress; "rally as much as **you**

please; but I hold my opinion:—the triumph, or grief, or joy o of this world, must be more touching than that of the theatre, because it is *real*."

"*Ma belle!*" answered the Marshal, with ready courtesy, "all is real when *you* are on the stage."

"Ah!" returned the lovely woman, "if you reply by compliments, I must give up the argument; but though I can say no more, I *will* see the baton."

The Marshal's principal attendant was summoned, and, at the lady's desire, the staff of office was produced. It was beautifully wrought, studded, or, to use the ancient heraldic phrase, *semé* with *fleurs-de-lis* in gold and enamel. The fair Adrienne snatched the glittering emblem of military domination from the hand of the attendant, and when he had left the room she kissed it passionately, and exclaimed, "May victory hover wheresoever 'tis raised! but the wish is needless—it *must*, in the hands of *La Maréchal de Saxe*."

"You can beat me at compliments," said the Marshal, "though you disclaim them."

Adrienne rose, and, assuming a military stand, waved the baton in the air, and with the happiest mimicry imitating the Count's manner, gave a series of the most absurd commands. The Count laughed, half at the close imitation of himself, half at the nonsense she was talking; while the admiration of her beautiful arm, as it waved to and fro in all the accustomed grace of the highest study, cast an Attic enjoyment over the scene, and almost made farce sublime.

"Sit down!" cried the Count, when his laughter permitted him to speak; sit down, lady fair—what nonsense you do talk. If Hercules was absurd holding the distaff, Venus makes as poor work with the truncheon."

The lively *tête-à-tête* was soon interrupted by the announcement that Mons. de Devenish, the commandant, waited the Marshal's pleasure.

"*Ma foi!*" exclaimed the Count, surprised, and consulting his watch, "*que le temps fuit!* it is indeed the hour I appointed;" and turning to the servant, he desired him to make his compliments to the commandant, and say he should be charmed to see him : the servant retired.

"Now," said the Count to the lady, "you will hear some very droll French spoken."

"I am used to that," said Adrienne, with a smile, alluding to the Marshal's own foreign accent.

"Ah! but I am an angel compared to Mons. de Devenish; he is an Irishman—one of the many thousands who, brave as Cæsar, and loving fighting in their hearts, are not allowed to araw a sword for the king of Great Britain, under whose crown they live; and therefore they help to win victories for other countries. I have known De Devenish many years; he was an officer in the first regiment I ever raised, and has been in many a hot place with me; he has elevated himself by his own merit to be commandant of this fortress, and a more deserving officer never held command."

The entrance of the commandant cut short any further praise or comment the Count might have felt inclined to make, and after returning the Marshal's salutation, he begged to present to him an officer who had entered the chamber with him. His aspect was stern, and his arm in a sling spoke of recent encounter; and when the commandant introduced him under the name of Captain Lynch, the Marshal seemed to receive him with peculiar courtesy.

"Charmed to see you, Captain," said the Marshal; "you have strengthened the brigade* wonderfully;—what dashing fellows you have brought from Ireland—are they all such hand-some, strong, straight dare-devils?"

"I believe, Marshal, we are pretty fairly provided with natural gifts."

"You have got hurt—how's that?"

"A sharp affair, Marshal," answered Devenish, taking up the conversation; "and in a quarter I would not have expected, which made me take the liberty of bringing the Captain with me, to give all the information you might desire."

The Marshal withdrew to a table at the further end of the room, and, after asking Captain Lynch some few brief questions, he turned to Devenish, and with an outspread map before him, began to guage distances with a pair of compasses. After a pause of a few minutes, he exclaimed to the commandant, "I tell you 'tis impossible; the Duke de Grammont is here—Mons. de Luttaux there. The Duke de Biron could not be forced— St. Sauveur commands an impenetrable point—the Count de Longaunai would not permit an enemy to steal a march—'tis impossible anything of moment can have taken place."

Devenish ventured certain suggestions, which the Marshal listened to with an attention which showed in what respect he held the commandant's judgment, but still he maintained the opinion that any serious movement of the enemy was impossible.

While this conference of so much moment was going forward, Lynch's attention was arrested by the occupation of Adrienne, who, still holding the Marshal's truncheon, used it for a play-

* The Irish Brigade—one of the most distinguished in the French army of the period.

thing to provoke her dog into activity. Yes; while the interest of kingdoms was in debate, the staff of honour, presented by a proud potentate to an illustrious soldier, was made the toy of the moment in the hand of a woman.

Lynch's mind was not of the mould to derive enjoyment from the piquant frivolity of such a scene; the staff of honour made a plaything for the amusement of a lap-dog, to his earnest nature only conveyed a sense of displeasure, and an expression of pity and sadness passed across his countenance while he watched the gambols of the lady's pet, pursuing in bounding circles the baton which the lovely woman waved above his head. Even the beauty of person and grace of action before him, to which, under ordinary circumstances, he was not insensible, became neutral- ised by the wound his sense of propriety received. The im- pressions of the man were less vivid than the feelings of the soldier; and the truncheon, which in his mind was associated with thoughts of honour and victory, and whose indication he would have followed with alacrity though the path led to death,—that type of command to be degraded, as he considered it, cast a deeper shadow over his stern and massive features the longer he looked. His attention was withdrawn from the displeasing incident by a word addressed to him by the Marshal, who, having finished the discussion of the important topics on which he was engaged with the Commandant, turned the conversation upon the passing trivialities of the time.

"I hope you, and Mademoiselle your fair daughter, enjoyed the ball the other night, Captain;—by-the-by, what a charming person she is. She was called by common consent in the *salon*, *La belle Irlandaise.*"

Lynch bowed and thanked the Marshal for his flattering speech with a formal courtesy.

" I hope she enjoyed our comedy too."

" Extremely, sir."

" No doubt she can appreciate the wit of Moliere, for I know she speaks French charmingly.—Has she ever lived in Paris ?"

" No, Count; she has passed most of her life in Ireland."

" Then how has she acquired so pure an accent ?"

" An old priest was her instructor."

" Ah, truly, I forgot that; all your priests get their educa- tion in France. We send you priests, and you supply us with soldiers. We have the best of the bargain," said the Marshal, laughing. " So a priest has taught her French ?"

" Yes, Count, and something better, I hope," replied the father, seriously.

" Oh, doubtless," returned the Count, with a corresponding

suavity of voice · "*but still she enjoyed our comedy*," added he, with a mischievous twinkle of his dark eye, and one of his merriest smiles.

"Certainly," replied Lynch; "we say in Ireland, sir, that we may be 'merry and wise,' and I think it quite possible."

"I'll go farther than that," said the Marshal; "I think it very unwise not to be merry when one can. But now I can offer to Mademoiselle a higher entertainment. Our camp is honoured with the presence of the first *artisté* in the world," and he looked at Adrienne as he spoke: "and I doubt not Mademoiselle has tears to bestow on tragedy, as well as smiles to reward comedy. I hope for the honour of seeing you, and your fair daughter, Captain, amongst our auditory."

"Thanks, Marshal;—but my daughter has left Courtrai."

"For shame, Captain! Beauties are not so plenty here that we can spare so fair a face. I hope Mademoiselle returns soon: besides, remember what an intellectual banquet is before her in seeing Mademoiselle Le Couvreur." He waved his hand towards Adrienne, and bowed courteously. She returned the salutation with a smile, and retired.

"I hope your daughter is within recall," continued the Count. "Where is she?"

Captain Lynch hesitated for a moment, and muttered something about the Marshal's too flattering courtesy.

"I insist on knowing," said the Count, with his most winning air. "I positively command her presence here, to grace our revels;—where is she? Answer, Captain, or dread a general-issimo's displeasure: if your fair daughter is thus spirited away, I swear you shall not have a forlorn hope to lead, or a post of danger to defend, for the rest of the campaign.

Lynch smiled at the nature of the Marshal's threatened punishment, and in reply to the reiterated questions of where his daughter had gone, he replied, "to Bruges;" but in despite of the entreaties made for her return, respectfully declined the honour of the Marshal's pressing invitation, and soon withdrew in company of the Commandant.

They had scarcely retired, when the Count ordered the immediate attendance of his favourite emissary, Lerroux.

A swarthy man, of powerful frame, overhanging brow, and quick dark eye, soon made his appearance. The moment he entered, the Count addressed him with something of reproach in his manner.

"How is it that you never told me Mademoiselle de Lynch had left Courtrai?

"I did not know it, *Monseigneur*."

"Then she has fairly given you the slip?"

" But I will learn where she is gone, if *Monseigneur* desires."

" I know it without your help;—so you see I have done without you this time—*prenez garde*."

"*Pardon, Monseigneur.*——And what is *Monseigneur's* pleasure ?"

" We must have the lady back to Courtrai ; we have no beauties to spare here—eh, Lerroux ?"

" *Monseigneur* is right."

" She is too charming a person to stay at Bruges while I am here."

" At BRUGES ;—thanks, *Monseigneur.*—But what address ?'

" Plague take you, rascal; am *I* to find out everything that belongs to *your* business ? "

" *Pardon, Monseigneur !* am I to go to Bruges, then ?"

" Yes: *you* know how to find out where anybody is any-where, and can discover the address of Mademoiselle. She is too handsome to be spared from Courtrai, and we must make some excuse to get her back again. Her father is wounded ; that is a good plea to draw her from her retreat."

" Admirable, *Monseigneur !*"

" You can make it serve, I think."

" Without doubt, *Monseigneur.*"

" Contrive it your own way ;—but of course *I* know nothing about it." He threw him a purse of gold as he spoke, and smiled.

Lerroux answered with a vile leer and low chuckle.

" Lose no time."

" Not a moment, *Monseigneur.*"

" And you shall *not* lose *money*—for there is *another* purse if you bring back the lady."

" *Monseigneur* is *too* good !" said the wretch, with a cringe, as he retired from the room, and left the Marshal to his alternate reveries of love and war.

CHAPTER VI.

THE Commandant insisted on the presence of Captain Lynch at his quarters on their retiring from the Marshal's presence. The latter pleaded his wound as "reason fit" why it were wiser to betake him to the retirement of his own lodging and the repose of his own bed; but the Commandant pleaded ancient friendship, with that oft-used clause, "the length of time since they had met;" and Lynch being an Irishman, the social disposition of his nature backed his friend's request, and yielded to his hospitable wishes, on the understanding that Lynch should "do as he liked;" which meant, that the Commandant would not enforce his guest to drink till he was tipsy. In the course of their walk, Mons. de Devenish, for so we must call our French-Irish commandant, alluded to the beauty of the Captain's daughter, and the universal admiration she created.

"Even the Marshal," said he, "though used to the blaze of charms in the French court, has been attracted."

"I wish he were not," returned the father.

"And why not?"

"Because I desire not such distinctions for my child. The admiration of wolves for lambs is something like that of your Count-Marshal for a captain's daughter; it is disproportionate, and any superstructure on so false a base, must fall; and in falling, whom would it crush?—the woman. The brilliancy of a warrior's reputation, and a courtier's manner, are an over-match for the natural weakness even of the most sensible girl; and I would not willingly expose my child to the trial:—not that I fear or doubt her good sense and her innate love of all that is honourable, not only in reality, but in seeming; nevertheless, I should shrink at the idle whispers of a clique commenting upon the courtesies of a man of the Count's gay reputation to my daughter."

"My dear friend," answered Devenish, "you think like a man who has lived in the hermit retirement of our native land, and is unused to the world."

"And you, my good Commandant," returned Lynch, "think —or, perhaps, I had better say, *don't* think of such matters— with the carelessness that long habit has engendered while living with these demoralised foreigners."

"It is possible," said Devenish; "but I hope I am not contaminated."

" Certainly not," replied the Captain ; " but your feelings on such matters are blunted : and so strongly do I feel on this sub-ject, that I am going to ask of you the favour of supplying me with some trusty messenger, to convey to my daughter a letter to warn her against any surprise that may be attempted to draw her to Courtrai."

" Surprise !" exclaimed Devenish, in wonder.

" Aye, surprise," repeated Lynch ; " there was something in the manner of the Count I did not like—it jarred upon me ; and I would ask the favour at your hands I have named."

" You shall have it, my dear friend."

" My wound, and the duties I have to perform here," said the Captain, " are obstacles to my own departure hence at this moment, or I would instantly go to Bruges and see my girl ; but a letter in *safe* hands must serve my turn for the present. You say you can furnish a trusty messenger ?"

" Depend on me," replied Devenish.

" Thanks !" said Lynch : " it is enough."

Their brief and confidential colloquy brought them to the quarters of the Commandant, where a few officers had been invited to share the hospitality of his table, and were already awaiting their host. He pleaded the commands of the Marshal for this breach of etiquette on his part, and ordered dinner to be served directly.

Most of the men were Irish, for Devenish loved to have his countrymen about him, and the after-dinner hilarity was mingled with various anticipations of the proposed descent on Great Britain in the cause of Prince Charles, and its probable result on Ireland. Lynch promised the most devoted adherence to the cause, on the part of all Ireland,—stating his personal knowledge of the feelings of the country, in the cause of their legitimate king.

" More fools they !" said Devenish—" pass the bottle, boys."

" Call you devotion to a sacred duty folly ?" said Lynch, in whom a romantic and enthusiastic nature produced a deeper love for a sinking cause.

" I call it folly," returned Devenish, " to adhere to a family through whom poor Ireland lost all, and got nothing. They ad-hered to the royal cause in Charles the First's time, and little thanks they got—only were *murthered* entirely by Cromwell for it after, and had not even pity from Charles the Second. Still, for all that, nothing would serve them but to stick to *dirty** James, with desperate fidelity ; and much good that did them,—

---

* King James is still remembered in the devoted land he abandoned by this complimentary *sobriquet.*

only got them *murthered* over again by Black Billy, and made the world just one big barrack for Irishmen to go live abroad in, for they dare not stay at home."

"And are we not as badly off under George?" asked Lynch, gloomily—"and is it not worth a struggle to make Ireland a land where her sons may live and die in honour, and not be forced to live in exile, if they would not live as slaves?"

"Ah, Lynch, leave your indignant eloquence, like a good boy, and pass the wine,—there is poor O'Donnell eyeing the bottle with a longing look, that is quite heart-breaking."

"I am of your opinion, Commandant, respecting the expedition," said O'Donnell, filling his glass. "The wit spoke truth, who told Louis that he would never see mass performed in London, unless he had three hundred thousand soldiers to serve it."

"We have yet to see what the expedition will do," said Lynch.

"And they are making all haste in their preparations," added Blake.

"Yet I have no expectation from it," said Devenish.

"Though Saxe commands it?" replied Lynch.

"Aye, even Saxe.—And, by-the-bye, I am not sure if he won't be *held by the leg* here—that wound of his is troublesome sometimes. I know it of old—for I was with him when he got it."

"By the way, that was a desperate affair, I believe?" inquired O'Donnell.

"Faith, you may say that."

"An extraordinary escape, was it not?" inquired another.

"Incredible, almost," replied Devenish, who was requested by all present to give the particulars of the encounter, as none of them had ever heard the details.

"It is upwards of twenty years ago," said Devenish, "and as one might forget a little or so in that time, I dare say you will imagine the half of what I shall tell you invention; but I give you my honour, the most fertile fancy could not invent half the wonders of that night's work. You see it was when I first joined the Count's regiment,—the first which his father allowed him to raise, and with which he certainly performed wonders in a former campaign,—it was then that the regiment was ordered to Pomerania to join the Prussians, and the Count sent off the lads before him, that they might be in for the first of the fun, he himself intending to follow in a few days; but as he could move faster than a whole regiment, they were sent ahead, he reserving only six of his officers, and about twelve servants well armed, for his escort, though we had to cross part of an enemy's country."

"Did he dare such a thing with only eighteen men?"

"Dare?" said Devenish; "of all the dare-devils I ever saw, —and I have seen a few in my time,—the Count surpassed, when he was young. He knows better now; for indeed the bit of advice Prince Eugene gave him one day was needed."

"What was that?" inquired Blake.

"When the general officers were praising the young Count one day, at Bethune, for some of his daring vagaries, Prince Eugene waited till they were all done, and then he took him down a peg, with these remarkable words:—'You mistake temerity for courage,' said he, 'but do not confound them, Count, for *connoisseurs know the difference.*'"

"But you are forgetting the story, Commandant."

"Well, we were but nineteen people in all, well mounted, and armed to the teeth; and we pushed our nags pretty smartly, till night brought us, after a hard day's ride, to a small place called Crachnitz. Here there was but a shabby little inn, which could not afford sufficient accommodation for our party. We • were obliged to distribute our horses in various stables up and down the village, reserving those of the inn for the officers' chargers, and the servants to sleep in. We stationed a couple of scouts to be on the look-out, to avoid a surprise, and then the Count ordered supper, with as much *nonchalance* as if he were safe at home in his father's palace. Well, just as we were sitting down to supper, in rushed our scouts, to tell us the enemy were pouring into the town in great force. What need of force, you will say, to take nineteen men? but, as we afterwards heard, the enemy had supposed us to be a much stronger detachment, having heard that Marshal Count Fleming travelled with the Count de Saxe; and so something to the tune of two hundred dragoons entered the town, while six hundred cavalry were posted outside, to prevent escape, and make our capture sure; for if they could have carried off the Count and the Marshal, it would have been as good as taking three thousand men.

"The Count immediately gave orders to barricade the door and lower windows—to pierce the wainscot of the hall, and place a couple of men in each of the side rooms, which commanded the passage, who could thus, under cover, pour a fire upon the first who should enter. The Count and the rest of his suite withdrew to the stables, which we could better defend, and where we saddled our horses, to be ready to run when we could no longer fight. We heard the clatter of the dragoons, as they galloped up the street, and drew up round the inn. A violent knocking at the door succeeded; and on the refusal to open, the officer in command threatened to force it. The threat was soon put into execution; the door was battered down with the butt ends of fire-arms. And while all this din was going forward outside, *the stillness of death reigned within,*—where the Grim King was soon to reign *himself.* A light was so disposed, that the hall was visible to us, whilst those who should enter could see nothing. The four men in the two rooms, with guns ready pointed through the loops, awaited the forcing of the door, to deal slaughter on the first who should enter. Bang! bang! fell the blows on the portal, and the creaking planks told how fast the work went on. At last came one grand crash, and in fell the door; a rush of dragoons is impeded by a slight barricade of furniture in the hall; the moment they are checked, four deadly shots are put in from the side rooms. We then, from the other end of the passage which led to the stables, hurl a murderous fire upon the assailants, whose own dead bodies become an additional rampart for our defence. The dragoons, treading over their fallen companions, are pressed forward from the rear,—they are met with the bayonet, and slaughtered helplessly; a panic seizes the assailants, and the hall is abandoned—literally barricaded with dead. An escalade was attempted at the same time, however; and just as we had cleared the hall, the tramp of the dragoons was heard in the apartments above, where the windows were undefended. The Count was the first to rush up stairs in the darkness. He had a pistol in one hand, and a sword in the other. The first man he met fell by the former; and then he laid about him so vigorously with his steel, that several were killed by his own hand, before we could back him. A desperate struggle now took place; it was pitch dark; we could not see where we struck, and the greater part of the conflict consisted rather of wrestling, and knocking our foes on the head with the butt-ends of our pistols. At last we drove them towards the windows, and *threw them out*—by St. Patrick 'tis a fact!—we threw them out *by handfuls!* A second attack was made, and a second time repulsed; and the enemy, finding the defence so complete, concluded a greater number were in the house than was anticipated; therefore, the officer relinquished further assault, till daylight would enable him to use his numbers with advantage; and as he considered himself sure of his prey, he only placed strong parties round the inn, and ordered the men to rest on their arms till morning, when he might summon the Count to surrender. When we found ourselves unmolested, a little council of war was held, and the first thing that we perceived, with surprise, was, that not one of us, except the Count, had received so much as a scratch;—he got a pistol wound in the thigh, but he treated it as nothing, and we proceeded to debate what was best to be done. 'We must *make daylight through them* while it is *night,*' said the Count; 'for if the dawn should show the paucity of our numbers, the game is lost.' The difficulty now was, the want of horses; for you remember the stables of the inn could only accommodate those of the officers. It was therefore agreed to wait till the enemy might be supposed to be drowsy, and surprise the post, which, we perceived, had been established behind the inn. One great difficulty now existed;—though we had powder, we had expended every ball, and a rummage was made through the house for anything we could substitute; any bit of brass or iron was a treasure. I crammed a nail *for some fellow's coffin* into my pistol, and the Count was busy cutting the buttons off his coat, to ornament some other gentleman's uniform, when a bright thought, as I imagined, struck me. 'Count,' says I, 'we say in Ireland that nothing can kill the d——l but a silver bullet. So suppose we club our dollars, and cut them up into slugs?' 'A most characteristic invention,' replied he; '*I never knew an Irishman who could not get rid of his pay faster than any other fellow in the world.*' Laughing at the Count's reply, we acted on my advice, however, and chopped up our dollars into slugs, determined to pay the enemy ransom in a new fashion. When all was prepared, we mounted our horses, opened the gates of the court-yard quietly, and ordered the servants on foot to steal cautiously forward, till they should get sufficiently close to the enemy to enable them to reach them as fast on foot as we should on horseback. Having contrived this combined attack of infantry and cavalry on *so grand a seale*, the Count at the proper moment yelled out 'Charge!' and every man shouting enough for a dozen, to make believe we were in force, rushed forward for death or liberty. This sudden and furious assault upon the guard, who thought themselves in such security that they had alighted from their horses, and were lying round a watch-fire, took them completely by surprise; and such as escaped our fire, and the edge of the sword, fled precipitately, and our servants picking the best of their horses, we set off at full gallop, and never drew rein till we arrived at Sandomir, the next morning, which we accomplished without the loss of a man, or a wound amongst the party, except that of the Count.

"Now," said De Devenish, when he had finished the story, "remember you *asked* me to tell you that; for, 'pon my conscience, I would not volunteer to tell so marvellous a thing and hope to be believed."

His brother-soldiers, while they acknowledged the affair to have been a wonderful feat, still avowed their belief that, favoured by darkness, a small determined party might keep fearful odds at bay; and many instances were remembered round the board.

"By-the-by, Commandant, was Burke with you in that affair?" inquired O'Donnell.

"He was, *poor fellow!*" said De Devenish, with an expression of true regret on the last words. "He had not long come from Ireland then, and was one of the four picked men who held the hall. He was my servant for many years, and, much as I valued him, I did not know all his worth till I lost him. I have never had such another. You remember him, O'Donnell?"

"I cannot forget the strange scrape he got into the night he mistook the pass-word."

De Devenish laughed at the recollection.

"Tell us, Commandant," was the general request.

"O'Donnell knows it," said Devenish; but as there are some here who do not, I will tell you; and it has the great merit of not being long. It was one night when I wished to make a communication with one of our outposts, commanded by a brother Pat, that Burke was the only disposable person I had for the purpose. He had to pass a line of sentries; and as it was not long since he came from Ireland, he did not know a word of French, so the only thing I wished to impress on his understanding was the necessity of remembering the pass-word. As it happened, our glorious marshal here furnished the same in his own ever memorable name—*Saxe*—ever memorable but in the case of poor Burke, who forgot it, though he swore he never would, nor *could* if he *tried*—'for your honour,' says he to me before he went, 'how could I forget that word? Sure, I can remember a miller aisy enough, and a miller has *sacks*—isn't that right?' 'Quite, Burke,' said I; 'remember a miller and sacks, and you can't go wrong—that one word will pass you to-night all through the camp.' Now you must remember, Saxe did not command us, and that Burke had never heard of such a person, and depended on his mnemonic system for remembering the charmed word; but whether it was thoughts of home, or 'the girl he left behind him,' that were busy with my poor Burke, or that his high-trotting horse shook the word out of his head, I won't pretend to say, but when he was challenged, the lively '*qui vive?*' of the sentry was answered by Burke singing out 'BAGS;' and as you may guess, Burke was laid hold of.

"'Let me go, you thief!' cried Burke—'*Bags*, I tell you!'

"He was taken before the officer of the guard, who asked him where he came from. Burke tipped him a knowing wink, and cried '*Bags;*' but the officer seemed as stupid to Burke as the sentinel.

"'What brings you here?' asked the officer.

"'*Bags!*' said Burke, with more emphasis than before.

"The same answer to two different questions roused the Frenchman's indignation; but the warmer he got, the more did Burke repeat 'Bags!' and cursed in his own mind the officer's stupidity; and though he rang the changes on 'Bags' in every possible intonation, it was not till the next day that my inquiries after my servant set him free. Many a laugh was had at Burke's expense on the subject of the pass-word; and for a long time after, if I ever wanted him to be particular not to forget any thing, I had only to say 'Bags' to put Burke on his mettle."

"What a smart soldier he was too!" said O'Donnell.

"And as brave as a lion," added Devenish. "In short, he was a noble fellow. Though in the ranks, he had a heart that would have done honour to a marshal. I knew his history, and it was touching. He loved a girl passionately, who treated him, nevertheless, with coldness; yet I firmly believe, that to the end of his life, she was the dearest thing in his memory. Too daring a devotion to what the poor fellow considered the cause of his country, obliged him to fly from it, and never was there a more home-sick exile at *heart;* but his pride, in both cases, was so un-flinching, that word or look would never betray to strangers that he regretted the girl and the land that were lost to him for ever. He fell, at last, on a hard-fought and victorious day; and a lock of jet-black hair, and a withered shamrock, were found enclosed in a small case of green silk, together with a gospel, suspended by a ribbon from his neck, and resting over the pulseless heart which in life never throbbed with an unworthy emotion.

"The incident suggested to one of our lads who was as ready with his pen as his sword, a song, which has often been sung round our camp fire, and which, if O'Donnell pleases, he can give us now."

The manly voice of the soldier was at once raised in accordance with the wishes of his comrades, and though he could not boast the perfections of an accomplished singer what was wanting in art was more then made up in feeling.

The Soldier.

I.

'Twas a glorious day, worth a warrior's telling,
  Two kings had fought, and the fight was done,
When, 'midst the shout of victory swelling,
  A soldier fell on the field he won.
He thought of kings and of royal quarrels,
  And thought of glory without a smile;
For what had he to do with laurels?
  He was only one of the rank and file.

But he pulled out his little *cruiskeen*,*
And drank to his pretty *colleen*,†
  "Oh darling!" says he, "when I die
  You won't be a widow—for why?—
Ah! you never would have me, *vourneen*."‡

II.

A raven tress from his bosom taking,
  That now was stained with his life-stream shed;
A fervent prayer o'er that ringlet making,
  He blessings sought on the loved one's head.
And visions fair of his native mountains
  Arose, enchanting his fading sight;
Their emerald valleys and crystal fountains
  Were never shining more green and bright;
And grasping his little *cruiskeen*,
He pledg'd the dear island of green;—
  "Though far from thy valleys I die,
  Dearest isle, to my heart thou art nigh,
As though absent I never had been."

III.

A tear now fell—for as life was sinking,
  The pride that guarded his manly eye
Was weaker grown, and his last fond thinking
  Brought heaven and home and his true love nigh.
But with the fire of his gallant nation,
  He scorn'd surrender without a blow!—
He made with death capitulation,
  And with warlike honours he still would go;
For, draining his little *cruiskeen*,
He drank to his cruel *colleen*,
  To the emerald land of his birth—
  And lifeless he sank to the earth,
Brave a soldier as ever was seen!

The applause which followed O'Donnell's song was still ringing round the table, when a servant entered, and addressed some words to the Commandant.

Devenish, ever since his holding the important station he filled at Courtrai, always made it a rule to examine English prisoners himself on their capture, to avoid the misunderstanding that might arise from question and answer being confused by an imperfect knowledge of language between parties, and now he was informed an officer was in waiting, having an English prisoner in charge. The Commandant desired he should be brought before him; and, in another instant, Ned was standing in presence of the dinner-party.

Though his air was somewhat sad, there was nothing of the

* A dram-bottle.   † Girl.   ‡ A term of endearment.

downcast craven about it, as he looked towards the Commandant at the head of his table; but when he heard himself addressed, not only in English, but with the accent of his native land, his face brightened as his heart told him he was not so friendless as he thought himself. After answering the Commandant's first question, he cast his eyes round the table, and they met those of Captain Lynch. A mutual look of surprise and pleasure passed between them; and as the Captain rose and advanced towards him with open hand, saying, "Well met, my young friend," Edward exclaimed, "What! Count Nel——"

The Captain suddenly stopped him by seizing his hand, and, with significant pressure, saying, "Captain Lynch is glad to see you—how came you to be a prisoner?"

A few words of explanation sufficed to show that Edward was clear of any charge that should limit his liberty, and the Commandant pronounced him free, and requested him to take a seat at the table, so that, by one of those sudden turns of fortune which are so surprising, he was transferred at once from a prison to the table of the Commandant, and instead of "supping sorrow," drinking most excellent wine, the first glass of which he filled at the courteous soldier's request that he would pledge him.

"I am happy to have the pleasure of seeing you, sir," said Devenish, with that air of high breeding, warmed with heartiness, that so much characterised the Irish gentleman of the period, "and I hope you will make yourself comfortable. We owe you a little extra civility, in consideration of the rough treatment you first had at our hands; but if you have seen something of the chance rubs of travelling in a country under military occupation, I trust, before you leave us, we will prove to you that soldiers can be very good fellows as well as sturdy."

Ned, who never before had sat in as good company, feeling that inevitable abashment which being made the subject of address in such presence always produces in a young man of his station, made a somewhat hasty and hesitating speech about the honour he considered he enjoyed, and the good fortune of an apparently unlucky chance affording him the pleasure and *honour* of such a distinguished society. So far, his native tact enabled him to say what was quite right under the circumstances, though given with the diffidence which betrayed a shyness, showing a want of intimacy with the high-bred, but by no means awaking a suspicion of vulgar habits.

"As for the pleasure, sir," said Devenish, (politely leaving the *honour* unnoticed,) "I believe I may, without flattery, opine that the apartments of the Commandant are more agreeable than those of the *prevôt maréchal.* I hope you will look over the little accident that befel you: these French fellows, you know, —these *fascinating* foreigners,—have a very *taking* way with them, as they say of the robbers in Ireland."

Ned assured him he felt more than repaid by the consequences that ensued from his capture.

"I hope you have not been taken much out of your way, Mister—by-the-bye, your examination was conducted in so very Irish and after-dinner a fashion, that we never inquired your name;—may I beg the favour?"

"Fitzgerald," answered Ned.

"A good name, sir,—I had some cousins of that name myself. May I ask, are you connected with the Kilkee family?"

Ned, feeling much puzzled to be asked about his *Fitzgerald* relations, answered in the negative.

"Or the Knight of Kerry?" continued Devenish.

A negative was still returned; and then politeness forbidding the Commandant to inquire further, he returned to the question of "hoping that our hero had not been taken out of his way."

So far from that, Ned declared Courtrai was a place he intended to visit.

"Then no bones are broken after all," said Devenish, who having performed the courtesy of conversing with a stranger introduced to his table under such peculiar circumstances, joined in the general conversation of his guests.

Ned was delighted to escape from the inquiries on the subject of his genealogical tree, which was anything but a tree of knowledge to him, as far as *Fitzgerald* was concerned.

"What a strange meeting this of ours," said the Captain. "We last met in a quiet town on the remotest shore of Europe, and here we come together again on the theatre of its most stirring incidents."

"True, sir," answered Ned. "And yet in that quiet town, you may remember, we met in strife better befitting the seat of war."

"I don't forget it," answered his friend, significantly; "and anything I can do for you here, pray command me.— May I ask what your object is in visiting Courtrai?"

Here was poor Ned puzzled again with the very second question put to him. He dare not tell to him who asked it the real object of his visit; and a second time within a few minutes he felt the painful difficulty of not being able to speak the truth. He said at last, that having a few days to spare, the natural curiosity of persons to visit strange places was his motive; and then, trying to make a virtue of speaking truth enigmatically, he added, that doubtless *there was that in Courtrai which he should be glad to see.*

The Captain assured him there were places of much greater note in Flanders, Courtrai being principally remarkable for its manufactures, not for the outward beauties which are attractive to the traveller, and recommended his young friend to leave Courtrai as soon as possible, as he should only *lose his time there.*

How dismally those words sounded to Ned. Despair stared him in the face; he scarcely noticed anything that took place afterwards till the party broke up. Then, as the Commandant politely offered the guidance of his own servant to conduct him to an hotel, Lynch declared it was needless, as he would give his young friend accommodation in his own quarters.

Despair fled at the words: the enthusiast saw Fortune smiling again; and the lover's heart jumped at the chances involved in the proffered invitation.

CHAPTER VII.

On retiring from the hospitable board of the Commandant, with what surprise did Ned find himself walking down the street arm in arm with a count—or a captain, as he chose to be called there— and a passing wonder was experienced by Ned, how any man could wish to conceal his rank—that is, when it was a high one. But the wonder was momentary; superseded by the ecstatic idea of seeing his enchantress in a few minutes; nay, of being under the same roof with her; but ah! what was his disappointment, when he found, on reaching the soldier's barrack-room, his fond anticipations unfounded!—"How many tricks hath fortune played me to-day," thought Ned—and he sighed at the thought. Hitherto, with the timidity of true love, and a young heart, he had not dared to breathe her name; but his impatience would no longer remain within bounds, and he hazarded a timid question after her health.

"I thank you, she is well;" said the soldier; "and may God keep her so—and in safety!" he added, and seemed, in uttering these last words, as if he thought aloud. Then relapsing into silence, a shade of deep reflection settled on his brow, and he did not speak for some minutes. Suddenly he addressed Ned, asking him, that, as there was no immediate business to detain him at Courtrai, if he would object to visit other towns, better worth seeing. Ned raised no objection, merely saying he should be on his return to Dunkirk in some few days.

"You can do that, and oblige me too," said Lynch; "and also see the person after whom you have asked so politely—my daughter."

Ned could hardly answer from sheer breathlessness of delight, but he stammered a hasty assurance of his happiness to oblige in the particular requested.

"Then you can carry a letter to her, for which purpose I require a trusty messenger, and you have already proved how stout and sure a friend you can be;—but if you would oblige me, you must start to-night."

Ned assented with alacrity; and the Captain, writing a short letter, which he placed in Ned's hands, took down a sword from the wall where it hung, and presented it to his young friend.

"You can ride to-night in perfect safety, with a detachment of dragoons going to strengthen Belem; but as you will have to proceed thence alone by the canal to Bruges, and, in these rude times, may meet blustering people, it is as well to be provided with the means of defence."

Ned, after expressing thanks for the gift, buckled it to his side, and they proceeded immediately to the quarter where the cavalry was already mustering for the march, and Edward being presented to the officer in command by Lynch, was allowed to join the party, and accommodated with a troop horse. As he departed, a single but deep and earnest "farewell" was bestowed by the stern soldier.

The night-march was rapid and fatiguing; but Ned, with the excitement produced by the novelty of the scene, and, beyond all, the promising nature of his mission, would glady have borne twice as much; the

"Pride, pomp, and circumstance of glorious war

were around him; the martial clang of arms, and rapid tramp of steeds, rang through the darkness. The glitter and flutter of gold and steel and plume, that dazzle by day, were not there, but snatches of moonbeams struggling through the clouds, lighted them more picturesquely than sunshine, and rendered the scene, if less brilliant, more romantic.

As soon as he reached Belem, notwithstanding all his fatigue, he sought not repose, but lost no time in embarking in the first passage-boat which proceeded to Bruges. In the boat, however, exhausted nature sought the rest she needed, and he slept for some hours, until the clatter of dinner aroused him. Here was another novel scene to Ned; smoking, eating, and drinking, all going on together, the women joining in the latter pretty freely, and the custom being that the wine bill should be defrayed by the men, travelling bachelors undergoing a sort of tax upon celibacy by paying for the wine of other men's wives and daughters, Ned found the Flemish fair sex had a tolerable capacity for the consumption of the article. There was but one person on board who could speak a word of English, and only a few broken scraps were at his disposal. This occasioned Ned to attach himself to the company of this person, though there was something in the man from which he was instinctively inclined to shrink, a sort of bird-of-prey look that was repulsive, yet through the desire to ask a question, so natural in a young traveller, our hero overcame his prejudices, and submitted to the companionship. Ned found he was well acquainted with Bruges; and as they approached the town, the magnificent tower of the town-hall (the *carillon*), the lofty steeple of Notre Dame and other spires were named to our young traveller by the obliging stranger, to whom Ned fancied he had done great injustice by his antipathy.

"You can tell me, then," said our hero, "in what part of the town I can find this address;" and he produced the letter he was bearing to Ellen.

Ned saw an extra brightness kindle in the swarthy stranger's eye as he glanced at the direction; but it was momentary, and he calmly answered, he should be happy to show him the house, warning him against trusting to any paid guides through the town, as they were the greatest villains unhanged. Ned remembered the Captain's parting words and his gift of the sword, and was therefore readier to give credit to the stranger's admonition.

"*I vill show good 'ouse to Monsieur*," said the friend, whom Ned thankfully followed; and the stranger led him to the *Singe d'Or*, where he proposed they should have *soam léetel refraish togezzer*, and that he would conduct him afterwards to the place he sought for; he then left Ned, on some pretence, saying he would be back by the time the "*refraish*" was ready, which, having been ordered with all speed, Ned expected to make its appearance in some twenty minutes; but when an hour elapsed, and the stranger returned not, Ned fancied he had forgotten him and the "*refraish*" altogether, and therefore determined to delay no longer the delivery of the letter; demanding a guide, he issued from the inn, and after traversing some intricate and unsavoury by-ways, his conductor indicated with his pointed finger that the house he sought lay up a street into which he had just turned. Ned saw a carriage with a door open, and a figure standing, as if in attendance, which struck him to be the hawk-eyed stranger of the passage-boat—the next instant a lady issued from the house: it was Ellen; and the stranger assisted her to the carriage. A thought of treachery flashed across Edward's mind, and he ran with all speed to the spot, where the stranger was employing his utmost haste to shut up the steps and close the door. But Edward arrived in time to present himself before Ellen, who grew alternately pale and red on beholding him, and saw in his excited look some occasion of unusual moment—while his urgent appeal to her to stop was met by the swarthy stranger's passionate exclamation that there was not a moment to delay; this he urged, speaking rapidly in French to Ellen, with much gesticulation.

"I fear there is treachery here," cried Ned, eagerly; but he was interrupted by the Frenchman, who, with some contemptuous gesticulation towards him, gabbled a torrent of talk to Ellen, which Ned could not understand, as the stranger spoke his own language. But our hero would not be thus put down; for, laying hold of the door, and shoving the intruder aside, he put his head into the carriage, and said,

"Dear lady, if this rascal is trying to persuade you that I am not your father's authorised messenger, he is a liar!"

"*Sacré!*" exclaimed the Frenchman, who, with gnashing teeth and eyes flashing fire, drew his sword fiercely, and with such evident murderous intent, that Ned quickly had his rapier out, but barely in time to parry the furious thrust of his assailant, whose rapid lunges, urged with great personal power lashed to its utmost exertion by rage, placed our hero's life in imminent jeopardy. Ellen screamed; and, opening the carriage door, was about to rush between the combatants, when a rapidly-returned pass from Ned laid the base Lerroux dead at the feet of the lovely creature he would have betrayed.

Ellen would have fallen to the ground but that Edward caught her in his arms, and bore her into the house, where the attention of the rapidly-assembled domestics recalled her from her swoon. Her first words, on recovering, were to urge Edward to immediate flight, but his answer was handing her the letter of her father, and saying, "I must not go until I know if there is any other duty I can perform."

She glanced over the letter, and exclaimed, "Oh! from what peril you have preserved me!—but you have slain a Frenchman, and are in the hands of his countrymen, in arms—Fly! for Heaven's sake, fly!" — Then wringing her hands, she exclaimed, "Alas! alas! am I doomed always to involve you in trouble?"

She looked with so much gentleness at Edward as she spoke, that a thrill of delight shot through his frame, and he exclaimed, with an emotion to which no woman's ear could be insensible,

" Think not for a moment of my danger; I would gladly lay down my life for you!"

The sound of commotion in the street without now became audible, and increased more while they spoke ; and when Ellen moved to the window and looked out, she suddenly withdrew, alarm impressed on every feature. " They are gathering fearfully,—it is impossible you can escape by the front ; the court in the rear opens on the canal, and a boat is at the stair.— Hasten, Ernestine!" she exclaimed to a fair-haired girl, her attendant; " put this gentleman across the canal, and you will escape immediate interruption. Lead him at once to the nearest gate,—get him out of the town, for Heaven's sake—and when once you gain the suburb," she added, addressing herself to Edward, "you can procure the means of escape, and neglect it not for an instant, as you value your life. Fly! I beseech you."

" Lady!" said Edward, " I have a word in private for you."

" There is no time."

"I cannot leave without."

Ellen rapidly waved the attendants from the room, and closed the door.

" Be brief."

" I may never see you again, but I cannot leave you without telling you, that a mad presumption has entered my heart,—Oh, do not start—I am going.—I hope and believe I shall yet have fortune, and one day *might* hope—Oh, say, if ever I come back, where may I hear of you? Do I presume too much?—Oh, be not angry with me!" he exclaimed, imploringly, dropping on his knee at her feet, and taking her hand.

" Against one who has been my preserver," said Ellen, trembling, " gratitude forbids I should entertain anger ;—but this is folly, and may cost you your life."

" Then answer—where shall I hear of you?"

" To save your life I *must* speak," said Ellen. " At the Convent of the Assumption, in this city, you are likely always to hear of me."

" A convent!" exclaimed Edward, with a look of horror.

A louder murmur rose from the street as he spoke, and Ellen's pallor and tremor increased.

" If you really respect me," she said, " fly."

He ventured to press the hand he held to his lips, and rose, and uttering a passionate farewell, hurried from the room. On the stairs Ernestine was waiting for him, and beckoned him rapidly to follow her. To run down the court, jump into a boat, and cross a canal, was the work of a very few minutes, and a **few more found them threading back streets towards one of the** gates. As they hurried along, a chime of bells rang out, and an expression of alarm overspread the girl's face, as she beckoned Edward to greater speed, and ran forward to the gate that was now in sight. They ran till they were out of breath, and reached the guarded portal only to learn that the gates were closed for the night, and none must pass.

———————

CHAPTER VIII.

ERNESTINE could not avoid betraying in her countenance alarm and anxiety, which might have been enough to awaken the suspicion of the sentry had he been a reasonable man; but, as he was a conceited fellow, he attributed the changing colour of the damsel to the result of the impertinent love-glances he cast from those bold eyes, which he fancied capable of conquering any woman alive, and, as he ogled the fair Fleming most unequivocally, the girl's agitation was set down to his grenadier gallantry.

Ernestine through all her alarm saw this, and with womanly readiness determined to make use of it; she pouted her ripe lips into the prettiest form of entreaty, and bent the most love-like gaze of supplication from her blue eyes as she urged every ingenious plea she could think of, to be permitted to pass the wicket. It was in vain;—to every appeal the grenadier only chucked her under the chin, and told her to "try again," till at last Ernestine, seeing he was making a jest of her, left off calling him "cruel," which she hoped would have made him kind, and saying he was an impertinent fellow, turned away from the gate, in bitter disappointment that all the powder and shot of her coquetry had been thrown away, and in much anxiety respecting the safety of the young gentleman who had been put under her charge. For some time the girl seemed absorbed in thought, as she traced her steps with speed across the bridge and down the main street from the gate, till turning into one less frequented she relaxed her speed, and, looking round to see that none were near to observe, she stretched forth her arms in the action of swimming, with a look of inquiry to Ned, who having answered by a nod of assent, she hurried forward again. Ernestine's pantomimic question arose from a little plot she had contrived for placing her charge in some place of safety *within* the city, as she

could not get him *out* of it; and as the only one she knew was in
a public part of the town, and not far from where the fatal affray
took place, the difficulty lay in getting the fugitive there without
observation.   This she feared was impossible by crossing any of
the bridges—at least it was perilous; and as the house she intended for his sanctuary had a water-gate which opened on one
of the canals, her plan was to go round by the bridges by herself,
and leave Edward to lie in some momentary place of concealment, till she could advertise the inmates of the house of her
intention, and give a signal to Ned from the opposite side of the
canal, which, as he could swim, would present no other obstacle
than a wet jacket between him and security.

The understanding between Ned and his guide had been so
perfect by the mere intervention of gesture, that no further explanation was required, for the present, to comprehend one another's
meaning,—he understanding she expected him to swim, and she
quite satisfied he could do so; therefore, she trotted on, and he
after her, through a multiplicity of intricate windings, which
reminded Ned of his native town in their high flavour and nar-
rowness.*   They soon debouched, however, from these unsavoury
labyrinths into the broader and more frequented part of the town;
but the relief to one sense gave alarm to another, for the eye
became painfully alive to passing groups, whose upraised voices
and gestulation showed they were moved by some event producing popular excitement, and many of the military were among
them.   Ernestine hurried across one thoroughfare thus occupied,
and cast a furtive glance backward to see that Edward followed
unmolested, and, when assured of this, she took no further notice,
but led onward with unslackened pace through the quieter inter-
secting street till she reached the opening on the next highway,
where a sight was before her enough to shake a stouter heart;
for a party of soldiers were at the moment bearing over the bridge
the body of Lerroux on a litter, and seemed excited even to
ferocity.

Ernestine grew white with terror, and, turning suddenly
back, absolutely dragged Edward after her till they reached a
low-browed arch leading up a dark entry, to the farthest extremity of which they quickly retired, waiting in silent anxiety
until the receding murmurs should tell them the savage crowd
was past.   They listened breathlessly, but the noise increased

---

* There are many points of similitude between Bruges and Galway.
The heavy portals forming the entrance to quadrangular buildings,—the
narrow passages through successive arches, not over sweet,—and the
Spanish look of the women with their ample cloaks. This may be
accounted for by the existence of Spanish power in the Nstherlands, and
Spanish intercourse with Galway in ancient times.

rather than diminished, and to their dismay the mob turned
down the street to which they were so close. Ernestine, trembling from head to foot, leaned for support on Ned, who grasped
the handle of his sword in readiness to sell his life dearly, if need
might be.   On poured the stream of the growling and swearing
multitude, past the little entry, which reverberated to their heavy
tramp, and whence the fugitives could see from out the friendly
shadow the grim faces that were passing.   The numbers grew
less and less—the murmur faded into distance, and soon the
tramp of some following straggler alone disturbed the quiet
street.   Ernestine ventured to peep out, and, beckoning Edward
to follow, they emerged from their hiding-place and again dared
the streets, over which the shadows of evening now falling,
favoured their retreat, which the careful girl still contrived
should lie through the most quiet ways.   At last they arrived at
an open square, whose odour proclaimed it at once a fishmarket,
and whose proximity to the water showed the fitness of the
locality.   Hurrying to the quay, Ernestine, after casting a few
inquiring glances about, thought a barge moored to the bank the
most favourable chance that offered for her purpose, and, stepping
on board, she was soon joined by Edward. She pointed to a house
nearly opposite, with a water-gate opening directly upon the canal,
and gave Edward to understand that he should remain in the
barge until she could get round by a bridge to that particular
house, to which, as soon as he saw *her*, he should swim. She
then departed hastily, and Edward cast a glance across the water
to measure the distance of his aquatic short cut.

  Not far from his promised asylum stood a building of such
quaint and peculiar beauty, that Edward, even amidst the reasonable anxiety of his situation, could not avoid remarking it. Its
graceful pinnacles yet sparkled in the sunset, and the elaborate
beauty of their form was more remarkable from being wrought
in brick, whose makers and layers in olden time must have far
surpassed all modern workmen, judging from the exquisite specimens still to be seen in Holland and Belgium. But though its
pinnacles were still bright, the greater mass of the building was
sinking into shade, relieved only by the small squares of glass
in its ample windows catching a light here and there, which, reflected in the canal beneath, broke the massiveness of shadow
which would otherwise have been heavy, and made one of those
pictures which only such amphibious places afford.

  He withdrew his eyes now and then from the sparkling pinnacles to cast a glance at the little water-gate, in search of Ernestine, and had not long to wait, for the assiduous girl had used all
speed to accomplish her object; and Edward soon saw her
standing within the recess of the opposite arch, and waving a

handkerchief by way of signal.   Letting himself down gently by
a rope from the barge's side into the water, to avoid the noise a
plunge would have made, he struck out boldly across the canal
and Ernestine received the dripping fugitive with smiles and tes-
timonies of admiration, and led him immediately up a winding
stair, at the head of which a fat old lady, the picture of good
living, was waiting to receive him.   She shook him by the
hand with an air of elaborate politeness, and said, "Velkim
velkim."   She then talked an immensity in her own language
with a word of English here and there, to Ned, who was shaking
the weight of water from his garments in the hall, while the fat
old lady poured a torrent of directions to Ernestine, who was
running up stairs after having received them, but was recalled to
get a fresh supply of orders.   Off went Ernestine again, and by
the time she was near the top of the house, the old babbler must
have her back for some fresh order,—and this was repeated
several times, till the girl's patience was exhausted, and, affecting
not to hear the recall still screamed after her, she pursued her
way up stairs to get fresh clothes for Edward.

The old lady then told him she could speak English, though
he would have scarcely found it out without her saying so, for
her few words, badly pronounced, were so crushed between her
native gutturals, with which she made up her conversation, that
no dictionary in the language would have recognised the disfigured creatures as acquaintances, and they could only be classed
amongst the vagrants and vagabonds that go wandering over the
world without a claim on any society : few and shapeless as the
words were, however, she made it intelligible that she acquired a
knowledge of English from her second husband, but that it was
to her third that Edward was to be indebted for his clothes.

"But yaw are vet, naut moche, I dink," said Madam Ghabbelkramme.

Ned shook his head, and the skirts of his coat. and said
"Very."

"Bote it vos soi droi here—very—dis zummer."

"Maybe so, ma'am," said Ned ; "but the canal is very wet
I assure you."

"Ah no—cannaut—dis year rain not moche."

"The little that was of it, ma'am," said Ned, "is very pene-
trating, however."

The feet of Ernestine were now heard pattering down stairs
and she soon made her appearance, bearing a bundle of clothes.

Madam attempted a long talk with Ernestine about the
clothes, which the girl strove to cut short by hurrying towards
a side room off the hall ; but madam held her back by her skirt
as she gained the door, and said that, as the garments had not

been worn since her poor dear good man had died, that they must
want airing. To which the girl replied, with an exclamation of
wonder at madam's absurd care, that they were certainly more
dry than those the young gentleman had on him. Edward,
seeing the tendency to discussion on the old lady's part, lost no
time in following Ernestine into the room; where the girl, de-
positing the clothes in a chair, gave him a significant nod to
make the most of his time; and, notwithstanding the old lady's
attempt to establish a parley at the portal, Edward contrived to
get the door shut sooner than his hostess thought consistent with
that politeness to the fair sex which she constantly preached, and
of which she considered herself a most deserving object.

She kept talking to him, however, through the door all the
time Ned was effecting his change, which presented two difficulties, the first to drag off the wet garments which clung to him,
and the second to keep the ample folds which had encased the
rotund proportions of the late Herr Ghabbelkramme from falling
about his heels; no possible buttoning would do it, and he was
fain to hold them up with his hands, which the capacious sleeves
and heavy ruffles of the portly burgher rendered nearly useless.
It was as much as Ned could do to get one hand free to open the
door, at which the fussy old lady began to knock impatiently,
and when she entered, her desire to give Ned a second shake of
welcome by the other almost produced a catastrophe which it
would have given us pain to record. Ernestine saw our hero's
difficulty, and, while she laughed at it, promptly set about its
removal; huge pins were put in requisition, and at length the
application of a scarf round his middle set Ned's mind at ease
and his hands at liberty, whereupon his fat hostess shook them
heartily, and remarked to Ernestine, how slender the youth
looked in the burgher's clothes.

"Augh!" exclaimed she in German, "Ghabbelkramme was
a fine man—but to say the truth, the youth is good-looking."
She then led the way to another chamber, where the supper
table, handsomely provided at all points, was laid, and, after
some words to Ernestine, the latter departed, and Edward was
left *tête-à-tête* with the old lady, who did not seem in the least
to regret that he did not answer one word, but appeared the
happier that she had all the talk to herself, in which she never
relaxed for one moment. There were a good many pictures in
the room, most of them daubs done to order; among them were
three portraits of the three former lords and masters of the extensive domain of female loveliness that now stood before
Edward, and this she contrived to make him understand by
pointing to them and saying, as each was indicated—

"Dat is mine von; dat is mine doo; dat is mine pree. Mine

von vos gooder; mine doo vos beaster; but, mine dree vos pigger. Dem is his goats;" and she pointed to Ned's coat and nether garments as she spoke. She then indicated several portraits of herself at different periods of life; and by reference to these and those of her husbands, and afterwards calling his attention to various composition pictures which hung round the room, gave him to understand that she and her former lords had sat as models for the principal figures. It would seem the tastes had varied at the different periods of these pictures being painted. In the earliest, the Pastoral prevailed—Madame figured as a shepherdess. In the second, Mythology was laid under contribution for the subject; and here, as Daphne, she was escaping at the very moment of metamorphose from a bloated Apollo, who seemed very much blown with his run; while the tree into which she was changing was by far the least wooden part of the picture. In the third era Scriptural subjects prevailed, and this mountain of "too solid flesh" had done some of the most renowned beauties of sacred history the favour of being their representative. In some of the accessory seraphic groups, too, she would indicate the handsomest, and say "*Dat is me;*—but here is 'noder—ver goot indeet;" and she pointed to the largest picture in the room, the subject being Tobit and the Angel. "Dat is goot to ebbery potty *ebbery time* (which was the old lady's way of expressing *always*)—Ghabbelkramme vos Tobit— de *hangel* is *me.*" Ned found it difficult to resist laughing, and commenced a voluble praise of the picture to escape such a breach of politeness, remarking how very naturally the fish was represented.

"Oh, yais," said madam, "ebbery ting from nature—de veesh vrom de market—ver goot—after bainter baint him, de cock made him for zuppers;—ebbery ting from nature, ebbery time, in goot vorks;—Ghabbelkramme vos Tobit—de veesh vrom de veesh—and de hangel is *me.*" Ned could no longer resist a smile, but perceiving which, she requested him to remember that she was much more beautiful *then* than *now;* and by certain applications of her hands squeezing in her present redundancy, and her pointed finger referring to departed dimples, and cutting certain figures through the air indicating various lines of beauty, she endeavoured to convince her guest that she was the remains of a Venus, somewhat enlarged.

"But dat is all mine goot humour,—I am so grabble, (agreeable, she meant to say), it is bleasant to live mid me, I do adsure you;" and she gave Ned a tender glance as she spoke.

"All mine von, mine doo, mine dree, zay I vos so grabble; dere is mek me happy-not, only von ting,—I am 'vraid zum day

I vill grow too tick:" she was eighteen stone, if she was a pound, as she spoke the words.

Ned would have given the world to have laughed out, and screwed his mouth into all sorts of shapes, to keep in the rebellious merriment that was producing internal convulsion.

"I zee," said the old lady, "you laughs at mine bat vorts of Hingelish; but you naut know notten *Deitch*—zo me petters dan you." Leaving the room as she spoke, Ned was left to his own observations of the chamber, which had much in it indicating wealth. There were an Indian cabinet and screen, jars and beakers of china, idols of marble and gilded metal, and monsters in porcelain of the direst forms of ugliness, rich cornices and mouldings, hangings of that stiff damask which we only now have a notion of through old pictures, and tall backed chairs of walnut wood and cut velvet inviting to sedentary ease. Everything in the room bore an aspect curiously coinciding with the figure of the mistress. The cabinet was square-built and thick, and one open drawer, crammed with a medley of things, gave some idea of the surfeit under which the rest were labouring; while another empty one seemed protruded by the poor cabinet itself to get a mouthful of air. The jars were of the most rotund forms, the dragons seemed bursting, the idols were bloated, and the very chairs seemed stuffed as full as they could cram. His further observation was interrupted by the return of his hostess, followed by a stout-built *frau*, bearing a tray holding several dishes; upon which, as they were laid one by one on the table, the lady who feared she would grow "too tick" looked with an eye of affection little in keeping with such an apprehension, and, when all was ready, she motioned Ned to a chair, and then, flopping down into one herself, squeezed as near the table as *her good humour* would allow her, and commenced operations. After helping her guest, she set to herself, and though Ned, as might be expected from his youth, and hardy calling, could play a tolerably good knife and fork, or was, in Irish parlance, a capital "trencher-boy," he was a fool to his hostess, who made astounding havoc with both eatables and drinkables. No sooner was one dish cleared, than an assault was made on another; and, though Ned did all he could to keep a lady in countenance, he was forced to give in long before she relaxed in her labour of love. Heavens! how she did gobble and swill! it was almost sublime, and, somehow or other, she contrived to talk all the time. At last she seemed to have done, and spoke to the servant, who partly cleared the table and retired, and the interval was made use of by Madame Ghabbelkramme to pull a large handkerchief from her pocket and rub down her face, which began to give some dewy evidence of the exertion she had gone through. She pulled a second handkerchief from another pocket, and before making use of it, said, "I am zo partic, ebbery time, mid mine ankleshift,—you zee I habben von—to make mine nose—and 'nudder vor to zweep mine face."

The servant returned bearing an enormous dish of salad,—a perfect stack of vegetable production, which Ned declined meddling with, though assured by his hostess it was an excellent thing after a hearty meal; but she remarked after his continued refusal to taste it, that perhaps he was right, as he was "too tin" to eat salad;—"Bickos," added she, "I take him vor to kip minezelf tin." Then plunging her weapons right into the whole dish of vegetable, she began to gobble salad in a style that might have shamed a Neapolitan bolting macaroni, and, as she paused sometimes to take breath, would pant forth this assurance to Ned: "Augh!—dat is goot for me!" But, as every thing in this world must come to an end, poor Madame Ghabbelkramme finished her salad at last, and, sighing, she followed the dish with her eyes as it was borne away by the attendant *frau*. The table, however, was replenished with dishes of fruit; and burly, round-bodied, jolly-looking bottles, filled with good wine, and long-stemmed glasses, ornamented with spiral lines of white, sparkled gaily on the board. In making free with these, Ned had a better chance of coping with the old lady, though it is not unlikely, if she had a mind, she could have put Ned under the table. The curtains being drawn, and the chamber well lighted with plenty of wax candles, which stood in handsome candelabra of bronze gilt, resting on richly carved oaken brackets, and the servant having retired, they were now left to themselves, and another avalanche of talk fell upon Ned. She told him she was very rich, with good houses, and good plate; "gelt and silber,—and blenty,"—and she "so grabble," that it was easy to live with her,—and Bruges was a very good town to live in. On asking Ned if he did not think so, he answered, that it was impossible he could judge, as he had but just arrived. To this she replied that he might stay in Bruges as long as he liked, where he might consider *her* house as *his*. She then told him something of her history, assuring him that when young she was extremely handsome, and even now that she had a more delicate skin than many a girl, and held out her arm to Ned that he might prove it by touch. He, young in the world, and never having had the opportunity of observing to what absurd lengths vanity can be stretched, did not attribute the old lady's absurdity to its true cause, but began to think she was a little mad; and, instead of being inspired with disgust, entertained pity for her, which gave such a softness to his manner, that the old dame entertained a notion she was making a conquest, and began to look round the room to see if there was a spare corner for Ned's picture. To Ned's great relief, their conversation was interrupted by the arrival of Ellen, attended by Ernestine, though the pleasure he experienced on beholding her, which at first chased every other idea, was a little dashed when he rose at her entrance; for the feeling of the fat burgher's clothes slipping off gave him such a notion of his own ridiculous figure, that it shocked him to be in such a plight by his charmer. She, crossing the room with exquisite grace, approached Madame Ghabbelkramme to make her salutation, which the old lady did not seem inclined to receive a bit too well, for it disturbed her in the pursuit of an agreeable idea. Ellen then turning to Edward begged him to be seated, with an air of the gentlest courtesy: he was glad to obey, being conscious he looked less ridiculous sitting, as he could stow away some of the extra folds and flaps and skirts of *Mynherr's* voluminous garments behind him, and show a better front.

"Vat vor you kummen here?" inquired Madame Ghabbelkramme, rather gruffly, cranching an apple while she spoke.

"I came to thank you, my dear Madame," replied Ellen, in the sweetest manner, "for the protection you have afforded this gentleman." As if she thought the ceremonious term of "gentleman" cold, she then said,—"my friend;" and then, as if she feared she had said too much, added,—"my father's friend."

Edward bowed low as she uttered the words, and felt himself elevated in the scale of creation, to have won such a name from *her* lips.

"And I am glad to tell you," she continued to Edward, "that I have interested the good Father Flaherty in your behalf, and he has promised to see you into a sure place of safety, and get you unharmed out of the town."

"He is 'nuff safe vere he is," replied Madame Ghabbelkramme, tartly; "ve vant naut Vader Flart."

"Remember, dear madam, that, in case of need, he could place him in sanctuary."

"Sanctum—fittle! de yhung mans is fer goot vere he is ;—vaut a vright you iz, mine loaf, to-night! you iz a vite as mine dabble-clout ;"—and she laid her hand on the table-cloth as she spoke; "vy iz you naut all rosen liken to me?"

"I have been much frightened, madam, this evening."

"Yais,—you looks liken to dead; you iz alfays too tin, bote now you looken like a skelter."

"Not *quite* a skeleton, madam," said Ellen, smiling.

"Yais,—skelleter ;—you never had proper-shins."

Edward, who had hitherto listened with amazement, became indignant at what he thought an attack on the symmetry of

tne young lady's legs, not being able to comprehend that old
Ghabblekramme meant *proportions*, when she said "proper-
shins."

Ellen only laughed, and the old lady continued:—

"You can laughen, mine tear,—bote you iz no peauty, dough
you tink zo,—maynbe;—young foomins tinks it peauty to be
tin,—but de mans knows petters. Now you looken, mine tear!"
and taking a knife in her hand and holding it upright on the
table, she said: "Dere! you are just liken to dat—stret before,
and stret behind, and *vairy* tin."

Ned could hardly keep his temper; but the gentle smile of
Ellen calmed him by its sweetness, and when he saw Ernestine
laughing behind the old woman's chair, it taught him to regard
the old lady's speeches as they did. As he looked at Ernestine,
he saw a dark figure emerge from behind a screen, and gently
approach the chair of Madame Ghabbelkramme, as she continued:—

"Yais, mine loaf, don't you be konsetted;—if you aff hearen
as I aff hearen de mans talk of de foomins, you vould know
petters: a poor tin tread of a ting is not grabble to de mans, I
do adsure you!—de talken of poor tin tings, as—cane chairs,
mine loaf;—as teal poards, mine tear!"

By this time, Father Flaherty, for it was he whom Ned had
been advance, laid his hand on the back of Madame Ghabblekramme's chair, and overlooking the mountain of conceit beneath
him, exclaimed in a rich brogue, after she had uttered the
words, "deal poards and cane chairs,"—"Arrah, then, Madame
Ghabbelkramme, *acushla*, did you ever hear of such a thing as a
feather-bed?"

Ned could "mind his manners" no longer,—he burst out
laughing, and even the trained courtesy of Ellen could not
repress her mirth. Ernestine, though she could not understand a word, gathered the meaning from the result of the
father's speech, and ran out of the room to enjoy herself at
freedom in the hall.

"Yais,—Vader Flart,—I know vat is vedder bet;—dere is
vedder bet in mine 'ouse."

"All the town knows *that*, ma'am."

"And you taken avay must not—dis yhung mans,—vor I aff
a vedder bet vor him dis neight, so kumfitab."

"It would be too much indulgence, ma'am, for a youth. I
must treat him to sackcloth and ashes in my own little gazebo."

"No, no!—not must be, Vader Flart!" Then turning to
Edward, she said, "You vill not go,—you vill not go to zack-
clout, and leaf your vedder bet,—you *vill* not leaf your
vedder bet?"

She said this so tenderly, that Ned, remembering its allusion to herself, could not repress a smile, though he answered respectfully, that, much as he thanked her for the offer of her hospitality, he was bound to go wherever *Mademoiselle* and the good Father desired.

"Den you are bat mans, Vader Flart, to take away mine *rent*."

Ned hurried from the room with the Father, who came provided with a proper disguise; and in the side chamber off he hall, where Ned made his first change, he assumed a clerical habit, more suited to his size than the garments of the fat burgher.

"'Pon my word, you are a good figure for the part, young gentleman," said Father Flaherty to Ned, when he was dressed; "only your hair has a very unsanctified twist about it; how ever, we can shave your head if necessary."

With this prospect of losing what it must be confessed Ned was a little vain of, and which, as he hoped to see Ellen again before he left Bruges, he particularly wished to preserve, he left the house closely tucked under the sheltering wing of Father Flaherty, who kept humming snatches of Irish tunes as they wended their way through the now silent streets.

Passing in front of the *Hotel de Ville*, they walked close beside a soldier, keeping guard beneath its massive and lofty tower; and the *padre* remarked, it was little the sentry knew who was close to him! Striking across the ample square in its front, the chimes of the *carillon* rang forth, and Edward recognised in the plaintive melody the very notes he found written on the music paper he made prize of at Hamburgh. With those who love, every circumstance that relates to their passion, culminating to the one dear point, increases its force, and so the merest trifles become important. Thus it was with Edward on hearing the chime;—he stopped suddenly and listened, and the sweet tones of the bells, as they rang out their liquid melody high in air, seemed like aërial voices speaking to him of his love.

"What ails you?" said the priest.

"Oh those bells!" exclaimed Edward in ecstasy.

"Why, then, is it stoppin' you are to listen to the clatter of *thim owld* pots and pans!" exclaimed the priest, dragging him onward.

What a savage Ned thought Father Flaherty, and what a simpleton the father thought Ned!

"Sure this is twice as purty a tune as that owld *cronan*," said the priest, lilting a bit of an Irish jig, which quickened their pace by urging them to step in time to it, and brought them the sooner to the end of their walk.

Ned thankfully refused the hospitable offers of refreshment on the part of the *padre*, as his supper had been so substantial; and after the excitement and fatigue of mind and body he had experienced, he began to feel the need of rest, and the kind-hearted priest showed him to his sleeping-room.

Now that he was alone and in security, the eventful circumstances of the last few hours crowded rapidly upon him, and, despite his need of rest, kept him wakeful: the thought that he had sacrificed a human life, though in self-defence, and what was to him still dearer, in defence of her in whose cause he would have laid down his own a thousand times, weighed heavily upon him, and he prayed long and fervently, ere he lay down to sleep, for pardon of his unpremeditated guilt. His conscience thus soothed, poor Edward flung himself on his bed, and exhausted nature yielded to that benign influence which can alone restore her—profound sleep.

CHAPTER IX.

It took some hearty shakes by the shoulder to rouse Ned from his sleep the next day, when, at rather an advanced hour, Father Flaherty told him it was time to rise. Resuming his clerical disguise, he descended from his dormitory, and joined the worthy father at breakfast, after which they quitted the house, and proceeded towards the cathedral of *Notre Dame*. The gigantic outward proportions of the building struck Edward with amazement; but when he passed into the interior, a sense of solemn admiration made him stand still and silent before he advanced many steps.

There is a reverential feeling, produced by the aspect of a large gothic interior, which even long habit cannot overcome: the first experience of it is almost oppressive. The cold vastness into which we at once are plunged on passing the portal has a chastening effect, and we pause; the lessened light permitted through its painted windows has a subduing influence, yet gratifies the sense of beauty by the tinted loveliness it sheds wherever it falls. The eye, raised in involuntary wonder up those lofty yet slender shafts that bear the over-hanging pile above, is lost in the complex beauty of the fretted roof. With slow and respectful steps, we move towards the centre of the aisle; we stand beside one of those apparently slender columns, and perceive it is a ponderous mass of masonry, to which the artifice of sculpture has imparted the seeming of lightness, and the presence at once of beauty and power commands our homage. We look through that long vista of columns that stand like mighty sentinels guarding the approach to the altar, shedding its glories of gold and marble and pictured art from afar, through the open arch of the elaborate screen, whose slender filagree seems to support, as if by magic, the gigantic organ above, whose melodious peal, should it then be waked, first bursting like thunder through the vaulted pile, and then fading to the faintest echo through the solemn vastness, fills the heart with a reverence bordering on awe, and lifts the mind above this world.

With what dumb-stricken admiration did Edward first behold the cathedral of *Notre Dame*, where the gorgeous ceremony of a high mass increased his reverential wonder! Imagine a young man from the remote shores of Ireland, where the humble chapel of a friary was all he had ever seen in the service of that religion, whose exercise was there and *then* little better than felonious;—imagine him, for the first time, entering a temple of colossal proportion and elaborate beauty, and witnessing a high mass, in all the pomp of a dominant religion, with its gorgeous altars, its massive wax-lights, the odour of incense flung from silver censers by numerous-acolytes before the train of bishop, priests, and deacons, clad in the utmost splendour of sacerdotal robes, amid the organ's plaintive notes or full-toned peal,—the wail of choral voices or their exulting burst, as they were subdued to the penitential spirit of the *Confiteor*, or rose to the triumphant outpouring of the *Gloria in excelsis*—imagine this, and think with what emotion Edward knelt at a high mass in Bruges! Though the service in word and act was the same, yet the difference in extrinsic circumstances might well suggest the internal question —"Can this be the same religion in which I was reared? Is this the poor frightened faith which hides in holes and corners in my native land?" And then the wish arose that those who sat in high places in Galway could only witness the splendour of the rites which appealed so powerfully to his own weak points. His passion for the lofty was flattered to its utmost bent by the "pomp and circumstance" he saw before him; and his father's apprehensions of the superior "gentility" of the protestant religion were no longer valid, for from that moment Ned was firm in the faith of Rome. It is not saying much for our hero, that such influences held sway in a cause where deeper and holier motives should operate; but it is our business to tell the truth of him, and not make him out to be either wiser or better than he was.

The service being over, Edward was conducted by Father Flaherty up a lofty winding stair, which led to a small chamber that seemed to be cut out of the thickness of the wall, and was desired to remain there until the priest should return to him. "And here is a book for you, my son," added he, handing him one of prayers. "You had better occupy your mind with good and holy thoughts while I am away, and chastise the proud spirit of humanity,—for though I don't want to be too hard on a poor fellow in distress, yet I must remind you, my son, that you must not forget you killed a man yesterday." Hereupon Edward expressed such contrition, and gave such manifest evidence of his sense of guiltiness, that the kind-hearted priest felt more inclined to comfort than to blame, and spoke words of hope to him.

"There, there, that will do now. You killed the man, 'tis true, but it was in a good cause—yet there is blood on your head, no doubt; but then, if you killed him, he was a blackguard, and no loss to king or country *agra!* so don't fret. Not but that I would put a good round penance on you, if you were staying here in quiet and safety; but considering that you have to run some risk before long, and might be taken off sudden, you see, I must not let you die in your sin, my poor boy, but must hear you make a clean breast of it, and give you absolution before you face the danger of the road: so while I am away, working out a little plan o' my own to get you out of the town, stick to that book like a good Christian, and chastise the proud spirit of humanity."

Leaving Edward with these words, the father went to make arrangements for an escape from the town; and an opportunity was offered by a procession of The Host being about to take place through one of the gates; and he conceived the stratagem of clothing Edward in the habit of an acolyte, and making him the bearer of one of the banners carried on the occasion, and thus eluding the vigilance of the guards. During his absence, Edward really did apply himself to the sacred book, the only interruption to his holy communings being the chimes of the *carillon*, which in the calmness of the day and the stillness of the high place where he sat, far above the noise of the town, he could distinctly hear. He felt it was sinful to wander from the sacred duty in which he was engaged; but as every thought of *her* in his mind belonged more to heaven than earth, the lapse, perhaps, was pardonable. When the chime ceased, he again applied himself to the book; and his attention never wandered from the sacred page until withdrawn by the reappearance of the kind *padre*, who came at once to confess and shrive and liberate him. Of confession there needed not much, for, to say truth, in knowing that he killed a fellow-creature, the priest knew the greatest of Ned's human offences; and as there was—

"Short time for shrift,"

he briefly received absolution of his sins, and was made ready for "rope or gun," as the case might be, in the gauntlet he was about to run for his life. He was then habited in a white surplice to represent an acolyte, and bade by the father to follow him. As they descended the long winding stair, the soft-hearted priest often paused to give Ned some fresh direction how he was to comport himself, and told him to be "no ways afear'd, nor *nervish*," though, in truth, the good father himself was infinitely more nervous about the matter than Ned. On reaching the church below, the persons to form the procession were assembling; and Father Flaherty, after a few minutes' absence in the vestry, returned in the sacredotal habit suited to the occasion, and placing Edward next him, joined in the line, which, emerging from the church, carried before it homage through every street. The doffed hat, and bended knee, and downcast eye of humility showed the fugitive what an admirable means it was of escaping not only interruption, but even observation; and a fresh wonder was revealed to him in the reverence the Romish faith obtained *here*. Encountering in their course a handsome *cortége*, where stately coach and prancing steed had place, the pageant made way, and the servants of the church held their road.

At last the gate came in sight, and Father Flaherty began to exhibit symptons of anxiety, while Ned was perfectly collected. The father was praying devoutly, mingling at the same time certain admonitions to the fugitive; and they were so rapidly alternated, that the good father sometimes looked to Ned when his addresses were meant for heaven; and he raised his eyes to the skies when he said something appertaining to his friend. For instance, winking at Ned, he exclaimed, "Holy Virgin, *purissima! pulcherrima!*—howld your banner straight. Holy saints and martyrs!—you'll be shot if you're discovered. Mind your eye when you come to the bridge, and don't look at them.— Guardian angels!—they've no mercy—but show a bowld face."

The sudden outburst of a bold strain from trumpets and drums now arrested their attention; and as they topped the middle of the bridge, they beheld a military column advancing, and close upon the gate. For the first time Ned felt somewhat nervous;—to be stopped just at the gate was awkward; but his apprehensions were only momentary; for the instant the advancing troops perceived the sacred procession, they halted; the serried masses filed right and left on each side of the road and as the procession of the Host passed uninterruptedly through the gate, it was met with a military salute as it progressed through the opened ranks; and when it reached that portion of the column where the standards were carried, the ensigns of a king were lowered before the banners of the cross.

———

CHAPTER X.

WE must now transfer our readers to the cabin of the Seagull, where, four days after his escape from Bruges, Ned was cracking an after-dinner bottle of most exemplary claret with Finch, luxuriating in repose and safety, rendered the more enjoyable from the fatigue and dangers he had undergone in making his way to Dunkirk. These fatigues and dangers, as well as his doings at Courtrai, he detailed to his friend while they sipped their wine; and the sparkling eye of the skipper, as he listened to the romantic recital, showed the ardent love he bore adventure. He congratulated his young friend on his having "done bravely," as he said, and foreboded brightly of the future. When Edward ventured a doubt of this, reminding him that Ellen would not have listened a moment to him but for the danger in which he stood, Finch met his doubtings with a laugh of derision.

"Tush, man! what a young hand you are at such matters! If she meant to crush your hopes, would she have gone to the old fat *frau's* house to see you?—answer me that."

"Consider," replied Ned, "that my life being endangered on her account, she came to see after my safety."

"Nonsense, I say," returned Finch. "Your safety could have been attended to by the old priest just as well; and take my word, if she was angry with you, you never more would have had a sight of her by her own act and will. I tell you, make money, lad; be rich, and the lady may be yours. Say no more about it for the present; you need rest, so turn in, and take no care."

The working of the windlass, and the song of the sailors, as they lifted the anchor, were now heard.

"Hark!" said Finch, "they are weighing, so I must go on deck now; to-morrow we shall talk more about this—good night."

Ned prepared to turn in with good will, and as the Seagull was standing out of the harbour before he got into his berth, the ripple of the water along her side helped to lull him to sleep ; for sweet to all who have ever known it, is the music of that sailor lullaby. When he rose the next morning, the gallant boat was bounding gaily over the waters, and most of the day was passed in talking of his affairs to Finch, who won more and more upon Edward as the intimacy increased. He could start no doubt for which Finch could not find a satisfactory answer; no adverse circumstance for which he did not at once name a countervailing expedient: there seemed in him such a fund of ready contrivance for the exigencies of every occasion, that he passed upon Ned for a marvel of sagacity, and he willingly rendered to his words that ready submission which in early youth is so easily yielded to those who have a command of glib language, and can adroitly make use of common-places, which pass as good as new on the uninitiated. Ned felt *very* happy ; he glided through the hours of the day as smoothly as the Seagull through the waters; and when the black cook had completed his work in the caboose, and the dinner was announced, he wondered how the time had passed, and could scarcely believe it was so late. The table still exhibited that superiority which Ned had first remarked, and when, after enjoying its good cheer, it was cleared, and that he and the skipper were left to themselves, he ventured to remark, that either the owners of the Seagull were much more liberal than those under whom he had had the chance to serve, or their trade must be far superior, to afford such enjoyments—"Unless," said Ned, suddenly catching at a thought, "unless you have a private fortune of your own."

"No fortune but what I make by the trade," answered Finch; "but then that trade is a glorious one! and the more a man knows of it, the better he likes it." He then enlarged upon the subject, and while discussing with his young friend seductive wines, and spirits, and liqueurs, discussed also some important questions of a fiscal nature; in the course of which all governments were shown up to Ned in the light of selfish and crafty tyrannies, whose only objects were robbery and oppression of the people, whose state would be too wretched for endurance but for the existence of free-hearted souls like the skipper, who endeavoured, by a generous and daring intervention, to counteract the baneful influence of the harpies who snatched from the labours of the industrious three-fourths of their honest earnings, by making them pay four times the original price of an article, which the skipper, in the spirit of philanthropy, was willing to supply to them for only twice the cost. Ned was fascinated by the glowing manner in which the skipper represented the case, yet, when all was done, he could not help saying, with great simplicity, "Why, as well as I can understand what you have been telling me, the traffic you speak of is very like what they call smuggling."

"That *is* the name the land-sharks give it," returned the skipper; "but we call it ' free trade.' "

"Well, now, isn't it odd," said Ned, " that, often as I've heard the phrase 'free trade,' I never knew what it meant before?"

"Not odd at all, my lad.—You are too young to know much yet, and the more you learn in my school the better you'll like it. Besides, instead of your paying your master, your learning shall line your pockets with gold, boy; and then—ah! I see your eye brighten!—then your heart's desire may be realised. Yes, when once you command the influence of what I call the magical letters—the £ s. D.—then you may ask and have the girl of your heart. But, even without this inducement, the romantic adventures we sometimes turn up—'splood! 'twould make a fellow of spunk a free trader, for the mere sport of the thing." A commendatory slap on the shoulder served for sauce to this speech; and the bright eye of the dashing skipper beamed upon Ned, as if he saw in him some future hero of free trade.

Ned went to sleep that night, his head heated with wine and the inflammable conversation of his friend; but in his dreams the glories of "free trade" always presented themselves in the shape of "smuggling;" and he saw his father's honest shop, and his father's honest face, and a frown upon it: he tossed and tumbled, and awoke rather feverish; but a walk upon deck in the fresh morning breeze, before which the Seagull was bounding over the bright waters, cooled his blood, and the activity of waking life dispelled every sad thought the visions of sleep had created. In truth, he must have been a determinately gloomy fellow who could be sad on board the Seagull, for a merrier set of fellows never stepped on deck than her picked crew, which was chosen by the skipper himself, whose skill in selecting the men suited to his purpose amounted almost to instinct. He made it a rule never to have an ill-tempered man in the crew; if he chanced to make a mistake in his selection, which was rarely, he always got rid of the sulker; the consequence was that the duty was done with a spirit and heartiness which was quite beautiful. It was this same quick perception of men's qualities that made him pitch upon Ned: he had lately lost his mate, and among his crew he did not know one exactly suited to fill the place, and he fancied he saw that in Ned which promised, in the service, a bold, active, and enthusiastic participation, without which the daring risks of a smuggler's life could never be surmounted. He was not long in proving his neophyte. Ned was soon engaged in running some goods under very trying circumstances, and acquitted himself so well that he won the praises of the skipper, who handed him over a purse with no contemptible number of gold pieces, as his share of the night's work. Ned would have refused them, but his friend was peremptory.

"The money is *your right*, lad!—the owners consider that short reckonings make long friends; and after each successful turn of traffic, every man in the craft has his purse the heavier for it."

"Yet I have a scruple of conscience about it, somehow," said Ned. "I am not quite satisfied this smuggling is right."

"It is not right to *let it be known*," said Finch,—"that is the only harm to avoid. Bless your innocent heart! If you but knew the worshipful men ashore who are engaged in it, you would soon be reconciled to the practice. I tell you, lad, the outcry and scandal raised against it is only a got-up concern by those to whose interest its suppression tends—those in high places—and men of sense *know it is so*; and therefore, while they would avoid the publication and penalty of their doings, nevertheless dare to do what they are convinced is not morally wrong in itself, and brings those who have hardihood to venture, large profits. Could you but see the smooth and silky man who reaps his thousands a year from the Seagull—a sanctified man; —goes to church three times on Sunday; a most worshipful man on 'Change:—an upholder of church and king; whose adversary, Charles Edward, he would gladly hang—though he thinks it no harm to get on the weather-side of his majesty's exchequer:—so take cash and counsel, and be the richer and wiser."

Ned never had so much money in all his life at once, and there is something in the chink of a purse full of gold amazingly attractive, as a young fellow chucks it up and down in his hand, with the internal complacent feeling of "*this is mine.*" Ned had some qualms at the notion of being, after all that could be said for it, engaged in an illegal traffic; for though he had been humbly, he had been honestly reared. So far the pursuit was repugnant to the earliest lessons he had received, and next, his acquired notions did not exactly chime with it—he was not sure that it was *genteel*, and there is no doubt he would have declined engaging in a contraband trade, but for the hope it held out of sudden wealth, whose first instalment was in his hand. Not that Ned loved money for money's sake:—we believe there are few souls base enough to be actuated by this wretched motive; but he saw in it the means to realise the fond dreams in which he had dared to indulge; to fulfil aspirations that, however wild, were those which the noblest spirit might entertain. And thus gold may become precious n the eye of the enthusiast for the sake of

6

what it may win. Refined in the fire of love, and bearing an ethereal impress, it ranks above the mints of kings and purposes of common traffic;—it becomes the coin of the realm of romance, and we may wish for its possession without being sordid.

Thus Ned was fairly enlisted—the bounty-money was in his hand, and he became a hearty contrabandist. Having made the first plunge, having gone through the trial with *éclat*, the golden harvest being suddenly reaped, with the increasing favour of the fascinating skipper, before whose plausible words all objections melted away insensibly, a few months discovered him to be, as Finch anticipated, one of the most ready, quick-witted, and daring followers of the "free trade." He soon became mate of the Seagull, and won so fast on the confidence and good-will of his chief, that the latter let him do very nearly what he liked; and to such a height did this esteem increase, that on one occasion, when a severe indisposition obliged the skipper to stay ashore, the craft and her cargo were entirely trusted to Ned, who won fresh reputation by the skill which he displayed in the conduct of the venture.

Ned's berth on board the boat was a picture of neatness, and a touch of his quality might be felt from the shelves of books with which it was stored. Histories of adventure, both real and fictitious, lives of remarkably daring persons, romances and books of poetry, abounded there. A few works of navigation also, with which science Ned had made it a point to become well acquainted, and instruments necessary for its practice as well. All these little possessions he had ample means to purchase, and had handfuls of money to squander beside in all the pleasures that might tempt a young man on shore, if by such pleasures Ned could have been tempted;—but he loved, and the poetry of passion preserved him through many a trial. Besides, his main object was to accumulate as much money as possible,—not that his present profits, liberal as they were, would have soon realised a fortune; but they made a handsome beginning, and Finch held out the hope of soon being enabled to purchase a vessel for himself, in which Ned should hold a share; and "then, my lad," he was wont to say, "then shan't we have the wind in our sails?—wait a while;— once let us possess our own craft, and a couple of years shall make us good matches for ladies even as charming as yours."

In one of their runs across the North Sea, after having made a safe landing of their cargo, Finch told Ned he had entered into an engagement to remove secretly from England a couple of his countrymen, who, becoming obnoxious to government, from being engaged in making enlistments for foreign service in Ireland, were obliged to fly; and, dreading the vigilance of the servants of the law at the ports, which were strictly watched, offered a handsome sum to be taken off at some convenient and secret place along the coast, where they might embark with less risk of discovery.

"One of them I know," said Finch; "his name is O'Hara, an officer of the Irish brigade. I promised to meet him at a little inn that lies some miles inland, and while I am absent you can stand out and keep a good offing, away from all observation from the land, and be back about the same time to-morrow, and hang about that point to the westward, where I know there is a little creek will suit our purpose.

All their measures being preconcerted, signals agreed on, and other necessary arrangements entered into, Finch doffed his sailor's guise, and assuming the landsman's attire, became at once the dashing looking fellow, who so won upon Ned at Hamburgh. A boat was lowered, which rowed the skipper to the shore, and afterwards returned to the Seagull, which stood out from the land, while Finch pursued his course to the appointed inn to meet the fugitives, who so anxiously sought the aid of his friendly vessel. A walk of some two or three miles brought him to a farm house, where, by the offer of a guinea, he obtained the loan of the farmer's horse for the next twenty-four hours. The good man proceeded at once to the stable to saddle his nag, which was soon ready for the road. Finch, as he was going to mount, addressed the farmer, saying, "By-the-bye, my friend, as you know nothing of me, had I not better leave you a deposit for the value of your horse?"

"Na, na," said the farmer, "yow'll bring un back, I's not aveard."

Finch was pleased with this exhibition of good faith, arising from an honest nature, which could not suspect guile in another; but willing to pursue his train of doubt regarding himself a little farther, he continued, "How do you know I won't steal your horse, and that you'll never set eyes on me again?"

"*Whoi*," said the blunt fellow, with a faint gleam of fun lighting up his habitually quiet eye, and casting a glance at Finch from top to toe, "whatever mischief yow'll be after, I don't think it's a stealing of a 'orse *yow'll* be 'anged vur."

Finch laughed at the rejoinder, and applied his heel to the side of his steed with a galliard air, as if he expected "Dobbin" was to prance off in a corresponding manner, but as his heel was unarmed, (for spurs are not articles in much requisition on board ship, though we have heard of "horse marines,") Dobbin only grunted, and stirred not a peg.

The farmer had the laugh against Finch once more, and said, "Ah—yow beant up to our honest country ways; that be an honest beast yow're a ridin on; he waunt do nothin' onless he be convinced it's roight, and I'll give yow an argument for un." So saying, he went into the house and returned with a heavy thong-whip, which, before presenting to Finch, he cracked loudly, and Dobbin pricked up his ears directly.

"I towld 'e so," said the farmer, chuckling, "I towld 'e he'd listen to reason."

Handing the whip to the rider with these words, the latter was not idle in reasoning Dobbin into a trot, though it cannot be denied that Finch was very much shaken in his argument; however, on they went wrangling over ten miles of ground, both right glad when the discussion was over. Calling for the hostler, and giving the beast into his charge with a good natured admonition to take good care of him, Finch entered the comfortable little inn, and, seeing the door of a snug parlour open, he at once took possession, and ringing a small bell that stood on the table, a plump and merry-looking girl answered the summons.

It is an established rule in travelling, that a bar-maid is fair game for flirting; indeed it would seem that there is something in the genus to inspire the propensity; for the stupidest fellows, who cannot exchange a word of the most distant pleasantry with a lady, are elevated into wits at the sight of a bar-maid.

Finch was a sort of man who does as the world does, so, just to avoid being remarkable, he chucked the buxom girl under the chin, swore she was very pretty, asked her name, and what he could have for supper.

"Jenny, please your worship, and chickens."

"Very good, Jenny," replied Finch; "I'll have the chickens first, if you please—and Jenny!"

"Yes, your worship."

"Send me Boots here, with a boot-jack and slippers."

"Yes, your worship," and Jenny vanished; but Finch heard her merry clear voice in the house, calling for Ralph to "go to the room and take boots." She came bustling backward and forward preparing the table, and never made an entrance or exit without some interchange of merry talk with Finch, who inquired every time when Boots would make his appearance. At last, after the fifth asking, when Jenny was bustling out of the room, Finch called her back, and requested her to put her "pretty little foot" on the toe of his boot, and he would do without the lazy, good-for-nothing fellow, who seemed determined never to come. Jenny obeyed. And as she stood close to Finch, he took occasion to lean on her for support, and then affecting to lose his balance, caught her hand to save himself from falling, declaring he was the most awkward fellow in the world, and still keeping hold of her fingers, which if he had not squeezed he certainly must have tumbled to the ground.

"Ha' done! do!" said Jenny.

"My dear, this confounded boot is so tight," and he clung closer to her for support.

At the moment a great lout, bearing a boot-jack under his arm, and slippers in his hand, entered the room, and exclaimed, "'Ere be the boot-jack, your worship."

"Thank you," said Finch, "but *I prefer the boot Jenny*—you're not wanted."

Boots stared, and left the room; and after a great many trials Finch contrived to get off his boots, and Jenny managed to get out of the room, protesting his worship was the funniest roisterer she ever met.

Finch was joined at supper by a gentleman who rode over to the inn to inquire for him. The visitor was the brother-in-law to O'Hara, whose sister had come over to England to see him in safety out of the country; and whose agency, with that of her husband, was of importance to one who, being watched, could not conduct his measures of escape in person without imminent risk. It was agreed that O'Hara and his companion in flight should join Finch at dinner at the inn the next day, and the visitor, after a hasty supper, departed, for he had far to ride that night.

The next day, accordingly, the entire party assembled at the little inn, and O'Hara, after a hearty salutation of Finch, introduced to him the friend, who was going with him to join the Irish Brigade in Flanders, "to strike," as O'Hara said, "a blow for the rightful king." O'Hara's sister and her husband were with them, and there was evident effort on all sides not to be sad —there was even a forced merriment among them. O'Hara's handsome companion seemed to be most unconcerned, (except Finch,) and showed his fine white teeth in many a laugh, as joke or repartee passed round the board. It was the woman whose smiles would have given most pain to an acute observer. There, beneath an outward show of much cheerfulness, the torture of an aching heart might be seen. While she openly expressed thankfulness that her brother was so near the moment of escape, it was plain that the thought of parting was little less painful than the thought of death: but she went through her task heroically;—with the most difficult of all heroism, that passive endurance of pain, in which the gentle fibre of woman puts the stronger nature of man to shame. She never winced for a moment; nay, she even joined the mirth, for mirthful they were, at least in seeming. Yes, they laughed—they even sang. Finch dashed off snatches about fair winds and flowing sails; O'Hara, like a soldier, did something in the "love, war, and wine," fashion; and to please the skipper, who professed an extravagant admiration of Irish melodies, the gentlewoman raised her voice in song, while her heart was steeped in sadness.

Oh, how hollow was all this—what a mockery—how false! what a deceitful thing is the human heart! Not only does it try to deceive others, but how often does it deceive itself!

The first check to the cheerful aspect of the party, was Finch looking at his watch, and saying, "'Time and tide wait for no man.' We must soon be at the shore;" and with good taste, wishing to leave the party alone at the last moment, he said, he would go order the horses to be got ready, and left the room; O'Hara's companion followed the example, and on reaching the stable-yard, was struck with the sudden change in Finch's aspect; his eyes being fixed with an expression of much anxiety towards the horizon that lay seaward. In a moment he spoke. "Go back to your friends," said he, "and hurry them—I would we were afloat—the weather looks threatening, and we are on a bad coast."

In the meantime, the sister and her husband were in the room with O'Hara, interchanging those last words of parting, which make parting so precious and so painful,—impressing on each other the many fond remembrances which, hurried over in a moment, are remembered through our lives; those half-uttered wishes that we understand before they are half spoken, and are replied to by a glance; or some promise exacted, which is better ratified by a pressure of the hand, than by the solemnity of an oath. In this endearing intercourse were they engaged, as their friend returned, to deliver Finch's message. O'Hara's sister grew pale at the words.

"Remember, Honora," said her brother, taking her hand gently, "remember your promise—you told me you would behave like a soldier's sister."

"And have I not kept my word, Charles?" she answered gently.

"You have indeed; but will you do one thing more for me?"

"Name it."

"You will think my request foolish—absurdly weak; but you know there is another besides you *very* dear to me—and—"

"Yes; what shall I say to her?"

"All that is kind at all times. But 'tis not that I would ask—"

"What then? do tell me."

"It seems a childish weakness—at such a time as this, it appears like trifling—but there is one song I wish you would sing me before I leave you—that *one* I love so *dearly!*" said O'Hara, with more sadness in his manner than he had yet prayed.

" Do not ask it, Charles; it is more than you can bear—more than either of us can—remember how much it touched us both *last* night, how much more will it on *this*—when we are to part for so long a time."

" Soon to return, I hope, in triumph, sister," he exclaimed with energy; " but I would hear that song once more before I part."

" It will make you too sad."

" No, no—sing to me—pray do! Let me take away that song and story of my native land fresh upon my ear—my *outward* ear:—in my memory it will dwell for ever."

Nerving herself to the utmost, his sister raised her voice, rendered more touching by the emotion against which she did her best to struggle, but which, nevertheless, tinged the strain with a peculiar air of sadness. Wedded to the melody were these simple lines, which told the tale of many a broken heart in Ireland, a tale of whose truth O'Hara himself was but too painfully conscious.

Mary Ma Chree.

I.

The flower of the valley was Mary *ma chree*,
Her smiles all bewitching were lovely to see,
The bees round her humming, when summer was gone,
When the roses were fled—might take her lip for one.
Her laugh it was music—her breath it was balm ;
Her heart, like the lake, was as pure and as calm,
Till love o'er it came, like a breeze o'er the sea,
And made the heart heave of sweet Mary *ma chree.*

II.

She loved—and she wept; for was gladness e'er known
To dwell in the bosom that Love makes his own?
His joys are but moments—his griefs are for years,
He comes all in smiles—but he leaves all in tears.
Her lover was gone—

Here the voice of the singer, whose eyes betrayed how deeply the subject of the song and the circumstances of the hour affected her, began to falter, but by a great effort she controlled her emotion, and continued—

Her lover was gone to a far distant land,
And Mary, in sadness, would pace the lone strand;
And tearfully gaze o'er the dark-rolling sea,
That parted her soldier from Mary *ma chree.*

The soldier's head drooped as the stanza stole to its conclusion, and at the last line he hid his face in his hand, while the voice of

the singer, no longer supported by the artificial exertion of sus-
taining the strain, was audible in stifled sobs.

O'Hara, dashing the gathering mist from his eye, wrung the
hand of the beloved singer with convulsive fervour, and said,
"God bless you—I am ready to go now."

Scarcely had he spoken, when a rapid knock at the door, and
Finch's voice outside, were heard. He was invited to enter, and,
on opening the door he said, with more of energy in his manner
than he was usually betrayed into, " *Pray*, gentlemen, delay no
longer—I like the look of the weather less and less every moment,
and it behoves us to be off the coast without delay ; as it is, we
must ride hard for it."

O'Hara turned to his sister—one glance passed between them.
Oh ! how much of affection and agony were mingled in that
look ! his lip was pale, and slightly quivered ; he did not dare to
say more than a parting Irish blessing, as he folded his sister for
the last time to his heart, and, after uttering that beautiful benison
of " God *be with you*," he yielded her to the arms of her husband,
on whose shoulder she drooped her head as her beloved brother
left the room. Nestling to her husband's heart, her eager ear
listened for every sound ; she heard the hurried tread of the
party leaving the inn, in another minute the clatter of horses'
feet told they were speeding to the shore, and then the struggling
emotions that had been so long pent up in her bosom had vent,
and the little parlour of the inn, that so lately rang with song and
laughter, echoed to the deep sobs of a bursting heart.

The husband sought not to interrupt her sorrow, but permitted
its first outpouring to have vent ere he attempted to soothe. Then
gently pressing her to his heart he spoke words of comfort, and
with kind patience awaited her recovery from the prostration
attendant on the violence of her emotion. Her head still rested
on his breast, and thus for a long time she wept in silence—till
suddenly she started up, as the heavy sough of the wind swept
past the window where she sat, and shook it in its frame. For
the first time she became conscious a storm was rising, and she
listened to her husband's wish that they should leave the inn at
once, and seek the retreat whence they came, before the weather
should break. Their horses were soon at the door, and when the
acclivity of a neighbouring hill enabled her to get a glimpse of
the sea, and the threatening sky that hung above it, her tears
ceased, for the chill of fear froze the fountain of sorrow ! Strange
operation of our passions ! Had it been a calm, she would have
wept throughout her homeward way—tears would have dimmed
her sight to the soft sunshine, which had indicated safety ; but a
dry eye was bent on the lowering elements which threatened
danger ; and sorrowing for the past gave place to fears for the
future.

CHAPTER XI.

OTHER eyes as well as those on shore were cast about, anxiously regarding the prognostics of the weather, and raising no favourable augury from the aspect of the darkening horizon, which seemed closing in on all sides, like some mighty net, which soon should make its sweep upon the waters, and gather within its deadly coil shattered barks and shipwrecked men. Ned had stood in for the land, according to his orders, before the lowering sky had given warning of the approaching storm ; or, with such a coast under his lee, he would not have run the pretty Seagull into such a point of danger ; and would have trusted to Finch's judgment for knowing why he did not, and acquitting him of blame for disobedience of orders. But there he was, as fortune would have it, and he should make the best of it. Already the wind had so increased as to oblige the topmasts to be struck, and sail taken in ; and, that not a moment might be lost in getting Finch on board, Ned despatched a boat to the creek before the appointed time, and beat off and on as near the point as prudence would permit. Alternately looking to the weather and the shore, to watch the increase of evil omens on one side, or the signal that should announce Finch's arrival on the other, Ned paced the deck of the Seagull impatiently, and passed at every turn an experienced mariner, who had never quitted the same place for nearly half an hour, and leaning over the bulwark, with his weather-beaten cheek resting on his sinewy hand, kept eyeing the weather with a steady gaze, as if he looked upon an enemy, and was measuring the strength with which he soon should have to contend.

Ned paused as he reached the mariner on his next turn, and said, " Dirty weather, Mitchell."

" As ever I see," was the curt answer of the man, who still kept his gaze fixed on the point he had been so long observing.

" And the change so sudden too—"

" Can't say I liked the looks o' the morning, sir.

" I wish you had told me so."

" Not my business, sir," replied he ; " besides I never likes croaking ; I never know'd it lucky yet—them as looks out for squalls is the first to catch 'em ; they're bad enough when they comes without invitin' of 'em, as I think growling often does."

"Do you think I was wrong in standing so far in?' inquired Ned, anxiously.

"Can't say you was, sir; for, as you say, the change *was* sudden for sartin, and the weather deceitful—besides, there was the skipper's order."

"True," said Ned; "but as the craft was in my care, I should be sorry to have run her blindly into danger.

"No, no, sir; don't you think that; the weather *was* deceitful, that's sartin, and might have deceived an older seaman than you; for I will say, Mr. Fitzgerald, you are, for your years, about as good as ever I see. You'll excuse me for saying so to your face; but it's true, and I wouldn't, only you was a blaming of yourself. But as you have hailed me on this here matter, I would recommend another reef taken in, sir."

"She carries what is on her well, Mitchell; doesn't she?"

"Yes, sir, for the present, and may be for the next half hour; but remember, six hands are away in the boat, and we mayn't find it so easy by and by to take in canvas, sir, if it comes to blow as hard as I expect before they come back."

Mitchell's advice was acted upon, and, as it proved, most wisely, for every ten minutes increased the violence of the wind, which howled louder and louder through the shrouds; the sea tumbled in more heavily, and the increasing line of surf along the shore gave rise to the conjecture that the boat would find it impossible to put back to the vessel. Ned kept a sharp look-out to the land with his glass, which he was forced to wipe from time to time, so thickly was the spray flying about.

"If they do not appear in five minutes more," said Ned, "it is impossible they can put through that surf, and after waiting that time I will put out to sea."

"I would, sir," said Mitchell; "for it will be a foul night, and a foul coast under our lee, and it will be as much as we can do, as it is, to weather the head; thof, if there be a thing that swims can do it, the Seagull can."

"Oh, we are safe enough yet, Mitchell."

"Yes—I don't say we are not, sir; but we've nothing to spare, I reckon."

The next five minutes were anxiously passed in watching the coast, and just as they were on the point of expiring, a black speck emerged from out of the fringe of foam that whitened the whole shore; and, riding over the white crests of the waves that rolled in with increasing violence every moment, the bold boat was seen putting her head to the storm, and pulling gallantly against it. How anxiously Ned watched them! Calling Mitchell to his side, he gave him the glass, and said, he feared they would never be able to reach the Seagull with such a sea

and tide making against them. "We must run in a little farther, Mitchell."

"Wait awhile, sir," said the old seaman; "don't be in a
hurry, they may make better way when they get more clear of
the shore, and if we go in farther, we shall never weather the
point to the southward."

"But we can't let them be lost before our eyes."

"Sartinly not, sir; we must all sink or swim together."

"If we cannot make sail, could we not ride it out at our
anchors?"

"Ah, master!" said Mitchell, "I know what's a comin', and
iron was never forged, nor hemp twisted, that would hold a ship
this night."

As he spoke they saw a flash from the boat.

"'Tis a signal, they cannot make way to us," said Ned; "we
must run down to them."

"Then we shall all have a squeak for it," said Mitchell.

The way that six stout rowers could not make was soon
skimmed over by the Seagull, that flew through the water before
the storm which gathered thicker and faster every moment.
Sweeping swiftly towards the boat, she approached it as near as
safety would permit. "'Bout ship!" shouted Ned to Mitchell,
who had gone astern.

Down went the helm, and the Seagull, turning her head
gallantly to the storm, swung up into the wind, leaving the boat
but a few oar strokes under her lee.

It was a service of danger to get on board with such a sea
running,—stout oars and lusty sinews bent to the work—a rope
was hove from the Seagull and caught—

"Lay fast hold of that rope when you spring," said Finch to
O'Hara. "Steady now!—wait till the boat lifts close to the
ship's side, and lose not that moment to jump on board."

It was done, and in safety by O'Hara, and the next instant
down swept the boat into the trough of the foaming sea. Again
she lifted, and O'Hara's companion, without waiting for the rope,
seized the favourable opportunity to spring to the chains, where
Ned himself was standing to assist in getting the unpractised
strangers aboard. Less lucky than O'Hara, the bold stranger
slipped his foot, as he sprang, and though he caught the shrouds
with one hand, the pitching of the vessel, and his own impaired
equilibrium, were swinging him back again into the hissing
surge below, but that the powerful grasp of Ned recovered him,
and in another instant he was standing in safety on the deck,
and Ned beheld in the man whose life he had saved young
Kirwan.

Even in that instant of commotion and of peril, the thought that Kirwan was going where Ellen was, brought with it a pang to Edward's bosom, that suspended all other considerations, and it was only the voice of Finch, who had sprung to the deck, shouting to him and giving orders, that recalled him to the business of the moment.

After issuing some few prompt orders, placing Mitchell at the helm, and seeing the craft beating out to sea, as close to the wind as she could run, Finch went below to rid himself of his landsman's guise, and assume a habit fitter for the rough work of the night he should have to go through. He took down O'Hara and Kirwan with him, requesting them to remain below as they would not only be exposed to unnecessary danger and discomfort on deck, but be in the way of those whose exertions were but too needful and urgent that night to bear interruption; "for I will not conceal from you, gentlemen," said Finch, " that we have an anxious night before us; the weather threatens to be worse even than it is, and we have a bad coast under our lee." Finch returned to the deck immediately, where an unpromising gloom sat on every seaman's brow, as they looked towards the dreaded headland that was now barely perceptible in the distance; for the evening was suddenly overshadowed by the storm, and premature night settling over the sea, added fresh horror to a scene already sufficiently appalling. They soon lost sight of any land-mark, and swept through the boiling surge by the guidance only of their compass. The gale was rising now to a perfect hurricane, and the increasing turbulence of the sea made every timber, plank, and spar of the Seagull "complain" as she strained, even under her diminished canvass, through the fierce elementary commotion which she faced so gallantly; riding up the over-hanging waves that threatened to engulf her, and dashing back their fierce assaults from her bows, as a lion flings the dogs of the hunter from his crest.

An intervening bank lay between her and the headland which was the ultimate danger, and this more immediate peril became a source of anxiety as they approached it. When a calculation of their run induced them to believe they were in its neighbourhood, the flash of a gun a-head was observed, and every eye was strained to watch for a repetition of the signal of distress, for such it was undoubtedly. At the expiration of a minute it occurred, and Finch, as he saw it, exclaimed to Ned, who stood beside him, "We are all right yet!—the flash was on our lee bow —and see, 'tis a large vessel—it can be but the tail of the bank we are near, and with our light draught of water we shall pass it in safety."

" With such a heavy sea running we might strike," said Ned.

" We shall soon know," replied Finch, " and escape at least the pain of suspense."

Again the flash broke through the gloom ; and it was almost on their beam.

" Huzza !" cried Finch, " the bank is passed!" He walked amongst the crew, and cheered them by remarking, so much of their danger was over, and expressed the fullest hope they should weather the head yet.

Another signal of distress flashed from the stranded ship, which was now astern of them ; and it was an unhappy response to Finch's speech of encouragement ; for it is enough to shake the nerve of the stoutest, when, at the mercy of the tempest, you witness one of the fatalities of which you yourself may be the next victim. Yet boldly and unflinchingly the gallant crew of the Seagull did their duty through the darkness and peril of the night, with that seaman-like skill, and heart of daring, that can best elude or readiest meet danger, which gives security in the tempest, and victory in the battle.

On sweeps the Seagull !—the darkness grows denser ;—the hurricane grows fiercer ! Scarcely can the speaking trumpet carry Finch's orders to his men, through the roaring of the wind. Higher rise the watery mountains, deeper rushes the boat down the yawning gulf before her ; heavier is the buffet of each sea that smites her, and makes her tremble throughout from stem to stern ; groaning at the instant she receives the shock, and then as she writhes with heavy pitching over each billow, the straining of her timbers producing plaintive sounds, like the painful whine of some living thing. Well may she complain, for the lash of the tempest is upon her ! She bounds under each blow—she flies—but the tempest is merciless, and lashes more and more, and madly and blindly she rushes onward through the darkness of that terrific night !

Land as well as sea bore the marks of that memorable visitation ; cattle were killed, and trees torn up by the roots : rivers burst their bounds, and the gathered produce of industry was swept away ; the inundations rendered roads impassable, and many bridges yielded to the pressure of the streams they spanned. Few were the sleepers in London that night, for terror kept them wakeful ; houses were unroofed and chimneys blown down, and loss of life and limb were amongst the accumulated misfortunes of that dreadful storm. Every hour brought tidings of the havoc made amongst the shipping; the shores were covered with wrecks, and many a merchant who held high his head on 'Change, drooped it under the ruin which the tempest made. .

But while there was individual wail for private loss, and much of public lament too, for this sweeping destruction of national property, still it was overpowered by the rejoicing which later news created. The tempest had utterly scattered and demolished the threatening navy which had been preparing, at such an enormous cost to France, for the invasion of England. Her marine had for the present received a blow which must require a large amount of time and treasure to repair, and The Guelph sat easier on a newly acquired throne. The loyalists had further cause for rejoicing. Anson had returned from his voyage round the world. His ship, the Centurion, had happily made her port, before the tempest had burst, and had brought back from the plundered possessions and ships of Spain a larger amount of treasure than had ever hitherto been taken.

The name of Anson was in every mouth. He had returned not only with the reputation of an able circumnavigator, but the glory of a conqueror. If the gamblers made long faces at the loss which had fallen on the merchant interest, the upholders of things as they were answered that the coffers of the bank would be filled with Spanish gold and silver; and the treasure, immense as it was, was magnified by the ever-exaggerating voice of rumour. If, on the one hand, the destruction of our shipping was lamented, the triumphant reply was, that the navy of France was annihilated.

But while joy-bells rang, and public feasting was held, the bitter wail of those whom that tempest had bereaved made mournful many a house in England. The noisy triumph of the hour soon passed; while the low wail of sorrow was heard for many a day.

CHAPTER XII.

A few days after the dreadful storm we have recorded, a certain merchant sat in a dark little counting-house in the city of London, anxiously looking over his books. He was a staid looking man, somewhat beyond the middle age; whose thin lips, small eyes, scant hair, and low forehead, bespoke a poverty of nature; and the pinched cut of his snuff-coloured garments accorded well with the character of his countenance. His spare neckcloth was tied simply, and smoothed down in a plain fall in front, without the least particle of border,—an excess in which Mr. Spiggles did not indulge even on a gala day. Snuff he did indulge in,—or it should rather be said he *took*, for it was not for indulgence he used it, but merely to give him the opportunity, when he was asked a question which he did not like to answer hastily, of taking out his box, tapping it leisurely, dipping his fingers into it slowly, and making three solemn applications of his hand to his nose, that he might thereby gain time to answer the aforesaid question in a manner the most advantageous to himself. He was sparing of everything—even his words—though they were worth nothing, unless they were written, and this, it would seem, was his own opinion, from the fact that he was quite regardless or forgetful of them *himself*, unless the inexorable "black and white" held him bound, or refreshed his memory.

Mr. Spiggles was consulting his books after the "terrible night," to see what amount of risks he had on the water, when a thrifty neighbour, as fond of money as himself, entered the counting-house. After the exchange of formal salutations between them, Mister Gripps remarked the sad visage of his neighbour.

"Ay, brother Gripps, and well may my visage be saddened as I look over the sums that I have trusted to the winds and the waves, which, mayhap ere now, have dispossessed me of the same."

"And yet, methinks," returned Gripps, "thou should'st rejoice rather that so much of thy ventures have come to port, when such a many of thy neighbours have been despoiled by the tempest."

" Thanks to Providence, truly, friend Gripps, I am a favoured man, doubtless, but still much is abroad. Yet, His will be done, —'the Lord chasteneth whom he loveth,' and these visitations may be for our good; for, alas! not only hath the tempest of the winds and the waves smitten us heavily, but, alas! the internal tempests of the factious and disaffected threaten us full sore."

" Verily!" said Gripps, " the adherents of the scarlet one waxeth bold: only think, as I passed by the Belle Sauvage just now, there was much ado about another discovery made of arms for the Papists."

" Have they seized those concerned therein?"

" No," said Gripps, " they know that a chest of basket-hilted swords and a cask of skull-caps hath arrived from Birmingham, and were on the road into Dorsetshire, and them have they seized."

" Ah!" exclaimed Spiggles, devoutly," would they could seize those who sent and those who were to receive: what matter for the arms in comparison with the hands that were to wield them, —of the skull-caps, with the Papist-heads they were to cover; would they were over Temple-bar for ornaments!"

" But still it is well," answered Gripps, " to keep the arms from the hands of the ungodly, that would work evil in the land."

" Truly, brother Gripps."

" And the nets of the godly are compassing the knaves round about. Just now have I seen two Irish rebels, in the pay of France, taken to Newgate. They were cast upon the coast by the hand of Providence, in the late storm, and were then fain to endeavour to escape, in the packet from Harwich into Holland; but the king's servants, who watch the ports narrowly, seized them there, and they were sent up by order of my Lord Cartaret, under care of two messengers."

" Heaven be praised!" piously ejaculated Spiggles; " these Papists would devour us with good will, but Heaven favours the godly and the righteous;—the church and state are under especial care from on high—yea, from above! But how heard you all this, brother Gripps?"

" From my friend Alderman Spiers, who looketh for news and salvation, as thou knowest; he told me, moreover, that it was a smuggling ship that cast them up, as pieces of her wreck which floated ashore did betoken."

" Ah! the vile and ungodly ones, that would defraud the king's revenue," said Spiggles; " Heaven be praised, they are smitten as with a rod!"

" A well-known and dangerous ship was the same," added Gripps.

" Heaven be praised!" again ejaculated Spiggles.

" Well known for her malpractices, though they never could take her."

" But the storm encompassed her round about as with a net," said Spiggles; " the finger of Providence pointed her out for destruction; praised be His name for smiting the ungodly!"

" She was entitled the ' Seagull,'" added Gripps.

" The ' Seagull?'" involuntarily echoed Spiggles,—looking more pinched and miserable than before.

" Yes, the ' Seagull'—dost know anything of her?"

Mister Spiggles began to take snuff, and after his usual manœuvres, answered, " Why, yes—I think—as well as I can remember, I have—that is, 'tis like a dream to me—"

" Well, Heaven be praised, she is a wreck at last," said Gripps. " What can honest dealers like me do, while such rogues are let to live?"

" True, neighbour—true," answered Spiggles, with a long-drawn sigh.

" Art not well, neighbour?" inquired Gripps, observing the increasing pallor of his friend.

" To say truth, brother, I am but ill at ease since this storm ;—I have not only my own proper risks at sea, but much of my money is out on bottomry, and the borrowers are not men of substance, so that if the ships reach not their port, my loans are in jeopardy."

A lank-haired clerk now entered the counting-house and whispered to his master, who grew paler than before, and telling his neighbour that a person on private business sought an interview, Gripps departed, and to his shuffling step of departure, succeeded the firm tread of the approaching visitor, who soon stood before the pallid Spiggles, in the person of Hudson Finch.

Neither spoke a word for some time, for both were startled at the other's appearance. The gallant skipper had been used to enter with a light and dashing air, and as far as a smile could take a liberty with the parchment features of Spiggles, it did, to welcome the man who was a valuable friend ; but now both looked haggard; a gloom and anxiety were on Finch's brow, where brightness and daring were wont to sit, and his usually trim attire was changed for the coarsest guise of a storm-beaten sailor. Spiggles was the first to speak.—"It is true, then?" said he.

" What is true?" returned Finch.

" The ' Seagull'——" said the merchant.

" What of her?" said the skipper.

" Is lost," faltered Spiggles.

" Yes," said Finch, sadly. " Do you read it in my face

7

"I heard it," said Spiggles.

"Zounds! but ill news speeds apace," returned Finch. "How did you hear it?"

Mister Spiggles had again recourse to his snuff-box, and the impatience of Finch in driving new questions at him before the preceding one was answered, gave the cautious merchant additional time to treat the headlong seaman's inquiries as he pleased. After some farther conversation, Spiggles began a long lament over the amount of his loss, but was suddenly cut short by Finch.

"Hang the money!" cried he—"It is not *that* loss I mind— of money there is plenty more to be had; it is not the money, but the *boat* I lament—there never was such a beauty swam the sea. Other craft we can buy, but never such another as the pretty Seagull." He said this with an expression of grief befitting the loss of a beloved friend.

"Captain Finch," replied the merchant coldly, "I shall never have such another vessel *at all*."

"What?" exclaimed Finch, eyeing him sharply. "You don't mean to say you are going to give up so thriving a trade?"

"Even so, Captain Finch. It hath pleased Providence to open mine eyes to mine iniquities," cried Spiggles, with a sniffling whine, "and I will wash myself from my abominations."

"That is as much as to say, you are so rich you don't want any more," said Finch.

"Nay," said Spiggles, "I am not a rich man—it is the inward yearning after righteousness."

"Well, my good sir," said Finch, cutting short his cant, "I neither want to pry into your accounts, earthly or heavenly, but as I have been a useful friend to you, I hope you don't mean to turn me adrift now, when your own turn is served; and if you intend to abjure the traffic, I hope you will give me the opportunity of repairing my present mishap, by getting afloat again."

"Your skill is too well known, Captain, to let you want for employment."

"It is rather a bad introduction to a new employer, though," said Finch, "to say, 'Sir, I have just lost one craft, will you give me charge of another?' No—that won't do. I don't want you, Mister Spiggles, to have anything to answer for in a new venture, if your conscience is against it; but, as I have been a faithful and profitable servant to you, I only ask you to lend me a couple of thousand pounds, to put me afloat handsomely again, and I will repay you, with interest, within a year."

Spiggles opened his little eyes as wide as they could open,

at the mention of two thousand pounds, and assured Finch he had not the money, nor a tenth part of it at command.

A mingled expression of indignation and contempt crossed Finch's countenance, as he said "That is, in other words, you *won't*."

"*Can't*, Captain."

"Fudge!" cried Finch. "You talk of conscience; how can you reconcile, I say, to your conscience to throw off one who has been the making of tens of thousands for you, and who now stands before you a ruined man? how, I say, can you reconcile the refusal of what is a small sum to you, to retrieve his fortunes—a small sum, were it even to be given—but when it is only a loan I ask. No, I am sure you cannot mean to refuse it."

"Could I even spare it, Captain Finch, my conscience would equally reproach me for aiding another in evil doing."

"Come, come, Gaffer Godly, that won't do. You can't humbug me, though you can the world—we know each other. You would not like to have the world know all I could tell of you."

Mr. Spiggles took snuff again before he answered. "You would find it difficult to *prove* anything against me, Captain Finch."

"More perhaps than you would like," said Finch—"but fear not—I would scorn to use so base a means to raise money, though I were starving. Once for all, will you lend me even a thousand?"

"I assure you, Captain—

"Even five hundred?"

"Not only do I disapprove of the illegal traffic in which you indulge, but I have heard you have gone so far as to aid the king's enemies—flying rebels—and I own I am loyal to my Church and my king."

"Pooh! pooh! put a stop on that lingo, you old hypocrite!" cried Finch, losing all patience. "Church and king, forsooth! much you care for either. Your religion you can put off and on like your coat, and, like it, 'twill be always of the sleekest outside—and your loyalty teaches you to cheat the king's exchequer. Church and king, forsooth!—If you could make a thousand pounds by selling both, you'd do it. Religion and loyalty, quotha!—Your false oaths at the custom-house are good proof of both! and yet *you* talk of virtue—you, you forsworn hypocrite, with a string of perjuries hanging round your heart as thick as beads on a blackamoor."

Spiggles grew more ghastly as Finch poured forth his fierce invective, and opened a little window that looked into the outward warehouse to call his clerk, but Finch interrupted him

" Don't be afraid, you paltry coward—I'll not narm you. Do you think I would soil my hands with such contemptible carrion—faugh!   I leave you to your religious meditations, you perjured, pilfering, stingy, old sinner ; and in the middle of your prayers, don't forget my *blessings* on you ! "

As he spoke he shook his clenched fist at the shrivelled-up Spiggles ; and as he showed his teeth in a fiendish grin while he uttered the word " blessings," there was something more appalling in it than if he had used all the curses in the world.   He strode from the counting-house, trembling and pale with passion, and thrusting his arm inside that of Ned, who was waiting for him at the door of the warehouse, hurried through the narrow lane without uttering a word, and did not speak until they reached the thoroughfare, as if his " great rage " could not get vent in a smaller space.

Then he copiously anathematised the miserly hypocrite who cast him off ; but getting cooler when they got over a couple of miles of ground, as they walked westward, the indignant Finch snapped his fingers, swore he did not care a curse for the old hunks, and that all would yet be right.   " I have another port still under my lee, lad, and though it is not the haven where I had most right to expect shelter, mayhap 'tis there I'll find it."

In this hopeful expectation they pushed onward towards the neighbourhood of Charing Cross, and turning into a tavern, Finch walked straight into the bar, where a very pretty child was dragging her doll about in a quart pot, by way of carriage.

" Hillo—is that Polly ?" cried Finch.

The child turned up her pretty blue eyes in wonder at hearing her name uttered by one whom she did not know.

" Where's mother ?" inquired Finch.

The child only put its finger in its mouth, and kept gazing as before.   The mother entered at the moment ; and the instant she espied Finch, uttered a glad exclamation of surprise, and seizing him by both hands, poured forth voluble assurance of how delighted she was to see him.

" I *must* shake hands with you, Captain !"

" You may as well give us a bus, mother !" said Finch, kissing the buxom landlady.

" You are as merry as ever, Captain ; though—bless my heart—you don't look as you used, saving your favour."

" Can't return the compliment, as they say, Mrs. Banks, for you are looking better than ever I saw you."

" And am better, Captain, thanks to you ; I have thriven ever since the day you lent me the money and got me out of trouble. I've got on ever since ; oh, you've been the saving of me and my orphans."   She stooped and took up the child, and bade her kiss the gentleman, for that he was the best friend her mother ever had.

The child put its little arms round his neck, and pressed its ruby lips to the bronzed cheek of the sailor, who seemed touched by the incident.

"And I can give you back all your money now, Captain," continued the widow; "ay, and more too," added she, in an under tone, "if you want it; for indeed, Captain, you do look bad; don't be angry with me—but if a hundred more—"

She stopped, for she saw Finch's lip quiver; he could not speak, but catching her in his arms, he gave her another hearty kiss; and as the landlady wiped her eye, which glistened with the dew of pure human sympathy (though it was in the bar of a tavern), Finch recovered himself sufficiently to say, "Bless you, Mother Banks! you were always a good soul!—I hope your house is not so full but you can let me have room."

"If a lord was in your way, he should turn out for you, Captain. The house is yours, and all that's in it!"

"Avast, mother, avast!—a woman's palaver always bothers me; so say no more—show my friend and myself to a room; and as soon as may be, let us have a dinner of the best, and a rousing bottle from your pet bin!"

Mrs. Banks showed them the best room in her house; and as for dinner, protested she only wished she could melt down gold and silver for their dinner, and give them distilled rubies for wine—or words to that effect, as the lawyers say.

"There!" cried Finch to Ned, as Mrs. Banks closed the door; "there, in a poor widow have I found the friendship which the man whose fortune I have mostly made, refused me. Oh Ned, Ned! how unequally, and 'twould seem to us how unjustly, are the riches of this world divided!"

Finch's spirits rose rapidly after he found himself under the roof of Mrs. Banks; her heartiness and gratitude chased the hateful recollections of Mister Spiggles from his mind, and the innocent kiss of the unconscious child that was told to love him, acted like balm upon his spirit; a spirit easily excited, but as easily soothed. Indeed, it was Finch's misfortune that he was too sensible to immediate impressions; he was capable of doing either a bad or a good action. But whatever his faults were, they were attributable rather to a headstrong nature than a bad heart, and were far outnumbered by his good qualities. Among these, generosity stood pre-eminent; and a loan of money, in an hour of need, to poor Mrs. Banks, had saved her from destruction; and it was perhaps the inward consciousness that the kiss of her innocent child was not quite undeserved, that made it the sweeter; for how much dearer is every enjoyment we have

earned. Finch's misfortune (to go a little further into his character) lay in not having a fixed principle about anything; and
this want, in conjunction with an excitable nature, often allowed
him to be betrayed into that, in heat of blood, which, in cooler
moments, he would not have committed, and in cooler moments
often regretted. He was fond of pleasure, whose road, though
generally smooth, has some rough places in it, which, without
careful driving, may overturn those who frequent it; and Finch
had had some upsets in his time. Now, in these cases it is found
that the warnings arising from experience do not always act as
correctives, but rather embolden; and that when people have
been flung very often, and escaped unharmed, they get so used
to the matter, that they think nothing about it. And so it was
with Finch. He had been so long following the bent of his will
merely, that he neglected any other form of guidance, and, of
course, his horses sometimes ran away with him, and consequently an occasional break-down was the result; but as his
energy and activity always put him on his legs again, he heeded
not the momentary bruises he received, which, as they healed,
hardened, and became insensible to future pain, as the culprit
often flogged, loses all terror of the lash.

Asking pardon of the reader for this slight digression from
the immediate story, to afford a general idea of the class and
"manner of man" to which Finch belonged we shall now proceed.

Finch, as his spirits rose, opened to Ned the bright prospects
the future presented to him; and, as they sat at the window, looking upon the busy thoroughfare before them, he suggested every five minutes a new plan to "be up in the world
again." His fourth proposition was just on the point of being
broached, (making exactly twenty minutes they had been at the
window), when his thoughts were interrupted by a singular
arrival at the door of the tavern. Two coaches drove up, having
their roofs occupied with four sailors each, while their interiors
were empty; and as an altercation commenced between the
drivers and the tars, which seemed to excite the indignation of
both the disputing parties, and the mirth of bystanders, who
rapidly gathered to listen, Finch threw up the window to hear
what was going forward. He found the dispute occasioned by
the sailors desiring the coachmen to drive them "back again,"
while the coachmen swore they wouldn't, for that their horses
were tired, and that they had driven them back and forward the
same road three times, and what could they want more?

" What's that to you if you're paid," said one of the Jacks.

" Well, I don't like it," said coachee.

" Well, no matter whether you like it or not—you've got the
bounty, and are under orders, and must sail—so weigh and be off."

" Can't you get another pair of coaches ?"

" We see none here," cried the sailors.

" There are plenty to be had," answered the coachman

" Well," said a more reasonable tar, " let them drive us to one of their anchoring grounds where the craft lie, and let these lubbers go into dock and be paid off, if so be they like it."

" But I like this craft," says another; " she's none o' your fair-weather cockle-shells—she pitches as if it blew a trifle, and 'tis a'most as good as being at sea."

The crowd laughed at the sailor's choice of a coach, but the coachmen turned to them and said, " Ah ! *you* may laugh, but if you knew what a plague we've had with them—and they won't even sit inside."

" Why, you lubber !" said the principal spokesman, "would you have us stay below while we can come on deck ?"

The absurd answer of the seamen always turned the laugh against the discomfited drivers, and the arrival of another coach similarly laden to the former ones, strengthened the party of the Jack tars. Indeed, this coach was stronger in attraction to the crowd, for amidst the sailors on the roof sat a piper, who was playing away for the bare life the most rollicking of tunes. Hitherto Finch and Ned had enjoyed the scene in silence, but now the latter involuntarily exclaimed,

' By the powers, 'tis he !"

" Who ?" inquired Finch.

" There—there !" said Ned, pointing to the piper, and made no further answer, but, rushing from the room, ran down stairs, and in another moment Finch saw Ned clambering to the top of the coach, and after addressing a word to the piper, beheld the most cordial marks of recognition pass between them. This put an end to the dispute between the drivers and their strange fares, for as *Phaidrig-na-pib*—for it was he—said he would go into the tavern with his friend, the sailors agreed to go wherever he went, so the coaches were discharged with ten times the amount of their proper fare ; and as the crowd saw the sailors showering money into the hands of the drivers, they cheered the open-handed liberality, whereupon some of the Jacks dipped their hands into their pockets again, and presented them full of coin to the crowd, many of whom were not loath to take advantage of such a windfall. The thoughtless sons of the sea, however, were soon housed in the tavern, the crowd dispersed by degrees, and after Ned had seen the sailors comfortably stowed in a room below, he conducted Phaidrig up stairs, and introduced him to Finch, who, he had no doubt, would be as glad to hear, as himself by what chance the blind piper had come to London.

" I'll tell you how it was," began Phaidrig.

"Stop," said Ned—"perhaps you would like a glass of something before you begin."

"Bless your sowl, not at all!—them divils of sailors keep me dhrinkin' mornin', noon, and night, so that in throth its refreshing to have a mouthful o' nothing. Faix I'm so full o' spirits, that I'd be afeard to blow out a candle for fear my breath would take fire. But to come to my story. You see, one fine day there put into Galway-bay three ships, and soon afther came a power o' sailors on shore with handfuls o' strange money, that no one could tell the value of, *not even the sailors themselves*, for I hear broad pieces of silver and even *goold* was scattered about like *dust*—and maybe the townspeople didn't *sweep it up*. Well, sir, the sailors was mad for divarshin, and av coorse coortin' and danein' comes undher that denomination, and as music is wanted for the fanatistical toe, to be sure they could not do without me—Phaidrig-na-pib was in request—and maybe they did'nt pay the piper. By dad, I was a rich man in a few days, and paid off all the incumbrances on my estate."

"Have you an estate, then?" inquired Finch, rather surprised, for Finch, be it known, was an Englishman, and had never met an Irish piper before.

"To be sure I have," said Phaidrig. "Haven't I the estate of man upon me, and what more throublesome estate is there to manage?"

"True," said Finch, with a smile. "But what were the incumbrances you spoke of?"

"It was all in consequence of a legacy was left me," said Phaidrig.

"Ah!" said Finch, anticipating—"and you sunk your own trifle of property in going to law with the exeeutors, I suppose?"

"Not at all," said Phaidrig.—"In the first place I could not sink my property much more than it was by nature, for it is undher wather nine months in the year—being in a bog; and as for the executioners, or whatever you call them, I never heard o' such people at all; but not to bother you with such bits and scraps o' nonsense, just let me tell you how I got here.

"The sailors, as I towld you, kept me busy, mornin', noon, and night, and at last the Captain himself came ashore one day, and heerd me, and swore nothing would content him but that I should go aboord and play for him, and by dad he pulled out some goold pieces and popped them into my hand,—not that I went for the sake of the money, but that he praised my playing powerful, and I remarked he liked the fine *owld airs*. His name was Talbot—and he took me aboord sure enough, and the way he came into Galway-bay was, that having taken some Spanish ships prizes, and the weather turning bad, he made for Galway-bay, until the storm was past, and the word was that the prizes was so rich, that Captain Talbot never touched the private goods of the people at all, only the cargo of the ship, although the people wor so rich that they had diamond rings on every finger, and goold-hilted swoords, and diamonds in *them* too—but not a taste the Captain would take av them, and was so pleased with the great haul he made, that he gave a present of twenty goold pieces to every sailor and sarvant in the ship. Well, I staid aboord for two or three days as happy as a king; when one mornin' as I got up, afther a pleasant night aboord, I began to stagger about and could'nt keep my feet. 'Ow wow!' says I,— 'I'm drunk yet,' and was going into bed again, when I no more could get into it than if it was the eye of a needle, and I was catching at everything in my way to lay howld of it, but nothing would make me stand ; and with that I heerd them laughing at me all round about, and my head began to reel, and I began to feel *quare* a bit, and down I fell on the flure as sick as a dog. To make a long story short, they had put to sea in the night, and that was the cause of my staggering and qualmishness all the time I was blaming the dhrink for it. Well, I was so bothered with the sickness for five or six days, I could'nt take bit or sup, or handle the pipes at all, so that the Captain was disappointed of all the music he expected to get out o' me while he was sailing from Galway to London, but when I got well, I paid off the old score, for I worked a power, and didn't lave a tune in the bag I didn't give them, and I got such a favourite with them that they made me put up with them here in London, and they pet me like a first child—and that's the way you see the Irish piper came to London."

"And how do you like London?" asked Finch.

"Oh, it's a fine place, sir."

"How can you tell under the deprivation of sight?"

"Don't I *hear* it?—Can't I tell what crowds are passing up and down, and what a power of waggons and carriages there's in it?—and all the different bells that's a-ringing tell me 'tis full o' churches. Sure fifty ways I know it's a big place."

"How would you like to live here, Phaidrig?" inquired Ned.

"Not at all—the air breathes thick to me, and wants the sweet smell of the mountains."

"When do you mean to return, then, to Ireland?"

"When these divils o' sailors will let me—and faix I'm beginning to get tired o' them—and would be long ago, only for the thundering lies they tell, that divarts me. And one chap, a new friend they have picked up to-day, bates all the rest hollow;

I give it up to him for the biggest liar I ever met, and I have met a few, and, indeed, am not a bad hand at it myself, on an occasion—but this fellow—Ow, ow!"

"Who is he ?"

"One of the sailors out o' the great ship come home lately; I forget her name, but the commander's name is Anderson."

"Anson, I suppose, you mean," said Finch; "Commodore Anson."

"That's it," said Phaidrig. "Well, if you were to hear this fellow tell of all their doings."

"He can scarcely tell more wonders than the reality, I believe," said Finch; "they say Anson's sufferings, and dangers, and triumphs, are beyond the wonders of fairy tales."

"Faix, the fairies are fools to the fellow I spake of, if the half of what he says be true."

Finch suggested to Ned that they should join the party of sailors, doubting not it would be good fun. Ned chimed in with the proposition, and Phaidrig undertook to make them welcome on his introduction. They at once acted on the suggestion, and found the jolly tars "tossing the can" gaily. Phaidrig was hailed with a shout of delight, and his friends heartily welcomed him; and, having been accommodated with seats and glasses, Finch and Ned were on as good terms with the lads of the ocean in five minutes as if they had been shipmates. Finch essayed immediately to draw out the principal romancer, of whom Phaidrig had spoken, and found it no difficult matter. Every sailor is ready enough to talk about his ship; and when a man had such a ship as the "Centurion" to brag of, he had reason to speak the more. He rattled away about the disasters and triumphs of the circumnavigation right willingly, every now and then bolting out some tremendous fiction, whereupon Phaidrig would make his pipes give out a little querulous squeak, that made every one laugh but the story-teller, who only swore the more stoutly to the truth of all he said, the more doubt was cast upon it. *He* was one of the principal people engaged in the attack on the shores of South America—*he* was the first to land—*he* made the Dons run—five-and-twenty of them—and the Governor at their head, *all with his own hand.*

Phaidrig's pipe gave a plaintive cry, as if it was calling for mercy.

"What's that you say ?" cried Jack. "D—d if I didn't, though; and I would have thrash'd twice as many, if they were there!"

On went the narration again. The town was burnt, after being emptied of its treasure, and the triumphant boats rowed back to the ship, all but sinking with the weight of gold they carried ; again they are afloat on the great Pacific Ocean ; again they traverse the mighty waste of waters ; again sickness attacks them.

"Then," said Jack, "we knew that unless we could make an island, we were lost—and, by hard work, we did make an island at last."

"You *made* an island," cried Phaidrig; "well, that is the best thing you towld yet!"—and Phaidrig made his pipe give a *screech*, while he shouted with laughter. "I suppose you'll tell us you made the world next."

"Put a stopper on that chap's lingo, will you?" cried Jack.

It was now explained to Phaidrig that "making" an island, in nautical parlance, meant arriving at an island.

"Oh, that's it, is it?" said Phaidrig; "then that's the way you sailoring gentlemen arrive at your wonderful stories, I suppose—by *making* them."

The story-teller swore he would carbonado the piper if he didn't take care; but the rest of the sailors overruled him in this, swearing Phaidrig was a treasure, and the best fellow in the world, and that he had the privilege of saying anything he liked.

"Well," continued Jack, "we made the island—mind, you piper-chap—we made it."

"Ay, ay!" cried Phaidrig.

"And then," cried Jack, with enthusiasm, "how we did enjoy the fresh water and vegetables—and such vegetables! You will hardly believe it, now, but as true as I'm here, there was little round loaves growing nat'ral on the trees, and as good bread as I'd wish to eat."

"I hope it was ready butthered," said Phaidrig

"No, it wasn't, you old piperly humbug. But if we hadn't butter, we had milk on the trees, though. Now, what do you say to that?"

"As far as milk is consarned, sir," said Phaidrig, "all I say is, that ' Kerry cows have long horns.'" *

"It was not from cows we had it, I tell you; but trees—out of nuts; there we found nuts that gave us more than a pint o' milk a-piece."

"That's the hardest nut to crack I ever met," said Phaidrig.

"It's true though, so hold your jaw; they call 'em *co-co* nuts."

"*Cow-cow* would be a fitter name for them " said Phaidrig.

---

* A saying in Ireland, applied to any incredible story. Kerry being a remote corner, it would be more difficult to detect any exaggeration promulgated as to its wonderful productions; hence the saying.

"Well," continued Jack, "after making all right and tight for sea, we made sail for China, and stood for ten days or so—"

"And why didn't you go on ?" cried Phaidrig.

"So we did go on, you nincompoop."

"Why, you tell me this minit you *stood*, and how could you go on while you were standing ?"

It was again explained to Phaidrig that the sea-phrase to "stand" for a place, meant to go towards it.

"Well, you have quare ways of talking," said Phaidrig; "and if a plain-spoken man can't make you out, it's your own fault, with your contrary words."

"Well," continued Jack, "we made China ;—you know *now*, I suppose," said he to Phaidrig, rather testily,—"you know now, old blowpipe, what I mean when I say we *made* China."

"O yis," said Phaidrig, mischievously, "you mean you made cups and saucers."

"No, I don't, old double-tongue," exclaimed Jack, while the sailors laughed at the continued quibbling by which Phaidrig annoyed him—"No, I don't ;—but it's no use talking to you— only don't vex me too much—that's all—mind your eye !"

"I wish I had one to mind," said Phaidrig.

The cheerful spirit of the man, jesting on his own misfortune, touched even the impatient story-teller, and he joined in the chorus of laughter which followed Phaidrig's last rejoinder. Phaidrig's spirit of jest was fully satisfied in making the man join in the laugh against himself; and when the noisy mirth abated, he begged Jack to go on, and said he would not annoy him any more, *if he could help it.*

"In China," continued Jack, "we did the grand thing. They wanted us to pay port dues there, and all that sort of thing, in going into harbour, but our commodore said he'd see 'em far enough first—farther than any of us would like to go, I reckon ; and told 'em the king of England never paid no duty at all, but took all he could get, and more too,—which stands to reason, or what would be the good of being king of England ? So we got all the 'commodation in life we wanted, and did'nt pay a rap to the long-tails ; and then, all being ship-shape again, we put to sea. The commodore said nothing to none of us, thof all of us suspected there was something in the wind, by the long walks the commodore used to take, all by himself, up and down the quar-ter-deck, with never a word to nobody ; and sure enough we were right. We were nigh a fortnight at sea afore he broke his mind to us ; but then, ordering all hands to be turned up, he tipped us the lingo. 'My lads,' said he, 'wouldn't you like to go back to old England with your pockets well lined ?' says he. 'Ay, ay, sir !' says every man in the ship. 'Well, then,' says the commodore, 'there's the rich Spanish galleon,' says he, 'a-sailing from Manilla to Akkypulky, and *that's* what I'd like to take.' The commodore's speech was hailed with a shout. 'Remember, my lads,' says he, 'I never want to deceive you;'—we shouted again;—'the galleon is strong,' says he, 'and we are wasted by sickness; our numbers are few, and that few are weak; we have only half our complement of hands; but, at the same time,' says he, 'a'nt we able to lick twice as many Spaniards, my boys?' We shouted louder than ever. 'That's enough,' says the commodore, 'we'll take the galleon;—keep a bright look out; let every lad have his eye open.' And sure enough we had;—then you might see the officers sweeping the horizon with their glasses every half hour, and night and day a man at the mast head. Well, about noon one day a sail to the southward was reported from the top;—up ran the officer of the watch, with his bring-'em-near;*—and when the commodore hailed him from the deck, to know what he made her out to be, he answered 'twas all right —a large ship, running to the southward. My eyes! what a shout did rise when we heard the news; we were all as nimble as monkeys; and, with a 'will O,' we made all sail in chase. When we had every inch of canvass drawing, and were going well through the water, 'Let the men have their dinner,' says the commodore; 'they have work before them.' Dinner we had soon, accordingly, tho' the thoughts of making so rich a prize almost took away our appetites, so we made short work of it. All this time we were nearing the galleon, that did not seem to notice us for some time, but soon we saw she was alive to it, for she crowded sail and seemed inclined to show us her heels : but all of a sudden, 'bout she comes, and bears right down on us. 'Twas such a comfort to see we were not in for a long chase, and maybe lose her in the night, after all, but to settle the matter out of hand at once; so we cleared the decks, and made all ready for action. Now, you see, it's a custom with these Spanish chaps, to lie down when an enemy comes up to them to deliver a broadside, thinking they have less chance of being killed crouching than standing; and then, when the broadside is over, up they jump and work *their* guns;†—it's a dirty dodge; but so it is;— so the commodore passed the word round the ship, that instead of firing a broadside into the enemy, we should give her our guns one after another, as we brought them to bear when we neared her, and so we did; so that the lubbers were lying flat, waiting for a broadside, while we bore up to her, going bang,

* Telescope.
† Such is described to be the Spanish mode of fighting. by the writers of the day.

bang, into her with our starboard guns as we ran past her, and then, going about, we had our larboard broadside ready by the time the Dons were on their legs; so that we exchanged with them, after giving them thirty guns before we got any answer. We had rather the advantage in metal, but they had twice our number of men—five hundred and fifty to little more than two hundred, weakened by sickness too ;—but what o' that?—they were Spaniards, and we were Britons! The Spaniard mounted thirty-six guns on his lower deck, besides twenty-eight lighter ones on his gunwale quarters and tops; they call them ' pidreros' "—

" Pattheraras, we call them in Ireland," said Phaidrig.

" Don't stop me, and be d—d to you! !" shouted Jack.

" Twenty-eight pidreros, and they peppered our decks pretty well; but as most of our hands were below fighting the heavy guns, they did not do us much damage, while our heavy metal was pounding them in their vitals; they were only scratching our face while we were digging them in the ribs ; and their hands were so numerous that every shot of ours was killing more on their crowded decks, than theirs among our spare crew. They did not fight badly, however—but at last down came the flag of the *Nostra Signora de Cabudonga*—that was her name; those Spanish chaps, men, women, and children, ships and all, have such confounded long names ;—and her commander *Don Jeronimo de Montero*—there's another o' them—came aboard the *Centurion*—now there's a tidy name—and delivered his sword to —*Commodore Anson*—that's short and sweet too—so there's how we took the *Nostra*——confound her, I can't say her name right over again."

" Bravo!" cried Finch—" well fought; and her treasure, they say, was a million and——"

" Avast heaving, messmate—we're not come to the treasure yet; there was worse danger than the battle, after the enemy struck. Just as we were conquerors, up walks the first lieutenant to the commodore to congratulate him on his victory— *as he pretended*—but it was to whisper to him that the Centurion was on fire below, close to the powder room. That was the time to see the cool courage of the noble Anson—not a word of alarm was whispered on the deck, and the commodore went below as unconcerned, to all appearance, as if he was going to dinner, and by his example kept the men so steady and quiet below, that the fire was extinguished in a few minutes. As it turned out, the danger was really less than it appeared, for some oakum had caught fire by the blowing up of a small portion of the powder between decks, and the smoke and the smother made matters seem worse than they were—but a moment's confusion might have blown gold and all, friends and foes, into the deep ocean, and no word would have been heard of Anson's glory."

"A brave tale, i' faith," said Finch.

"Stay, there is one thing more I have to tell," said Jack. "What I told you, partly is credit to ourselves; what I'm going to tell you, is to show how Providence watched over us all the way home. Our sickness diminished, we had good weather round the Cape, and prosperous winds home, and just as we were entering the Channel it fell thick and hazy, and this we were ungrateful enough to call bad luck, when, as it turned out, it was our salvation, for in that very fog we passed unseen right through the middle of a whole French fleet."

"Providential indeed," said Finch.

"Yes," said Jack thoughtfully—"I will say Heaven was special kind to us all through, though we had some sore trials and sufferings."

"But how amply rewarded you are by the tremendous treasure you have brought home! Near a million and a half, I hear; you must have prodigious prize money."

"Why, yes—pretty picking," said Jack. "Every man before the mast got three hundred pounds on account the other day, and we have a heap more to get still—so call for what you like; I'll pay for all."

"No d—me!" you shan't, cried another of the revellers; "I'm not a Centurion man, and didn't sail under a commodore; plain Captain Talbot was my commander, and my ship only a privateer, but as far as prize money goes I pouched eight hundred guineas to my share, so *I'll* pay—you can pay for me when you get the rest of yours!"

"Eight hundred?" exclaimed Finch.

"Ay—eight hundred hard shiners!" cried the sailor; "there's a sample," said he, thrusting his hand into his pocket and dragging out a fistful.

Finch exchanged a look with Ned, and said, "*That's* the trade!"

"And though a commodore didn't command us," added the tar, "we had a pretty tightish fight of it, as I could tell you, if so be you'd like to hear it."

"I should, of all things," said Finch, who, wishing to ingratiate himself with these roving gentlemen, knew the surest road to a sailor's heart was through his story. The sailor popped a fresh quid in his cheek, hitched up his trousers, and put himself into an attitude—in short, "squared his yards" to tell his story, when, just as he had got over the preliminary sentences, his yarn was suddenly cut short by a very sharp sound of hooting in the street; and as the noise grew louder the whole party rose and ran to the windows to see whence the hubbub arose. A dense mob of people preceded a carriage, which was guarded by some strange-looking soldiers, whose singular uniform seemed matter of special dislike to the populace. They wore grey jackets turned up with red, and there was a very un-English cut about them altogether. They were, in fact, a body of Swiss, resident in and about London, who, in the absence of the greater part of the regular troops abroad, in the prosecution of the king's *foreign* wars, volunteered to do military duty, and were embodied accordingly; and this seeming confidence in foreigners in preference to Britons was a most odious measure, and rendered the king very unpopular with the great mass of his subjects. The crowd seemed inclined to impede as much as possible the progress of the guarded carriage which contained prisoners, who were on their road to examination at the Cock-pit, where the Privy Council then held their sittings. Reproaches were showered on these Swiss guards, and terms of disrespect loudly shouted against the king and his ministers by the growling crowd, which pressed more and more on the guard, who seemed half inclined at last to use their bayonets.

"Kill Englishmen if you dare!" roared the crowd.

"Down with the Hanoverian rats!" was thundered from another side.

"Why won't the German good-for-nothing trust his own people?" cried a third party.

"Down with the badgers!" was echoed round about—alluding to the grey regimentals of the Swiss.

At this moment the carriage which bore the prisoners came within full view of the window, and Ned recognised Kirwan in one of the captives. For an instant he almost rejoiced that the man whose presence in Flanders he so much feared was retained in England; but in an instant his better nature triumphed over the selfish thought, and he called Finch's attention to the carriage, at the very moment that *he*, too, had caught a glimpse of O'Hara. Exchanging a significant look with Ned, Finch made a rapid and impassioned address to the sailors, saying the prisoners were friends of his, and as innocent as babes unborn; winding up with an appeal to their feelings, as "men and Britons," if they would allow free-born Englishmen to be dragged to slaughter, like sheep to the shambles, by a pack of beggarly foreigners?

"Will you, who have thrashed the Spaniards, let a parcel of hired strangers make Britons slaves in their own land?" cried Finch.

"No, no, no!!" was indignantly shouted by the thoughtless and generous tars, who, headed by Finch and Ned, made a rush from the tavern, and, further inflaming the crowd by their fierce invectives and daring example, a bold dash was made at the carriage, the doors dragged open, the guard overturned right and left, and Kirwan and his companions in bondage were freed in an instant, and hurried through the rejoicing crowd by the posse of sailors down the narrow streets of the favouring neighbourhood; and, while the tumult raged wildly behind them, and all pursuit was successfully retarded by the mob, the two men, so late in deadly jeopardy, sped securely onward towards the river, where they effected an embarkation in safety; the broad Thames was soon placed between them and their pursuers, and the obscure haunts on the Surrey side of the river gave sanctuary for the present to the rescued prisoners.

CHAPTER XIII.

THE storm which had so nearly made an end of the persons most prominently engaged in our history, which dealt such heavy blows on the mercantile interest in England, as almost to amount to national calamity, had not inflicted such smarting wounds as those under which France suffered. She had been for months preparing a great blow against Britain, which the winds in one night had paralysed. And as this threatened movement was known to all Europe, its defeat was bitterly felt by the sensitive nation that looked on it so hopefully.

But still they could attribute their failure to the elements in *that case*; but another occurred which was more difficult to support with patience. Admiral Roquefeuille, having made a junction of the Brest and Rochefort squadrons, sailed up the British channel with the intention of making an attack by sea, while Saxe should make his descent by land, and, having run up channel as far as Dungeness, the British fleet hove in sight, bearing down upon him. The lateness of the hour, and state of wind and tide, prevented the gallant old Norris from at once closing in action with him, and Roquefeuille took advantage of the night to get away in the dark, and return to port, while Norris had the credit of clearing the channel of the enemy without firing a shot.

But the extreme vigilance which our fleet and cruisers were

8

obliged to exercise for great national purposes, gave facility to minor adventurers, who dared the channel, and the safety which could not be obtained by the guns of a line-of-battle ship, was secured by the insignificance of a fishing-boat. Under cover of such protection, Kirwan and O'Hara reached the coast of France in safety, in a few days after their rescue in London; and at Gravelines joined Lynch, who was deeply engaged in the interests of Charles Edward, and in constant communication with the prince, who kept quiet at this little spot under the name of the Chevalier Douglas. *His* hopes had been fearfully dashed by the disasters of the storm. His cause, which had hitherto been so popular, fell into disrepute; for that great element of popularity—success —seemed to be denied to him, and the unfortunate Stuart was blamed for all the failures. Some few faithful and untiring friends still clung with desperate fidelity to his cause, and his small house was the rendezvous of these devoted adherents, where the prince was still cheered by their hopefulness, and assisted by their advice. Of the latter he stood much in need; for the chevalier was deplorably deficient in judgment, and allowed trifles to attract or annoy him, when greater interests might have been expected to engross his mind at that important moment.

Lynch had been on a mission to Paris, to make interest amongst the friends of the prince in the capital, and, through them, to endeavour to influence those in power in his favour; but he found the cabinet as much disgusted with the failure of their last grand effort as the people in general; and, so far from having the interests of Charles Edward discussed in council, their best energies were employed to send a sufficient force into Flanders, which was seriously threatened by the Dutch, who seized this favourable opportunity to join England in the war more heartily than they had yet co-operated.

A little council of four sat in the small house of the Chevalier at Gravelines. The Prince himself, Lord Marshal, Drummond of Bochaldy, and Lynch, just arrived from Paris. After he had laid his statement of how matters stood in the capital, Drummond asked him if he had seen Marshal Saxe.

"Yes," said Lynch.

"And what said he?" inquired Charles; "he seemed to be all heart and soul in the cause."

"Yes, sir," answered Lynch, "as he would be heart and soul in any cause that promised daring military achievement. The Marshal is essentially a soldier, and loves war for war's sake."

"I am quite of Captain Lynch's opinion," said Lord Marshal.

"Then he," pursued Charles, "does not seem to care about following up the expedition?"

"His attention is now turned towards the Low Countries, sir, where the French will soon take the field under his command—that is, if the Marshal's health permits him to leave Paris; for he is reduced to a state of great exhaustion, and when he allowed me the honour of an audience, he was in bed."

" His debaucheries, I suppose, have reduced him to so helpless a state," said Lord Marshal. "'Tis a pity so great a man should be such a slave to pleasure."

"Tush!" exclaimed Charles. "What were life without pleasure? I vow to heaven I would rather be on a sick-bed in Paris, than stuck up in a vile corner like this, where one earthly enjoyment is not to be had. I am *ennuyé* to death. I have neither hunting nor shooting: I have not had a gun in my hand for two months."

This was said with a petulance and levity that was shocking to the devoted men who heard it; and glances were exchanged among his followers, that, if Charles could have read their eyes, should have made him blush.

"'Tis very hard the king refuses to see me," continued the Chevalier, in the same tone of complaint. "If he would even permit me to reside in Paris—the Duke de Richelieu promised to intercede for me in this particular,—did you see *him* ?"

"I did, sir," said Lynch.

"Well ?"

"He strongly recommends a continuance of quiet residence here for some time."

"Plague take it!" cried Charles. " The deuce a thing there is to do here but buy fish."

"Is there not such a thing as ' *mending our nets?*' " said Lord Marshal, pithily.

" Pshaw !" said Charles, pettishly; " my patience is worn out."

"I think we shall not have so long to wait before we see clearly, one way or the other," said Drummond. "Much depends on this campaign. Let the arms of France be successful again, and our cause prospers beyond a doubt. Let victory remove the remembrance of recent disasters, and they will be ready to back your cause again, sir."

" I agree with you, Bochaldy," said Lord Marshal.

" And even then," said Lynch, "though the French government should not give all the aid your highness may reasonably expect, still *their* success makes *your* success. You remember, sir, the Irish merchant at Bourdeaux, of whom I spoke ; he is ready to advance money, and if we watch the moment of England's defeated arms abroad, a well-arranged descent on the shores of Scotland and Ireland at that time must be successful.'

" You always tell me I may depend on Ireland."

" Sir, she has been always faithful to the eause of your royal house, and is so still."

" And all Seotland would die for you," said Drummond.

" So be not impatient, my prince," added Lord Marshal. " Await the result of this campaign."

" Then I will join the army," eried Charles Edward, "and share in the eampaign myself; for I must have something to do."

" Oh, my prince!" exclaimed Lord Marshal, reddening to the forehead with shame for his master's folly, "think not of so rash a step. Consider, sir, your position. For God's sake think not of raising your arm in battle on the side of a foreign power, against the people over whom you seek to rule!"

" It seems I am never right," said Charles, pecvishly, seeming quite insensible to the noble rebuke his faithful servant gave him; and, rising suddenly, he left the room.

He retired to his own chamber, and employed the remainder of that day in writing to his father bitter abuse of the devoted and high-minded exile who sought to direet his folly. And the men who had abandoned home and eountry, and were ready to sacrifiee their lives for him, were the objects of this ungrateful trifler's anger, beeause his humour was thwarted by their good sense. He also wrote to Paris, to obtain permission to join Louis' army in Flanders; but the king felt, as Lord Marshal did, the indeeeney of sueh a proeeeding, and positively forbade his presence.

Lynch, after the prinee retired, had some further eonferenee with Lord Marshal and Bochaldy, who were much better able to eoneert measures for their master's good in his absence; and when the future ehances in favour of the Stuart cause were canvassed by the three adherents, till no topie was left untouched, Lyneh bade them farewell, as he was going to join Dillon's regiment—so called after its gallant colonel, than whom a more devoted adherent of the Stuarts did not exist. Repairing to his own lodgings, he rejoined Kirwan and O'Hara—the latter bearing a commission in the Irish Brigade, the former about to join, less perhaps with the love of arms than of Lynch's fair daughter; for it is more than prebable that to be near Ellen was one of the objects, if not the principal, which made Kirwan quit Ireland. For the present, however, he was not likely to see her; for, as the army was about to take the field, it was now concentrating on the frontier, and the following day Lynch and his two eountrymen set out for Douay.

CHAPTER XIV.

IT was a beautiful morning in spring, when the active inhabitants of two neighbouring villages in the province of Hainau, adjoining French Flanders, had just finished their morning meal, and were outgoing again to the fields, to continue the healthful industry with which the morning opened, when the blast of a trumpet attracted their attention, and the peaceful peasants were startled at the sound ; for who could live in that province and not know that any day might bring the horrors of war to their door, and, though the little villages of Fontenoi and Antoine had hitherto escaped that perennial scourge of the Lower Countries, the sinking heart of every inhabitant foreboded that their hour was come at last ; and the happy hamlets which hitherto had known no greater excitement than a wedding-feast or a christening, were about to have a burial-service celebrated on a large scale. The implements of husbandry, which had been cheerfully flung over the shoulders of sturdy men as they went a-field, were suddenly cast downwards again, and the listeners to the trumpet leant thoughtfully on spade and hoe, as they caught the first glimpse of the party whence the warlike warning proceeded, and some squadrons of French horse were seen approaching ! Women and children now crowd the village streets, as the cavalry ride in and dismount, and appropriate houses and stables to their use, as they are billeted by the proper officer,—and when houses and stables can hold no more, the horses are picketed and the men bivouac. When all is, so far, settled, the peasants go to work, but they cannot work with that heart-free spirit which makes toil pleasing. The demon of war

' Casts his shadow before,"

and all is darkened beneath it. The women in the villages are busy with ordinary cares; they are preparing " sops for Cerberus," and hope to soften the hearts of the men of war by roasting and boiling. So far, so well. But, in another hour, the engineers arrive, and, shortly after, a group of officers of the higher rank gallop into the town,—rapid orders are given, and the officers depart swiftly, as they came, and then a terrible work of destruction commences. Whole families are turned out of their houses; the engineers set to work, the rafters of the cottages are sawn through—in tumbles roof after roof, and each house is made the platform for a piece of artillery. Yes, the smoke of the happy hearth that curled in the golden mist of evening, and invited the weary traveller from afar, was to be replaced by the repellant vapour of the cannon's mouth!

> " The war clouds rolling, dun,
>   Where furious Frank and fiery Hun
>   Shout in the sulphurous canopy."

The hospitable village that afforded welcome and healthful fare, and wholesome slumber to the wayfarer, was preparing to hurl destruction on all who should approach it. The homes that heard the first fond whispers of bride and bridegroom, and the after holier blessings of fathers and mothers on their children, were soon to hear the roar of cannon thundering above their ruins.

When this work of destruction began, the men ran back from the fields, while the women and children stood in the streets into which they were turned, and looked on,—some with horror, others with the clamour that bereavement will produce in the most patient. Here was a woman, in silent despair, looking on at her dwelling tumbling into rubbish,—there was some youthful girl, struggling with a swarthy pioneer, endeavouring to stay the upraised axe, about to fell some favourite tree. The men, returning breathless from the field, add to the clamour in a different fashion; but curses or prayers are alike unavailing,—the work of destruction goes on.

Far apart, sitting by the road-side, was a woman, whose tears fell fast, as she held her baby to her bosom,—the fountains of life and of sorrow were both flowing. The unconscious baby smiled ever and anon, and looked up with its bright eyes at the weeping mother, while an elder child, who could just lisp its thoughts, was crying bitterly as she told her little grief—that the soldiers had trampled down all the pretty flowers in the garden. An officer approached this group, and attempted words of consolation. It was Lynch; for the vanguard of the French army was a portion of the Irish Brigade.

" Do not cry so bitterly," said Lynch to the weeping woman.

The woman only answered with her sobs.

" Do you not see the other villagers are getting away their furniture and making the best they can of it?"

The woman looked up gently through her tears; for, though she could gather no comfort from his *words*, there was charity in the sound of his *voice*, and even *that*, to the wretched, is something.

" You would find relief in going to help your husband."

"I have no husband to help," said the woman.

"What! a widow?" exclaimed Lynch.

"No, thank God!" replied the woman. "But my husband is not here,—Pierrot is gone some miles away to see his mother, who is dying, and I don't know what to do. I think less of the destruction of our house and the loss of all, than the thought of what poor Pierrot will think when he comes back and sees his house in ruins, and won't know what has become of his wife and children. O! if Pierrot were only here I wouldn't mind it; but what shall I do all alone?"

"Show me which is your house," said Lynch, touched by the woman's agony, "and perhaps I may be able to preserve it."

"You can't," replied the woman sadly; "there it is!" added she, "there—there, where they are dragging up the cannon now."

'Twas true; the artillery had arrived, and they were mounting the guns on the ruins of the houses. A dragoon rode up and handed a note to Lynch, saying, as he made his salute, "From Colonel Dillon, sir." Lynch, after glancing at the brief contents of the missive, turned his eyes towards the weeping woman, with much sadness and pity in their expression; he looked as though he wished to speak, but, feeling he could give her no comfort by his words, he hastily told the dragoon to lead him to Colonel Dillon, and galloped from the spot, heartily wishing he had escaped the scene of suffering he had witnessed. He soon reached a rising knoll, where Colonel Dillon and some other chiefs were issuing orders to numerous officers, who, arriving and departing in rapid succession, were scouring over the broken ground that lay between the villages of Fontenoi and Antoine and the wood of Barri on the opposite side of the narrow little valley, directing the operations that were going forward with speed and energy across the entire line of this point of defence. Spade and mattock were busily plied in thousands of hands, and deep trenches were cut across the pass, and trees felled and made ready barricades, behind which cannon was judiciously planted, to sweep, with cross fires, the intermediate points where an enemy might dare to force a passage. Thus went on the day; every hour making the approach to the bridge of Calonne more terrible; and *there* were the engineers constructing a *tête du pont*, which soon bristled with cannon, and gave the French complete command of the passage of the Scheldt; for Saxe chose to fight with the river in his rear, thus giving himself the means of throwing the river between him and the enemy, in case the day should go against him, and hence the powerful work constructed to hold the bridge, which afforded retreat, if retreat were needed. And now the gentle slopes which rise from the banks of the "lazy Scheldt" began to show upon their crests battalion after battalion crowning the heights and making a brave array of the French force; and soon the hill sides, whitening with their tents as though a sudden fall of snow had taken place, show that the army of Louis is encamped. Ere long a burst of trumpets and saluting cannon is heard, one universal shout arises where the lilied banners float:—these sounds announce the arrival of the King and the Dauphin; the chivalry of France is to fight under the eyes of their monarch and their prince, and all is enthusiasm.

"Where is the gallant Marshal?" inquired the King, as he missed the presence of Saxe, in the crowd of chiefs who surrounded him.

"Sire," said the count D'Argenson, "the Marshal is so reduced by sickness that the fatigue of superintending the preparations of to-day have obliged him to retire to rest."

"What trumpets are those?" said the King, as he caught the distant sound of the warlike blast coming from afar.

"Those of the enemy, Sire," said D'Argenson, looking across the Scheldt, and beholding the distant columns of the English advancing.

"They are welcome," answered the King; "we shall measure our strength to-morrow."

But the English seemed not inclined to wait for the morrow, for a smart fire opened on their side, the French outposts were driven in, and the Marshal de Noailles paid a tribute to the ready gallantry which the English always exhibit to join battle. And now, not content with driving in the outposts, and taking up their position, they even commenced a cannonade against the French lines, although the evening began to close; and it was deemed advisable to consult Saxe on the subject. The Marshal was no way disturbed by the news. "Let them fire away," he said—"the Duke of Cumberland is young and precipitate; he bites against a file; he little knows what I have prepared for him; he has no time this evening to force a single point, and must wait till to-morrow to find out the trap into which he is running his head.—So never mind this demonstration to-night—they will soon stop."

The event proved the truth of Saxe's word. The cannonade soon ceased, and the Duke of Cumberland called a council of war. He held the chief command, though the Prince de Waldeck had some share of authority at the head of his Dutch troops, and burned for military glory which had been so brilliantly won by the English prince at Dettingen; but the ardour of these two young men was held in check by the old Marshal Kœnigsec, who commanded the Austrians, and was entrusted by the States-General for the very purpose of overruling the temerity of the fiery young princes.

On the English side the arrangements were soon made. On the left, the Prince de Waldeck promised to seize Antoine. The Duke of Cumberland undertook all the rest with his British and Hanoverians.

In the French camp all was gaiety. The king held a banquet in his pavilion, surrounded by his chiefs—he was never known to be more lively; the discourse ran on battles and feats of arms, and Louis remarked, that since the fight of Poictiers no king of France and his son had been together present in battle. The remembrance of a fight so fatal to the French chivalry was looked upon as an evil omen by many, and rather darkened the end of the festive evening.

On retiring to his quarters Dillon met Lynch, who, at his colonel's request, was awaiting him. Unusual gloom sat on Dillon's brow; he grasped Lynch's hand with fervour as he told him he wished some parting words with him before the morrow's fight, as he knew that fight would be fatal to him, and, he feared, disastrous to the cause they both loved.

Lynch endeavoured to dispel such gloomy forebodings.

"I fear they are too true," replied Dillon.—"Only think of a French king, by way of inspiring his soldiers, refreshing their memories with Poictiers on the eve of a battle!"

"'Twas less felicitous than Frenchmen generally are in their allusions, certainly," said Lynch ;—"but what of that?"

"Let it pass," returned Dillon ; "but for myself I feel—I *know* I am to die to-morrow, and would bid you, my staunch friend and faithful adherent to the Stuart cause, farewell ; and request you to bear to the prince my dying wishes for his prosperity, and the assurance of my fidelity to him to the death, for I shall fall to-morrow in making my best charge for the regaining of his crown." *

"My colonel—my friend !" exclaimed Lynch ; "why this—"

"Say no more, my dear Lynch," said Dillon ; "such presentiments as mine are always fulfilled. I shall fall—but it will be at the head of my gallant regiment, and *I prophesy* it will be a charge that England will long remember, and make the wise

---

* Though the gaining of a battle in Flanders could not immediately replace the Stuarts on the throne of England, still every success against England was looked upon by the exiled Irish as favourable to their cause; and the brigaded Irish in their gallant aid to France were not actuated by love for the French, but by a desire to favour the Stuarts, whom they regarded as the legitimate race of their sovereigns; and, though fighting under the banners of Louis, it was the *feeling* for their own exiled king, and their own persecuted faith, that inspired them, and whetted their courage—it must be owned not unnaturally—against the English *of that day.*

regret the cruel laws that convert Irishmen into exiles and enemies."[*]

The friends then parted with a " Good night," and " God bless you," and Dillon offered up his soul devoutly to God before he slept ; for he felt his next sleep would be that of death.

Night and slumber now wrapped the two camps in darkness and in silence, save the pale glimmer of the stars, or the faint ripple of the river which reflected their light. But this repose was of short duration : drum and trumpet startled the quiet dawn, and the first rays of sunrise glittered on the ready arms of both the powers.

The king of France was one of the first to rise in the camp, and Count D'Argenson sending to Marshal Saxe for his last orders, the Marshal replied that all was ready for his Majesty to enter the field. The King and Dauphin, each followed by their splendid suites, wound down the slope, crossed the bridge, and entered on the field of battle, of which, to obtain a better view, many of the followers of the court climbed into trees to feast their Parisian eyes with slaughter.

Saxe was in such a state of exhaustion, that he was obliged to be carried through the ranks in a litter made of osier, to give his final orders ; and the soldiers, looking with fond admiration on their glory-loving general, who made a sick couch serve for a war chariot, hailed his presence with applauding shouts. Around him rode a brilliant staff, and, as he had completed his arrangements, he pointed towards the enemy as various generals and commanders departed for their respective posts, and said, " Gentlemen, I have but prepared for you the road to victory— alas! I cannot lead you myself; but you need not the guidance. None know better how to follow the road to glory !"

The English guns open as he speaks, and the generals ride to their respective posts. The Count de la Mark gallops to Antoine, where he is received by the brave Piedmontese with cheers. The Marshal de Noailles embraces his nephew, the Duke de Gram- mont, ere he departs for his post; but he quits the embrace of his uncle for the embrace of death; he is struck by a cannon-shot, the first victim of that sanguinary day. The old man hides his face in his hands, but the soldier triumphs over the mortal, and, dashing a tear from his eye, he bows to Saxe, and cries, " *I* will take his place, count. Let Fontenoi and vengeance be mine !" The Marshal puts spurs to his charger, and rushes to the defence of Fontenoi, on which the English and Hanoverians make a

* George the Second, on hearing of the terrible and triumphant charge of the Irish Brigade at Fontenoi, uttered these memorable words: " *Curse on the laws that deprive me of such soldiers.*"

joint attack; the slaughter is terrific; never was seen a fire so rapid and so terrible: the valour of the assailants is only to be equalled by the bravery of the defenders; but the village is one blaze of fire, sweeping destruction on all who dare approach. No living thing exists before it—the English retire, the French shout in triumph, the taunting sound stings the brave Britons, and again they assault the village. So rapid has been the French fire that the ammunition is nearly exhausted; *aide-de-camp* after *aide-de-camp* is despatched for a fresh supply—it does not arrive —the English continue the assault, every ball in Fontenoi is exhausted; but they still have powder. " Let them fire with powder only, then !" cried the brave old marshal ;" we must keep up the appearance of defence, at least." On press the English— Fontenoi is almost theirs, when a fresh supply of ammunition arrives, the fire is no longer a mockery, and the English are mowed down; they are too much weakened to hope for success, they retire till a reinforcement arrives.

The Duke of Cumberland, in the centre, passes through the village of Vezon under a tremendous cannonade, and, though not more than fifteen or twenty men can march abreast, still, undauntedly, they press through the fire, and file off to the left, forming line with the cool precision of a parade, while the iron shower makes wide gaps in their ranks, which are instantly filled up, and rapidly a column of undaunted British infantry forms, and advances across the broken ground of the centre; they are suddenly checked—the ground is *escarpé*—an enormous trench is before them. Old Kœnigsec whispers the Duke, he dreaded his attack was rash, and that *he told him so.* The Duke makes no answer, but, rushing to the front, exhorts the men to remember Dettingen, and, dashing through the trench himself, he leads his gallant guards forward, who drag with their own nervous arms six guns across the trench, and again move forward at the command of the duke.

Four battalions of the French guards now confront them, and the picked infantry of both armies prepare for deadly conflict. The Scotch guards under Campbell and Albemarle, the English under Churchill—a descendant of the great Marlborough. When fifty paces interpose between the combatants, the English officers advance, and, with a courtly air, take off their hats and salute the French guard. The Count de Chabanes, the Duke de Biron, and all the French officers return the salute. Such were the chivalrous customs of that time, that even an invitation to fire was made, which seems absurd in these more matter-of-fact days, when " Up, guards, and at 'em !" was the pithy and unceremonious phrase of Waterloo; but, in the polished day of Fontenoi, the gallant Lord Charles Hay exclaims, "Gentlemen of the French guards, fire!"

The gentlemen of the French guard would have been shocked to do anything so rude, and Count d'Auteroche replies, "Fire yourselves, gentlemen—*The French guards never fire first!*"

The English take them at their word, and when they did once set about it, they certainly fired in good earnest, for nearly the whole front rank of the French guard fell. The incredible number of 380 killed and 485 wounded was the result of that first volley, to say nothing of officers, nearly all of whom bit the dust; indeed Fontenoi presents a more fearful list of leaders killed than any other action on record; such was the heroism on both sides with which the men were led to assault, or inspired to resistance.

The second rank, appalled by the utter annihilation of the first, look back for support; they see the cavalry 300 toises behind them, they waver, but throw in their fire; it is fearfully returned by the English, and when Luttaux and D'Aubeterre at the heads of their regiments attempt to support the guards, they arrive but to witness and join in the rout. Luttaux bit the dust. The Duke de Biron had his horse shot under him. On press the victorious English, and the Duke of Cumberland pours fresh masses into the field. An impenetrable body of 14,000 men is firmly established. The Duke looks to the right, and expects to see Ingoldsby driving the enemy in before him—alas! he only receives a message from Ingoldsby asking for fresh orders, as he has hitherto done nothing, being kept in check by the skirmishers, and intimidated by the batteries. The Duke of Cumberland curses him for a coward, and swears he shall be tried by court-martial for it—*and he kept his word.* This is a fatal mistake. The Duke must either dare all, and pass between the batteries on his right and left, or retire; he chooses the desperate resolve to hazard all, and the invincible British bayonets drive all before them, though a cross-fire of batteries rips up the English ranks, and carries fearful slaughter into the advancing column, *but still it does advance.*

Saxe is alarmed for the fate of the day, and the thought of defeat lends him strength: he calls for a horse, and mounts, but his weakness prevents his carrying a cuirass, and a sort of buckler of quilted taffeta is placed before him on the pommel of his saddle. For some time Saxe permits it to remain there, but he soon cries, "Curse such mantua-making!" and, flinging it down, dashes into the hottest of the fight in a light, open dress. He retrieves the disorder, but sends the Marquis de Meuze to the king requesting him to retire. The king refuses, and determines to remain in the fight. At the moment, his suite is scattered by the broken regiments rushing back upon them. The body-guard, of their own accord, without waiting for orders, interpose their columns between the king's person and the fugitives. Saxe heads the second column of cavalry himself, and makes another charge upon the unflinching column—the cavalry are flung back from the serried bayonets, as a broken wave from a rock—the column is unshaken, and Kœnigsec already congratulates the Duke of Cumberland on his victory. And so it might have been, had the Dutch then advanced; but alas! for the Prince de Waldeck, his fame is tarnished. After the first assault upon Antoine, which he undertook to secure, he retired, and never attempted to do more. Saxe rode amidst a tremendous fire all along the centre British line, to reconnoitre their state with his own eye. They were firm, but quite unsupported by any other portion of their troops; charge after charge, nevertheless, they resist, and the Marshal saw nothing for it but to prepare for a safe retreat for the king. To this end he ordered Fontenoi and Antoine to be abandoned, which bravely held out against a third attack of the English, who, from that quarter, were in vain looked for by the Duke of Cumberland, as the Dutch were as vainly expected from Antoine. The Count de la Mark would not obey the order to retire from Antoine; and Fontenoi was held also. Again Saxe orders the French infantry to advance and revenge their comrades—"Men of Hainau, you fight on your own fields—drive hence the enemy! Normandy, remember your ancient chivalry! you conquered all England once—shall a handful of Britons resist you?" Thus inspiring regiment after regiment with his words, he ordered them to charge, calling on their leaders by name as he passed them. Saxe watched the result of the charge—the English were still invincible. The Prince de Craon fell as he led his troops to the charge, and the regiment of Hainau was swept from the field by a terrible fire of musketry and cannon; for the English had some few guns with them which they used with great judgment; and as their musketry was fired in divisions, it kept up a continued slaughter amongst the French, which drove them back in utter disorder. Saxe now gave up the day for lost —the English column, though it did not advance, was master of the field. It remained motionless, and showed front everywhere, only firing when it was attacked.

Seeing this state of things, a rather noisy council was held round the king, and Saxe despatched fresh orders to have Fontenoi and Antoine evacuated, telling Count de la Mark to refuse at his peril. Just as these orders were despatched, the Duke de Richelieu, the king's *aide-de-camp*, arrived at full gallop.

"What news?" cried Saxe.

" That the day is ours, if we only wish it! The Dutch are beaten, and the English, too, at Fontenoi—the centre only holds out. Muster all our cavalry and *fall upon them like foragers,* and the victory is won."—

" I am of that opinion," said the king to the Marshal

" Then we'll do it," said Saxe; " but first shake them with some cannon. Pequingny," cried he to the Duke, " advance four heavy pieces. D'Aubeterre, Courten, head your regiments! Ride, Richelieu, to the household troops, and bid Montesson charge! Jumillac, head your musqueteers! let the movement be concentrated. Dillon"—for the colonel was among the knot of officers round the king,—"Dillon! let the whole Irish brigade charge!—to you I commend its conduct. Where Dillon's regiment leads the rest will follow. Let the Irish brigade show an example!"

" It shall be done, Marshal!" said Dillon, touching his hat and turning his horse.

" To VICTORY!" cried Saxe, emphatically.

" Or DEATH," said Dillon, solemnly, kissing the cross of his sword, and plunging the rowels in his horse's side, that swiftly he might do his bidding; and that the Irish brigade might first have the honour of changing the fortune of the day.

Galloping along the front of their line, where the brigade stood impatient for the order to advance, Dillon gave a word that made every man clench his teeth, and grip his weapon for vengeance; for the word that Dillon gave was talismanic as others that have been memorable; he shouted as he rode along, *" Remember Limerick!"* and then wheeling round, and placing himself at the head of his own regiment, to whom the honour of leading was given, he gave the word to charge; and down swept the whole brigade, terrible as a thunderbolt, for the hitherto unbroken column of Cumberland was crushed under the fearful charge. Dillon was amongst the first to fall; he received a mortal wound from the steady and well-directed fire of the English column, and as he was struck, he knew his presentiment was fulfilled; but he lived long enough to know, also, he completed his prophecy of a glorious charge,—he saw the English column broken, and fell, fighting, amidst a heap of slain. The day was won; the column could no longer resist; but, with the indomitable spirit of Englishmen, they still turned their faces to the foe, and retired without confusion; *they lost the field with honour,* and in the midst of defeat it was some satisfaction to know, it was the bold islanders of their own seas who carried the victory against them. It was no *foreigner* before whom they yielded. The thought *was* bitter that they themselves had disbanded a strength so mighty; but they took consolation in strange land in the thought that it was only their *own right arm* could deal a blow so heavy. Thanks be to God, these unnatural days are past, and the unholy laws that made them so are expunged. In little more than sixty years after, and not fifty miles from that very spot, Irish valour helped to win victory on the side of England; for, at Waterloo, Erin gave to Albion not only her fiery columns, but her unconquered chieftain.

CHAPTER XV.

THE battle of Fontenoi may be said to have decided the campaign it opened. Town after town rapidly fell into the hands of the French; and though gallant defences were made here and there on the part of the allies in detail, no general movements could be effected; and the greater part of French Flanders was once more under the dominion of Louis. Nevertheless, while plumed with victory, he offered peace; but whether England thought the offer insincere, or fancied that at such a moment favourable terms would not be obtained, she rejected the pacific overture, and France and England continued belligerent powers. This circumstance was considered by the adherents of Charles Edward most favourable to his views, as it was hoped the successes in Flanders would be followed up by striking a home blow at Great Britain, and his partisans flocked to Paris, whither the prince himself had been now allowed to proceed; and although yet refused a personal interview with the king, he resided in the vicinity of the capital, and was in constant communication with those about the court who were favourable to his interests. Here he could pursue the amusements he so much regretted at Gravelines, and awaited his happy hour with better temper than on the sea-coast, the interregnum being agreeably filled up by the pleasures of the chase and the charms of a society which, though small, was brilliant, and offered a foretaste of St. James's in the observance of courtly etiquette and homage to his rank. Not only some of the *haute noblesse*, and many gallant cavaliers, but fair and stately dames made the small country house of the handsome young prince an enviable residence. And pre-eminent amidst the beauty which graced it was Ellen—no longer the inmate of the cloister at Bruges, but mingling in the gaieties of

Paris, under the protection of Madame de Jumillac. To none
were the little meetings of the mimic court of Charles Edward
more agreeable than to Ellen, whose personal charms won homage
from all the cavaliers, and whose sweet manners almost reconciled her triumph to her own sex. As the daughter of one of the
most active and devoted of the prince's agents, *he*, too, was studious in his attentions to her ; and wherever the fair daughter of
Captain Lynch appeared—at masque, or ball, or theatre—she
attracted universal admiration. Madame de Jumillac particularly
loved the opera ; and one night, as she and her fair *protégée* had
taken their seats to witness the representation of *Armide*, an
unusual commotion was observable among the audience ; whispers
seemed to pass from box to box, and eyes were eagerly directed
towards a conspicuous place near the stage which was yet unoc-
cupied : the pit catches the movement from the boxes, and are
equally anxious gazers at the vacant place. The overture commences ; and though, of course, that strict silence which the
severe etiquette of the French theatre most fitly enjoins, immediately ensued, still it was manifest the audience were inattentive ;
and the vacant seat near the stage carried it hollow against the
crammed benches of the orchestra. In a minute or two the door
of the box opens, and, ushered with profound reverence to his
seat, appears an officer in brilliant uniform. It is the victorious
Marshal himself, just arrived in Paris—it is the temporary idol
of the people, the glorious Count Maurice de Saxe, and all
etiquette is forgotten by the audience. The pit rises *en masse*,
and loud *vivats* ring through the house ; the powerful orchestra
is drowned by that burst of popular admiration—sweeter music to
the hero's ears than if Apollo himself led the band. The musicians
themselves have lost self-control, and the bewildered leader can
scarcely keep them together, while Saxe returns repeated obei-
sances to the applauding audience. At length order is restored,
and the last few bars of the overture are audible. The curtain
rises, and an impersonation of Glory appears, and sings a species
of prologue ; some lines occur in the verses which singularly
apply to the hero of Fontenoi, and the actress, catching the
enthusiasm of the moment, directs her gaze upon the Marshal as
she pours forth her strain of triumph ; and finally, as she com-
pletes her heroic *roulade*, she advances to the box, and presents
the laurel wreath she bears, as one of her attributes, to the Marshal. Again the pit simultaneously rose ; and so taken by
surprise were *all* by this impromptu of the actress, that even the
courtly boxes were urged to a breach of decorum ; and *vivats*
from the men, and white handkerchiefs waved by fair hands,
hailed the conquering Count, who seemed sensibly touched by
the enthusiastic welcome. Again and again he bowed to the

audience ; and when, after some minutes, order was restored, he might be seen making slight marks of recognition, as his brilliant eye wandered round the house, and, piercing the deepest recesses of the farthest boxes, caught some smile or glance which beauty cast upon him. But suddenly his attention seems particularly arrested ; and he makes a salutation in which there is more of devotion than he has yet manifested—his glances wander no more—he continues gazing on the same place—and all eyes, by degrees, turn to see who has enthralled the *voluge* Count. It is the box of Madame de Jumillac that is the point of observation. It cannot be *Madame* who has made the conquest —she is *passée*—it must be *la belle Irlandaise.* Yes; the unaffected graces of the beautiful Irish girl put the overdone Parisian *belles* into the shade ; and the coquettes of the capital are indignant, while Madame Jumillac, in the second-hand triumph of a *chaperon,* whispers to Ellen with a smile—" My dear, you have conquered the conqueror.''

Ellen would have given the world to have escaped from the theatre. A host of disagreeable emotions crowded upon her ; and the natural repugnance of a woman to speak of herself as the object of an unbecoming admiration, prevented relief in words. No woman of delicacy, even to one of her own sex, chooses to admit that she has inspired aught than an honourable passion; and, therefore, Ellen preferred keeping to herself the knowledge of the Marshal's atrocious attempt, through his emissary at Bruges.

She knew that Madame de Jumillac was a woman of honour and reputation, and that under her protection she was in security, and that speaking as Madame did, she only made a sportive use of the phrase, which, in that age of gallantry, meant nothing; for where so much of gallantry—not to use a stronger phrase— was then tolerated, the tribute of open admiration to a lady's charms might go much further without being blamed, than in the modern times. Ellen, therefore, sat patiently under the disagreeable trial to which she was exposed, though the blushes with which the concentrated observation of the whole theatre suffused her cheek were sufficiently painful, without the deeper and hidden feeling of maiden indignation. Still, with all her desire to conceal her emotion, Madame de Jumillac saw the triumph of the moment was not pleasing to her whom most it concerned; and she attributed to the recluse nature of her early education this shrinking from what a court-bred belle would have enjoyed.

" My love, do not think so seriously about it," said Madame de Jumillac.

9

"Seriously, Madame!" replied Ellen, echoing the **word**; "how could I think seriously of such folly."

"But it makes you uneasy:—pray be tranquil, child, **or all** our friends will laugh at us."

"But it is *such* folly," said Ellen.

"My dear, such follies may sometimes be made to serve good purposes. Remember the Marshal's enormous interest at the court at this moment, and how signally he may benefit the cause of your exiled king."

These words gave a new turn to Ellen's thoughts. She felt how much truth there was in the observation; and in her devotion to the cause of the royal Stuart her personal feelings were sunk. In that devotion she had been early instructed by her father, than whom a deeper enthusiast in the cause did not exist; and the seeds thus sown, taking root in a heart full of affection and sensibility, produced that unalloyed attachment, which can supersede all selfish considerations—an attachment to which the tendril nature of a woman's heart and mind conduces, and has furnished so many examples of heroic self-devotion.

The thought of enchaining the Marshal to the Stuart cause in the rosy bondage which Madame de Jumillac hinted, thus entered Ellen's mind for an instant; but that sanctuary was too pure to permit it to remain there longer;—its temporary admission was obtained through the generosity of her disposition in preferring the cause of her king to her own, but the dignity of her nature revolted at the idea, and she almost blushed for herself, that any cause could have made her harbour a thought repugnant to honour. In thus speaking of honour, of course the word is used in its most *refined* sense; for Ellen Lynch was too strongly fortified in virtue to feel any evil consequences to herself from the attentions of the most accomplished *roué* in the world. She had also sufficient confidence in her own powers of attraction (of which every day gave evidence), and reliance on a sufficiency of woman's wit, to hold a hero in her chains, if she had looked upon coquetry as allowable; but her simple dignity of nature, and a deep sense of moral rectitude, were above the practice of what she held to be wrong; and even for a cause in which she would willingly have laid down her life, she could not stoop to a course of conduct which would have forfeited her own self-respect. She was so absorbed in thought, that the pageant on the stage passed before her eyes as unseen as though she gazed on vacancy; her whole mind was preoccupied in anticipating circumstances that chance might combine to force her into intercourse with the Marshal, and forming thereupon resolutions as to how she should act: and after much consideration, her final determination was, that prudence made it advisable to appear unconscious of any cause of anger against the Count, should they meet, and that she must rely on a punctilious politeness to protect her from any advance that could offend.

This, perhaps, was the most delicate course she could have adopted in her present situation. Her father was absent at Bourdeaux, concerting measures with an Irish merchant, named Walsh, in the cause of Charles Edward; and confided, as she then was, to the protection of a lady moving in the court circles, and the wife of an officer in the army, it might have placed Madame in an awkward position had Ellen spoken the real state of her feelings, and the cause; to say nothing of the repugnance, already alluded to, which she entertained against speaking of such matters at all.

Besides, she expected the return of her father soon, and, for a few days, she reckoned it impossible any evil could result from the silence she had determined to observe.

As soon as the first act was over, the Marshal's box was crowded with a succession of visitors, some *few* really glad to interchange words of kindly greeting; the *many* proud to be seen as of his acquaintances, thus deriving a reflected light from the star of the evening. One, however, remained longer than the rest, and took a seat beside the Count—it was Voltaire. They seemed mutually pleased with each other's company, and ere long the eyes of the philosopher were turned towards the box where Ellen sat. It was the first time she had seen him, and she was forcibly struck by the intellectuality of that face, where keenness of perception and satire were so singularly marked, while he was as much attracted by the expression of simplicity with intelligence which characterised the beauty of the Irish girl. It is difficult to say which had most pleasure; she, in gazing on distinguished ugliness, or he in admiring the beautiful unknown.

"What are you about there, Sir Poet?" said Saxe, noticing the rapt gaze of Voltaire.

"I am not a poet at present," answered he, "but an astronomer. I am making an observation on that heavenly body."

"Heavenly, you may well say!" ejaculated the Marshal.

"Your cynosure," said Voltaire, slyly.

"I should rather call her Venus," returned the Count.

"I should think *Mars*," said Voltaire, eyeing the Marshal, "would like to be in conjunction."

"Or *Mercury* either," rejoined Saxe, with a glance at the poet.

"You are getting too close to the Sun, now," answered Voltaire. "We shall be dazzled in the light of our own metaphors, so we had better return to the earth and common sense. Who is she?"

"The daughter of a captain in the Irish Brigade."

"*Ma foi!*—those Irish are victorious every way. We have heard wondrous rumours of then at Fontenoi, from the Stuart party here"

"The fact is," said Saxe, in a whisper to the historian,— "*they won the battle*—but for heaven's sake don't say I said so, or, you know, it would not be relished in France."

"Don't fear me," said Voltaire, "I won't make either *oncdit* or history of it.* But *revenons à nos moutons*—the lady is very charming; I wish we had a brigade of such."

"A brigade!" cried Saxe, in surprise; "why, there are not as many *such* to make it in all the world!"

"*Parbleu!* Count!—You are positively *entêté* on this point."

"I'm over head and ears in love with her!" said Saxe; "I confess it—and the worst of it is, she is a piece of snow."

"From the top of a mountain in Ireland," added Voltaire, with a sneer.

"Provokingly pure, on my honour," said Saxe.

"But snow melts when it is no longer on the top of the mountain," said the scoffer.

"Would I were the valley it would fall upon!" said Saxe.

"I should think the air of Paris sufficiently warm to thaw your frozen beauty."

"She's not so easily melted, I assure you."

"*She's a woman,*" said the leering cynic, who had no faith in any virtue.

"By my faith, she has more of Diana about her than ever I met yet," said Saxe.

"'Tis most natural," returned Voltaire, "with your love of sporting, that you should liken your fair one to the hunting goddess; but, Marshal, if I mistake not, you admire the *chase* more than the *chaste.*"

"The difference is but a *letter*," said Saxe.

"How can you say *letter*, in your present state of mind," said Voltaire; "you should say *billet-doux.*"

"Hold! hold!" cried Saxe, "I cannot play at *jeu de mots* with you."

Here a fresh visitor entered the box, and made his salutations to the Count in the most obsequious manner. He was one of

---

* The historian of *Précis du Siècle Louis XV.* kept his word. He behaves shabbily to Ireland in the account of the battle. It is from other sources we hear the whole truth of the memorable charge of her gallant brigade.

those useful persons whom nobody likes, yet nobody can do without; who is always abused in his absence, but whose presence seems always welcome; who, by a species of ubiquity, is present at every party, where every one votes him a bore, yet smiles at his sayings, and asks him to forthcoming fêtes and suppers. He had the singularly appropriate name of "*Poterne*." The Marshal was delighted at the sight of him, shook him by the hand, and invited him to a seat. Even the great Voltaire gave him a pleasant nod of recognition.

"Charmed to see you, my dear Poterne," said the Marshal. "As usual, I find you in the midst of fashion."

"And as usual, Count," returned Poterne, with a monkeyish grin, "I find you worshipping beauty—" and he made a grimace, and looked to *the* box as he spoke.

"By the bye, Poterne," said the Marshal, in a confidential whisper over the back of his chair, "I wish you could find out for me where Madame de Jumillac sups to-night."*

"I can tell you already," said Poterne, with a knowing look. "I thought you would like to know, so I found out and came to tell you."

"My dear Poterne, you are a treasure!" exclaimed the Count, squeezing his hand in a fit of momentary friendship: "where?—where?"

"At Madame de Montesson's."

"Bravo!" exclaimed Saxe, "I can invite myself there."

"You need not do *even* that," said Poterne, with a shrug. "*I* managed all that—the whole thing I imagined, à *l'improvisé*, and I have just come to tell you that Madame de Montesson hopes for the honour of your company."

"You are my good genius, Poterne!" said Saxe in ecstasy; "pray bear my compliments to Madame de Montesson, and say how happy I am in accepting the honour she proposes, and add that I will bring with me the wit of Voltaire to season my stupidity."

The "fetch and carry rascal" departed to do his message, content with being seen in close converse with the great man, as the payment of his dirty work.

"*Mon ami*," said Saxe to Voltaire, "you must come with me to supper. I depend on you to engage Madame de Jumillac in conversation, while I talk to her *protégée*. You alone can serve me, for she is given to virtue and letters—therefore you must make a diversion in my favour."

---

* The "*petits soupers*" of this period were brilliant things, and matters of course after the opera.

"I will prevent sport being spoiled as much as possible," answered his friend.

Again the door of the box was opened, and a servant in the livery of the theatre made his appearence, but remained in the back-ground.

"Well?" was the brief exclamation of the soldier.

The servant still remained within the shadow of the back of the box, and exhibited a small note.

"Give it me," said the Marshal, without leaving his seat.

The servant advanced, and placed the missive in his hand; Saxe broke the seal and read—

"Glory waits you!
"Supper at 10. Quai d'Orfèvre.
"CELESTINE."

"A Monseigneur
"Le très illustre
"Le Maréchal
"Comte de Saxe."

It was a note from the actress who had personated "Glory" in the opera, and this very brazen invitation to supper so displeased *even* Count de Saxe, who was not very particular, that he tore a slip from the note, and, borrowing a pencil from Voltaire, wrote,

"Glory should not seek a soldier,—
A soldier should seek Glory."

And twisting up the paper, handed it to the servant for answer. He made a low obeisance and retired; and as he was hastening back along the corridor to the stage, he was met at the head of the staircase by Adrienne le Couvreur, who arrested his further progress. She had been in the auditory of the theatre, and all unseen had witnessed the presentation of the laurel branch to the Marshal by Celestine, who was a very pretty woman, and a desperate coquette, and had avowed her determination to rival the tragic queen with the gallant Marshal. This demonstration had put Adrienne on the *qui vive*, and a little ruffled her temper; but when she saw the servant of the theatre hand a note, (for with all his care to keep in the shade, the vigilant eye of Adrienne saw him, and her suspicions told her his mission,) her jealousy and indignation were no longer under her control, and instantly hurrying from her box she rushed down stairs to intercept the servant, and was successful in her manœuvre.

"Give me that note, sir," said Adrienne.

"What note, Madam?" faltered the messenger, his eyes

wandering from side to side as if he dared not meet the vivid glance which was fixed on him.

"You dare not look me in the face and repeat that question," said Adrienne quickly. "That note in your hand behind your back."

"*Vraiment!* Madame!" said the messenger, holding forth his empty hands with a seeming candour.

"Then you have put it up your sleeve," said Adrienne. "You can't impose on me—I know all about it—it is an answer to a note you bore from Mademoiselle Celestine to Marshal Saxe—"

"Really, Madame!"

"I must have the note. I do not expect it for nothing—here," she said, drawing forth her purse, and handing the servant a couple of *Louis d'or.*

"Madame!" exclaimed the fellow in a deprecatory tone, "consider my honour!"

"Well sir, tell me the price of your honour."

"Pardon me putting a price on my own honour, Madame," said the fellow, with an air that was very whimsical, "but I think a note from a field marshal is worth five gold pieces."

"There!" said Adrienne, handing the money.

"And now, madame, consider my character, I pray you? For pity's sake order a couple of these gentlemen to force me to deliver the note," and he pointed to some of the servants of the lobby, who were standing near and laughing.

"You are a gentleman of the nicest punctilio!" said Adrienne, smiling, and giving the order he requested to the attendants, a mock scene of forcing the note from the messenger was gone through, who with a tragic air wrung his hands, and swore he was in despair, while Adrienne seized the *billet,* and gave another *Louis d'or* to the attendants for their service. Hastily untwisting the *chiffon,* she read the Count's answer with intense delight, and observing one of the principal persons in the stage direction passing at the moment, she addressed him, and requested the favour of being allowed the advantage of his private key, and being passed at once to the stage. This little favour was immediately granted, and *La belle Adrienne,* flushed with victory, and meditating vengeance, trod the boards with lofty dignity, seeking for her would-be rival. Soon she espied "Glory" at the front wing, surrounded by many subordinates; and entering the *ring,* that at once made way for the approach of so distinguished an *artiste,* she made a most dignified inclination of her head to Celestine, and, handing her the billet open, said, "Allow me the honour to return Marshal Saxe's answer to your *obliging* invitation," laying great stress on the word "obliging," and making a low curtsey as she spoke.

Celestine might be seen to grow pale, even through her *rouge*. She bit her lip, and could not refrain from bursting into spiteful tears, which contrasted strangely with the emblems of triumph with which she was decorated.

Adrienne, with a scornful curl upon her lip, said scoffingly, "What a Glory, to be sure? This is not French glory," she added, to the women who stood by and enjoyed the scene: "'tis a glory of the Dutch school."

The words were received with a titter, for Celestine being rather a full-blown beauty, and the Dutch behaving so dastardly at Fontenoi, the words bore a double application; and, satisfied with having raised the laugh against the vanquished Celestine, Adrienne returned to her box, first having despatched a messenger with another note to the Marshal.

He was much surprised to see a second theatrical messenger hand him a second billet, and exchanged a laugh with Voltaire as he broke the seal. The note ran as follows :—

"I am glad you are not *too* fond of Glory. Come sup in peace and quietness with   "ADRIENNE."

"*Embarras de richesse!*" exclaimed Saxe, with a shrug, to his companion, who lending his pencil again, the Count, taking a leaf from a pocket-book, wrote a few words to Mademoiselle le Couvreur, regretting he could not accept her invitation for that evening, having a pre-engagement.

To that engagement he looked for much gratification, and with the eagerness of a new passion longed for the moment that would enable him to make his compliments to Ellen ; and as soon as the opera was over, he lost no time in seeking his carriage, and driving with the poet to the hotel of Madame de Montesson. He had but just alighted when his quick eye caught sight of Ellen in the carriage that was drawing up to the door, and waiting till she was going to alight, he stepped forward, and offering his hand with an air of the most courtly attention, he assisted Ellen from the coach, and ushered her into the hall with the most respectful assurances of his great delight in having the good fortune to meet her in Paris.

It was lucky that Ellen had, by anticipation, prepared herself for the occasion, as it gave her an ease and composure of manner most calculated to serve her under the circumstances, and which rather took the Count by surprise ; for where he expected a certain amount of apprehensiveness and timid reserve, which his practised address was to reassure and overcome, he found a calm but faultless politeness which puzzled him excessively, and induced him almost to believe that Ellen could not be aware of the nature of his design at Bruges. On entering the drawing-room where Madame de Montesson had arrived but a few moments before, the Count, after paying his compliments to Madame, followed to where Ellen had taken her seat close beside Madame de Jumillac. The proximity to her *chaperon* prevented the immediate adoption of any urgent strain of compliment which he might otherwise have attempted, and he waited till the announcement of supper would give him the opportunity of monopolising her attention out of inconvenient ear-shot, when his friend should have drawn off the elder lady to a distant corner of the table. In the meantime he addressed polite inquiries after her father, and took occasion to flatter Ellen's nationality by high praise of the Irish Brigade. Of this Ellen took immediate advantage, by turning the conversation into a channel the farthest removed from that into which the Count could wish it to flow; she spoke of the death of Colonel Dillon in terms of affectionate regret, saying she knew the whole family well in Ireland, and could tell the Count many anecdotes connected with their history, which she had learned during her early intercourse with them in her childhood, and which, she was sure, would interest the Count much, from the great regard he was known to entertain for the late colonel.

The Count protested the most devoted friendship, but would have willingly made the anecdotes a present to his Satanic majesty; but so well did Ellen feign great interest in the recital, that he was bound to hear, without the opportunity of saying one gallant thing till supper was announced.

"Now," thought Saxe, "my time is come," as he offered his arm to Mademoiselle, and led her from the drawing-room, while Voltaire held the delighted Madame Jumillac, proud of the poet's attention, one of the last to leave the *salon*.

The Count seated himself at supper most favourably for his purpose, and was studious in his attentions to Ellen, who, having worn out the Dillons, bethought her of a new subject. She, after some preliminary askings of thousands of pardons, *et cetera*, hoped the Count would excuse her if, as he had already spoken of the brigade, and so far touched on public affairs, he would allow her to mention the cause dearest to her heart.

The Count here edged in some speech about hearts in general, and *her* heart in particular, at which Ellen only smiled, and said a woman never could make use of the word "heart," but the gentleman beside her thought it his bounden duty to make love on the spot. "But I absolve you from that duty, Count," said Ellen, "you know the cause *I* mean is that of my king,—what think you of his prospects? brightly, I trust."

Hereupon she engaged the Count on the business of the Pretender during the whole of supper, that is to say, the *eating* part of it, when people are so engaged in their own immediate interests that they care very little about their neighbours' doings, and, therefore, such time is the most propitious to a tender *téte-à-téte*, when well managed by a practised *cavalier*; but so quickly did Ellen put question after question, and suggest fresh and *sensible* matter for discussion, that all the *soft nonsense* the Count had hoped to utter he was forced to keep to himself. The business of supper advanced, the champagne circulated, conversation grew brisker, laughing more frequent, as if mirth and champagne had been bottled together, and every cork that popped out emancipated hilarity. And now, what sharp ringing laughter comes from the other end of the table?—'tis the tribute to the pleasantries of Voltaire, who, in endeavouring to enchain the attention of Madame de Jumillac (quietly though he does it), enchains the attention of all besides—for Madame's laughter attracts notice—'tis something Voltaire has said has made her laugh; who would not like to hear Voltaire's *bon mots?*—all became attentive by degrees. The Count now thinks his time has arrived; he makes a desperate dash at compliment, and hopes to have Ellen all to himself; but she, with a well-acted air of innocent rudeness, turns to him and says, "Oh! Count, pray don't talk now; I want to hear Monsieur de Voltaire,"—then, suddenly stopping, as if she recollected herself, she said, "Marshal, I beg your pardon; I fear I have been very rude."

"By no means," said Saxe, with a smile, though he really *was* very much stung, wished Voltaire where the whole Catholic Church wished him, and vowed in his inmost heart he would never call upon a wit to help him when he wanted to make himself agreeable.

Voltaire had now every eye and ear devoted to him, and after a brilliant hour the *petit souper* broke up.

Saxe handed Ellen to her carriage, without having advanced his position one step since he handed her out of it.

"Well," said Voltaire, as he drove away with the Marshal from the house, "how have you fought your battle?"

"Never was so beaten in my life," said Saxe. "That girl is either the most innocent or the cleverest woman I ever met."

CHAPTER XVI.

THE day following, when Madame de Jumillac and Ellen met at breakfast, the latter complained of head-ache. This was true, but not quite to the extent that Ellen feigned. The excitement of the previous evening was sufficient to account for the throbbing of her temples, but the pulsation under ordinary circumstances would not have been sufficient to make her forego a very gay *fête champêtre* given that day in the neighbourhood of Paris; but, as she had heard over-night that Marshal Saxe was to be present, she made her head-ache serve a good turn for once, and excused herself on that score from being of the party.

"My dear child, the air would do you good," said Madame de Jumillac.

"Not to-day, dear Madame—I feel it is too bad a pain to play with."

"And such a charming party too!" added Madame.

"So charming," said Ellen, with a sweet smile of suffering, "that they won't miss me."

"Dear girl, half my pleasure will be gone if I have not you with me."

"I am sorry, dear Madame, to deprive you of any pleasure, but pray enjoy the other half without me."

It was in vain that Madame de Jumillac urged arguments or persuasions or coaxings. Ellen would not go; and, therefore, when in due time the carriage was announced to be at the door, Madame de Jumillac was destined to be the sole occupant, and drove to the *fête champêtre* alone.

On arriving at the tasteful *château* where the fête was held, Madame de Jumillac was accosted by many a gallant cavalier as she sauntered through the shady walks and gaily dressed *bosquets* of the pleasure-grounds, and the salutation graciously tendered to *her* always finished by an inquiry after *Mademoiselle* whose companionship in the dance was ever held a high favour. On hearing that a slight head-ache was the cause of her absence, there were a thousand "pities!" uttered;—some hundreds were "*very* sorry"—and about fifty "in despair;"—nevertheless, they all contrived to enjoy themselves. It was when she was almost wearied out with the eternal regrets of all her friends at the non-appearance of her *protégée* that Madame de Jumillac saw the Marshal Saxe passing through a crowd of distinguished persons to make his respects. After observing all that courtesy could desire to a lady at her time of life—in short, paying the *octroi* that is due at the gates of the *chaperon* before you can deal for the goods that lie within her circumvallation—the Count made a polite inquiry after Mademoiselle de Lynch, and Madame de Jumillac thought he exhibited more real emotion when he heard that poor Ellen was all alone at home, than any person who had heard of her indisposition. And true it was that the Count *did* exhibit more emotion—but it was emotion arising from very different causes than those for which Madame de Jumillac gave him credit—'twas an emotion which his quick spirit of stratagem excited; for, in this circumstance, he perceived a chance of obtaining a *tête-à-tête* with Ellen, and determined at once to act on the suggestion of the moment; therefore, bowing and smiling his way towards the point of egress, he seized a favourable opportunity to retire, and, finding his carriage himself, without making the *éclat* of having it called, he was driven back to Paris with all speed.

Ellen, in the hours of Madame de Jumillac's absence, had devoted her time to reading a heap of old letters, some of which (in the accumulation that time will bring) it became necessary to destroy; as, in the rambling life she was forced to lead by her father's occupation, the most portable luggage was of importance. Perhaps there is no sadder occupation than reading old letters— particularly where you are obliged to burn some of them. Sometimes their words recall pleasures of the past—such pleasures as you feel you may never taste again; sometimes assurances of affection, or some expression of sympathetic endearment which you are loth to destroy, and which you read over and over again before the paper is given to the flames; sometimes a trait of un- looked-for friendship—of distant kindliness that has cheered when most we wanted, and in some desolate hour had made us feel we are not forgotten. Such are the things that render old letters dear, and make the burning of them painful. The ancients used to keep the ashes of the dead in urns. Might we not do the same with letters?

It was in the midst of such employment—her mind attuned to the tenderest pitch of sentiment, that Ellen was startled by the loud rattle of a carriage and a commanding knock at the door; and, in a few seconds afterwards, the door of the sitting-room she occupied was thrown open, and a servant announced Marshal Saxe, who approached Ellen with the most courteous ceremonials, but at the same time with a devotion of manner far above the level of common-place politeness, and which no woman could mistake.

"Mademoiselle," said the Marshal, "I have hurried hither

from a scene of pleasure, where I went in the hope of seeing you; you being absent, it was no longer a scene of pleasure to me; and I came to throw myself at your feet, and tell you so."

Ellen was so taken by surprise at this sudden avowal, that it absolutely took away her breath, and she could not answer; while the Count, profiting by her silence, poured forth a voluble flood of passionate protestation. At length Ellen, recovering her self-possession, though still pale with mingled alarm and indignation, answered; her voice, though less sweet, retained all its clearness, and fell with that cutting distinctness which irony imparts.

"Count," she said, "I must suppose you have been at a masquerade, and, retaining the spirit of the scene you have quitted, have come here but to mock me."

"No mockery, by heaven!" exclaimed Saxe, "and you know it, lovely one! Did you not see, last night, how I was watching for one look of tenderness at the theatre, which you refused to grant? Did you not see, in the midst of all that engaging scene, my thoughts were wholly yours? Why were you so cruel? Could you not afford one kind look?"

"Sir," said Ellen, "in the midst of that scene of your triumph, I should have thought it a vain and unseemly intrusion had so humble a person as I am dared to claim your attention."

"Humble person!—scene of triumph!" exclaimed the Count, echoing the words—"yours is nature's nobility; and as for *triumph*, I swear to you by a soldier's honour that, in the midst of all the flattery showered on me last night, I had no thought but *you*. The applauding shouts of all France would charm me less than one sigh of yours—if *I* might win it."

He fell on his knees as he passionately uttered these words, and, seizing Ellen's hand, impressed several kisses upon it.

After a momentary struggle she disengaged her hand, and the tone of irony was instantly changed to that of dignity, and as her noble brow was slightly knit, and her bright eye dilated with emotion, she said, "You have spoken of a soldier's honour, sir; remember, I am a soldier's daughter, and that *his* honour is involved in *mine*. I hope I need say no more." She was rising to leave the room, but the Count, again seizing her hand, retained her in her seat.

"You must not leave me thus! not without some word of hope to me—"

"What would my father say, sir, if he saw you kneeling at my feet?"

"It is not what your father would say I want to know, but what his daughter would say," returned the unabashed Marshal;

"by heaven, you are the most enchanting creature in the world. My angel, my goddess, my—"

Thus was the Marshal pouring forth his raptures, attempting to kiss Ellen's hand between every two words, when she became alarmed at his impetuosity, and bethought her of a stratagem to relieve herself from her painful predicament. Feigning a new apprehension, she held up her finger in token of silence, and exclaimed softly, "Hush!" Affecting then to listen for a moment, she muttered quickly, "'tis *he!* I am lost? Oh! Count, if you would not have my future prospects utterly destroyed, pray conceal yourself for a moment; if you are seen here I am ruined."

"Where shall I hide?" exclaimed the Count, springing to his feet.

"Here," said Ellen, opening the door of a china closet.

"Oh! you rogue!" said the Count, laughing, and looking archly at her, as he obeyed her command, and entered the open portal.

"You dreadful man!" said Ellen, with a coquettish air, as she was shutting him in.

"Remember you owe me something for this," said Saxe, popping out his head.

"Take care!" said Ellen, affecting alarm; "be quick."

Saxe entered the closet, and Ellen locked the door upon him, and withdrew the key. Then throwing a light mantle round her, and casting a veil over her head, she hastened down stairs, and entering the Marshal's carriage, which stood at the door, ordered the coachman to drive back to the *château* where the *fête* was held. Here she was soon enabled to find Madame de Jumillac, to whom she communicated what had happened, briefly relating the Bruges adventure, and giving her reasons for the silence she had observed on the subject. "But now," said Ellen, "I am convinced nothing will cure him but to make a scoff of his gallantry; he is locked up in the china closet; here is the key. I leave his exposure to you, Madame, the sanctity of whose roof he has dared to disrespect."

Madame de Jumillac was deeply indignant at the Marshal's conduct, and, quite approving of the punishment Ellen proposed, bethought her how she could make it most severe. She determined his own particular friends should be the witnesses of his discomfiture, as well as hers to bear evidence of the affair; and with this view she sought for Voltaire and Poterne; for anything in which Voltaire bore a part must become celebrated; and Poterne was the man of all men to give currency to a piece of scandal. Having found them, Madame promised them a piece of the richest ridicule they ever witnessed if they would come with her, and so successfully piqued their curiosity, that the wit and the tale-bearer joined her party back to Paris, whither they speedily drove.

In the meanwhile the gallant Saxe remained locked up in the china closet—not the first, by many a dozen, he had been in—exulting in the success of his bold move: for the moment a lady proposed to conceal him, he was sure he had triumphed. He looked upon a china closet as the very citadel of love, which having carried, it was his to propose the terms. Not that he imagined the lady in this case would have yielded so soon. He thought her the very slyest person he had ever encountered, and set her conduct down as one of those strange varieties of the sex, of whose caprice he had such extensive experience; but this example, he admitted, surpassed by far any he had hitherto met; and he laughed to himself at the sudden turn affairs had taken. She all honour and indignation; and then, in a moment, is proposed a china closet. "Capital!" thought Saxe—"capital! —to be sure, she would not have yielded so soon, I dare say, if she had not heard her *other* lover on the stairs, and dreaded my being discovered. Good!—her *other* lover—and she playing injured innocence all the time—and at a word proposes a *china closet!* Oh, woman! woman!! woman!!!"

Such were Saxe's reveries (though they have not appeared among his *published* ones) while he was awaiting liberation and love. He began to get very impatient, however, towards the end of his imprisonment; and it was with no small satisfaction, after the lapse of a couple of hours, that he heard a tap at the door, and Ellen's sweet cautious whisper outside. After some soft mumblings through the key-hole, the key is employed, the door is opened, and forth pops the Count, expecting to embrace a charming girl, when, to his horror, he sees a *group* of his particular friends, who are as much surprised as he, for Madame de Jumillac had not told the nature of her piece of ridicule, nor the name of the principal actor.

Madame de Jumillac advanced with an air of serious dignity, and said—

"Marshal, I hope this lesson will prove to you that there are some virtuous women in the world. That you should offer an affront to a young lady under my protection, at once grieves and surprises me; and I think your violation of my house justifies the severe revenge I have taken in thus exposing your defeat to the world."

Saxe looked, first very foolish, and then very angry, as he saw every one grinning ridicule upon him, and knew the story would be all over Paris next day. Poterne was the only looker-on who did not enjoy it; he was really sorry to be made an unpleasant sight to a great man, and advancing with a cringe towards the Count, requested him to believe that he had no idea *he* was the person engaged, or he would not for the world have been of the party.

The Count only pushed him aside, with a half-muttered malediction, as he passed towards the door, near which Voltaire was standing looking on in ecstasy.

"My dear Count," said Voltaire, with a smile of malicious delight, and a tone which clearly implied he did not mean a particle of what he said, "you may be certain *I* will not mention one word of this affair."

"Of course not," answered Saxe in a corresponding tone. "I dare say I shall have an epigram at breakfast to-morrow."

"Unless you would like it better at supper to-night," replied his friend.

"Plague take you!" muttered Saxe. "As for you, ladies," he added, with a severity on his brow that seldom sat there, "since you have chosen to play at lock and key with me, I beg to remind you that *two* can play at that game, and perhaps my locks and keys may be stronger than yours."

He left the room as he spoke, and the spirit of jest was chilled under the terrible influence of his words. An involuntary shudder passed through the heart of every woman in the room; for Saxe, hero as he was in the field, was known to have been, on occasions, very unscrupulous about the means of indulging any and all of his passions, and the fearful *lettre de cachet* had been employed by him more than once to accomplish his purposes. With such reminiscences on the minds of all, the reconnoitring party of Madame de Jumillac broke up suddenly, and with that embarrassment which the dread of something unpleasant produces; and the affair of the china closet did not turn out so good a joke as was expected to the parties who made it, though Paris laughed at it considerably; and Saxe's prediction was fulfilled by his receiving a note next morning, containing the following epigram :—

"Love's empire is celestial!—Yes!
And so is China.——Count, confess."

CHAPTER XVII.

IT is necessary, now, to return to the fortunes of Ned and Finch, whom we left in London, after assisting in the escape of O'Hara and Kirwan, who, it has been seen, got out of England in safety.

The rescue of prisoners from the Swiss guard made a great commotion in London. It gave a colour to those who wished to carry high-handed measures, for the exercise of the law in its greatest severity against all those who had the misfortune to fall within its compass; and tirades were uttered by the upholders of government against the daring disaffection of the times, when state-prisoners were rescued in open day from the king's soldiers. At the moment the circumstance occurred, the Privy Council were quite taken by surprise, on hearing of so bold a movement of the mob, and they instantly set measures on foot to inquire into the circumstances of the case, and punish the guilty, if they could be discovered. Knowing that some sailors had been the instigators of the riot, and that they had issued from a certain tavern, an order of the Council was despatched to the magistracy, to make diligent inquiry at this house of entertainment, touching the offence and its perpetrators.

It was not long, therefore, ere Mrs. Banks had a domiciliary visit from Sir Thomas de Veil (an active magistrate of that day), and a posse of constables, who searched the house, high and low, for any against whom suspicion could lie, of having taken part in the riot. Mrs. Banks, *of course*, knew nothing about any of the party; they were, according to her account, a pack of noisy sailors, not one of whom she had ever seen before, and devoutly hoped never to see again. She would have been the last woman, so she would, to let an enemy of the king, God bless him! into her house. *She* harbour rebels!—no, no—she knew better than that;—what would become of her licence if she would permit such goings on!

In the midst of her torrent of eloquence, the officer who commanded the guard, and who had accompanied the magistrate, caught sight of Phaidrig, and pointing him out as having been in the window of the tavern while the affair was transacting, at which he seemed in great delight, and that he was playing on his pipes at the time, as if to encourage the rioters, and yelling forth some most unearthly cries, enough to make one's heart sink in their bodies.

The fact was, Phaidrig *had* been lilting one of the wildest of the pipe war-tunes, and shouting the battle cry of "Kierawaun aboo," during the fray; and when this fact was brought home to him before Sir Thomas de Veil, all Phaidrig had for it was to mystify the magistrate as much as possible.

"What were you playing on the pipes for, sirrah?" asked Sir Thomas, fiercely.

"That's my business, your honour."

"You had no business, sirrah, to be playing when rebels were impeding the king's officers."

"I beg pardon, your honour. I had no business, it's thrue for you; and when I said business, it was all through modesty."

"How do you mean modesty, sir?"

"Why, your honour, I said business, when, in fact, I should have said profession, and that was all through modesty; for mine is a profession, I being a musicianer."

"You're an Irishman," I perceive.

"Faix, I am."

"Then you're a papist?"

"No, sir—I'm a piper."

"No quibbling, sir: a piper must have a religion."

"Excuse me, your honour—pipers never has any religion at all; they must make themselves plazing to all companies."

"Then are you a heathen, you vagabond?"

"No, your honour,—I'm only a pagan."

"Dare you acknowledge yourself a pagan in my presence, sirrah?"

"To be sure, your honour: there's no law agin pagans; it's only agin Christians the laws is."

"But there are laws against unbelievers, villain!"

"That'll do me no harm, your honour, for I believe every thing."

Here some persons amongst the many who were listening to Phaidrig's examination, laughed, which was all Phaidrig wanted; for nothing damages the intention of a serious examination so much as a hue of ridicule cast over it.

"But you were of the party of the sailors, however," said Sir Thomas. "Did he not come with them?" added he, addressing Mrs. Banks.

"To be sure I did," said Phaidrig, before she could answer, and to relieve her from any difficulty as to her reply.

"Silence, sirrah! I did not ask you—but the woman of the house."

"He did come with them, your worship," answered Mrs. Banks.

"See there!" exclaimed Phaidrig triumphantly—"I towld you so; do you think I want to tell you a lie?"

"Then if you came with them, you must know something of them," said the magistrate. "Who are they?"

"Not a one o' me knows," returned Phaidrig.

"How did you come into their company?"

"I did not *come* into their company at all. It was they *took* me into their company agin my will."

"How did that happen?"

"Why, your honour, its a long story, but I'll make it as short as I can. You see they are wild divils of sailors that was out looking over the wide ocean for the Spaniards, to rob and murdher them, accordin' to rayson, as your honour knows, is only right and proper; and so comin' back they wer dhruv in by hard weather to Galway bay, which is the finest bay in the world, and came into the town of Galway, which is the finest town in the world, barrin' this town of London, of which your honour's glory is a chief governor, and long life to you. Well, I must tell you, sir, the Galway people is very proud of being descinded from the Spaniards, and they are always braggin' of it evermore, and by my sowl, when the wild divils o' sailors heerd the Galway people, one and all, saying they wor Spaniards, the sailors swore they would thrate them as sitch. And sure enough they lived at free quarters, and robbed right and left, and not a thing in the town they took a fancy to they wouldn't take without have your lave or by your lave; and among other things, sure they took a fancy to me, God help me! and took me a prisoner, and made me play for them mornin', noon, and night, and divil a penny they paid me; and not contint with that, nothing would sarve them but to carry me off in the ship with them all the way here, sore agin my will, and when I said I wouldn't play for them, they said they'd hang me—and I b'lieve they'd ha' kept their word, for I don't think any thing is too hot or too heavy for them."

"Well then," said Sir Thomas, hoping to incite Phaidrig through personal motives to disclose all he knew, "you have a heavy charge to make against these men; and if you can only bring all, or any of them to justice, they shall be punished, and I will endeavour to obtain for you ample compensation for the loss you have sustained."

"Long may you reign, my lord!" exclaimed Phaidrig; "it's the first word of pity or justice I have heerd for many a dav."

"Then you'll swear against them for this offence?" said Sir Thomas."

"I'll swear *sthrong* agin them!" thundered Phaidrig.

"You know their names, I suppose?"

"'Twould be hard for me to forget them, for they had **the** queerest names I ever heard of with cat or dog. One fellow was called 'Bumbo,' and another 'Nosey;' and there **was** 'Dasher,' and 'Slasher,' and 'Smasher.'"

"These are not surnames," said Sir Thomas.

"No, your honour, but they had very fine surnames with them for all that. There was 'Alexander.'"

"Alexander is a Christian name," remarked the magistrate.

"No, your honour, beggin' your pardon, *this* Alexander wasn't a *Christian* name, but an *owld anshint* name—it was Alexander the *Grate* they meant all the time, together with Pompey, and Saizer, and Nickydemus."

"But these are not surnames. Were there not amongst the crew some one of the name of 'Smith,' 'Brown,' or 'Jones,' or some such name?"

"No, your honour! I never heerd sitch a name at all. There was only one smith aboord, and he——"

"There now, you are contradicting yourself," said Sir Thomas, hastily. "You said you never heard such a name on board as Smith, and in the next breath you acknowledge there was a Smith on board."

"Yis, your honour," returned Phaidrig, in a most soothing tone of voice, "so there was a Smith—that is what I was going to tell your honour; but *that* Smith was a *blacksmith*, that they had to make and mend iron things when they wor broke with fightin', or storms, or the like."

"Then you never heard regular English surnames amongst them?"

"No, indeed, sir. My own private opinion is, they thought it better to leave their names behind them when they went to *say*, for their doings there was not likely to do their names any credit; and maybe they thought it would be saving the magisthraits throuble to make themselves as little known as possible."

"Ah—I see—each man was provided with an *alias*."

"I can't say I ever heerd of sitch a thing among them, sir."

"I mean they all had nicknames."

"Faith they had; and owld Nick himself never gave his name to more desarving childher, for they are the greatest set o' divils I ever came across. Oh, your honour, won't you do me justice, and sthrive and nab them, and get me my lawful due agin them?"

"What can I do, when you can give no clue?—You don't know anything of them."

"That's thrue, your honour; and I wish I knew less. Oh, weira! weira!—ruined I am. Maybe it's your honour could give me a thrifle o' money to take me home to Ireland?"

Sir Thomas did not relish this proposal, and asked, had the piper no friend in London? He answered, by asking, how could he have one in a city where he had first set his foot that morning? The magistrate asked, by what conveyance he came to London? Phaidrig answered, "by the river." The functionary demanded the name of the ship. Phaidrig replied that the desperadoes had quitted their own ship a long way off, and came up the river in a smaller one, the name of which he did not know. To various other questions tending to find a clue to the sailors, Phaidrig pleaded his blindness, as preventing his making the observations other men, blessed with a sense of vision, could; and continued, by his seemingly simple and queer answers, to baffle all the efforts of the magistrate to implicate him in the transaction, or to make him implicate others. Sir Thomas de Veil and his satellites departed, and left Phaidrig to the care of the kind widow, who was right well pleased when she saw the authorities cross her threshold, and charmed with Phaidrig for his address throughout the affair.

"You are staunch and true, and right honest," said Mrs. Banks, "and it is a pity so clever a fellow should want his eyes."

"'Tis a loss to me, ma'am, certainly," said Phaidrig, with an air of gallantry, "since it deprives me of the pleasure of seeing you."

"Ah! you rogue," said the widow, "you' have a tongue worth more than a pair of eyes. Isn't it enough to have talked over Sir Thomas de Veil, without palavering me?"

"Veal, is it, you call that janius?" said Phaidrig. "Faix, he'll never be veal till he's dead."

"You mean he's a calf while he's alive," said Mrs. Banks.

"Mrs. Banks, ma'am," answered the piper, "you're a mighty purty-spoken, sinsible woman."

Here their conversation was interrupted by the entrance of Finch and Ned, no longer in their rough sailor's trim, but rather handsomely dressed in laced coats, embroidered waistcoats, and the rest of their attire correspondingly beauish. Mrs. Banks was rather surprised at the sudden metamorphosis, which Finch readily explained.

"You see, mother, the sooner I cast my sea-skin the better, after the row; so I took the loan of a handful of doubloons from one of the Jacks, and at a respectable establishment of cast-off finery, rigged myself and friend afresh, and under our new canvass the sharpest thief-catcher in England would not know us."

"But you *do* look handsome, captain!" exclaimed the widow.

"Yes, the clothes are not much the worse for wear—they'll do well enough for a turn on shore."

"And the young gentleman, too, becomes the fine clothes well; my certie! but he has a nice leg of his own."

"Hold up your head, Ned," said Finch, laughing, "here's money bid for you! And now, mother, a word with you in private; this day's rough work is like to turn out well for me, if I can make all things requisite *fit*. A few of these bold dogs, who left you to-day in such a hurry without paying their score, are going to fit out a slashing privateer to cruise against the Spaniards, and if I can lay down some rhino in the common stock, I can have a share, and then my fortune's made. Now, mother, you told me you can let me have the cash I lent you—"

"And a hundred more I told you, if you like."

"So you did, mother, like a good soul as you are; but the matter is, can you spare it?—not but that I'll pay it back again all safe to you, but do not inconvenience yourself for me—that's all."

"Lor! Captain, wouldn't I lay down my life, let alone my money, for you! But consider, my dear captain, this fighting work is very terrible, and maybe you may lose your precious life, and then what's all the money in the world to you—or to me either, indeed?—for I should break my heart, I think, if anything happened to you."

"As for that, Mother Banks, have no care. Thrashing the Spaniards is simple work—just as easy as paying out cable."

"But a bullet may reach you as well as another; for somebody must be killed in these affairs."

"I may get a hole in my jacket, certainly, mother, but I might get run over on shore; or my head split with a falling tile from a house-top; or my windpipe slit by some of your city Mohawks as I am going home some night. We must all die, mother, some time or other; and I'd rather have a bullet out of one of those long smooth Spanish guns—"

"Lor! don't talk so, Captain!" exclaimed the widow, writhing as if she felt a bullet had gone through her.

"I'd rather die at sea than ashore any day; and if so be in fighting the Dons, all the sweeter. I hate 'em! Zooks! I could eat a Spaniard without salt. And as for plundering them on the high seas, I think it a good deed."

"No doubt of it, Captain, as long as you come home safe."

"No more o' that palaver, mother; I don't think my yarn is quite spun yet. The money I can have, you say."

"Whenever you like, Captain. May heaven preserve you!"

"Fiddle-de-dee, mother!—Come, Ned, we'll have a jolly day of it; I'll show you a good week's sport on shore before we go afloat again—for afloat we *do* go, lad; it's all right!—the mother here, bless her—" and he gave her a hearty kiss as he spoke— "she'll furnish the cash, as I knew she would; so we're before the wind again, hurra!" He snapped his fingers above his head gleefully, and tucking Ned's arm within his own, forth they sallied on the town to have a surfeit of amusement.

CHAPTER XVIII.

In about a fortnight after their London adventure, Finch and Ned were at Portsmouth, where the privateer lay, in which they were going to seek their fortune. In playing this game, in this particular way, many hundreds of Englishmen were at the moment engaged; and even some of the Irish ports sent out cruisers against the Spaniards, so infatuated had the whole kingdom become with the spirit of privateering. In England it was a perfect rage at the time; scarcely a port that had not her little cruiser out to harass the enemy in detail along their coasts, and make them suffer in their minor merchant trade, while many a dashing craft of heavier metal scoured the ocean in search of larger and more valuable prizes. In this pursuit not merely the love of gain inspired the undertakers; a deep and rooted hatred to the Spaniards rendered them more energetic in their measures; and the British pride, so long wounded by the right of search which Spain, in all her treaties, continued to enforce along the coasts of South America, found balm in this opportunity of wreaking vengeance on an arrogant foe, now that the king had declared war by the reluctant advice of his ministers, who were almost forced by popular clamour to that measure; the public indignation being roused to its highest pitch of fever by the accounts constantly brought home by almost every British ship that traded to the West Indies, of the insults and cruelties exercised upon them by the Spanish *Guarda Costas* in those seas.

It sounds strange to English ears, in these triumphant days of our navy, to hear that right of search was ever submitted to by us; but the fact was, that our ships of war were then very inferior to those of other powers, particularly those of Spain, at that day the first in the world; and the scientific writers of England on the subject lament the inferior build and power of our vessels, which, in all their classes, were so weak in comparison with the enemy's, that it was overtaxing the valour of British seamen to expect them to cope with such fearful odds against them; and though they kept the British flag of that day untarnished, yet they could not add many laurels to the national wreath of glory, inasmuch as that in some instances, when an English ship had absolutely beaten a Spaniard, she was not strong enough to take possession of her, from sheer want of the proper power belonging to her class.

This was a cause of much national vexation, and was attributed to the love of having an army in Flanders on the part of the king, instead of triumphant fleets at sea. And when the activity and courage of privateers were so successful, these deeds of daring on the ocean were welcomed by the people with a rejoicing which, in other times, might not have been given to such a questionable mode of warfare; and the taint of piracy which, to a certain extent, must ever tarnish privateering glory, however brilliant, was overlooked at a time when vengeance upon an enemy was the predominant feeling.

So thoroughly did this sentiment pervade all the seaports, that the crew of a privateer were held rather in more repute than a man-o'-war's-man, and the chances of rich plunder held out to all able hands engaging in the service, brought the most dashing fellows flocking to the privateer flag; insomuch, that if a group of particularly fine seamen were walking up the main street of a seaport town, it was reckoned certain a privateer was in the harbour. Then, while all the men of the port liked them for the cause they were engaged in, the women admired them for their good looks; and the little boys, who are always glad of any excuse to make a noise, used to go hurraing after them up and down.

Thus it was that Finch and Ned and their companions were greeted as they paraded Portsmouth in very trim attire; and when their equipment was complete, and their beautiful craft, the Vulture (a snow), had her "blue peter" flying swarms of boats put off from shore, and cheered her as she made sail. Thus it was that, with the good wishes of all England and a favouring breeze, Ned was afloat again, and yet he was not quite happy. He could not divest himself of the idea that privateering was only a sort of *licensed* robbery, far worse than smuggling, which was *illegal*. Whatever is wrong in smuggling, its evil effects are not so immediately apparent, and are spread over a wider and less tangible surface; whereas, in the case of the privateer, the success of the victor can only be based on the immediate loss, perhaps ruin, of some very few; and thus, the wrong being more apparent, is more startling, particularly to a nature like Ned's, where sensibility and want of reflection were so dangerously blended. But the old temptation lured him on; the phantom which love prompted him to pursue. "Riches and Ellen," cried hope. What chance had a whisper of conscience after the "voice of the charmer?" So bracing himself up for the consequences he had determined to dare, he bade conscience be silent; he looked onward over the bows of the bounding bark, that was cleaving her way into those "blue waters" of which Finch had spoken when first he fired Ned's brain with the love of adventure. He was going to share in the excitement and peril of battle, in which he was yet untried, and that thought strung his nerves with new fortitude. With clenched hand he smote his breast, and muttered, "Conscience, be silent; *I must be a man!*" When his watch was over, and he slept, he dreamt of a Spanish galleon of enormous magnitude; they board her; he sees her deep hold crammed full of treasure; in the heat of the fight he tumbles amidst the ingots and the doubloons, which open like water to receive him, and he sinks into the metallic mass, which closes on him, and he feels himself crushed to death by the enormous weight of the wealth he has won. He started and woke, but soon slept again, and Ellen smiled on him in his second dream, and his waking in the morning was happy.

Every depressing thought was cast to the wind—to the wind that gave them wings, and sped them onward on the path they hoped to make golden. Onward they ploughed into the deep Atlantic, and the bold and merry hearts of the treasure-seekers expanded in revelry every night over the "flowing can." There was one joyous fellow in particular, who was the life and soul of the company. He abounded in anecdote. though now and then a dash of bitterness was perceptible in his sallies, which his companions attributed to his having been engaged in literary pursuits wherein men got so used to "handling the foils," that they cannot help hitting their friends now and then, to keep their hands in practice. He had been, to a certain extent, soured by some of his early experiences. Born in a small town, the paltry jealousies which beset any aspiring man who offends his brethren by trying to do more than *they* can, stung young Tresham, and gave an occasional unamiable turn to his thoughts.   Having left his native town in disgust, he proceeded to London, and won some literary reputation.   He became a contributor to the *Gentleman's Magazine*, and wrote pamphlets for parliament-men, who wished to have the credit of wielding a stinging pen.   But his love of pleasure ran him into difficulties, from which his literary pay could not extricate him; so he joined the privateering speculations of the time, and had already done something in the small way, near the coast.   Ned admired Tresham extremely, and Tresham sufficiently liked Ned, only he said he was too sentimental by half. "You are always talking," he would say, "about your 'native land,' and all that sort of thing, which is pure nonsense, believe me.   Excuse me, my dear fellow, for the word; I don't mean it offensively—but nonsense it is.   Now, I am of the pure cosmopolite breed; that's the thing, nothing like it; cosmopolite for ever!"

Notwithstanding such discourse, however, Ned persevered in his love for his country, and was not ashamed to avow it—nay, he even would *sing* it; and one night, while enjoying their grog, as songs were going round the board, Ned, in his most sentimental vein, gave the following:—

Love and Home and Native Land.

I.

When o'er the silent deep we rove,
  More fondly then our thoughts will stray
To those we leave—to those we love,
  Whose prayers pursue our wat'ry way.
When in the lonely midnight hour
  The sailor takes his watchful stand,
His heart then feels the holiest power
  Of love, and home, and native land.

II.

In vain may tropic climes display
  Their glittering shores—their gorgeous shells;
Though bright birds wing their dazzling way,
  And glorious flowers adorn the dells;
Though nature there prolific, pours
  The treasures of her magic hand,
The eye—but not the heart, adores:
  The heart still beats for native land.

Tresham only laughed at Ned's sentimentality.   "You Irish

fellows are the most incurable patriots in the world; there's no curing you. Now, I'll volunteer a song on a native subject, gentlemen, if you allow me."

"Bravo! bravo!" exclaimed all.

"It is not about my whole native land, for that is too extensive a subject for my limited genius; it is only the thumping heart of an Irishman can entertain so gigantic an affection; I am content with a town." Then off he dashed as follows:—

My Native Town.

I.

We have heard of Charybdis and Scylla of old;
Of Maelstrom the modern enough has been told;
Of Vesuvius's blazes all travellers bold
  Have established the bright renown:
But spite of what ancients or moderns have said
Of whirlpools so deep, or volcanoes so red,
The place of all others on earth that I dread
  Is my beautiful native town.

II.

Where they sneer if you're poor, and they snarl if you're rich
They know ev'ry cut that you make in your flitch;
If your hose should be darn'd, they can tell ev'ry stitch;
  And they know when your wife got a gown.
The *old* one, they say, was made *new*—for the brat;
And they're sure you love mice—for you can't keep a cat;
In the hot flame of scandal, how blazes the fat,
  When it falls in your own native town.

III.

If a good stream of blood chance to run in your veins,
They think to remember it not worth the pains,
For *losses* of caste are to them all the *gains*,
  So they treasure each base renown.
If your mother sold apples—your father his oath,
And was cropp'd of his ears—yet you'll hear of them both,
For loathing all low things they never are loth
  In your virtuous native town.

IV.

If the dangerous heights of renown you should try,
And give all the laggards below the go-by,
For fear you'd be hurt with your climbing so high,
  They're the first to pull you down.
Should Fame give you wings, and you mount in despite,
They swear Fame is wrong, and that they're in the right,
And reckon you *there*—though you're far out of sight
  Of the owls of your native town.

v.

Then give me the world, boys! that's open and wide,
Where honest in purpose and honest in pride,
You are taken for *just what you're worth* when you're *tried,*
    And have paid your reckoning down.
Your coin's not mistrusted—the critical scale
Does not weigh ev'ry piece, like a huckster at sale;
The mint-mark is on it—although it might fail
    To pass in your native town.

Before a word of comment could be made upon the com-
parative merits of the two songs, the report of " a sail " from the
deck soon cleared the table, and all rushed to join in the look-out.
It was soon agreed she was a merchantman; and the most experienced made her out to be a " Spaniard for sartin," so all sail
was made in chase.   For some time the stranger seemed to take
no notice; but soon it was perceived her course was altered, and
sail crowded upon her, and this made the pursuit more urgent.
The evening now was closing ; but before sun-down, they found
they were gaining on the chace; and ere darkness settled over the
deep, they had neared her sufficiently to be convinced she was
" foreign " and to prove they could outsail her; so vigilant look-
out was kept during the night, that they might not lose her before dawn, as in case they could but have her *then* within view
they could run her down before night.   Fortune favoured the
privateer.   With every effort of nautical stratagem to get away
during the darkness, the Spanish ship was visible in the morning,
and an anxious chace ensued during the day, which caused beating hearts on board both vessels.   At last the Spaniard saw she
must fight, and she prepared for action :—she was a large merchantman, well-armed and ably manned; but the superior
sailing qualities of the privateer enabled her to choose her position,
and her better-handled guns gave her a decided advantage. the
results of which were soon apparent.   The Spaniards, nevertheless, defended their ship gallantly; and it was not until a large
proportion of her men lay dead upon her deck that she struck.
Then, what a thundering shout arose from the privateer; how
eagerly pushed off the boat to take possession of the prize.   She
was found to be a rich one; a large amount of treasure and a
valuable cargo secured to the captors ample reward for their
enterprise.   The bullion was at once removed to the privateer,
together with a portion of the crew of the Spaniard; while a draft
of men from the victorious ship was put on board the prize,
leaving a portion of her own people free, under the armed control
of the captors, for the purpose of working the vessel; and the
few passengers on board were allowed to remain, and enjoy the

conveniences of their berths, but under the authority of the person put in command.

That person was Ned, who had behaved most gallantly in the action, and who, from his seamanlike reputation, was accounted the fittest person to entrust with the prize, as Finch could not be spared from the privateer, where his presence was indispensable.

The first care was to repair on both the ships the damage done in action; and after the requisite "fishings" and "splicings" and "knottings" were completed, they both made the best of their way in company towards England.

The prisoners were let up on deck by turns, and it used to go to Ned's heart to witness their dejected looks. But one of the passengers in particular excited his deepest compassion. He was an old man, of venerable aspect, on whom an Indian climate had set its mark, rendering the traces of time more decided; but since the taking of the ship, ten years seemed added to his age; and the sunken and lustreless eye, now and then cast up to heaven, as if accompanying some inward prayer for pity, but chiefly bent downwards despairingly, as he paced the deck, bore heart-rending evidence of suffering. Up and down that deck would he pace with slow and tottering footsteps, occasionally uttering such heavy sighs, as though his heart were breaking.

The Spaniards called him Don Jerome Carcojas, but the old man spoke English so fluently, that he would not have been taken for a foreigner by his accent. Ned sought every opportunity to exercise little acts of kindness towards the old man, who seemed soothed by his attentions, and sometimes entered into conversation with Edward, who did his best to divert his melancholy by the most amusing anecdotes he could recall; and by degrees he so won upon the captive, that their conversations lengthened daily, and the poor old gentleman at last used to leave his confinement below, less for the sake of the refreshing breeze of the deck, than the society of Ned.

One very beautiful morning, as the captive made his appearance, Ned was pacing the deck with a light and joyous step, and singing snatches of sea-songs. In short, Ned was in great spirits. The ship was going swiftly through the water before a favouring breeze, the sea sparkled brightly, all external things were calculated to cheer, and Ned was anticipating how many hundreds he should have for his share; and it must be owned, that in the frequent indulgence in this thought of late, it was wonderful how fast he was getting rid of the conscientious scruples that suggested themselves when he first set sail on the expedition. As he turned lightly on his heel to pace forward on his beat, he caught sight of old Don Jerome, and instantly ceasing his merry carol, accosted the old man in a gentler tone.

"Yes, you are all life and merriment," said the old man, sadly. "Ah! there is one about your age, as light of heart as you are now: light of heart in expecting me, and in anticipating riches in my coming, who if he could see me here a captive, and bereft of all my wealth, would hang his head, and maybe weep."

Ned attempted some words of comfort, which the old man heard with a silent shrug.

"Comfort to me!" he exclaimed, after some minutes' silence. 'I will tell you with what hopes and intentions I was going homewards, and then you yourself may answer how a poor disappointed and ruined old man may ever hold up his head again. But God's will be done! 'Man proposes, but God disposes.' Many years ago I left my native country. Indeed, I ran away from it; abandoning parents and friends in a wild and wilful spirit, that possessed me in my youth, and maybe this heavy blow in my old age is a punishment intended by Providence for the waywardness and disobedience of my early years."

The old man paused and sighed, as if recollections of the past brought with them bitter regret, and Ned, in thus witnessing the grey-headed sorrows for youthful disobedience, bethought him of his own infraction of parental authority, and abandonment of the course wherein his father had ordered him to walk.

The old man resumed. "Years and years rolled on, and I never heard of home or kindred; but in the bustle of young and active life, I thought nothing of that; and as I prospered fast in worldly affairs, and not only all comforts, but pleasures were at my command, the present hour always drove both the past and the future out of my head. But when age began to creep on me, I had no one to care for, nor to care for me. and then regrets for past ties began to steal upon me, and self-reproach for early heedlessness used to disturb my hours of solitude. At last, by a chance intercourse with a trader, I learnt that my brother was still alive in his native land, and had a son, the prop of his age—a blessing I did not possess, and I took the resolution of going back to Europe with all my wealth. I converted every thing into treasure—the treasure which you took, and is now on board your ship—and was returning in the hope of embracing my brother, and my nephew whom I intended making my heir, and in the enjoyment of kindred to end my days, with the hands of one who should love and honour me to close my eyes when it should please Heaven to call me away, not to be left in the last hour to the cold care of heartless hirelings in a strange land. Such were my intentions; but worse is before me than the death

I wished to shun; for where I expected to go back a welcomed benefactor, I shall return but a burden and a pauper."

Tears trickled down the old man's cheeks as he spoke, and he sunk down exhausted on a gun-carriage.

"'Tis a sad tale," said Ned, laying his hand gently on the old man's shoulder—"a bitter tale!"—and he wished in his heart he had not heard it.

"You are compassionate," said the old man, "and compassion to the wretched is much. There is kindness in the tone of your voice that is welcome to me;—an accent belonging to the kind-hearted land you came from."

Ned was surprised at such a remark upon accent coming from a foreigner, and asked him to explain himself.

"Are you not Irish?" said Don Jerome.

"Yes."

"No wonder then I recognise the accent of a countryman," returned the old man.

"I thought you were a Spaniard."

"I lived amongst them in their American possessions for forty years, and in the course of that time have become like one of themselves."

"And how comes your name to be Don Jerome Carcojas?"

"It was only a slight alteration which the Spaniards made, to accommodate my real name to their pronunciation—which is Corkery."

Ned started—gasped for breath, and had he not laid hold of the bulwark, must have fallen upon the deck.

CHAPTER XIX.

WHAT a confused rush of contending emotions whirled
through Ned's brain, as, gasping for breath, and his heart
thumping against his ribs, he held on for support, and cast a
fearful gaze upon the old man, who, with one word, had made
him miserable. Poor fellow! his case was a hard one. He saw
before him his own uncle, of whose wealth he himself was the
intended heir; and of that wealth he had helped to despoil him.
The compunctious visiting of conscience he experienced before
he entered on this course of pillage had been disregarded in his
greedy desire for wealth, and they all recurred to him at that
moment, adding weight to the blow which had fallen. He felt
the chastising hand of Providence was upon him; and that,
when he went forth in violence to plunder others, the bitter retribution was ordained that he should despoil himself. Then in
what fearful relation he stood to this new-found relative! His
heart prompted that he should embrace him; but how could he
dare acknowledge himself his nephew—he who was amongst his
captors and his plunderers?

The old man looked up, and Ned could hardly fortify himself
against the kind expression of his glistening eye, as words of
thanks were given to him for his sympathy.

" You are a good-natured fellow," said the Senor—" God
bless you! "

The benediction was worse than curses to Edward's ear, and
he writhed under it.

"Do not think me a poor, weak old driveller, because I
droop so. I would not grieve so much if the boy had not
heard of it; but I lately sent home word of my being alive, (for
they thought me dead,) and of my wealth, and good intentions
towards my nephew; and of course he, poor boy, is full of joy
and hope; and when he knows the result, 'twill be hard for him
—hard—hard! It is crushing in early youth to receive a blow
so heavy."

Bitterly the truth of these words was felt, while the unselfish
nature of the old man's regrets increased Ned's anguish.
"Wretch that I am!" thought he, "that all this solicitude
should be entertained for the worthless fellow who has helped to

work his ruin; and these kind considerations be given to one whom he imagines far away, while the miscreant is at his side."

"*I* have not long to live," said the old man; "the grave will soon shelter me from worldly woe; but *he*, full of youth and health, has long years of regret before him for this mischance."

"True," was the response, uttered with a pang.

"While with the wealth I could have left him, he had a future of enjoyment in prospect."

A heavy sigh followed from Ned.

"Proudly might he have claimed the girl of his heart."

These last words were as coals of fire on the head of poor Edward, who could endure no more, but rushed from the spot, and, hiding himself in his berth, gave vent to the convulsive feelings with which his heart was bursting.

When these had run their rapid and violent course, calmer musings succeeded; and then it was that Ned saw his case presented one point of consideration which was downright ludicrous. He was a brilliant specimen of an Irish heir, who had destroyed the fortune to which he was to succeed. He was his own cut-purse.—He had come forth to shear, and was returning shorn.—He dare not confide his case to any one.—Finch would only laugh at, while his uncle would abhor him; therefore must he be doomed to imprison the fatal secret in his own bosom, saddening his heart, and gnawing at his conscience. What prolonged misery he endured, on the homeward passage, as day after day he was forced to meet his uncle, and experience frequent repetitions of his griefs, his thanks, and his yearnings towards his nephew! This became at last insupportable; it was a load his conscience could no longer bear, and he felt it would be some alleviation of his misery to confess the relationship at once, and, by the voluntary exposure of his shame, make some atonement for his transgression. But this he found was not so easy. Often he essayed, but, as the words of confession were rising to his lips, his courage failed, and pride was stronger than conscience—he could not so humiliate himself. But as the old saying hath it—

"Continual dropping will wear a stone."

And one day the expressions of affection for his nephew, on the part of the old man, were so fervent, so full of thoughtful tenderness, that Ned could stand it no longer—he felt almost choking; his eyes glistened with rebellious tears, and asking the Senor to follow him to the cabin, he there "made a clean breast of it," relating his adventures from the time he left home—love, smuggling and all,—and finally disclosed his name and relation-

11

ship to the old man, who, when the first shock of astonishment was over, folded Ned to his bosom and wept over him.

"Can you forgive me?" said Ned.

"Forgive *you?*" returned his uncle. "My poor fellow, *you* are more to be pitied than I am," were the only words of reproof the generous old man uttered, and Ned wrung his hand with gratitude.

"What I blame you most for is your not writing to your father."

"I thought he would have disapproved of my course of life," answered Ned, "and I did not like to give him unhappiness."

"No unhappiness like uncertainty about those we love," said his uncle; "you should know that from your own experience."

"Oh, as for my love," said Ned sadly, "I told you of it because I determined to confess all. Of course you think it a wild and absurd vision—as it is; nevertheless, it has led me to all I have dared."

"Where will not love lead?" returned the old man, with a sigh, and a tone of tenderness in his voice, and his sunken eye lighted with a gleam that Edward never had marked before. "What will it not make us dare! what will it not make us hope! Think not I blame you for entertaining a love so much above your station You could not help it—I know it, boy—for I could not help it myself. I loved as you have, Ned. But don't fear an old man is going to prate of his love—no, Ned, no. Love is for youth. I have said it, boy, only to show you I could not blame you. *My* days and hopes are past and gone, but the thoughts still lie here—here!" and he laid his attenuated hand on the slowly-beating heart, which still carried in its lessened current the unlessened tenderness of an early and hopeless passion. "Ah, Ned!" he added, with an expression of the deepest longing in his voice, "Would to God my fortune had been yours—that you might have claimed your love—that I might have seen in one of my own kin, at least, the happiness hat was denied to me! it would have been making real before my old eyes a dream of the past to me!"

Ned suggested that their present conference must cease, as too protracted a *tête-à-tête* might create remark on board, and remark excite questions; "and I would not for the world they should suspect our relationship," said Ned. "How the rascals would laugh! and, though I have borne the shame of avowing myself to you, I could not bear the humiliation of being the jest of these dare-devils."

"The laugh of scorn is a sore thing," said the old man; "but the humbleness which repentance makes is consoling—do you not feel the happier, Edward, for your confession?"

"Oh, so much happier!" said Edward; "but to what merciful ears I confessed!"

"Boy!" said his uncle, solemnly, "remember that repentance ever begets mercy. And now let us part for the present—fear not discovery from me."

With these words they separated, and met no more for that day; but every four-and-twenty hours afforded them the ordinary meeting, and uncle and nephew enjoyed the interchange of affection.

Ned's spirits returned as soon as he had unburthened his conscience, and, without saying a word of his intention to his uncle, he had determined that, whatever his share of the prize should be, he would hand it over to the old man; and, though this placed as wide a gulph as ever between him and the object of his love, it brought peace to his conscience, and the inward conviction of doing what was right proved, as it ever must, a great consolation.

The ships were now nearing the shores of Europe, and, one morning, Ned was asked by his uncle for a few minutes of secret conversation. "Be sure there is not a creature within ear-shot of us," said the old man.

Ned took his opportunity for obtaining the privacy his uncle required, and the old man told him he had a secret to reveal which might in some measure retrieve their fortunes.

"It sometimes happens," said he, "that, when ships are taken by privateers, some strong-handed plunderer, under another flag, may wrest the prize from the first captor; and this has happened so often of late, that privateers make it a rule to seize upon all the treasure they can find, and convey it on board their own bottoms, in case of the worst; and that, however ships and cargoes may slip through their fingers, they, at least, will make sure of the pieces of eight. Now my boxes of treasure have been so served by your friends, and are on board the privateer yonder; but, when I left the main, in case of accident, I—"

The old man paused and cast a look of alarm towards the door.

"Did you not hear a noise?" said he, in an under tone, to Ned.

Ned answered in the negative; and, opening the door to see that no one listened, his uncle was reassured and continued ·

"In case of the worst, I—" again he paused, looked round, and, lowering his voice to a whisper, continued—"I concealed no inconsiderable sum of gold in the bags of snuff which are among this cargo."

"Well," said Ned, breathlessly, "what then?"

"If you could only procure some trusty agent on shore to buy all this snuff when the cargo is put up for auction, as it will be soon after we get into port, then—"

"We should possess the gold," interrupted Ned.

"Exactly."

"Uncle," said Ned, after a moment's pause, and with a heavy sigh, as if he regretted what he was forced to say, "It would be dishonourable."

"Dishonourable!" exclaimed the old man in surprise. "Talk of honour with thieves like these?"

"Yes," said Ned, "the principle has passed into an old saying—

'Honour among thieves,'

and I will not violate it—I am of them—I came out with them, as we all came, to risk our lives for gold—banded together in daring and in danger; and, though the fates have been unkind to me in the venture, nevertheless, I cannot reconcile myself to play this trick upon my shipmates."

"You are a romantically-honourable fellow, Ned!" said his uncle. "I would not have you obtain wealth if you have a scruple about the means."

"If you think of any way in which you yourself could manage to procure an agency for this purpose," said Ned, "I will say nothing about it; though I am not sure if that is not a breach of trust; and question if I am not bound in strict honour to tell them this."

"I cannot have such an agency," said his uncle; "that is quite out of the question, utter stranger as I am in England; but, as for telling them, Ned, do not tell them yet; they have not got us into port, and there are slips 'between the cup and the lip' —France and Spain have their privateers and ships of war as well as England, and, if a Spaniard should retake us,—"

The old man became suddenly silent, for a hasty step was heard descending the companion-ladder; the door of the cabin was opened, and the mate popped in his head to say the privateer was making signals.

Ned hurried to the deck, and, glass in hand, was on the alert to answer his consort. The signals gave notice of a strange sail, and also told the prize to keep closer company. To achieve this, the privateer shortened, while the prize made all the sail she could; and, when a couple of hours had brought them sufficiently near, a boat was ordered from the Spaniard to the privateer, where Ned received orders how to manage the ship through the night;—for the night was approaching—and so was the strange sail, whose aspect was not pleasing to the company on board the *Snow*, for it looked ship-of-war-ish, and not friendly; and though the privateer might be equal in sailing, the prize certainly was not. It was debated for some time whether the two ships in company might be able to beat off the enemy, should she prove such; or if it would not be more advisable to throw overboard the guns of the prize, which, thus lightened, might have a better chance to run for it. It is scarcely necessary to say which way the question was decided. When did the question ever lie between fighting and running, that the British seaman did not throw up his hat for the fight? Ned was sent back, therefore, with orders to keep close to the privateer during the night, and, in case of an attack from the strange sail, to make a good bull-dog defence of it, while the privateer should take every advantage of position, and make her shot tell. That the prize might be the better able to keep her colours to the mast, an additional draft of men was given for the working of her guns; for, hitherto, as she sailed under the protecting cannon of the privateer, she only numbered hands enough to work the ship, without any view to fighting; but, now that danger threatened, this necessary supply to her guns was afforded, while, at the same time, Ned received the order to make all possible sail he could during the night, to avoid the necessity of hostile collision. Reversing the order of the noted sea-song, which says—

"We'll fight while we can—when we can't, boys, we'll run!"

Ned's duty was precisely the reverse—

"We'll run while we can—when we can't, boys, we'll fight!"

As the boats rowed to the prize the last red rays of the sun tipped each wave with crimson, and seemed to forebode blood; at least, so fancied Ned, who went back silently and full of thought. The announcement of a strange sail at the very moment his uncle suggested such a chance, struck him as remarkable, and was received with the superstitious reverence of a sailor. Then, if the sail should turn out to be Spanish, that he should be entrusted with the defence of a ship which, for his uncle's, and for his own conscience' sake, he should wish to be retaken, was an embarrassing circumstance, for here were wishes divided against duty; and in such a frame of mind, what man could wish to fight?

With a depression of spirits rare with Ned, he stepped
on board and resumed the command of the ship, whose deck he
never quitted throughout the whole of the night; during which
gloomy forebodings overcast his spirit, when the intervals of the
anxious duty he had to perform gave thought a moment's
liberty. A presentiment that he was doomed to fall, haunted
his midnight watch ; and when, as the dawn revealed the cold
dead level of surrounding waters, the strange sail loomed larger
in pursuit, he felt the fight was inevitable, and braced himself
with the manly determination honestly and resolutely to defend
his ship.

The sun now rose above the horizon, and morning, with its
freshness and its brightness, sparkled over the waters. In
another hour the pursuing ship fired a gun, and showed French
colours. The privateer and her prize took no notice. In half-
an-hour more the chace-guns of the Frenchman were opened on
the flying ships, and every ten minutes, as Ned looked over the
taffrail of the Spanish merchantman, he saw the shot falling
closer astern.

CHAPTER XX.

The affair of the china closet had spread over Paris rapidly, and the defeat of so able a strategist as Marshal Saxe was looked upon as too good a joke to be laid on the shelf: the consequence therefore was, that the redoubtable Count, hitherto invincible in love and war, felt so much of ridicule attach to the adventure, that he quitted the capital and retired to his *château*. But before he withdrew he prepared a terrible retaliation upon Ellen, fully in the spirit of the threat with which he quitted the house of Madame de Jumillac on the day of his defeat. He procured *lettres de cachet* against Ellen and her father, on the ground of their being in reality nothing better than English spies, while they were apparently attached to the cause of the exiled Stuart.

Lynch, it was his intention to consign to the Bastile, where he would be irrecoverably beyond all means of counteracting the Marshal's designs, and protecting his beautiful daughter, whom the Count destined for an imprisonment not so dismal, but more detestable, than that of the Bastile itself.

It was not the first time the Count had availed himself of that most iniquitous engine of all tyrannies, the *lettre de cachet*, for the accomplishment of his libertine desires; and he was not the only one who made it serve other purposes than those for which it was supposed to be intended. This unquestioned measure of imprisonment, for whose exercise no one in the executive was responsible, invented to uphold the despotism of the crown, was too frequently used to serve the purposes of a licentious court; and the person whom the *lettre de cachet* dragged from the bosom of home, was not always consigned to the Bastile. *That* place served for troublesome fathers, husbands, or brothers, while the surrounding *châteaux* of the voluptuous capital more frequently were the prisons of ladies who fell within the grasp of this secret instrument of unscrupulous power.

This seems almost incredible now, when the tyranny that disgraced France has been subverted for ever, and popular privilege based on the ruins of regal oppression; but, in the days of which our story treats, the crown, its minions, and the *seignorie* of France, held undisputed power over all the lives, liberties, and honour of the people,—that people who, driven at last to des-

peration, rose in maddened masses on their tyrants, and took swift
and terrible vengeance;—a vengeance so bloody, and so fraught
with human suffering, that we shudder to remember; but at
which, if we consider the provocation, we can scarcely wonder.

The Marshal had retired, we have said, to his country retreat.
It was the celebrated royal *château* of Chambor, which had been
presented to him by the king as a mark of his favour for the brilliant services of the soldier; and the gift was the more prized by
the gallant Count, that it had been a favourite retreat of one
whose name stands highest in the list of chivalry. Here Francis
the First had enjoyed his voluptuous leisure; and this palace,
built by the gallant king, had been since dedicated by many
a monarch to pleasure, and was not likely to have its celebrity
impaired, in that respect, by its present occupant. Saxe had determined to make a double capture of father and daughter; and,
armed with his terrible warrants for their arrest, waited till
Lynch should return to Paris before he should consign him to a
dungeon, and carry off Ellen to the *château*.

At last that moment arrived, and Saxe was awaiting the arrival of an emissary he had summoned, in that very chamber which,
doubtless, had often been the scene of intrigue,—that little room
which yet bore evidence on its window-pane of the presence, in
bygone days, of the gallant founder of the fabric, whose hand
had traced there the well-known couplet—

> "*Souvent femme varie*
> *Mal habil qui s'y fie.*"

The Count was not alone. Voltaire, who was then on a visit
with him, had just risen from the breakfast-table, and was scan-
ning the couplet on the glass with his keen eyes, marking the
form and cut of every letter. In the meantime the servant of
the Marshal's pleasures entered, received some sealed *pacquets*
from his master to be delivered in Paris, together with strict in-
junctions to be *sure and swift* in the matter of which he before
had received the *private* commands of the Count.

The emissary, with the assurance that "*Monseigneur* might
depend on him," bowed low, and left the chamber on his fearful
mission. The Marshal flung himself back in his *fauteuil*, and
watched Voltaire as he was still looking at the couplet of Francis.

"That seems to fascinate you," said Saxe. "Is it the auto-
graph or the sentiment you admire?"

"I am amused," said Voltaire, "at the vanity and conceit of
the royal rhymer."

"I cannot see either in the lines," said the Marshal.

'The man" said Voltaire, who puts a couplet thus *en evi-*

dence, thinks his production very clever; and I do not see any great exercise of ability in discovering what he has taken so much pains to engrave."

"But is it not true?" returned the Count.

"Certainly.—But I only said it was not clever."

"Yet the saying is known all over Europe; and that which has lived two centuries has some claim to distinction."

"It has lived because it is true," said Voltaire.—"Truth is immortal. At the same time it must be avowed this is a very common-place truth, and derives its immortality not from Francis: for I doubt very much if a king had not written it, and written it thus, that every sight-seer in Europe might tell, on going home, he had seen the celebrated writing on the window of the *Chateau de Chambor,* that the lines would have survived his reign. No. Its immortality may be derived from a more respectable antiquity than two centuries, for women were much the same two thousand years before as two hundred after Francis."

"All I pretend to say is," said the Marshal, "that Louis now might just as fitly and truly write those lines as Francis."

"Yes, my friend," returned Voltaire; "and so might Pericles have written of Aspasia, or Cæsar of Cleopatra; or, to go back to the beginning, I believe, if there had been another man in the world immediately after the creation, Adam might have carved the same saying on the tree of knowledge."

The Count laughed at the conceit, and Voltaire smiled at the success of his sally; and, according to the tactics of wits by profession, who are glad to retire after saying a "good thing," he made the excuse of being obliged to write, to make his bow for awhile; and, after these two sceptics in human virtue had amused themselves at the expense of the oft-abused gentler sex, the Marshal, settling himself into a position of greater ease in his chair, dropped into a luxurious doze, and dreamt of *La belle Irlandaise.*

It was the third day after, that the Marshal's messenger was approaching Paris, and about the same time Prince Charles Edward and his adherents were holding council at his little court in its neighbourhood. The French cabinet had refused open aid in his cause, and seemed disinclined, if not unable, to give him anything more than good wishes:—these were at his service in abundance,—but good wishes will not supply the sinews of war. Many of his adherents went so far as to believe that the professions of the French government were all hollow; and that the desire for peace with England made them hesitate in making any movement in favour of the young Pretender.

Lynch was most indignant of them all. He had run the ex-

tremity of risk in extensively recruiting in Ireland for the Irish
Brigade in the service of France, believing (as he was led to
believe) that the entire brigade would be given to the service
of his "rightful king," as he called Charles, and believed him to
be: but when he found that this was not to be the case, his indignation was deep, and partook of that disgust which honest
and earnest natures feel at breach of faith.

"Did they think," he would say, "that I would have made
myself a recruiting officer for Louis?—Did they imagine I
would enlist Irishmen to shed their blood for French quarrels
and French glory?   Insolent!—I enlisted my countrymen for
the cause of their King—to strengthen that gallant brigade
which I fondly hoped should have the largest share in placing
him on his rightful throne;—and what is my reward?—I see
not only their swords refused in that holy cause, but even worse;
many of the brave fellows I enlisted have not been enrolled in
their native brigade, but drafted here and there into French
regiments, in utter violation of the understanding with which I
embarked in the desperate cause of enlistment in Ireland. Curse
them!—And he, their great Marshal,—gallant and able though
he be, staining his laurels by a profligacy so unblushing, that
even the honour of a soldier's daughter, which should be sacred
in his eyes, is held as nothing!—Oh, the profligacy of the time
and place disgust me, and I long to be quit of the infected land."

While debating the affairs of the Prince he would say,—
"Strike at once!—While the terrors of Fontenoi still hang over
George, make a descent on Scotland."

This he had repeated more than once at the present council
held by Charles Edward, and the Prince declared himself to be
of the same opinion.

"If I go alone," exclaimed Charles, with energy,—"I will
show myself in Scotland, and trust to the loyal hearts there to
rally round their Prince."

"If we could even get a thousand regular troops," said
Drummond.

"The happy time is more to be considered than men," said
Charles.

"And if we bring arms, we'll find men to bear them," added
Lynch.

"True," said Charles,—"And some expert officers will accompany me, who will soon teach them discipline."

"The arms you can have, Prince," said a secret agent of the
government.

"And a swift brig of eighteen guns lies this moment at the
mouth of the Loire, ready for your Highness's service," said Lynch.

" And *I* will venture to promise," said the government agent, " that one ship of war shall sail in your company, and give protection ; while a portion of the officers of the Irish Brigade can be allowed leave, and may join the expedition.—So far the government is willing to wink at the aid rendered; but, under existing circumstances, any more open demonstration in your cause, Prince, is impossible."

After some further debate, in which details were entered into, unnecessary to particularise here, it was agreed that the adherents of Charles should proceed to the mouth of the Loire, and hold themselves in readiness for embarkation, for which the arrival of the promised frigate should be the signal. Lynch informed the Prince that Walsh, the Bordeaux merchant, was already at Nantes, and had three thousand gold pieces at his Highness's service, and also a house there ready for his reception.

Lynch was called from the conference, at this moment, at the urgent desire of a messenger, who had manifestly ridden hard, for his horse was reeking and dripping wet, as he stood at the door panting for breath. The messenger handed him a note,— he broke the seal hastily, and read—

"BELOVED FATHER
        " As you value all that is dear to you and to me, return here instantly.—Your own
                                        " ELLEN."

The urgency of the note made him contract his brow as he read; he cast an eager glance of inquiry at the servant, who answered the look by words.

" Mademoiselle desired you should take my horse, sir."

In another minute Lynch was in the saddle, and riding at speed to Paris. On reaching the house of Madame de Jumillac, and asking for his daughter, a servant told him he would conduct him to where Mademoiselle was, and, opening the hall-door, led the way to the street."

" Has she been taken from the house, then?" asked her father, in alarm.

" Mademoiselle left the house suddenly, Monsieur, with Madame and another lady in a carriage."

Lynch's uneasiness was somewhat appeased at the thought of Madame de Jumillac being still in Ellen's society; but he urged the servant to speed, and, walking at a rapid pace, they were not long in reaching a handsome house; there, on Lynch presenting his name, he was immediately ushered into an apartment, where, amidst objects of taste, which adorned the chamber, and furniture of the utmost elegance, a quantity of shabby-looking clothes were strewed about the floor, or hung upon the chairs, making a contrast too startling not to be observed by Lynch, whose wonder was increased by seeing Ellen standing amidst a heap of boddices, petticoats, caps, and jerkins, of all fashions, she herself wearing a peasant's costume, which was nearly completed, the finishing touches being in the act of completion at the hands of a very lovely woman. There was one remarkable trait in this affair; it was, that, though engaged seemingly in preparing for a masquerade, which usually inspires mirth, there was rather a serious and business-like air about the whole proceeding, and an expression of anxiety shadowing every face.

On Lynch's entrance, he was received by the beautiful lady who was acting tire-woman, with an air of supreme elegance; and, as he was taxing his memory to recall where he had seen her before, Ellen advanced to her father, and, hastily expressing her delight at seeing him in safety, begged to present him to Mademoiselle le Couvreur.

An involuntary expression of something between surprise and displeasure passed across his face, as Lynch saw his daughter thus engaged in offices of intimacy with one whose reputation was not stainless; and Madame de Jumillac, with all the quickness of a Frenchwoman, advanced, and said—

"You know not, *Monsieur de Capitaine,* how deeply we are indebted to Mademoiselle le Couvreur."

She then commenced an explanation of the affair to Lynch; the purport was, in brief, this: Adrienne had, in some way, which she did not think it necessary to explain, got information of the Count de Saxe's infamous design; and she, though herself not a model of purity, had, nevertheless, enough of a woman's sympathies remaining to shudder at the thought of the Marshal's plot, and hastened at once to the house of Madame de Jumillac to give warning of the impending danger, and suggest a mode of escape. Adrienne, aware there was no time to lose, hurried Madame and Ellen away instantly from their home to her own house, where she ordered the superintendant of the wardrobe of the theatre to be in attendance, with a choice of peasant costumes, both male and female.

It so happened that the day was the octave of the feast of *Corpus Christi,* on which day the Bastile was always thrown open for public inspection, and was visited by the surrounding peasantry of Paris in thousands, who were anxious to see the interior of this prison-fortress, whose name carried with it so much of mystery and terror. Adrienne, therefore, suggested that Ellen and her father, in the disguise of peasants, should visit the Bastile; and, wandering about there all day amidst the crowd, find safety, by being in the very spot to which there was a government order to convey them; judging, truly, that, of all places in Paris, the Bastile must be the last where they would be sought for, and that in the evening they could pass the barriers securely among the groups of country people then quitting the city,

Ellen's disguise was now completed; the only difficulty Adrienne experienced being to keep down her beauty as much as possible. Contrary to all the regular rules of the toilette, her object was to make the lady look ugly instead of handsome; but, with all the skill of an experienced and accomplished actress, used to the artifices of personal disguise, this was more than even Adrienne le Couvreur could accomplish.

When Lynch heard of the infamous design on foot against him and his daughter, his indignation knew no bounds; he lost all patience, and burst into a fierce and terrible invective against the Marshal, clutching the handle of his sword at intervals, as though he longed for the extremity of vengeance, and even suggesting the possibility of his hastening at once to the libertine's retreat, and demanding satisfaction at the point of the sword. From such fruitless passion and vain attempt he was at length cooled down and dissuaded by the persuasive words of the ladies, who now retired from the chamber with Adrienne, she promising to Lynch the immediate attendance of the theatrical wardrobe-keeper, who would do as much for him as had been accomplished for Ellen.

"Observe," said Adrienne, "I have made believe that all this masquerading is but for the fulfilment of a little bit of private fun; so clear your brow, *Monsieur*, and seem to treat the affair as a bagatelle."

With these words she retired, and the dramatic dresser made his appearance, and in some twenty minutes the captain of the Irish Brigade was converted into a rustic, and might have passed for the "Antoine" or "Basil" of some pastoral farce.

When the ladies were allowed to return to the room, Adrienne gave some finishing strokes to the "making up" of Lynch, and father and daughter were prepared to go forth on their pilgrimage. The next point of consideration was, whither they should fly when they were past the barriers, for concealment for any time near the city was impossible.

"Opportunely," said Lynch, "I was on the point of departing for Nantes, and this only hastens the journey a few days."

"Your road thither lies directly towards *Chambor*," said Madame de Jumillac, in alarm.

"All the better," said Adrienne. "When it is found that the birds are flown, none will suspect that they are flying towards the net of the fowler."

It was then arranged that Madame de Jumillac should drive to Prince Charles Edward, tell what had occurred, and ask him to procure a passport as if for one of his own adherents, who were in the habit of being permitted to travel under feigned names; and that, under favour of night, they should meet at a safe place of rendezvous near Paris, named by Adrienne, and thence Ellen and her father hasten to the coast. Such necessary preliminaries being arranged, Ellen uttered unfeigned and touching thanks to Mademoiselle le Couvreur; and receiving in return kind wishes for the success of the plot, father and daughter, as Basil and Annette, went forth upon the streets, and proceeded to the Bastile. As they approached the fortress, they mingled in the crowd of peasantry, and assimilated themselves as much as possible to their gait and manner, and imitated the upturned looks of surprise and gaping wonder which were bestowed on the lofty and ponderous towers. They crossed the drawbridge, and as they passed under the low-browed arch, and Ellen felt herself within the prison, she shuddered at the thought of discovery, and clung closer to her father. An admonitory look, and a whispered word of caution, recalled her to self-possession, and she affected an ease to which her heart was a stranger.—Sometimes they stopped to hear the remarks of some spokesman of a group, who pointed out something worthy of observation, or made some remark in a levity of spirit ill-suited to the place, which made his hearers laugh.

"Heaven pity the poor captive," thought Ellen, "who hears the thoughtless laughter of those who come to see the place of his misery! How bitterly must a laugh sound to him!"

Ellen observed a turnkey eyeing her intently; the gaze was, in fact, attributable to the brute's admiration, but to her it seemed as if he suspected her, and, with the cunning peculiar to his craft, saw through her disguise. Her heart sank within her; and as her arm touched her father he felt her shudder. Again his words were used to reassure her, but she took occasion to point out the turnkey to his observation.

"How that man looks at me!"

"Because he thinks you are pretty, Nell, no more.—Steady, my girl, and fear nothing."—The turnkey approached, and chucking her under the chin with as galliard an air as the savage could assume, said,—

"There's a pretty girl!—you're pretty enough for a lady, my dear."

"Pretty enough for a *lady*!—Could he mean anything?"—

Ellen attempted a smile, but it was very faint.—The turnkey thought it was shyness.

"You are too pretty to be bashful, my dear," he said.—"I should think you have soft things said to you too often to be surprised.—This is your father, I suppose, with you."

"Yes, sir," said Ellen; "but he is deaf; and, as he cannot hear what is said, he never speaks much."

She said this to exonerate her father from the necessity of speaking, for his accent had not that purity which hers possessed —a purity which could deceive a native;—besides, her power of imitation was such, that she could mimic the *patois* of many districts, and dreaded not present discovery on the score of language.

"Then, if he is deaf, I may say what I like to you—eh?— that was not a bad hint of yours," said the fellow, with a wink.

Ellen shook her head, as much as to say he must not go too far.

"You're the prettiest girl in your village, I'll be sworn.— Where do you come from?"

"Lonjumeau, sir."

"Lonjumeau!—ah, I like the girls of Lonjumeau, well.—Do you know Etienne Barolles, who lives there?"

"No, sir," replied Ellen, sorry she had hit on a village in which he had acquaintances.

"I expect him to-day."

"Ellen devoutly hoped he would not come.

"But, as he has not arrived, I'll wait no more here, where I promised to stay for him; and I'll show you the whole place, if you like."

Ellen thanked him for his offer; and a group of peasants taking advantage of this guidance, won through a pretty face, were permitted, on asking leave, to join the party, of which Ellen was quite the queen; and no peasants ever had such satisfactory sight-seeing in the Bastile as that group that day. There was nothing deserving of notice neglected by the turnkey; the narrowest spiral stair of its topmost tower, and the lowest and most noisome depths of its *souterrains*, were exhibited in the truest pride of a showman, who cared little whether it was their knees, or their hearts, he made ache, so he excited their wonder; for the more they wondered the greater man was he; and as the greater man, of course, the more acceptable to the pretty girl for whose sake all this was done. Occasionally, a halt was obtained, by his stopping at some particular place to point out where a stone had been once ingeniously removed, or an iron bar cut through, to achieve an escape; and such recitals made within the walls of this terrible prison, whose very stones seemed to deny the possibility of the tale, added such wonder to these stories, that they surpassed the marvels of fairy lore. The turnkey, seeing the incredulous looks sometimes cast upon him, and sometimes even called upon to answer doubting querists, who would venture to question the janitor in that peculiar excitement which an interest in an escape from bondage always makes, would beg to remind them that only few, *very few*, had ever succeeded in such achievements. "No, no," he would say, "when once people get in here, they don't go out in a hurry. There, for example,"—and he banged his ponderous bunch of keys against a door as he spoke—"inside there is a prisoner who has never been out of his cell for thirty years!" What a chill the words cast over his hearers! As for Ellen, she felt it to her heart's very centre, and put up an inward prayer for God's special mercy over her father and herself in that day of danger, and prayed that, with the shades of evening, his guardian spirit might descend to shield them through their many perils. This thought for self-preservation once passed, her gentle nature winced as her imagination reverted to the poor captive within that door whereon the crash of those ponderous keys had fallen. What did he think of that startling noise?—was it the executioner come to claim him?—was the hour arrived when death should relieve him from his misery?—did he hope so; or did the love of life still exist in the withered heart of that poor captive? —or did he remember that this was the day when his prison was open to public view? Did he rejoice in hearing the hum of human voices—this evidence of the presence of his fellows, even through his prison door?—or did the contrast of *their* freedom with *his* captivity make bondage more bitter? Or was some remnant of human pride still left to be wounded at the thought that *his* door was pointed out, like some cage in a menagerie, as containing some special monster demanding heavier bars, and peculiar watching?

Link after link of such heavy thoughts weighed down her spirit till she almost wept, while the turnkey thought he was doing the most amiable thing in the world, and making himself particularly agreeable.

Passing along one of the broader and more airy passages, he stopped at another door, and, shoving it open, said to Ellen, "You may look in there," and pointed the way. She hesitated; her ordinary courage was subdued by the appalling influences with which she was surrounded; and a thought shot through her brain, that, if she entered within that door, it might be shut upon her! She shuddered at the terrible imagining.

"What are you afraid of?" said the Cerberus, laughing. "'Tis only my own room; come in!" and he led the way, beckoning Ellen and her father to follow, while the crowd remained outside.

The chamber seemed to be nothing more than a hollow in the thickness of the wall, but was made as comfortable as such a place could be. Its owner opening a little cupboard that hung in a corner, produced a bottle of wine, and a glass, which he filled, and offered to Ellen, remarking that sight-seeing was tiresome work, and that there was yet much more to be gone over.

Ellen had experienced that sinking of heart which makes a restorative so desirable, and therefore gladly accepted the proffered hospitality; and though the wine was but poor stuff, it was most welcome. After giving another glass to her father, the turnkey pledged them both in a brimmer himself; and as he smacked his large protruding lips, assured Ellen a girl might do worse than marry a turnkey. This was said with a very significant look of admiration at *her*, and a self-satisfied grin, which showed that the gentleman stood on very good terms with himself.

"I cannot often get leave to go out," said he, "but the first time I can go to Lonjumeau, I will call and see you."

Ellen assured him it would give her and her father much pleasure.

"Whereabouts do you live there?"

This was rather a puzzler, for Ellen had named Lonjumeau on the spur of the moment, when he asked her where she came from, and knew but little of the place; she therefore was obliged to shelter herself under fresh inventions every step she took, and, for the present, said she knew but little of the village, as they had only removed to it within a few days.

"Oh, new comers," said the turnkey. "But then you know where your own house is."

"Oh yes," said she, "to be sure. I am not so silly as not to know my own house, though I *am* only a country girl."

"No, you don't look much like a fool," said the turnkey.

"La! how ready you gentlemen of the city are at making compliments," returned Ellen.

"Why, who could be uncivil to *you?*" said he, with a smirk. "But where do you live?—tell me that."

"You know the post-house;" said Ellen—that being the only place in the whole village she herself knew anything about, and only knowing that by having changed horses once in passing through.

"To be sure I know it," said the turnkey.

12

"Well, as you pass the post-house there is a turn down to the left."

"I know it," said the turnkey—"there's a grocer's shop at the corner."

"I believe there is," said Ellen; but I have such a bad memory, and have been such a short time there—but turn down at that corner, and there are some houses—"

"A great many," said the turnkey.

"Well, there's where we live," said Ellen.

"But in *which?*" said the turnkey, who was determined on making a visit.

"Do you remember any palings there?" asked Ellen, fishing for knowledge.

"To be sure I do—on the left."

"Just so!" said Ellen. "La! how clever you city gentlemen are! you know everything, if you only see with half an eye!"

"Oh, I remember quite well," said the turnkey, stimulated to further description, "some small houses, with vines on their front."

"The very houses," said Ellen.

"There is a house near," pursued he, "with a remarkable chimney."

Ellen, afraid of engaging too much in particulars, said she was not sure.

"You must have seen this chimney."

"I'm not sure about the chimney, sir, but I'm sure I have seen smoke," said Ellen, with well-affected simplicity.

"Tut! you pretty simpleton," said the turnkey, "your eyes are too good not to make better use of them."

"'Tis the fourth house, sir," pursued Ellen.

"The fourth.   Very well, I'll find you out."

"You can't miss it, sir."

"But in case of accident, you may as well give me your name, too, that I may inquire in the neighbourhood."

"My name is Annette Claudet, sir," she answered; and her admirer, satisfied with his inquiries, and promising a visit the first opportunity, offered another glass of wine, which being declined by father and daughter, he played turnkey on the bottle; and having locked it up again in his corner cupboard, pursued his course of exhibition over the prison.

There was a garden he showed, where the more favoured prisoners were permitted to take exercise.   To Ellen it seemed as if the few sickly flowers were languishing for liberty, and could not bloom in bondage; and the weakly trees appeared to have outgrown their strength in stretching upwards, in the hopeless endeavour to get a peep over the wall at the nature outside for which they pined. "What melancholy reflections," thought Ellen, "is this garden calculated to excite in those who are indulged in the use of its walks, if they look on it as I do!" Thus every fresh object she saw impressed her more and more with a sadness approaching despondency; and though she knew the place afforded her temporary concealment, she longed for the approach of evening, which would place her once more outside its walls, and permit her and her father to pass unsuspected amidst the peasant groups beyond the barriers of that city, where, even now, they were sought for by the myrmidons of power.

The wished-for time at length arrived; the Bastile began to pour forth the gaping crowds of idlers; and amongst the earliest of the departing groups were the disguised fugitives, who had the good fortune to pass the barriers in safety, and breathed freer as they found themselves on the open road; and when half an hour more placed them among quiet hedges, then Ellen, taking her father's hand, and uttering a fervent ejaculation of thankfulness to Heaven, ventured to express her belief that they were now in safety. A walk of a few miles brought them to the appointed place, where they might expect to see their friends; and as they approached the house, they saw one of the windows open, which commanded a view of the Paris road; and, peeping from behind its curtains, the lovely face of Adrienne beamed with a benevolent joy as she caught the first glimpse of the fugitives, and knew they were safe. After waving a welcome to them, she retired from the window; and by the time they reached the little entrance gate, the hand of Adrienne herself had drawn its bolt, and father and daughter were received in a pretty little parterre, and gratulations were warmly exchanged among the party.

"Is Madame de Jumillac here?" inquired Ellen.

"No," answered Adrienne. "But before you ask any questions, you must sit down, and submit to regular eating and drinking; for neither you, nor *Monsieur le Capitaine*, can have had any refreshment for many hours, and remember, you have a long journey before you."

Ellen and her father obeyed the hospitable command, given with so much grace and kindness, and partook of an elegant repast prepared for them; after which Adrienne told them how matters had fared since they had parted in the morning. It was not long after their disguise had been completed, that Madame de Jumillac's house was visited, and strict search made for Lynch and his daughter; which, failing there, was pursued in other quarters, the rank even of Prince Charles Edward not screening his retirement from invasion.

"Under these circumstances," said Adrienne, "it was im-possible that Madame, or even the Prince, could be of the slightest use in conducting the affair; therefore you must pardon me if I undertook to act in the place of your friends, and I hope you will not think me intrusive in thus becoming an agent in your safety; but you must perceive at once, that any passports obtained through those channels would have put your pursuers on your track, and, therefore, I advised Madame de Jumillac to let me procure them, and further entreated her to forego the desire she had of bidding you farewell.—Here is a letter she entrusted to my care for you, Mademoiselle,"—hand-ing Ellen a note, which was hastily opened, and read with suffused eyes, as the expressions of touching tenderness reached her heart.—"And here, Monsieur, is your passport. You had better look over it to see under what name you travel; and then the sooner you both cast your disguise and prepare for the road the better, for a post-chaise will be here anon, and it is needless to counsel speed under such circumstances.

Her advice was followed; and when Lynch and Ellen had resumed their proper attire, and returned to the apartment where they had left Adrienne, they found her engaged in pack-ing up a little basket, which she handed to Ellen, saying that, as they must travel all night, she had put up a few *confitures*, and some little restoratives, which might be agreeable in the morning, when she would feel exhausted after her night's fatigue.

"How thoughtful!—even to such trifles as these—you have been for my sake, *dear* Madam," said Ellen, offering her hand.

Adrienne pressed it tenderly, touched at the earnestness of her manner; and the word "dear," so uttered, and coming from such pure lips, sounded to her sensitive soul little short of a blessing.

"Let me kiss your hand!" said Adrienne respectfully, and as if she felt she asked a favour.

The gentle soul of Ellen was touched at this proof of an erring woman's sense of her loss of caste,—and that at a moment when so much was due to her. With all the warm heart and enthusiasm of her country, Ellen threw wide her arms, and, while heaven-born tears sprang to her eyes, she exclaimed, "My hand!—how can you ask for my hand only?—Come to my heart!"

In a moment they were locked in each other's arms; and Lynch, stern though he was in his morality, blamed not the noble nature of his pure child in thus mingling her embraces. He looked on in silence, through which the sobs of the two women were audible, and for some minutes neither could speak

At length Adrienne assumed her self-command, and, clearing the tears from her eyes, gazed on Ellen for an instant with a look of admiration and gratitude. "You are a noble creature," said she, "and worthy of all that could be done for you."

"And what have you not done?" answered Ellen,—"preserved to me my father!"

"And deeper still *my* debt," said Lynch, "you have preserved to me a daughter."

"We must part," said Adrienne. "The carriage waits, and time is precious.—Come!" She led to the entrance as she spoke; and as they stepped out into the parterre, the soft beams of the moon shed a soothing light on all things.

"And now, farewell, and Heaven speed you!" she said, turning to Ellen. The moonlight fell full upon her fair forehead and deep and lustrous eyes, and Adrienne thought she seemed more like a being of heaven than earth.

"You are like an angel," she said, with almost devotion in her voice, "and those soft sweet eyes beam peace into my very soul." She stooped and plucked a stem from a rose tree; "I will keep these roses," she said, "in remembrance of this hour; and whenever I see them they will recall the benign look of those angelic eyes, and I can fancy that a seraph, for once, looked kindly on me."

"Give me one of those flowers," said Ellen, "'twill be precious to me as to you."

They divided the stem between them; and, after a few last parting words, and a fervent blessing from Adrienne, Ellen and her father entered the carriage, and started on their toilsome and perilous journey.

For many miles they were silent; both were occupied with their thoughts,—those of Ellen reverting to the scene in which she had been engaged, while Lynch's were cast forward to the journey before them, for the accomplishment of which one serious consideration pressed upon him, namely, that he doubted if the money he had about him would be sufficient to carry them through. He entered into conversation with Ellen on this point at last, and they held a gloomy council of war as they drove through the darkness, for by this time the moon had set. It was decided at last that they should exert themselves to pass Blois as soon as possible. for, until then, while between Paris and the seat of the Marshal, they must run the risk of encountering his emissaries, should they be delayed at any intermediate post. A calculation of miles *versus* money was entered into, and Lynch, on reckoning up his cash, almost doubted being able to accomplish this object. They dare not write to Paris for money, as a letter might tend to trace them, therefore **they** must send a letter all the way to Nantes to obtain supplies. It was in such anxious debate the night was passed, and horses changed throughout the darkness at the successive posts; and the dawn began to break on the sleepless travellers, as they approached the town of Etampes. There is something peculiarly grateful to the senses in the return of day, when you have been journeying for many hours through darkness; and to spirits like those of our travellers, overcast with anxieties for the future, that darkness was yet more drear. It was with peculiar welcome, therefore, that they saw the first rays of the sun burst from their purple bondage in the east, and sparkle on the dewy vineyards through which they now were travelling. Pleasant slopes, too, here and there, were stretching down to the river Juine, and the sweet aspect of smiling nature shed balm on Ellen's spirit. The spires of the town appeared in the distance, rising among its surrounding meadows, and the morning chimes of the bells of St. Martin floated on the refreshing breeze; the postillion cracked his whip with more energy, and the jaded hacks pricked their ears, and seemed to step out more cheerfully, in expectation of the rack and manger of the hostelrie. In half an hour they were entering on the skirts of the town, and Lynch suggested to Ellen that she should refresh herself with breakfast, but assuring him she felt no inclination as yet for the morning meal, they merely changed horses, and pursued their journey. The truth was, Ellen was anxious to spare their purse as much as possible, and had determined that the little basket of *confitures* should satisfy any craving of nature until she had passed Blois. On reaching their next post, however, her father again urged her to take some breakfast, but Ellen commenced unlacing her little basket, and told him, with a significant nod, that breakfast, dinner, and supper, for the next two days, were in that little basket.

Lynch understood her motive in an instant, and urged her to be sure that she was not overrating her strength; but Ellen, with a sweet smile of assurance, bade him be content on that point. He called her a brave girl, declared she might give even an old soldier a lesson on prudence, and, acting on her suggestion, said he would subsist on an occasional crust and *buvette* (as a hasty cup of refreshment was called) until their point of danger was passed. He quitted the post-chaise, and entered the little inn to call for a cup of light wine, for Lynch, being an old campaigner, was not afraid of that beverage in the morning. As a pretty lively grisette was handing him the drink, Ellen suddenly entered the house, her face beaming with excitement, and having ordered the girl to bring them breakfast directly, took her father's arm, and led him into the parlour of the inn. Lynch could not account for this sudden revolution in Ellen's determination, and her change of manner.

"Oh, father!" she exclaimed, while the flush of emotion restored the colour to her cheek,—"that noble creature!"

The words would have been unintelligible, but that she opened the little basket as she spoke, and there, lying amongst the *confitures*, was a purse well stored with gold.

Lynch could not speak, nor Ellen utter another word, but with trembling lip and glistening eye she stood looking at her silent father till her heart was full to overflowing, and, unable longer to repress her emotion, she threw herself on his breast **and wept.**

Ellen was not a crying lady by any means; but her tears on this occasion may be pardoned, when we consider the sudden revulsion of her feelings. At this point of need, when, to save a few *livres*, she was willing to abstain from needful sustenance, and opened her little basket, content with the slender support it contained—heedless of hunger in the more necessary desire for flight—at such a moment to see a full purse was enough to make a full heart, and a stoic only could be calm ; the difficulties and dangers which beset them were lessened by this timely supply, and the demon, Want, that so lately threatened to be in league with their enemies, was overcome.

The smiling grisette now made her appearance, the table was soon spread for breakfast, and cheerfully did father and daughter sit down to their morning repast.

"What is the name of this village, my girl?" inquired Lynch.

"It is called Montdésir, *Monsieur.*"

"An appropriate name," said Ellen to her father, "for the place where we have found what was so much to be wished for; *à Montdésir j'ai trouvé mon désir.*"

"Come!" said her father, "I am glad to see you are merry to make a *calembourg.*"

They both, however, displayed renovated spirits ; and he was as willing to listen to as she to utter lively sallies—for lively she was. She had quite shaken off the gloom which oppressed her overnight; for it seemed to her that fate was inclined to favour their escape, and Ellen augured well of the remainder of their journey. No time was lost, however, in pursuing it; fresh horses were ordered, and now that they had got those golden wings which can transport the traveller with accelerated speed, a trifling *douceur* in the stables always secured the best pair of horses, and a bribe to the postillion pushed them to their best pace, so that the next fifty miles were much sooner passed than the former, and they were enabled to dine at Orleans. Here Lynch offered Ellen a few hours' rest; but she preferred the prosecution of their journey, and another night of travel was undertaken. The next morning saw them approaching Blois; this, the point they were anxious to pass, was reached in safety; and now they were within twelve miles of the man who sought their capture: little did the Marshal know how near to him was the prey his myrmidons were then seeking in Paris. This proximity to their enemy made Ellen very anxious, however, and she begged her father to make no further delay than change of horses required. Even at Chousy and Veuve she refused any refreshment; and it was not until reaching Haut Chantier that she took a slight breakfast. On they sped again, and reached Tours in time for dinner, which Ellen enjoyed more than her breakfast, as her courage rose in proportion to the distance placed between them and their enemy. Her father suggested some rest at Tours; but as there were still some hours of the day available, Ellen declared herself strong enough to pursue the journey farther. Fresh horses were therefore ordered; and now, leaving the southern route, they struck off to the right, westward, making for the coast; and having achieved two posts and a half, Ellen was content to give the night to sleep, and they rested at Pile St. Marc.

CHAPTER XXI.

IT was one morning, early in July, 1745, that a large merchantman was seen, under jurymasts, making what sail she could up the Loire, assisted in ascending the stream by being in tow of a handsome French corvette, whose prize she seemed to be. On reaching Port Launai they dropped their anchors, as the sands prevented vessels of their burthen proceeding higher.

A boat was lowered from the corvette, and the Captain went on shore to report himself. Being congratulated on bringing in a prize, he replied, the prize was not so very much, as she was a Spaniard, retaken from an English privateer; and, therefore, as the vessel of a friendly state, they could only claim salvage upon her.

" To judge from her masts," said the officer with whom he spoke, " you did not get her without blows."

" No; the Englishmen fought like devils, and a great number were killed ; such as there are I will send up to Nantes when the tide makes. By the bye, that is a very pretty brig that lies in the river; do you know what she is?"

" It is suspected she is meant for the service of the Chevalier St. George. You know whom I mean !"

" To be sure I do. Wasn't I at Dunkirk when the troops were embarked in his cause, and did't I barely escape going on the rocks? Parbleu! I shan't forget that gale in a hurry! So he has got something in the wind again ?"

" So it is rumoured here."

" Well, I wish him better weather than he had last—that's all—good-bye!"

As the naval officer was returning to his boat, he was accosted by a gentleman, who held out his hand, and claimed acquaintance.

" Do you not remember me ?" said the stranger.

" I have a recollection of your features, and yet I cannot recall where it was we met."

" You don't forget Dunkirk?" inquired the stranger.

" Ah! I have it now.—The Irish Brigade—you were on board my ship—"

" The same."

" Glad to see you," said the sailor, shaking him heartily by

the hand. "But you are not in uniform now, that is the reason
I did not remember you."

"Is the corvette here, Captain?" asked the stranger.

"Yes, there she lies yonder."

"Might I speak a word in private with you?"

"Certainly. I am going on board this moment; will you
come?"

"Willingly."

"Something brewing, I suppose," said the Captain, with a
significant nod, and pointing to the pretty brig.

"We will speak of that when we get on board," returned the
stranger.

With these words he followed the Captain to his boat, and
they were rapidly rowed to the corvette; and as they passed the
prize, which was lying close alongside, a voice shouted loudly,
"Captain Lynch! Captain Lynch!!"

Lynch—for the strange companion of the naval commander
was he—looked up, and, with no small surprise, saw Ned leaning
over the bulwark of the merchantman, and waving his hand as
he called to him, saying he wished to speak with him.

Lynch explained to the Frenchman Ned's desire, which the
Captain said should be gratified, as he would send for him to
come on board the corvette. "'Tis a strange chance that you
should meet here," said the Frenchman. "Do you know him
well?"

"Not intimately," said Lynch. "But all I know of him I
have reason to like, for he has laid me twice under obligation—
once deeply so. He is a very spirited young fellow."

"I'll swear to that," said the Frenchman; "for I never saw
a man fight a ship more gallantly."

"But what brought him fighting on board a Spanish ship?"
inquired Lynch.

"That is a most extraordinary piece of romance, which I
can't pretend to tell you, but which of course he can enlighten
you upon when you see him. His uncle, who is owner of the
ship, and a Spanish subject, interceded with me not to confine
your young friend with the rest of the prisoners. but to grant
him *parole;* and as I had proved him to be a gallant fellow, I
made the old man happy by acceding to his request. And now
for this private affair of your own," he added, as he led him into
the cabin of the corvette, and pointed to a seat.

"You are right in your suppositions about the brig yonder,"
said Lynch.—"I need say no more,—for the less said about
secret expeditions the better: and, however you may receive
what I have to propose, you, of course, will affect to know

nothing about our designs. We are all ready on ooard, but we dare not, in so lightly-armed a vessel, venture to sail in British waters. We have been led to expect, in an underhand way (for the government will do nothing for us openly), the protection of a sixty-gun ship, but she is not yet arrived, and we may be disappointed in the end, while every day's delay is detrimental to our cause. Now, as you are cruising in the Atlantic, could you not just as well take a turn with us to the northward, and I an prepared to promise the Prince would not be ungrateful."

The Captain said he dared not act without orders ; that everything connected with the marine was cavilled at in those days,— that no commander might risk the slightest overstepping of duty.

Lynch continued to tempt the sailor, suggesting many modes whereby he might excuse or justify " a *little* run towards Scotland." " For instance," he said, " could you not *suppose* you saw a sail, and say you chased it ?"

" You forget, my friend, that there are other eyes than a Captain's on board ship, and that there are accounts kept of our doings.—I dare not comply with your request."

Lynch, finding it vain, gave up his attempt, and returned to the deck, where he found Ned had already arrived, and cordial was the greeting he gave him, reminding him they had not seen each other since the night they parted at Courtrai.

" And that you presented me with a sword," said Ned.

" Which I heard you made brave use of," returned Lynch.

Ned hereupon ventured to hope Ellen was well, colouring so deeply as he spoke, that it was plain the inquiry was not uninteresting to him.

Lynch answered in the affirmative, and said she would be glad to see him if the Captain would extend his *parole* to a visit on shore ; " for I hear you are a prisoner," said he, " and that there is some very strange piece of romance about this affair in which you have been engaged."

Ned owned it was so, and that he should be delighted to relate to him the circumstances of the adventure, if he would favour him with a visit on board the merchantman

Lynch consented, and Ned was delighted, for he had many objects in view in getting Lynch on board. In the first place, though he would not join in practising a deceit on his shipmates regarding the gold concealed in the snuff, he had no such scruples about Frenchmen, and hoped to obtain through Lynch an agency by which this money might be recovered. In the next place, he wished Lynch to understand that he was his uncle's heir, and was anxious to set before the eyes of his fair one's father the wealth to which he should succeed. Great was Ned's joy, therefore, when he saw Lynch set his foot on the deck of the merchantman, and presented to him Senor Carcojas, for he still assumed the Spaniard, while Ned retained the name of Fitzgerald.

After giving a rapid account of his privateering adventure, Ned then confided to Lynch the secret of the hidden gold, and the means whereby it might be saved, concluding with asking Lynch's assistance.

Lynch paused for a moment, and, after some consideration, said he knew a little of the Captain of the corvette, with whom he had once sailed, and though he should be glad to oblige Ned, yet, for the interest of a gentleman to whom he had only just been introduced, he would not like to interfere in such an affair.

"Allow me on that point, sir," said Ned, "to set you right.— My uncle's generosity permits me to say, that what is *his*—is *mine;* therefore, in giving us your aid in this, you oblige me rather than him."

"Well, that alters the case," said Lynch, "and as I owe *you* my good offices, perhaps I may assist you."

"Ah, sir!" said old Jerome,—"do not say perhaps,—say you will. Did you but know the ardent desires that have put this boy of mine on his adventures, I am sure you would sympathise with him. He has been acting under the dominion of a romantic passion, which spurred him to seek sudden wealth in desperate adventure, in the doing which he unconsciously despoiled me, his uncle. Chance led him to discover this, and though he might have kept the secret, his conscience would not let him; he humiliated himself in repentant acknowledgment before me, and that act of grace won him lasting favour in my eyes. Since then, the honourable spirit to his companions in adventure, which urged him to defend this ship to the utmost, against his own interest, has raised him in my esteem, and therefore I beg to repeat to you, sir, that whatever is mine is his; and as I have told you the love of a lady has been the prime mover in all his affairs, I may as well be candid with you, and tell you also, that not only whatever is mine is his—but is also—your daughter's—if she will do him the honour to share it with him."

This was a most unexpected proposition to Lynch, who was silent for some minutes, during which Ned, who was rather "taken aback" by his uncle's out-speaking, hung down his head, and dared not look at Ellen's father.

When Lynch broke silence, it was in a question to Ned.— "Does my daughter know **you love her**?" said he.

"She does."

"Is the love returned?"

"I dare not hope *that*," said Edward.—"It was in those few hurried moments of danger at Bruges, which you alluded to, that I had the hardihood to throw myself at her feet."

"And what did she answer?"

"Nothing, in fact," said Ned. "She did not encourage—but—I may say—neither did she disdain me."

"Fairly answered," returned Lynch; "and I will as fairly tell you, my intention for her is another alliance."

Ned could not answer in words, but there was an expression of despair in the look he cast upon Lynch more eloquent than language,—so eloquent that it *touched him*. And he continued,—"At the same time I must confess *she* has given no answer on the subject; and on a subject so serious, she shall never be controlled by me to *accept*—however I may consider myself justified in the authority to *object*,—or, at least, *delay*."

Peculiar emphasis was laid on the last word; and it was painful to watch the changes that passed over Edward's face as the sentences followed each other.

"Now I have two propositions to make," continued Lynch. "There is an expedition undertaken to replace the rightful king of England on his throne; in that expedition we want brave men and ready money. Now, sir," said he, addressing the old man, "if I get your valuable snuff out of jeopardy, will you advance a loan of a thousand pieces to Prince Charles, to procure arms and ammunition, which we need?"

"Willingly," said the old man. "I wish his cause well."

"And will you," he said to Edward, "give the aid of a bold heart and able hands to the cause, as the price of my consent?"

"With all my heart!" said Ned.

"I must make this additional proviso," added Lynch, "that until our expedition has struck its blow, no word of love must pass between you and my daughter."

This damped Ned's rising spirits; but it was such a brightening of his hopes to have his pretensions entertained in the least, that he agreed to the condition, but hoped he might be permitted to see her.

Her father consented to this, and Ned's heart bounded with joy; but a sudden difficulty presented itself to him in the recollection that he was a prisoner.

"That is a difficulty easily got over," said Lynch; "offer to enlist in the Irish Brigade, and the commandant of Nantes will be ready enough to give you your liberty; and, when once enrolled, it will be easy to manage that you join the expedition."

Lynch set out for Nantes at once, where Ned's liberation was effected; and the secret of the gold was confided to Walsh, the merchant, who, in consequence, became the purchaser of the snuff when the cargo of the prize was offered for sale, which it was in a few days. This valuable lot of tobacco was sent off to a private store, where the peculiar virtues of the snuff were extracted; and though, in modern times, much is asserted in flaming advertisements of the rare qualities of certain eye snuffs, we venture to affirm that no snuff was ever so good for anybody's eyes as that proved to Don Jerome's.

The thousand promised pieces were handed over for Charles Edward's service, and a commission promised to Ned in the first regiment the Prince should raise on his landing.

Ned was now amongst the most impatient of all for the arrival of the promised convoy; he longed to embark in the expedition, which, by engaging him in the honourable profession of arms, would elevate him at once to the rank he desired,—a rank entitling him to the company of a peer, or the hand of a lady. But as yet he had not seen Ellen, though her father assured him he should before they sailed; day after day passed, however, without this promised pleasure being fulfilled. At length the *Elizabeth*, a ship of sixty-seven guns, was reported to be waiting at Belleisle, to convoy the brig; and the stores were at once forwarded to the man-of-war, and the Prince's adherents given notice to hold themselves in readiness for embarkation on the morrow. In the meantime they were all invited to an entertainment that evening, which the Prince gave before his departure. There were a few young nobles and men of rank who had followed him to Nantes,—some to join him in the expedition, some to witness his departure, and breathe good wishes for speed and safety to his sails. Among this goodly company were some noble ladies; and his fast friend, the young Duke de Buillon, graced this gallant little circle. Hitherto, all these gay people, as well as the Prince, observed great quietness while waiting for the arrival of the convoy, wishing the intended expedition to be as little bruited as possible; but now that the hour of departure had arrived, one brilliant meeting was agreed to, where hopeful hearts might cheer the adventurer with parting gratulations, fair lips whisper blessings on his course, and brimming glasses foam to the heartfelt toast of success to the throne-seeker.

There are times when the great find it their interest to be gracious; and at this parting reunion given by the Prince, there were no exceptions made among his adherents. Walsh, the merchant, was there, and Ned, as the young gentleman who was to have a commission, was presented to the prince; and his uncle, who had advanced the thousand pieces, was also a guest.

It may be imagined how Ned's love of gentility was gratified by being presented to a real, live prince—joining in the same party with noble ladies, and a whole duke, to say nothing of some clippings of nobility that were scattered about. But beyond this was his joy at seeing his lovely Ellen once more. She received him with a most gracious smile, and spoke with him for a good while; sharing her conversation, however, with Kirwan, who kept near her, and seemed studious in his attentions. "Ah," thought Ned, "there he is again." It was manifest her father favoured the suit of Kirwan; and the promise under which Ned was bound, placed him at a sad disadvantage; he was pledged not to speak one word of love; but Ned, however, could not help *looking* it; and he met Ellen's eyes two or three times in the course of the evening in a way no woman could misunderstand. She—*La belle Irlandaise*—received the choicest courtesies of the most distinguished men in the room; her foot was lightest in the dance, her lip most eloquent in repartee, though fair forms and quick wits were there. Brightly passed that evening; every heart seemed wrought to its highest beat; and flashing eyes and brilliant smiles met Charles Edward on every side, shedding hopefulness over his spirit, and seeming to prognosticate triumph to that expedition which ended so fatally.

> "Brightly then, to Fancy's seeming,
> The wily web of fate was gleaming;
> The warp was gold, of dazzling sheen,
> But dark the weft she wove between."

So wrote one in after years; one who then was present, and smiled and hoped like the rest. And sweet voices were there, and lays of the gallant troubadours were sung, as befitting such a meeting. One beautiful girl gave an old romaunt of Provence; one of those strange conceits which breathe of love and chivalry. We shall try a metrical version of the quaint old thing, which was called—

The Hand and The Globe.

I.

"To horse! to horse!" the trumpet sings, midst clank of spear and shield
The knight into his saddle springs, and rushes to the field!
A lady looked from out her bower, the stately knight drew near,
And from her snowy hand she dropt her glove upon his spear.
He placed it on his helmet's crest, and joined the gallant band;—
"The lady's glove it now is mine, but soon I'll win the hand!"

II.

Above the plunging tide of fight their plumes now dance like spray;
And many a crest of note and might bore proudly through the fray;
But still the little glove was seen the foremost of the band;
And deadly blows the fiercest fell from that fair lady's hand!
Before him every foeman flies; his onset none can stand;
More fatal e'en than ladies' eyes was that fair lady's hand!

III.

And now the trumpet sounds retreat, the foeman drops his crest;
The fight is past, the sun has set, and all have sunk to rest—
Save one—who spurs his panting steed back from the conquering band;
And he who won the lady's glove—now claims the lady's hand.
'Tis won!—'tis won! that gallant knight is proudest in the land;
Oh, what can nerve the soldier's arm like hope of lady's hand!"

The song, of course, was received with enthusiasm, where so many soldiers were present; and as the exclamation of "*brave*," and "*charmant*," ran from lip to lip, Ned was curious to know what the meaning of the song was which pleased so much, and inquired of Ellen, who hastily gave him the point of the romance.

Ned was quite charmed with the idea, which inspired him with the notion of making it serve himself a good turn. He had promised not to speak of love to Ellen, but to "give her a hint" now lay so fair before him, he could not resist it. Bowing low beside her chair, he said in a voice, sweet with lovingness, "Do you know that I have got a *glove* of yours *already?*"

"A glove of mine?" said Ellen, in surprise, and blushing at the obvious implication.

"Yes," he said, and was going to tell her how he obtained it, when Lynch approached, and he could say no more. She was soon led again to dance, and Ned had no further opportunity of exchanging a word with her. Supper soon after was announced, and a bright last hour was spent; foaming pledges of champagne passed round the brilliant board; and, at last, the parting toast of success to the expedition was given. The glasses were drained, and flung backward over each man's head, that their brims, so honoured, might never bear a toast less precious. The ladies rose and waved their handkerchiefs, and tears of excitement glistened on bright cheeks that were dimpled with smiles of gratulation. The joyous party broke up, and soon the dawn appeared of that busy day which was to see the adventurers on the water. Port Launai was a scene of bustle at an early hour: a swift cutter lay ready to bear the larger portion of the Prince's adherents on board the *Elizabeth*, which lay outside the harbour of Belleisle, while a chosen few should bear the Prince company on board the *Doutelle*. Among these were Lynch and his daughter; and before Ned embarked on board the cutter, he had the mortification to see Kirwan hand Ellen into one of the *Doutelle's* boats, and seat himself beside her, followed by her father and Walsh, who sailed on board his own brig, to do the honours to the Prince.

Thus was he separated again from Ellen, while his rival had the advantage of bearing her company. Ned was ungallant enough, however, to make a very horrid speech to himself: "She'll be sea-sick," thought Ned, "and won't be in much humour for love-making—that's a comfort."

Oh, fie! Ned!

He, at the same time, felt a pride in being on board the ship which should protect the bark that bore his "ladye-love;" and when, with favouring breeze, the two vessels in company stood out to sea, there was no eye watched the beautiful *Doutelle* so eagerly as Ned's.

For three days they thus kept company, and were unobserved by the British cruisers; but on the fourth a ship, bearing the English flag, hove in sight, and bore down on them. Under present circumstances, to avoid a hostile collision was desirable; therefore every effort was made to get off without an action; but from the point the wind blew, the Englishman had the power to force them to battle; and though inferior, by ten guns, to the *Elizabeth*, determined to engage her, and the brig of 18 as well. The French man-of-war cleared for action, and took a position between the enemy and the *Doutelle*, whose men were at their quarters also, ready to assist her consort, and annoy the British ship, who now opened her guns, as she bore down gallantly against such odds. The Frenchman returned the fire with promptitude, and the shot soon began to tell on both sides; in ten minutes more the *Lion* and *Elizabeth* were hard at it, pouring broadsides into each other with murderous effect. And now it was that the *Doutelle* might have done good service; though her weight of metal could not have damaged much so large a ship as the *Lion*, yet her guns, well used, might have annoyed her considerably, while engaged with a vessel of superior force; but, shame to tell, she sheered off, and made all sail, in a disgraceful flight, leaving her consort to sustain the whole brunt of the action, which was fiercely maintained for six hours; after which, both ships were so damaged, that they mutually gave up the contest. The *Elizabeth* was in too shattered a condition to keep the sea   therefore she returned to her own shores—a fatal

mischance for Charles Edward, for she bore all the military
stores.   How drooped the hearts of his adherents on board
as they thought of the unprovided state in which their Prince
would reach Scotland, should he dare to continue his course;
but heavier drooped the heart of poor Ned, who saw himself
again separated from all that was dear to him on earth, without
the smallest chance of knowing where or when he might ever
see her more.

CHAPTER XXII.

WHILE Ned was grieving for his separation from Ellen,
Finch was regretting the loss of Ned. The gallant fight Ned
sustained in the merchantman enhanced his value in Finch's eyes;
and when the overwhelming fire of the corvette drove the privateer from the support of her prize, and forced her to seek in
flight her own safety and that of the treasure she had already
secured, Finch was moved to a deeper regret for Ned's mishap
in falling into the enemy's hands than his nature was often susceptible of entertaining; while in this mood, and while Ned's
gallantry was fresh in their memories, Finch proposed to the
crew, that, in the division of their booty, when they should
return, Ned and his gallant companions in the prize should not
be forgotten, but their shares allotted and set aside, in case they
should survive and return to England to claim them. This,
with that generosity which characterises seamen, was readily
agreed to, and the privateer having suffered considerably in the
action, it was considered advisable to return to port, to secure
what they had already got, and refit before they should seek
more, unless some small prize should fall in their way. Their
good luck prevailed in this respect; they picked up a little
French merchantman after a run of a couple of days, which
raised the spirits of the adventurers, and greatly consoled them
for the loss of the Spaniard. They should have the satisfaction,
too, of "lugging something after them" into port,—a great joy
to Jack,—and when, after much vigilance to keep clear of the
swarm of privateers, both French and Spanish, that hovered
about the mouth of the channel, they caught the first glimpse of

their own cliffs, where security awaited them, how the heart of every seaman bounded! There is no one has the same delight and pride in his native land as a sailor,—it beats that of a landsman hollow;—nor can we wonder at this if we consider the circumstances that engender the feeling:—Is it not most natural, that, after long and dangerous absences on the waste of waters, the sight of his own shores should touch the seaman's heart ?— that he should rejoice in the coming pleasure of embracing those who wept his departure and shall smile at his return :—

> " 'Tis sweet to know there is an eye to mark
>   Our coming—and grow brighter when we come :"—

and though the thought could not be so beautifully expressed by the rough tar, still is it felt as deeply. In anticipation he pictures the bright glance of joy with which his wife or his sweetheart will rush to his embrace,—he opens his arms on empty air, and folds them on his breast,—he fancies the loved one is within them, and in the delusion of the moment exclaims, "Bless her !"

Even such gentle emotions stirred some of the hearts among the dare devils on board the privateer ; and as they filled the cup to drink "Welcome home to old England," Tresham found a ready echo in every bosom as he raised his voice in praise of the " white cliffs." Never was song hailed with louder welcome, nor joined in with heartier chorus, than these careless rhymes which picture the vessel returning "from foreign," lowering her boats over the side, and bearing the islanders to their native strand :—

Our Own White Cliff.

L

THE boat that left yon vessel's side,
  Swift as the sea-bird's wing,
Doth skim across the sparkling tide
  Like an enchanted thing !
Enchantment, there, may bear a part,
  Her might is in each oar,
For love inspires each island heart
  That nears its native shore ;
And as they gaily speed along,
The breeze before them bears their song:
  "Oh, merrily row, boys—merrily !
    Bend the oar to the bounding skiff,
        Of every shore
        Wide ocean o'er,
    There's none like our own white cliff !

> Through sparkling foam they bound—they dart—
>   The much-loved shore they nigh—
> With deeper panting beats each heart,
>   More brightly beams each eye !
> As on the crowded strand they seek
>   Some well-known form to trace,
> In hopes to meet some blushing cheek,
>   Or wife, or child's embrace ;
> The oar the spray now faster flings,
> More gaily yet each seaman sings:
>   "Oh, merrily row, boys—merrily !
>   Bend the oar to the bounding skiff,
>   Of every shore,
>   Wide ocean o'er,
>   There's none like our own white cliff !"

Before sun-down the privateer had dropped her anchor in a native harbour, and the scene represented by the fancy of the bard was enacted in reality. The shore-ward boats—the plashing oars—the eager eyes and expectant friends—all, all were there ; and the sailors flushed with prize-money, and their friends willing to spend it with them, made the town boisterous with their festivity ; and

> Midnight shout and revelry,
> Tipsy dance and jollity,

ruled the "small hours" of the four-and-twenty.

Finch came on shore, but did not join in such rude mirth. He proceeded to London, preferring to spend any spare time he could afford, there ; and really anxious to tell the good-hearted landlady the luck of his adventure, and return the sum she had lent him. On reaching the capital he proceeded at once to his old haunt ; and the first object which attracted his attention in the bar, was Phaidrig-na-pib petting the landlady's little girl on his knee ; and the familiarity of the child with the blind piper indicated that he had something like a family position in the establishment.

Finch hailed the piper

"Arrah, is that yourself, then, so soon back?" exclaimed Phaidrig.

"You know me, then," said Finch.

"To be sure I do."

"What's my name, then ?"

"Sure I heard you spake more than once, Captain Finch ; and once is enough for me. Why is not the young master with you?" He meant Ned

"How do you know he is not with me?" enquired Finch, in surprise.

"Oh, by a way of my own :—where is he?"

"I am sorry to tell you he is a prisoner."

"Oh, my poor fellow!" exclaimed Phaidrig, in distress, clapping his hands :—"A prisoner!—Who cotch him?"

"The French."

"The Lord be praised!" said Phaidrig, as if his mind was greatly relieved.

Finch, in surprise, asked why he gave thanks for his friend being taken prisoner by the French.

"Bekaze I was afeerd it was the English had him," said Phaidrig.

"And would you rather he was prisoner in France than England?"

"Faix, I would; sure, he might meet with some friends there. *The Brigade* is there, and if all fails, can't he list?— Throth, that Brigade—my blessin' on it—is as good as a small estate to the wild young Irish gentry. Besides, if a sartin person I know is in France, and knew of the lad being there, he'd give him a lift, I go bail."

"I guess the person you mean."

"Throth, you don't :—how could you?"

Finch whispered a name, and a few secret words, in Phaidrig's ear, to which the piper replied by a long low whistle; and, turning up his face, and fixing his sightless eyes as though he would look at Finch, exclaimed in a suppressed tone, "Tare-an-ouns—how did you know that?"

"Oh, a way of my own—as you said to me just now."

"Come up, come up," said Phaidrig, rising and leading the way :—"Come up to the little room, and we'll talk—we mustn't spake in the bar here."

He led the way up-stairs, and Finch and he were soon seated in a snug little bed-room, where Phaidrig's hat and pipes, hanging against the wall, indicated the apartment to be his own.

"You seem quite at home, here," said Finch.

"Oh yes," answered Phaidrig; "the misthris is a kind cray-ther :—Afther you and Misther Ned went off in that hurry, she took pity on me, as a dark man, without friends, in a strange place, and offered me shelter till it plazed me to go back to Ireland; so the few days I was resting here I used to play the pipes below-stairs to rise the money for the journey, and, by dad, the people used to like it so well—(the pipes I mane)— that they came twice to hear me, and brought a frind with them, so that when I was thinking of making a start of it for Ireland,

Mrs. Banks, the darlin', comes to me, and, says she, '*Faydrig*,' says she, for the English can't get their tongues round the fine soft sound of our language at all, and does be always clippin' it, like the coin*—the crayther could no more get the fine mouthful of soft sound, than climb the moon—she couldn't say *Faw-dhrig* for the life of her; but she has a fine soft heart for all that; and, says she, 'I wish you'd continue playing in the house,' says she, 'for you are bringing custom to it, and, to make you as comfortable as I can, and not give you the throuble of groping your way along the streets,' says she, 'you shall have a room in the house, and share of the best that is going."

"I suppose the end of all this is," said Finch, "that you have married the widow?"

"Oh no, captain," said Phaidrig, laughing; "faix I niver tried to get at the soft side of her heart; and I'll tell you why—because it might get her into throuble—as you'll see, when I tell you all in a minute or two more—and I wouldn't hurt or harm her for the world, for she's as fine a hearted crayther as ever breathed the blessed air of life."

"That she is indeed," said Finch.

"Well, I staid when she asked me—and, somehow or other, there wor many genthry came about the house when they heerd an Irish piper was here, and among them, from time to time, I got the 'hard-word'† that there were warm hearts here in London for one that was 'over the water,'‡ and they used to ask me to private parties to play—'by the way;'§ but it was probing me deep, they wor, about the hopes of the 'blackbird' in the bushes in ould Ireland: and I have seen more than one noble lord about the matther."

"*More*, I have no doubt," said Finch, with emphasis.

"What do you mane?" inquired the piper.

"Put a *Barry* to that," was the answer.

"Wow, wow!" ejaculated Phaidrig; "I see you know more than I thought. Well, my Lord Barrymore hears from Scotland regular; and we are towld that we may be expectin' somethin' there afore long."

"I have no doubt of it," said Finch.

"Ah then, now, captain," said Phaidrig, "don't be angry if I ask you one question"——

"Not if you ask me fifty," said Finch.

---

* Coin-clipping was a common offence at the period.
† Secret intelligence, or signal.
‡ The well-known phrase indicating the Stuart.
§ A pretence.

"How comes it that, being in with our side, you go on the sea and attack the French and Spaniards, that would help us?"

"A fair question, Phaidrig; and I'll give as fair an answer: When I was engaged in the 'free-trade,'* as we call it, I had occasional communications with adherents of 'Somebody,' and was always willing to give a cast across the water to gentlemen in d'stress; and I don't say but I would as soon see the man who ' sits in Charley's chair' out of it; for, to be candid, I care very little for either of them; but as, in those great affairs, poor men, like me, seldom come in for anything but blows, and the profits are only for the few and the rich, I don't see any harm in making my own fortune in my own way, and feathering my nest while I may; and while the war is a-foot, and English privateers *will* go out and seize French ships, I don't see why I shouldn't pick up my crumbs as well as others, for whichever side is uppermost won't care a curse for me when peace is made: therefore, though I would not betray any man engaged in this political game—and perhaps go as far as to wish them well— neither will I join in it, but get on as fast as I can in lining my pocket with French and Spanish prize-money—I don't care which."

"But suppose you wor made a captain of a man-of-war, where you would have prize-money all the same, and honour and glory into the bargain?"——

"But where's the man-of-war, Phaidrig?"

"Sure, we'll take them!" said the piper.

"Easier said than done, Phaidrig."

"I wish you'd talk to Lord Barrymore—maybe it's an admiral you'd be?"

Finch laughed at the sanguine expectation of the Irish piper.

"You might as well have a word with him—I'm going there to-night."

Finch declined, and expressed his wonder that Phaidrig should have anything to do with such desperate affairs, more particularly under the privation of sight, which rendered him so helpless in case accident should throw him into the hands of his enemies.

"I can't help it," said Phaidrig; "though I have no eyes, I have a heart all the same, and it beats for the rightful king—and whenever the row begins, I must be in it."

"You don't mean to say you'll join the fighting parties?"

* In one of the early chapters of this work, the term "free trade" was objected to by a critic, as an anachronism; but it is frequently found in the writings of the time.

"To be sure I will. Won't him I love best in the world be there—the bowld Lynch, I mane?—and won't I folly him to the death?—and one comfort is, that though I am blind, and worse off than others in that regard, I'm not worse off in another, and that is—I can die but once."

"But you run greater risk; for should danger hem you in you could not escape."

"That would be an advantage; for when I could not see to run I'd stand; and don't you think many would stand with me? —for who, with a heart in him, would desert the poor blind man in the front of the fight?—and it's there I'll be (plaze God!) lilting away for them, rousing the blood in them!—Hurroo!"

He waved his hand wildly above his head as he spoke, and Finch looked in admiration upon the heroic blind man, who, unable to restrain his enthusiasm, jumped up, hastily reached down his pipes from the peg where they hung, and began playing a wild battle tune. The noise of the music in the house attracted attention, and in two or three minutes the door was opened, and Mrs. Banks made her appearance; her joy and surprise were great at the sight of Finch, who, as usual, saluted her heartily; and Phaidrig, hearing the smack, cried out—

"Ah, Captain, you divil, you're at it again."

"Don't object, Phaidrig—she's not yours yet," said Finch, who saw in the heightened colour his words called up to the cheeks of Mrs. Banks, that his suspicions of the favour in which Phaidrig was held, were not unfounded.

CHAPTER XXIII.

Not many days after Finch's arrival in London, rumour, with her thousand tongues, began to whisper alarm to the timid, and hope to the disaffected. Rambling reports reached the capital of a descent upon Scotland, and at last it was beyond doubt that Charles Edward was landed. It was true, the adventurous prince had dared to do this with seven devoted men, trusting to the well-known attachment of the Highlanders to his cause for further support; but the horror-mongers of London had strengthened him with a French army of ten thousand men, and the old women were in hourly dread of the capital being sacked by the wild Highlanders. The town was in a ferment. The proclamation, warning the papists not to come within ten miles of London, was posted up afresh in all the public places—the guards were doubled—the corporations met and voted addresses, assuring the king of the attachment and unshaken loyalty of his good city of London, though these addresses were not passed without opposition, some being found stout enough to dispute that England had no right to prefer the existing government to any other, unless they would promise a redress of grievances, curtailment of expenses, and consequent reduction of taxes rendered necessary by the king's passion for foreign wars, and desire to aggrandise his Hanoverian subjects at England's expense—"Where is he now, for instance?" exclaimed Alderman Heathcote, in the common council. "He is at Hanover, this moment, which he seems to think more of than his goodly kingdom of England, invaded during his absence. Why is he not on the spot to guard his throne and people?"

"As for his people," exclaimed a second, "he does not concern himself much about them—however danger to his throne may alarm him."

"Let him look to it, or he may lose it," said Alderman Heathcote.

"Order! order!" was loudly exclaimed by the loyalists.

"Take down his words!" cried a hanger on of the court party.

"Do!" cried the Alderman—"Few words uttered here are

worth taking down; they make a pleasant variety. I am
an Englishman, and love my liberties; and I do not see any difference in being under the evil dominion of a Guelph or a Stuart.
We are taxed for the benefit of foreigners—the interests of
England are sacrificed to the interests of Hanover. Are the
many to be sacrificed for the few? The navy is going to ruin,
though the only force we can depend on. Where is our army?
Abroad, to fight the battles of strangers; our petted army is reduced, year after year, in numbers, in wasteful, useless, and
costly campaigns. Dettingen and Fontenoi are wet with English
blood; the one a worthless victory, the other a disastrous defeat.
On whom are we to depend for the safety of our own shores?
On Dutch and Hanoverians? In the good old days of England's glory, Englishmen had hands to defend their own heads,
and needed not the aid of foreigners. Who decided the battle
against us at Fontenoi? The Irish Brigade. Why should we
deprive ourselves of the natural aid of such brave brotherhood?"

"They are papists, and not to be trusted," said Finch's friend,
the liberal Mr. Spiggles.

"But the government refuses to trust even the Irish Protestants," returned the Alderman.

"No, no!" cried the court party.

"I repeat it," cried Heathcote. "The Earl of Kildare offered
to raise a regiment, *at his own expense*, to support the government,
and was told the king did not need his services; * while English
lords who offer and are allowed to raise regiments, demand also
that they shall be put on the government establishment, like the
rest of the army—there's a contrast for you! Our government
refuses the loyal Irish earl's disinterested offer, while it accepts
the bargain-and-sale loyalty of your English whig lords. Not
one of them has offered to raise a regiment *gratis*."

"The Archbishop of York," replied one of the court party,
"has organised a body of armed men without asking government
money."

"Yes," said Heathcote, "and put himself at their head."

Loud cries of "Bravo!" and "Hear, hear!" resounded in the
hall.

"Yes," said Heathcote, "you cry, Bravo! when your own
prelate puts himself at the head of a warlike movement; but how
often have I heard my Protestant brethren blame a Romish
prelate for the same act! Why do you praise the act in one
churchman that you blame in another? Because you rave under
the influence of a popish fever."

* Pict. Hist. Eng.

Thus spoke the independent alderman, and many were of his opinion, though the pressing emergency of the times prevented their outspeaking; and the clamour of the court party carried the address with very big words. But it is easy to be courageous and talk boldly on the side of "the powers that be."

With all this show, however, of the court party, they were in truth, uneasy at the signs of the times—there was an apparent apathy in those who did not oppose them, as if they did not much care which side won. It was said at the time by one whose words were worthy of noting, "We wait to know to which of the lion's paws we are to fall." Another, a member of the administration, writes, "We are for the first comer;" and asserts that five thousand regular troops would then have decided the affair without a battle, so unprepared was the government, and so disaffected the people. These apprehensions, therefore, produced extraordinary measures. The rich merchants subscribed a sum of 250,000l. for the support of additional troops; and the more rich, who always dread political changes, were, in self-defence, obliged to enter into a further subscription for the support of the Bank of England, for public credit was shaken, and a run on the bank had already begun. Great vigilance was exercised for the security of the city; guards were everywhere doubled; the Tower was watched with a caution almost ridiculous; the city called out the train-bands, and watch and ward was kept night and day; the city gates were shut at ten o'clock at night, and not re-opened again until six in the morning. The proprietors of public places of entertainment, such as jelly-houses,* taverns, and the like, were ordered to beware what persons they harboured, and were restricted in their hours; and all suspicious-looking persons were taken up in the street, without anything more than their looks against them. It was at this period of distrust and excitement, that, one night, some time after Mrs. Banks had closed her house, a cautious tap was heard at the door, which at such a time she dreaded to open, for spies were about, endeavouring to entrap the unwary into opening their doors by some specious story, and then giving them up for a fine to the authorities, which fine was pocketed by the informer. Mrs. Banks would not open the door, yet still the knock was repeated; and if caution and solicitation were ever expressed in such a mode, the present tapping at the door was a case in point. To Phaidrig's fine ear it pleaded so powerfully, that he

---

* Favourite places of resort at the time.

begged to be allowed to go to the door and endeavour to find out who sought admittance.

"Don't be afeerd—I'll make no mistake," said the piper; "none but a friend shall get in."

He went to the door and addressed a word to the person outside, who answered.—The first word of response was enough for Phaidrig—the bolt was drawn, the door hastily opened, a person admitted, and the door as quickly shut. Finch, who was in a back parlour with Mrs. Banks, heard the voice of Phaidrig in great delight in the dark hall, through which he led the belated guest to the apartment, and both landlady and Finch were startled with astonishment when, in the person of the new comer, they beheld Ned. With what wondering and hearty welcome did they receive the man who was supposed to be a prisoner in France, who absolutely reeled under the sudden rush of questions which assailed him, as to the manner of his escape. When "one at a time" was content to be answered, he replied that the story was too long and intricate to be entered into at that moment, and that he would reserve for Finch's ear on the morrow the entire account of his adventures in France. For the present, they must be content to know that, obtaining his liberty, he trusted to a fishing-boat for the means of crossing the channel; that, under cover of night, he had landed unobserved and had made his way up to London without difficulty, and did not know, until reaching the city, the risks a stranger ran after nightfall of becoming the prey of the watch, and that he had had a narrow escape of being picked up by these worthies, into whose hands he must have fallen, but for the timely opening of the door. Mrs. Banks, like a "sensible woman," saw, after some time, she was one too many, so, leaving plenty of creature-comforts for their benefit, she took her leave, and left the three men to discuss among themselves that which her natural quickness told her they did not choose her to be a party to. As soon as she retired, Ned confided to his companions the part he had undertaken as regarded the Pretender, and declared his intention of proceeding immediately to Scotland. Phaidrig recommended him to communicate with certain influential persons in London he could mention, before he started, as he would be all the welcomer at head quarters for being the bearer of confidential intelligence. Finch coincided in this opinion, and Ned agreed to wait for an interview with the Lords Barrymore and Bolingbroke, which Phaidrig promised him the day following. They continued to discuss the exciting topics of that momentous time with an energy and interest sharpened by the sense of personal danger which attended those who had determined to engage in the struggle, and they did not separate until the pale dawn, breaking through the chinks of the window-shutters, told them how heedless they had been of the passing hours.

At all times the light of returning day seems to look reproachfully on those who have passed in watching, the hours which Nature intended for rest; and the pure dawn shames the dull glare of the far-spent candle which burns near the socket, itself worn out by over-taxed employment; but when such hours have been spent in secret and dangerous conclave, the vigil keeper starts at the dawn with something like a sense of detection, and hurries to the bed which the fever of excitement robs of its accustomed repose.

Thus felt Finch and Edward, who each took a candle and withdrew to their chambers; while Phaidrig, unconcerned, found his way to his pallet, unchided by the light he had never enjoyed. The blind man, for once, was blessed in his darkness.

The next day, an unreserved communication was made by Ned to Finch of the entire of his adventures since they parted, and the romantic meeting of the uncle and nephew startled the skipper not a little; though, as Ned guessed, he laughed heartily at the notion of a man committing a spoliation of himself, as our hero had done, and, so far from being angry at the successful trick of the concealed gold, was delighted that so much had been got "out of the fire," and told Ned of the additional sum he would have in his share of the plunder the privateer secured.

"But the old gentleman, your uncle," said Finch—"what has become of him?"

Ned told his friend that it would have been too great a risk for the old man to run, to dare the chance of a debarkation from a French fishing-boat on the English shore; that, therefore, he had proceeded to Spain, where he hoped, in families of some of his mercantile correspondents, to find friends, which he could not expect in France, where he was an utter stranger, and whose language he could not speak; and that it was agreed, on their parting, should Prince Charles be successful, and a consequent peace with Spain ensue, the old man should return to Ireland; while, in case of a reverse, Ned should seek an asylum in Spain.

After being engaged in the exchange of this mutual confidence for some time, they were interrupted by the entrance of Phaidrig, who came to conduct Edward to the interview he promised him; whereupon the friends parted for the present, and agreed to meet again in the evening, for Finch, as Ned had avowed his determination to set out for the North the next day, pledged him to join in one merry bout before their parting.

How one in Phaidrig's station could obtain the confidence of men of rank, and be so trusted in dangerous affairs, may seem, at first, startling; but let it be remembered that the old saying, "Distress makes us acquainted with strange bedfellows," peculiarly applies to all associations of a revolutionary character. In such movements, the highest may have their most confidential agents amongst the lowest, as under that unflattering denomination we generally class the poor, though, to their honour be it spoken, experience proves that the betrayal of companions in such dangerous enterprises has rarely been chargeable to them, though their betters (so called) have not been above temptation. Ned sought not to know the sources of Phaidrig's influence, but certain it was, that confidence was not only reposed in him, but that his word was taken for the faith of another; for after driving a few miles to a house in the neighbourhood of the Thames, Edward, on the piper's introduction, was admitted to an audience with the Lords Bolingbroke and Barrymore, and many communications of great trust and importance were made between them touching the interest of the Stuart cause. Edward was urged to speed on his northern journey, and the most earnest desire expressed for the immediate descent of the Prince and his adherents upon London, as, in the present unprepared state of the Government, with a scanty exchequer, a shaken public credit, a want of troops, and a wide-spread disaffection, the triumph of their progress would be certain. In the course of the conference, which was long, extensive promises of aid were advanced, and numerous names and places, and plans of co-operation were read to be communicated to the Prince.

Ned suggested that when so much had to be communicated it were best to commit all to writing; but the noblemen started the objection of papers being dangerous instruments in the hands of enemies, in case the bearer of them should be arrested. Phaidrig here smoothed all difficulties, by assuring them that his memory was "as good as writing any day," and that anything repeated twice in his hearing would be retained with accuracy.

He gave evidence of this on the spot, by repeating, word for word, the contents of a document read to him, and having proved himself so unfailing a register, the desired communications were confided to the tenacity of the piper's recollection.

"It is all here now," said Phaidrig, raising his hand to his forehead—"here, in my brain; and search-warrants wouldn't find it, though the seekers should blow out the brains that hold it."

"I don't think killing men is the best way to make them speak," said Lord Bolingbroke, smiling, as he noticed the bull Phaidrig had made.

"Oh, my lord, remember I'm a musicianer, and most of *them* make no noise till they're dead "

"Well answered, Phaidrig," said Lord Barrymore; "and then their strains live in glory."

"Faix, then," returned Phaidrig, "that's more than them that made the strains ever did, for you know, my lord, what "piper's pay' is—'more kicks than halfpence.' "

After a few more words of good-humoured raillery with Phaidrig, he and Ned were dismissed with a parting injunction to make all haste to Scotland, and our hero almost wished he had not promised to spend the evening with Finch, for, though the day was far spent, still some miles might have been accomplished before night. Phaidrig comforted him, however, with that good old Celtic assurance which is made to reconcile so many Irish calamities, "maybe 'tis all for the best," and held out the prospect of an early start on the morrow, and a long day's journey.

On returning to town, Ned found Finch awaiting him at the tavern, and, having deposited Phaidrig safely at home, the two friends sallied forth to spend a jolly evening as they agreed. They first sauntered into one of the principal coffee-houses, the resort of the bloods and wits of the day, expecting to hear something piquant on the existing state of affairs; but there was little of a political nature handled; it seemed as if men were indifferent about Hanoverian interests, and of course, no word implying favour to the other party would be uttered in a promiscuous company. The coffee-house not proving so attractive as they hoped, Finch proposed a visit to Vauxhall, and they strolled down to the river's side, where they engaged a boat. As they stepped aboard, the waterman, touching his hat, hoped they would not object to "the young woman," pointing as he spoke to a girl who was sitting in the bow, indicating grief by her attitude, and whose eyes betrayed recent tears. Having pushed from the wharf, and being fairly engaged in pulling, the waterman commenced explaining the cause of the woman's presence.

"She's my sister, you see, your honours, and in trouble because her husband is a sojer, and is marched away to-day to Scotland to join the army, and she's in such grief, that I didn't like leaving her at home alone for fear she'd make away with hersel'."

"Oh, don't 'e, Tom, don't 'e," said the girl, in an under tone.

"Why, you said you would, you know," answered Tom over his shoulder. "Well, your honours, as I was telling of ye, I thought it better to bring her out with me here to keep her company; for you see she's not long married—there's where it is, and is a fretting more nor reasonable for a raff of a sojer, 'cause she's not tired of him yet."

"Now don't 'e, Tom," said the girl again.

"Why you know it's true, and it was agin my will that you ever had un, and you can't say no to that. But it's nat'ral, as your honours know, at the same time, she'd be sorry."

"Of course," said Ned.—"Have many soldiers marched?"

"Lor, no, sir, there's where it is, just a handful, and they've no chance, and they say them Highlanders be mortal vicious. I hear they eat their enemies sometimes."

"Ah, don't 'e, Tom!" cried the girl piteously.

"Why, how can I help if they do?" said the strangely good-natured brother; "besides, if they do kill un, you know my partner Dick will have 'e, and well for 'e if it was so before; a waterman's better than sojer."

"S'help me God, Tom!" exclaimed the girl, somewhat roused, "I'll throw myself out o' boat and drown, if 'e don't ha' done."

"Better not!" said Tom, "water's deep here, and I can't stop t' save you, for the ge'men's in a hurry."

"Who commands the troops?" said Ned.

"Oh, some o' them outlandish chaps; we ha' nothing but outlandish chaps now in all good places. It's well for watermen theirs is hard work, or I s'pose we'd be druv off the river."

"But of course you wish the King's cause well?" said Finch.

"To be sure I do, sir, as in duty bound : not that it makes any difference to the likes o' me, for whoever is uppermost, they'll want boats on the river, and there won't be a tide more or less in the Thames, and so I say, on all such matters, it's no affair o' mine, but God's above all, and them's my principles, sir."

"Excellent principles," cried Finch; "and becoming a Christian."

"Oh, I am a Christian," said the waterman, "that I am, and wouldn't be nothing else. I have no chalks up agin me at the tap; no, no! and loves my fellow creatures—all, 'cept the Hanoverians—and as they are so plenty in all other places in England, I do wish, I will say, that some o' them as couldn't swim, were in the middle of the Thames, without a boat under them, and a strong ebb tide a-running."

"You think that would be good for the country?" said Finch.

"Sure of it," said the waterman; "only the river would be dirtier with them."

As they rowed up towards Vauxhall they found in the course of their chat with the waterman, that not only he was no lover of "the Hanoverians," but gathered from his conversation that there was no great affection for them throughout his class; and this, together with learning the popular impression, that there were not sufficient troops for defence, was good intelligence for Ned to have picked up, and, in thankfulness for the same, when they arrived at their destination, he gave an extra sixpence to Tom.

The gardens were not as gay as usual—not for the want of the ordinary routine of entertainments; these went on as ever; but there seemed wanting that air of careless cheerfulness which characterises such public places. The fact is, the body politic, like the human body, is not fit for enjoyment when something not easy of digestion lies in the system, and impending events of an important and dangerous nature, however much people may affect to be unconcerned about them, partake of this character, and the public mind is not attuned to mirth. The bold may bluster, and the silly vent the empty laugh, but even with them, amidst the swagger of the one, and the folly of the other, the spirit of the momentous hour will sometimes assert her sway, and bring all within her power.

Thus it was at Vauxhall; the rope-dancer did not bound an inch lower than usual, the singers were as great favourites as ever, and sung as favourite songs; the fire-works burnt as brightly, and people paid as much for invisible slices of ham as usual; but still there was an indescribable dulness about it, which so affected Finch and Ned, that they left it long before the accustomed time. Engaging a hackney coach, they were driven to the suburbs of the town, and there they alighted to pursue the remainder of their way on foot. As they were passing through a narrow and ill-lighted street, they encountered a person just under the rays of one of the few lamps, and the imperfect light sufficiently revealed to Finch the person of Spiggles, shambling along as fast as he could, but Finch intercepted him, and, tempted by the opportunity of giving Spiggles a fright, he laid his hand on his shoulder, and said he was delighted at the pleasure of the meeting. Spiggles trembled from head to foot, and begged to be released, pleading his desire for haste, and the lateness of the hour.

"Tut, tut, man," exclaimed Finch. "Old friends must not part so; I want a few words with you, and you *must* stop;" and he jammed him against the wall at the words, while the wretched miser shuddered, fear depriving him of the power of calling for the watch, which he would have done if he could. Finch upbraided him with his want of gratitude, and reminded him of his refusal to lend him a small sum.

Spiggles, dreading violence, protested he had no money about him.

14

"Miserable niggard!" cried Finch, "do you think I want to rob you? No, no, others will save me that trouble, for I *do* rejoice to think how you will be plundered by the Highlanders when the city is sacked, which it will be in a day or two. The clans are close upon you. I rejoice how you will be fleeced—how your ill-gotten gold will be rummaged." Spiggles groaned at the thought, and trembled while Finch ordered Ned to take the old sinner under the other arm, and walk him along with them. Spiggles would have refused, but was unable, and borne by Finch on one side, and Ned on the other, he shambled on between them, while continued volleys of threats, plunder, Highlanders, and throat-cutting were poured into his ears on both sides. This jumble of horrors, which the two friends made as terrible as they could for the benefit of Spiggles, being spoken rather loudly to increase the effect, was overheard by a party of the watch which chanced to be unseen in a dark entrance; the party passed, and the guardians of the night followed stealthily, and hearing what they believed to be "flat treason," they fell suddenly on the trio, and having secured them, took them off to the round-house.

They were charged before the constable of the night with uttering of treasonable language, and as persons of evil intent, and were ordered to be locked up for the night. Spiggles protested that he was a peaceful and worshipful man, a man of substance and good repute in the city, and that a round-house was no place for him to spend the night with rogues and vagabonds.

"Rogues and vagabonds, indeed!" exclaimed a virago, in a fury, who had been just committed, but not yet locked up. She rushed at Spiggles and boxed his ears, calling him all sorts of foul names, and belabouring him, until she was laid hold of by the constables, and dragged away. Finch uttered not a word in defence, and Ned, by his advice, also maintained silence. To all the appeals of Spiggles, who said the gentlemen in whose company he was walking could explain it all, Finch only shook his head, throwing doubt more and more on the miser, whose ill-favoured aspect, further disfigured by fear, was anything but prepossessing.

Before being locked up, the parties were secretly informed by a watchman, that a message could be carried to their friends, if they were willing to pay for it. On inquiring the price, half-a-guinea was named, which Finch readily gave, and sent to Mrs. Banks, requesting her presence early in the morning. Spiggles of course refused to pay so much, and was content to wait till the magistrate should order a messenger to go for any person to whom it might be necessary to refer. This saving of half-a-guinea, by depriving him of evidence at the moment of need, laid him open to loss, through a device of the skipper's.

As for passing a night in durance, Finch thought nothing about it, as it was not the first time; nor would Ned, but for the delay it occasioned. Finch whispered him not to make himself uneasy, as he would manage their speedy liberation, and hoped to make Spiggles pay dearly for the frolic; and, afterwards, in some private words with the miser, he threatened, that if in his defence, he cast the smallest blame on him for the affair over-night, he would make certain disclosures respecting him that would cost him dearly. Spiggles, knowing he was in Finch's power, and supposing him to be in desperate circumstances, promised to cast no imputation on him, and the skipper then insisted, in assurance of his good intentions, he must permit him to make their common defence in the morning, and that he would get them out of it bravely. Spiggles was forced to consent to these conditions, and then groped his way to a corner. The prisoners were all huddled together in utter darkness; those who could find a seat, sitting, others stretched on the floor, whose curses were evoked as some lively gentleman danced over them. Some were moaning and crying, while others were laughing at the jokes cracked on the misfortunes of their fellow-prisoners. Spiggles had sunk into a melancholy trance, when he was roused by a shrill female voice exclaiming near him, " I wish I could clap my claw on the old rascal, that said rogues and vagabonds. Come out if you're a man!" shouted the virago, " and I'll fight you in the dark for a dollar!"

Spiggles sneaked as far away as he could, and when the morning peeped into the cell, he shrunk behind Finch for concealment and protection.

Mrs. Banks, as soon as admittance could be obtained, was in attendance to render Finch what assistance he needed. He merely desired her to go to the ship-agent who transacted the affairs of the privateer in London, and request his attendance before Sir Thomas de Veil. This was done; and when Finch, Ned, and Spiggles, were charged, and called on for their defence, the skipper became spokesman.

He admitted that they had been speaking in the street of an attack on London, and of Highlanders, and cutting throats, but that it was only in dread of it they spoke, not in hope.

Here the watch deposed that they spoke as if with knowledge of the movements of the rebels.

" Ha! ha!" said Sir Thomas, " knowledge?—what say you to that?"

" Please your worship, such knowledge as we all have from report, no more."

"Now, your worship," said Finch, "does it not stand to reason that persons to be suspected would be the last to speak loud, but would, on the contrary, be secret and silent? Speak loud, indeed! Well might this worthy and wealthy gentleman speak loud in the fear of his riches being swept away by these wild Highlanders; and the best proof your worship can have of his loyalty is, that he was going to Garraway's yesterday to subscribe to the merchants' fund for raising troops, but was prevented by urgent business."

"It is true, so help me God!" said Spiggles.

"But as he intends doing it to day," continued Finch, "and it would be troublesome to send to the city to obtain proof of his respectability, the shortest way to evince his loyalty is to hand your worship his cheque for two hundred pounds, to be forwarded to Garraway's."

The miser gasped, as if he would have spoken, but Finch, fixing his eye on him with a meaning he could not mistake, said, "Do you wish I should say any more?"

Spiggles quailed under the threatening glance; and supplied by Sir Thomas at once with pen, ink, and paper, he wrote the cheque with an agony little short of the bitterness of death.

"As for myself and my young friend here, so far from being favourers of the Pretender, we have been privateering against the ships of France and Spain, and that does not look like disloyalty."

The ship-agent came forward in proof of his words; Finch and Ned were at once discharged, and left the office in company with Spiggles, who looked more dead than alive at the loss of his money.

"A word in your ear," said Finch, taking the miser under his arm, and walking apart with him—"Now I have had a sweet bit of revenge on you for your cold-hearted ingratitude to me; I would not wring money out of you for my own purposes—I would scorn it,—but as you were base enough to refuse me a loan, which should all have been returned, I rejoice in having plucked you of a couple of hundreds, which you will never see again; and in case you ever meet in the course of your worthless life another servant as useful and faithful as I have been, use him better than you did me, and remember Finch and the two hundred. And now farewell—I've done with you—I wish you a good appetite for your breakfast;—don't eat eggs, nor fried ham;—don't be extravagant, try and make up in saving the loss of this morning—perhaps your high character for loyalty may throw something in your way—eh, skinflint?—but I think your loyalty is the dearest bargain you have been let in for, for some time. Good bye,—remember Finch and the round-house!"

"But they spoke fierce and loud, your worship," interposed the watch, "like suspicious persons."

So saying, he turned the old wretch adrift, and went off in an opposite direction with Ned and the agent, while the steps of Spiggles were tracked by a secret agent of the police, despatched after him by Sir Thomas de Veil, that he might be traced in case the cheque should turn out a hoax. But the document was proved true in another hour, and the money of Spiggles was converted to public uses—the first of his that ever found its way into so good a channel.

Through Finch's influence, the agent advanced Ned a hundred guineas on account of his prize-money, and after a hasty breakfast and a hearty farewell to the skipper, he started on his journey, accompanied by Phaidrig, who did not leave the tavern without some applications of the corner of Mrs. Bank's apron to her eye.

CHAPTER XXIV.

WHEN the young Pretender embarked in the daring enterprise of regaining the throne of his fathers by force of arms, one of the elements of success on which he counted was an immediate rising in Ireland so soon as it should be known his banner was unfurled in Scotland. But it so happened, that the one particular year he selected was the only one for many before or after in which Ireland would not have joined in the rebellion.

The cause of this absence of disaffection in Ireland, while there was anything but a well-grounded loyalty in England and downright revolt in Scotland, was attributable to one man—that man was Philip Stanhope, Earl of Chesterfield, chiefly known in England for his trifling letters to his son, but remembered in Ireland by all readers of her history as the most enlightened, benevolent, and successful of her viceroys. On assuming the reins of government in that oppressed and distracted country, he declared that he would be influenced by no dictation of minor personages *there*, but would "judge and govern himself." *

* Liber Muncrum Publicorum Hiberniæ. Report of Rowley Lascelles.

Acting firmly on this resolution, he discarded the counsels of
severity and injustice under which the great mass of the Roman
Catholic people of Ireland had been suffering, he administered
the laws in the spirit of justice, and he won the confidence of the
nation,—a confidence not only won but maintained during a
period of peculiar peril to the British crown.   He is thus spoken
of by an historian not particularly favourable to popular Irish
interests.*   "The short administration of Philip Stanhope, Earl
of Chesterfield, was a kind of phenomenon in Irish history.
This highly accomplished, liberal, and judicious nobleman,
to whose character such injustice accrues from the posthumous
publication of his letters, intended for a peculiar purpose,
by no means for general advice, was appointed at a dangerous
juncture, when in the midst of an unsuccessful war against
France and Spain, an alarming rebellion had been raised in
Scotland in favour of Charles Edward Stuart, son of the
Pretender.   Vested with ample powers, this Viceroy acted from
his own judgment, uninfluenced by the counsels of those who,
to prevent an imaginary, might have excited a real rebellion by
violent measures against Catholics, the bulk of the nation.   He
discountenanced all party distinctions."   In another history he is
spoken of as governing Ireland "with rare ability, and a most
rare liberality."†

After all, the successful government of Ireland at this
momentous period is less attributable to ability, than to a pure
spirit of justice,—a gift much rarer in statesmen than talent.
Actuated by this spirit, he received no tale on the *ipse dixit* of
the tale-bearer—he would have proof.   Alarmists were peculiarly odious to him; he sometimes got rid of them playfully, as
in one case when a person of importance assured him the " Papists
were dangerous," he replied, he never had seen but one, and that
was Miss ——, a particularly lovely woman.

This lady, as well as many other Catholics, won by Lord
Chesterfield's liberal policy, flocked to the Castle and graced the
viceregal court with an accession of charms to which it had long
been a stranger.   The particular beauty in question was so
delighted by Lord Chesterfield's noble conduct, that on some
public occasion, to mark how thoroughly she could overcome
political prejudice, she wore a breast-knot of orange-ribbon; the
earl, pleased at the incident, requested St. Leger (afterwards
Lord Doneraile), celebrated for his wit, to say something hand-

* Hist. Irel.   Rev. James Gordon, Rector of Killegny, in the diocese of
Ferns, and of Cannaway, in the diocese of Cork.
† Pict. Hist. Eng.

some to her on the occasion, whereupon St. Leger composed the following, not generally known, impromptu :—

> "Say, little Tory, why this jest,
> Of wearing orange on thy breast,
> Since the same breast, uncovered, shows
> The whiteness of the rebel rose?"

An alarmist one day asked him, in a very mysterious manner, if he knew that his state-coachman went to mass: "I don't care," replied the earl, "so long as he don't drive *me* there."

But when the landing of the Pretender, and the raising of his standard in Scotland, were announced, the alarmists became bolder, and besieged the liberal Lord-Lieutenant with tales of terror; he had no peace of his life; he was continually baited with buggaboos fabricated in the heated imaginations of partisans, whom he was unwilling to dismiss unheard, and whose cure he hoped to effect by a courageous incredulity.

The rumour of a popish plot soon brought down upon him one alarmist after another, who all were much discomfited at the coolness with which he received their reports. The first, one morning, was Alderman Watson, who arrived while his Excellency was at breakfast, and, sending in his name with an importunate assurance that he had intelligence to communicate which was of the deepest interest to the state, was immediately admitted.

There was a striking contrast between the ease of the accomplished Lord Chesterfield and the fussy embarrassment of the Alderman. The cool and accomplished courtier almost felt hot to look on the flushed face of the civic dignitary, who was mopping it with a snuffy pocket handkerchief while he assured the Lord-Lieutenant he had come in a great hurry.

"That is manifest, Mister Alderman," returned my lord; "and may I ask the cause of all this hurry?"

"I have it, your Excellency, on undoubted authority—"

"I beg your pardon, Mister Alderman," returned Chesterfield, smiling; "but I cannot help telling you that all the wild reports I hear are universally accompanied with the same assurance."

"On undoubted authority, your Excellency.—I have it from the fountain-head—"

"Whose head, do you say?"

"The fountain-head, my lord," said the Alderman, betraying some displeasure.

"Oh—I beg your pardon," said the Viceroy, with provoking suavity; "pray proceed."

"I came to tell your Excellency that there is a plot—a popish plot—"

Here he was interrupted by the sudden entrance of Mr. Gardner, the vice-treasurer, who, in great perturbation, and scarcely observing the common courtesies of salutation in his hurry, exclaimed, "My lord, the Papists of Connaught are to rise this day!"

"That's the very plot I came to tell you, my lord," said the Alderman; "remember, I came first to give the alarm."

To this intended "alarm" of the Alderman, Lord Chesterfield's calmness was intensely provoking.—Taking his watch carelessly from his pocket, he replied, "It is nine o'clock, and certainly time for them to rise." *

"I see, my lord, you make little of my information," said Gardner.

"My good Sir," said Chesterfield, "I cannot make it less than it comes from your own mouth. You offer a most startling piece of rumour, without any name, place, or time, direct fact or corroborative evidence of any sort,—you make a naked assertion—assuring me it is on 'undoubted authority,' and from the 'fountain-head.'—Would to heaven these feverish loyalists had heads like the fountains—cooler and clearer."

"Your Excellency must allow me to say, that loyal men might expect to meet more encouragement in the head of the government," said the Alderman.

"That is a very smart saying of yours, indeed, Mister Alderman; but you will allow me to say that you corporation gentlemen seem to have a very strange notion about loyalty. You are devoted to government as long as government does all you wish, and believes all you say, and will back you through thick and thin; but the moment government entertains a view superior to that—ventures to look beyond the bigoted boundaries to which your illiberality confines you, your loyalty is of a very doubtful character; for, in short, the self-made charter of your loyalty is simply this—'as long as the government lets us do what we like, we will support the government.'"

The Alderman protested he was the most loyal man in the world.

"I am so wearied with these eternal tales of plots and risings," continued Lord Chesterfield, "that I am in the condition of the shepherd in the fable, to whom the idle boy called 'wolf' so often, that I know not when to believe the cry; therefore I am obliged to depend on my own sources of information

---

* Liber Munerum Publicorum Hiberniæ   Report of Rowley Lascelles.

—and allow me to assure you I have them, Mister Alderman, and can depend upon them ; and have also the means of repressing any rebellious movement that may be attempted, but of which I have not, at this moment, the slightest apprehension."

"May divine Providence grant," said the Alderman, piously, "that your Excellency's confidence in the present deceptive calm be not ill-placed; for what should we do in case of a rising at this moment, when your Excellency has sent away so much of the army to reinforce his Majesty in Scotland?"*

"I have as much military force as shall be wanted while *I* am here," said Lord Chesterfield, smiling.

"It is fortunate, my lord, that the city has done its duty in furnishing forth the militia. And further, my lord, we have offered a reward of six thousand pounds for the head either of the Pretender or any of his sons—*dead or alive.*"†

"I should be sorry to interfere, Sir," returned the sarcastic lord, "with the bargains of the corporation, however injudicious I think them : for, in my opinion, the heads of all three are not worth the money."

An official now entered to inform his Excellency that Governor Eyre sought an audience. Hereupon the disappointed and indignant Alderman Watson retired, and the Governor of Galway was introduced.

Eyre was a fierce old soldier, whose only notions of law or government were derived from a drum-head court-martial, or the rule of a regiment, and his horror of "popery" was as absurd as that which a child entertains of a "buggaboo." Frequent written communications he had made to the Lord-Lieutenant‡ were not treated with as much consideration as he thought they merited, and he, therefore, went up to Dublin to make his representations in person. The courteousness of his reception by the polished lord softened the asperity of temper

---

* Rev. James Gordon's Hist. Ireland.

There is a singular resemblance between **Lord Chesterfield in 1745,** and **Lord Normanby** nearly a hundred years later.　Both men of fashion, suddenly grappling with a difficult government, and elevating their reputations by the largeness of their policy.　Both essentially exclusive—the men of a *coterie* in private life, were nobly above such influence in dealing with public affairs.—They legislated not for the few, but the many.　Both inspired with a sense of justice to, and confidence in the people, found ready obedience to the former, while the latter was never abused.　They were the only viceroys who could spare troops out of Ireland.　It is to be regretted, there was a lapse of almost a century between two such governments : "Like angels' visits, few and far between."

† Gent. Mag.

‡ Hardiman's Galway.

with which he entered the presence; and though he came
prepared to throw shot and shell, he was forced to exchange
salutes.

He entered on his business, therefore, with calmness and
precision; but as he was disturbed in the course of his representations by some searching question of the Viceroy, his
irritability was roused, and he began to warm thoroughly to the
subject of his complaint. Like all other complaints of the
time, the blame for every misfortune was laid at the door of the
poor and powerless Roman Catholics. According to Governor
Eyre, the safety of Galway was not worth a day's purchase;
and after detailing anticipated horrors enough for a dozen of
the darkest romances, he besought the Lord-Lieutenant to grant
him additional powers to keep down the " Papists."

" My dear Governor," said Chesterfield, in his blandest
manner, " I do not think my views concerning the ' Papists,' as
you call them, and yours, can ever agree."

" Do you not grant they are very daring, my lord, to
assemble and celebrate mass, in defiance of the law ?"

" Governor, people will say their prayers in spite of us; and
I cannot wonder they would rather worship God than man. It
is we who are wrong in making laws which it is impossible to
enforce. It was but the other day an old house in a secluded
street fell down from the overcrowded state of one of its rooms,
where the mass was celebrated, and many broken limbs were
the consequence."*

" I hope, my lord, the offenders will be prosecuted. It may
prevent a recurrence of the crime."

" I am not sure that a prosecution would save old houses from
falling, Governor—but I have recommended to the King and
his ministers a way to prevent a recurrence of such an accident."

" May I beg to ask it, your Excellency ?"

" It is to permit the Catholics to build chapels, and worship
in public."†

The Governor was thunderstruck. " And would you tolerate
the celebration of the mass ?" he exclaimed.

" Certainly," said Lord Chesterfield. " It is wisest to tolerate
what we cannot prevent; the laws that can be defied or defeated
are soon despised—good laws never are."

" Would you trust them, my lord, when they are ever ready
to enlist in the armies of our enemies ?"

" I have a cure for that, too," said Lord Chesterfield;
"I would enlist them in our own."

*" Lascelles' Report.   † Ibid.

"Our own!" echoed the Governor, in amazement.

"Yes; the Irish are essentially a military people; and it is much better to have them fighting for us than against us—for fight they will. You know I have used strong measures to repress foreign enlistments; I have issued a proclamation, offering a reward of a thousand pounds for the discovery of any one who enlists a British subject for foreign service*—yet what has it done?—Let Fontenoi answer: 'The Irish Brigade is stronger than ever.'"

"But how could we trust these pestilent Papists, my lord—who have poisoned the springs all round London to sicken the cattle, and kill the loyal Protestants with foul meat?"†

"So you believe that vulgar rumour, do you?—Let me assure you that the London physicians all declare the disease of the cattle to be an infection imported from Holland. What do you think of that, Governor?—Holland!—from our allies! But I fear the Dutch murrain will stick to us closer than the Dutch cavalry at Fontenoi. *Their cows are more fatal than their horse!*"‡

"Would, my lord, that you had seen the swagger of the Galway merchants the other day, when they fancied that some large ships, descried off the coast, were Spanish men-of-war come to help them!"

"I heard of no such armament, Governor."

"No, please your Excellency—they were not Spanish ships, only a portion of the East-India fleet driven up hither by stress of weather, but the Papists thought they were Spanish, and rejoiced accordingly."§

"Are you sure, Governor, they did not rejoice at the thought of their being East-India ships coming once more to trade to their harbours? For I have had many petitions from the same merchants, setting forth that the exorbitant port-dues, levied by the corporation of Galway, have ruined their trade, and caused a once flourishing port to be deserted."‖

The Governor here entered into an explanation with his lordship, setting forth, that it was necessary for the protection of Protestant interests that the members of the corporation should be protected by certain privileges and immunities, and that many of these imposts were to be avoided if ships were cleared or entered belonging to members of the corporation.

"Notwithstanding which," returned Lord Chesterfield, "if I

---

* Gent. Mag.   † Pict. Hist. England
‡ The Dutch Cavalry showed no fight at Fontenoi.
§ Hardiman's Galway.   ‖ Hardiman.

am informed aright, the trade has not increased under such protection to one class of the townsmen—not even amongst those it
was meant to benefit."

The Governor was obliged to admit this was true.

" And surely you cannot think it beneficial, Governor, that
the commerce of a port should be limited ?—Commerce breeds
wealth, and I cannot see any good to be derived from making a
country poor."

" I have written to the East-India Company myself," said
Eyre, " requesting them to recommend their ships to trade with
the loyal Protestant merchants of our town."*

" I cannot help thinking your efforts would be better bestowed, Governor, in urging the corporation to relax their heavy
imposts against their fellow-subjects, and let trade take care of
itself. In a few years more your port will be ruined, otherwise.
I am informed, that so late as seven years ago, fifteen ships belonged to the port, and traded on the high seas, but the grinding
exactions so discourage the merchants, that they are dwindling
away year by year, and the prosperity of the town is manifestly
impaired."

" The town is going to decay in many ways, my lord, I grieve
to say. In one point, most material to me, who have its safe
holding in trust : the walls and fortifications are in a dilapidated
state, and in many places holes are absolutely broken through
by the audacious smugglers, who, under cover of night, intro-
duce their goods to avoid paying the dues,† and I hope Government will look to the repairs, or I cannot answer for the town's
safety in case of a rising of the O's and Macs in the neighbouring
highlands of Iar Connaught."

" Well, Governor, you have certainly made an ample admission in favour of all I have been saying. The exorbitant tolls
which ruin fair trade, produce smuggling. The honest merchant
is wronged—rogues and vagabonds prosper instead. In despite
of you they make holes through your city walls, rendering the
king's defences unsafe, and then you call upon Government to
repair the damage which the blind injustice of your corporation
has produced. The town's defences I shall issue immediate
orders to the proper officers to look after—for the safety of no
part of the kingdom which my sovereign has entrusted to my
care shall be neglected—but at the same time I will address a
recommendation to the corporation of Galway to relax their
illiberal code of laws ; for be assured, Governor, it is far from
pleasing to his Majesty that one portion of his subjects should

* Hardiman.   † Ibid.

be sacrificed to the interests of another, or that any should be oppressed. I should think it manifest to any capacity, that if you let people lead quiet lives, and accumulate wealth, the preservation of their own comforts will be the best guarantee for their preserving public tranquillity; while if you oppress and impoverish them,[*] you cannot wonder they should wish to throw off your yoke. In my experience of the people of Ireland, since I have been their Governor, I have found them a generous and warm-hearted people, sensitive alike to kindness and confidence, or severity and distrust,—easily led by the one, or provoked by the other. I have tried the former, much the easier and more gracious mode of rule, and have found it succeed to admiration; and I am proud to believe, notwithstanding all the tales of the alarmists, that in spite of the contagious example of rebellion in Scotland, the disease will not spread into Ireland while a liberal course of policy is pursued towards her people."

The Governor, finding Lord Chesterfield impervious to alarms, withdrew, and returned to Galway, with no very pleasing intelligence for the corporation, who did not include Lord Chesterfield's health in the "loyal" toasts of their festive board, and who paid no attention to his remonstrance against their excessive imposts, which, as he predicted, ultimately ruined their town. So rapid was the progress of decay, that instead of fifteen ships belonging to the port and engaged in trading, only three had owners ere long, and of these only one traded in 1761, and one other in 1762.[†] So much for municipal monopoly. But these local plague-spots in various parts of Ireland were prevented from working a fatal result, in consequence of the general excellence of Lord Chesterfield's administration: for the confidence and good-will inspired by his liberal course of policy awakened in the people the hope of better days for the future; and though some enthusiastic Jacobites endeavoured to organise a rising, they found it impossible, and were fain to join the adherents of the young Pretender in Scotland.

---

[*] I cannot resist quoting a phrase from the recently published letters of Sir James Brook (ten years later than this passage of mine). Speaking of the bad government of the Dutch over the Malay States, he says, "It will be conceded that oppression and prosperity cannot co-exist."—*Author*, 2nd edition.

[†] Com. Jour. vol. viii.

CHAPTER XXV.

ANXIOUS was the watch kept on board the *Doutelle* when she parted from her consort, the *Elizabeth*. Deprived of that protection, her own guns were too few and light of metal to dare an encounter, and all she had to rely on for the safety of the precious freight she bore was her speed. This she was obliged to exercise more than once; and when closing with the Scottish coast she was chased for many hours by a British cruiser, whose swiftness put the sailing qualities of the French brig to a severe trial. Indeed, at one time it seemed impossible to avoid an action, but a sudden change in the wind gave the *Doutelle* an advantage in a point of sailing, and soon distancing her pursuer, she doubled a headland of one of the islands abounding on the western coast of North Britain, and dropped her anchor under its shelter. An eagle at the moment swept down from the rocky heights of the island, and wheeled in majestic flight over the *Doutelle*.

"Behold, my Prince!" exclaimed old Tullibardine, "the king of birds has come to welcome you to Scotland."

It was reckoned a good omen, and Charles landed, but his rank was not revealed to the islanders. He whom he hoped to find, Clanronald, was absent, therefore the *Doutelle* weighed anchor and stood over to the main land, whither the chieftain had gone. The following day, in obedience to a summons from the Prince, Clanronald repaired on board the brig, attended by several of his clan, and Kinlock Moidart bore him company.

The chieftains were sadly disappointed to find but one small and lightly armed vessel, where they hoped to have seen men-of-war and a supply of regular troops, and told the Prince that without such aid a rising would be madness—a hopeless adventure in which they would not join. Charles urged them by every artful appeal he could summon to his aid—their hitherto unfailing affection to his house—their promises, from which the honour of a Highland chieftain never yet flinched—their proverbial bravery, which no odds could daunt; all these stimulants were applied to the excitable Celts, but as yet in vain, and both parties grew louder in argument and answer as they paced rapidly up and down the deck. Ellen was reclining under an awning spread above the after-part of the vessel, sheltering from the noon-day heat, while her father and the rest of the adventurers kept aloof in a group, the Prince still engaged with the chieftains.   How her heart beat as she watched the expressions of *their* faces and that of Charles.   She could see the conference was not satisfactory, and she felt for the humiliating position of a prince suing to a subject and suing in vain.   At this moment she observed a young Highlander, who had taken no part in the debate, but who, as he caught the meaning of it, seemed suddenly enlightened as to the real rank of the person who was engaged with the chieftains, and became deeply interested.   It was Ronald, the younger brother of Kinlock Moidart, who had no idea of the objects of visiting the *Doutelle*. He had been leaning listlessly against the bulwark of the ship, seemingly careless of everything but his picturesque costume, which in every point was perfect.   Completely armed, he seemed the very model of a Highland warrior ; and as he caught the import of the Prince's words, his former listlessness was turned into eager watchfulness—his glistening eyes followed the parleying party backwards and forwards.   Ellen could see his colour come and go, his lips become compressed with the energy of high resolve, his hand fitfully grasp the hilt of his broadsword, and his whole figure heave with the tumult of emotion. It was at this moment the Prince passed over to Ellen, as if he had spent all his arguments in vain, while the two chieftains turned on the heel and paced the deck back again.

" Pardon me, your highness," said Ellen, in an under tone, "but pray look at that young Highlander, whose eyes are so enthusiastically bent upon you."

The Prince looked and saw that he had won the young man's very soul, and suddenly approaching him, he exclaimed, " You at least will assist me."

" I will, I will !" cried Ronald ; "though no other man in the highlands shall draw a sword, I will die for you !"   In the wild emotion of the moment he suited the action to the word ; snatching his bright claymore from the sheath, the steel flashed in the sunbeam, as he waved it above his head, and uttered the wild shout of the Celt.

The enthusiasm was infectious ; the hearts of sterner men were moved by the impetuous youth ; there was not a sword remained in its scabbard, and the clash of steel, and the war cry of the Mac Donalds, startled the silence of the smooth bay with a wild clangour, that was sweeter music to Charles's ear than ever he had heard in the palaces of kings.

Assured by the adhesion of these bold few, he landed, and

messages were despatched to every hill and glen to tell that Charles Stuart had come to fight for the throne of his fathers. Lochiel was the first to obey the summons of his Prince, but he came to dissuade, not to encourage him. He, unconscious of the scene that had fired the Mac Donalds, represented the madness of attempting a rising without aid from abroad, and recommended him to re-embark.

"No," said Charles, "as soon as I land what stores yet remain to me on board the brig, she shall return to France, and thus will I cut myself off from all retreat; for I have come determined to conquer or to perish. In a few days, with the few friends I have, I will raise the royal standard, and Lochiel, who my father has often told me was our firmest friend, may stay at home, and learn from the newspapers the fate of his Prince."

The blood of the "gentle Lochiel" curdled at his heart at these bitter words, and his prudent resolutions were forgotten when his honour was impeached, and his courage doubted.

"My Prince!" he exclaimed with warmth, "whatever be your fate, be the same fate mine, and the fate of all over whom nature or fortune hath given me power. I will love and serve you while I have life, and follow you to the death!"

Preparation for a general rising was now rapidly made through the highlands. Glenfinnin was named as the point of general rendezvous, where the Jacobite clans might assemble in detail, until their congregated force was sufficient to make a descent on the lowlands. The glen was admirably suited for this purpose—a deep and narrow valley, with a river running through it; steep mountains guarding it on both sides; while at either end it was shut in by a lake, thus preventing surprise from enemies, and rendering cavalry utterly useless.

With his few immediate followers the Prince set out for the glen; on reaching the shores of the lake, a shrill whistle from their highland guide called some wild gillies to their aid, a couple of small boats were brought forth from the concealment of some deep rocky creeks and low underwood, and launched upon the calm dark waters. About midway across the lake, the valley became gradually visible, like a deep rent in the mountains, presenting the picture of security. On landing at the opposite shore, the party sought the hovel of a shepherd, the only house within sight, and there leaving Ellen to rest, for the journey had been somewhat fatiguing, the Prince and his little band sauntered about the valley awaiting the arrival of the clans. For some ours not a sound disturbed the silence of the glen, and its savage grandeur and oppressive loneliness began to impart a tone of melancholy to Charles, who had never till now beheld the wild and solemn majesty of our northern hills. But that which made him sad, gave delight to Lynch, and Kirwan, and Sullivan (the Prince's prime favourite, who was his companion in all his subsequent perils and wanderings). They saw in these bold hills and wild glens the counterpart of their own dear western mountains of Ireland; and after the dead levels of Flanders, and the tame champaigns of France, on which their eyes so long had rested, the sight of cliff, and fell, and torrent, brought the features of home to their hearts, and the memory of early days,—when in boyhood they followed their careless mountain sports, and dreamt not, in that happy time, of future exile from their native land, a return to which was risking death.

Oh, happy boyhood! which sees no joy nor sorrow, but that of the day in which it breathes; or whose future, whenever it dares to speculate, seldom extends beyond a week. Whose highest enjoyments are in the whistling whirl of the rod and line across the lively stream, the sharp ring of the fowling-piece, and the *whir* of the flying covey, the neigh of the impatient steed, anticipating, in the warning tongue of the hound, the start of the game and the headlong chase. Happy boyhood! which cannot believe, however wisely preached, that days will come when such joys shall be as nothing; that the mind shall create for itself a world within more attractive than the external; that the questions of civil right and public good shall supersede all private considerations; that the present shall display its attractions in vain against the interest which the past affords in its historic lessons, and the future in its political hopes.

To our daring adventurers, the mountains revived such images of their boyish sports; these mountains that were now to become the theatre of their manhood's sterner game. The stream was valued not for its bounding fish, but as it might strengthen a position; the gun was now to threaten men, not birds; and the neigh of the steed was to be roused, not by the bay of the hound, but the blast of the war trumpet.

The old Lord Tullibardine continued near the Prince, but he became reserved, even to this gallant and faithful adherent of his house, and sat apart upon a rock, seemingly overcast with saddening thoughts, and at length leaning his head upon his hands as if in dark communion with himself. Did the spirit of divination which gifts the children of these misty hills then hover over him? Did he see the " rally and the rout " of Dark Culloden? Did he see the royal Stuart forced to hide his manhood in a female garb, to wander, hunted like a wolf, to shelter in a savage cave, and herd with robbers?

But soon the visions of the Prince, whatever they were,

15

vanished, like the mist of the morn before the sunbeam; he was startled from his trance by a wild peculiar sound which broke the solemn stilness of the glen. It was the pibroch of the Camerons.

Old Tullibardine waved his bonnet in the air, and his practised eye caught the first glimpse of the clan as its vanward men passed the crest of the hill, and might be seen glancing here and there through rocks and heather, with which their tartans blended, that none but the initiated could mark their progress. He pointed them out to the Prince, who, after some time, could discern them, while louder and louder rang the pibroch, startling from the cliffs the eagles, which boldly came forth and answered with their shout the war-strain, as if they challenged those intruders on their solitary domain. And now the clan became more visible, they had defiled into a mountain-gulley, and came pouring onward,—a rush of living men down the path of a winter-torrent. On reaching the valley they formed in two lines, each line three deep, and advanced in good order to where Charles Edward and his little staff were awaiting them. Lochiel was at their head, and when he brought them to a halt before the Prince, the first rank opened, and discovered, between the two lines, a small detachment of English soldiers and their officers, prisoners.

"Behold, your Highness!" said Lochiel,—"the first blow is already struck, a party of my clan yesterday intercepted a detachment of the red coats and beat them without the loss of a man on our side.* So far the game is well begun."

" Your conquest would not have been so easy, Sir," said the English officer, " but for the nature of the ground, and your peculiar mode of fighting."

"As for that," said Lochiel, " we fight in the way we best understand, and though it may not be according to your notion of tactics, you cannot deny you were beaten.

"Sir," said the Prince to the officer, with his peculiar courtesy of manner, "I at once liberate you on your parole. Rest here for the present after your fatigue, and be my guest for this evening; on the morrow you may return to General Cope, and tell him I shall soon give him battle."

The Prince was surprised to find the greater part of the clansmen carrying guns, and inquired of Lochiel how that came to pass, while a strict parliamentary act had disarmed the Highlands.

Lochiel laughed, and said the Highlanders had been *nominally*

---

* Fact.

deprived of arms by a stringent law : "But," said the acute mountaineer, "the sharper the law the sharper the people." He went on to say that extreme laws were the easiest evaded : "Fools may give up their arms," said he, "but wise men keep them." And he protested, that however cunning and vigilant the officers of the government might be, he defied them to discover arms amongst a bold and acute people, who were determined not to give them up. "Those who hide can find," said Lochiel ; "and signs by it," he added, pointing to his clan ; for, despite of the Arms Bill, he had brought six hundred out of his eight, armed at a short notice.*

Then turning to Tullibardine the Prince exclaimed, "Raise my standard, my Lord !" The old nobleman received it from Ellen, whose own hands had worked it ; and as the silken folds of mingled white, blue, and red were unfurled, and lifted upwards in the breeze that flaunted the colours gaily about, a deafening shout arose from eight hundred stalwart mountaineers, that made the echoes of Glenfinnin ring again, and once more disturbed the eagle in his eyrie.

How proudly beat Ellen's heart, as leaning on her father's arm she saw the ensign of her King displayed, and heard it recognised in loyal shouts, while his royal proclamation was read beneath it. And yet a shudder crossed her woman-heart as she thought that the gay and silken work of woman's hand, in peaceful hour, should muster the hands of men around it in deadly fight,—that the banner which had been her favourite occupation and companion in the quiet convent of Bruges and the luxurious boudoir of Paris, should float for the future amidst the thunder of the battle and the hardships of war.

How rapt in admiration was Kirwan, as he marked the enthusiastic gaze of the beautiful girl upon the standard. He

* "By an act of the first of the late King (George I.), intituled, 'For the more effectually securing the peace of the Highlands,' the whole Highlands, without distinction, were disarmed, and for ever forbid to use or bear arms, under penalties. This act has been found, by experience, to work the quite contrary effect from what was intended by it ; and, in reality, it proves a measure for more effectually disturbing the peace of the Highland and the rest of the kingdom. For, at the time appointed for the disarming act, all the dutiful and well-affected clans truly submitted to the Act of Parliament, and gave up their arms, so that they are now completely disarmed ; but the disaffected clans either concealed their arms at first, or have provided themselves since with other arms. The fatal effects of this difference at the time of a rebellious insurrection must be very obvious ; and are, by us in this country, felt at this hour."—*Letter of Andrew Fletcher, Lord Milton, Justice-Clerk to the Marquess Tweeddale Secretary of State for Scotland.*

fancied he divined her thoughts, and approaching her, whispered gently,—"Ellen, while within reach of my sword he will be a bold foe that plucks that standard down." And in saying this the lover thought less of his loyalty to his King than his devotion to the work of his mistress' hands.

A marble column marks the spot where that ill-fated banner was raised; even now we may stand where the enthusiast Lynch and his gentle daughter, the devoted lover, the loyal Lochiel, the faithful Sullivan, and the ambitious Prince, then stood, and trusted in hopes that were doomed to be blighted.

Yet why mark with a column that spot of blighted hopes ?— Alas! there is no spot on earth which might not thus be celebrated, save that spot where we kneel and pray in the hope of the Christian—the only hope that deceiveth not!

CHAPTER XXVI.

AFTER the reading of the proclamation the Highlanders were dismissed from their parade, and occupied themselves in preparing for a feast; gathering what would suit for fuel in the glen, they lit fires, and cooking commenced, in which they were assisted by many of their women, who came dropping in at the rear of the clan, carrying loads of provisions and kegs of whisky. Long wattles were placed in the ground, and small arcades of successive arches formed, over which blankets were thrown to make shelter for the women and children, for even children were among them, while shorter sticks, tending in the form of a cone, and thatched with fern plucked by the boys and girls among the rocks, made a more primitive retreat, and the valley soon assumed the air of an encampment. The shepherd's hut served for the accommodation of Ellen; for though it was intended for the prince, as the best shelter the place afforded, he, with a courtly gallantry, refused to take it when a lady was in his "little court," as he playfully called it, and the hut therefore was allotted to Ellen, and, as a point of nice punctilio, to her father.

"As for myself," said the Prince, "I shall sleep, like the brave fellows who come to fight for me, on the heather in my plaid;" for Charles, to flatter the nationality of the Highlanders, had assumed the tartan, and, as he said himself, in the parlance of Italy, to which he was most accustomed, "to lie *al fresco* was no great penalty in the month of August."

As the evening advanced, other forces poured into the valley. Again the echoes of Glenfinnin were waked by the pibrochs of Mac Donald and Mac Leod, and upwards of four hundred devoted men strengthened the force of the Prince, who greeted his adherents as they arrived.

And now the wild feast was spread. Charles and his little staff and the chieftains were stationed on a gently rising knoll, which served as a sort of natural "dais," whence they might be seen by all the clansmen who were huddled around without much attention to order. Game of various sorts served for viands; and while some claret was thoughtfully brought by Lochiel for the Prince, who might not like their stronger mountain beverage, whisky was the favourite liquor of the evening. When all the eatables were disposed of, Lochiel rose and addressed the assembled clans in a speech quite unintelligible to him whom it praised and meant to serve, for the Prince did not understand a word of Erse, (though his Irish adherents could gather most of the meaning,) but, judging from the effect it produced, it was spirit-stirring in the extreme, for the Highlanders yelled in delight as he proceeded, and quaffed their brimming cups to the last drop, as the chieftain wound up his speech with the toast of " *Deochs laint an Reogh !*"[*]

The pipers struck up the tune of "The king shall have his own again;" and as the mountaineers warmed to the spirit of the scene, the music had an electric effect upon them, and up they jumped and began dancing. Those who could get women to join them, all the better, but the absence of the gentle sex was no bar to the merriment, for the men pranced away amongst each other with as much seeming glee as if each had the "bonniest lassie" in all Scotland for his partner.

The chieftains were not exempted from the exercise, for two of the women coming up and dropping curtsies to Lochiel and Mac Donald, challenged them to the dance.[†] Forth stepped the chieftains as ready for the front of the festival as the front of the battle. The Prince, full of that "condescension" for which great people are so famous when they have a point to carry, wished to

[*] God save the King.

[†] This custom exists still, I believe, in Scotland, but certainly in Ireland, at harvest-homes and such festivals, where the highest gentleman would be considered recreant who would refuse the "challenge" of a peasant girl.

join in the common revelry, and offered his hand to Ellen if they would play a cotillon, but the Highland pipers knew no such outlandish stuff.   Lynch seeing the Prince's desire that all about him should make general cause in the mirthful spirit of the hour, said his daughter would dance a jig with "any comer" if there was a piper present who would play one.

"Hurrah!" exclaimed a voice, not unknown to Lynch, "Faith, then, it's I will play the jig for the masther!"

Lynch turned to the spot whence the voice came, and beheld, to his astonishment, Phaidrig-na-pib led up to him by Ned.

"Here's the music, sir," cried Ned to the Captain; "and mad I," he said, with all the humility and devotion he could impart to his voice, "have the honour of leading Miss Lynch to the dance?"

Ellen uttered an exclamation of surprise at sight of Ned, and eagerly asked what extraordinary chance had thrown him there.   He told her he would explain all to her when the dance was over, and Phaidrig, losing no time " for the honour of Ireland," in lilting up the very merriest of his jigs, Ned and Ellen set to, and won rapturous applause from the surrounding lookers on.   Ellen had that sound spirit of nationality, unfailingly allied to good sense, which made her not slight, even if she did not love, any customs of her native country.   She could tread the stately minuet or lively cotillon with courtly grace, but equally well could she bound through the tricksy steps of the merry jig; and the arm a-kimbo, and the

"Nods, and becks, and wreathed smiles,"

so peculiarly belonging to that flirty dance, were never more attractive than in the person of Ellen Lynch.

Now Ned could dance a jig right well too, and with the readiness of an Irishman he seized the occasion of showing off his good point, while he secured at the same time what he considered the highest honour on earth.   All his exertions were called forth by the sight of the beautiful girl whose graceful action even to one who was not already in love with her might have made him so; and whether it was the peculiar occasion, the presence of the Prince, or the honour of her country, it is impossible to say, but Ellen certainly danced uncommonly well; in short, she seemed to "take share of the jig" with all her heart.

The bystanders cheered the dance amazingly, and the point of honour of "who should give in first," was made more precious every minute. Ellen strove hard to "dance her man down," but Ned would not be beaten, and when breathless and panting, his flushed and exhausted partner almost dropped with fatigue, Ned tripped forward with the air of a true cavalier, and supporting his lovely burden firmly yet delicately in his arms, he led her, amidst loud applause, to a gentle slope, and seated her on a bunch of heather with as much ceremony as though it had been a velvet chair. As he retired, after thanking her for the honour of her hand, and receiving in return a gracious glance of her sweet eyes, he met the gaze of Kirwan, looking thunder.

Whether it was that the fitful light of the fires imparted an unusual flashing to the eye, and that the ruddy light tinged his glance with an *outward* glare rather than it burned from a fire *within*, Ned could not at the instant determine, but he felt it was the most repulsive look he ever encountered :—the more so, as Kirwan's aspect was generally good-humoured ;—handsome though he was, it was the expression of cheerful good-nature which rendered his countenance so prepossessing, and over such the shade of evil passions makes its most startling impress. Kirwan, for the moment, looked almost fiendish, and at the instant felt an agony of soul he had never before experienced ; for as the eyes of the rivals met, there was in Ned's look a joy so bright, a something more akin to the skies than the earth, so expressive of unlooked-for joy, of hope realised, that its brightness shot infinitely more of anguish to the soul of Kirwan, than *his* lowering aspect did of regret to Ned, in this passing encounter of their eyes. That glance was but instantaneous, and yet in that one moment those men felt that they were for ever and for aye, deep, deadly, irreconcilable foes.

This was the more painful, because both had rather desired to be friends. Ned, for Lynch's sake, would scrupulously have avoided a quarrel with Kirwan ; and he, on the other hand, could not forget that to Edward's hand he owed his life, when he missed his footing in springing on board the *Seagull* in the storm. He would have given the world not to be thus indebted. To owe a favour to the man you hate is indeed terrible, and Kirwan all on a sudden thoroughly hated our hero, for until that moment he had never dreamt of him as a rival ; but there was an indefinable something about Ellen's dancing which made Kirwan's heart sink within him. It is true, he had never been received as Ellen's recognised suitor ; a long and attached friendship was the highest claim he ever held to be so much in her society ; and though Lynch would have been glad of Kirwan's alliance by marriage, Ellen's bearing towards him, while replete with friendliness and confidence, could never for a moment be mistaken for love.

This, however, Kirwan hoped by long devotion to achieve at last; but, though the smiles of the gentle sex were no strangers to him, though a general favourite with the fair. and often envied for his ready access to their good graces, he felt that he had not made impression on Ellen's heart, though he was conscious of her utmost esteem. Can it be wondered at, then, that thus suddenly discovering a rival in a man he was inclined to consider, if not quite an adventurer, at least much his inferior in rank, he should look upon him with peculiar aversion; that the hopes he had been long building up being thus suddenly overthrown, should as suddenly engender hatred for the author of his disappointment?

Conscious that his aspect might betray the emotions which struggled within, he turned away from the group, and walked apart for some time. On his return he had no greater reason to be satisfied, for though Ned was not in the neighbourhood of Ellen, he saw him closely engaged in conversation with Tullibardine, Lynch, and the principal men of the party, and even with the Prince himself; and this argued an importance in his position which afforded fresh cause of uneasiness, for whatever made him useful to " the cause," would give him interest in the eyes not only of Ellen, but of her father.

It was immediately after the dance, when Kirwan had walked away, that Lynch inquired of Ned how he came to make so sudden and unexpected an appearance in the glen. Ned gave a brief sketch of his adventurous measures to join the expedition, but with great tact dismissed personal affairs, as soon as possible, and entered upon the subject of the secret Jacobite interests as entrusted to him by Lord Barrymore; whereupon Lynch praised him much for his zeal and activity, and led him at once to the Prince; who, on learning the importance of what Ned had to communicate, retired with him and his principal adherents to a neighbouring hillock, and received, with the aid of Phaidrig's memory, such detailed accounts of the assistance they might expect in England, that the hearts of the adventurers, exulting in the hopes before them, opened in welcome to the bearer of the glad tidings, and Ned found himself suddenly a person of some consideration. The Prince repeatedly addressed him, and at the conclusion of the conference praised him for his zeal, courage, and activity; and when the party separated to throw themselves on their beds of heather, Lynch had some more parting words with Ned as they walked together towards the hut whither Ellen had already retired. As they parted at the door, Lynch told his young friend he must find the best bed he could for himself on the heather, to which Ned replied that to one who had often kept the middle watch in a gale, a heather bed in August was luxury.

But Ned did not feel himself inclined for immediate repose; for although he had walked many a weary mountain mile that day, the excitement of the evening countervailed the natural desire for rest. His meeting with Ellen, and her gracious bearing towards him, raised hopes which Lynch's manner and the Prince's condescension were calculated to heighten, and which Ned had no wish to drown in slumber for the present, so he sauntered up the glen which was fast sinking into quiet. The whisky had done its duty; the Highlanders were stretched in drunken sleep beside their watch-fires, already beginning to burn low, whose dull red light, as it glinted upon some overhanging rock, contrasted in picturesque relief to the pale light of the moon, which now illumined the silent depths of the valley.

It was the very region of romance; and in such a region Edward might well indulge his own. Oh, what living, real romance was there! A prince had come to claim a crown, and with a daring few had commenced the bold adventure. Those faithful few, forgetful of all other ties, the dearest and most real nature knows, clung to that ideal one which from boyhood upward had held a secret, and therefore precious place in their enthusiast hearts—the tie of loyalty. They, in turn, had their followers, educated in the blind but affectionate and generous motive to follow the fortune of their chief, whithersoever it might lead; and here were prince, and chieftains, and clansmen, all sunk alike into the forgetfulness of slumber; slumber on the edge of doom! even that royal head, which now, resting on wild heather, might in a few eventful days lie beneath the palace canopy or on the scaffold's block, forgot itself in sleep. The ambitious prince—the devoted adherent—the reckless clansmen —all could sleep, but the travel-tired lover could not repose. No. Nought can disturb the heart like love—nought else so chase the soul of rest. Kingcraft and loyalty are of the world's making; but love is of nature's creation, and therefore more absorbing in its influence.

Edward had a confused consciousness of all this around and passing within him, though he could not have defined his sensations in words; but he apostrophised the name of his mistress, asking himself why he alone should be waking in that valley, as he walked amidst the sleepers. He looked towards the hut which sheltered Ellen, and approached it with the pleasing notion of making his couch where she rested.

As he brushed briskly through the heather in the eagerness of the fond idea, the rustling attracted somebody already in the neighbourhood of the hut, who, raising himself on his arm from his recumbent position, demanded, " Who goes there?"

"A friend," replied Ned, still advancing.

The challenger sprung to his feet and confronted him; and Ned beheld in the person who barred his path, Kirwan.

The moonlight perfectly revealed both the men to each other, and neither spoke for some time, but stood gazing silently on each other. Kirwan's visage was sad and pale, and it seemed as if he made an effort to be calm. At length he asked some vague question, to which Edward returned as vague a reply; and after the interchange of some broken sentences they seemed as much perplexed how to part as they were startled by their meeting. Each knew the other's motive for being there, as well as if the motive had been his own, yet dared not hint at such a knowledge. Each knew the working of the other's heart, as well as if he were inside it, yet tried to appear as indifferent as if they had not a heart between them. Both the men at that moment would have gladly seized each other by the throat, and struggled to the death, or gashed each other with their swords, yet were forced to assume the formalities of acquaintanceship; and when they stumbled on an excuse for parting, mutually uttered a hurried " good-night," while they wished each other at the d——l.

The following day was full of bustle and activity. An early council of war was called to consider the propriety of an immediate march to the south, but Lochiel and the other chieftains recommended the delay of one day more at Glenfinnin for the reception of small straggling parties of Highlanders which might be expected, and would be disheartened, or perhaps turn back if they found no friends awaiting them in the glen. This being decided on, the remainder of the day was given up to amusement. Athletic sports were engaged in by the mountaineers for the entertainment of the Prince, while Ellen and a few who loved the picturesque, made a little party to explore the beauties of the glen. It was after the fatigue of a steep ascent which they had made in their excursion, that the little basket of refreshment was opened, and their simple repast spread in a pretty sheltered nook of the hills, where a rivulet, crystal-bright, bounding down the rocks, offered ready beverage to the party. Here it was that Ellen called upon Ned to tell her of his adventures since they had parted at sea, and by what extraordinary means he had contrived to follow them. This he did in more detailed form than the night before to her father, but still without making himself offensively prominent in the story ; and all listened with pleasure to the adventurous little history—his contriving to get away from France, his fishing-boat passage of the channel, his secret landing in England, escapes in London, and northern journey, which latterly became dangerous, from the suspicion of the authorities in the lowland towns attaching to all southerns travelling to the north. All the incidental questions that were asked him in the course of his narrative were answered with so much clearness and good sense, that he obtained consideration among his hearers.

Kirwan was not among these; his duties obliging him to remain in the camp, much to his chagrin, as he saw Ellen departing with Ned in her train. As for Ned, it was the happiest day of his life. The beautiful girl he adored listened with pleasure to the recital of his adventures, and there was a nameless charm in her manner towards him which gave him joy for the present and hope for the future. How lovely did she seem in his eyes, as she reclined in that little rocky dell upon the short aromatic grass, where the tiny flowers had crept for shelter. Her fairy foot was playing with an hare-bell which lay close beside it, and Ned would have given the world for the painter's power at that moment to record the beauty of its arched instep and rounded ankle.

Young Ronald Macdonald was of the party, albeit not insensible to Ellen's beauty, and she called on the young chieftain to arouse them from their too luxurious quiet by one of those spirit-stirring songs with which he was wont to gladden the hearts of the king's friends : one of those strains whose fiery poetry roused men to action, and outlives the cause by which they were inspired.

The young chieftain poured forth his very heart in the song, which well suited the genius of the place, and as he arrived at its burden,—

> "Come through the heather,
> Around him gather,
> You're a' the welcomer airly,"

every voice joined in the chorus, and felt the aptness of the strain, for the heather was around them, and they were " a' the welcomer airly,"—they were the first of the adherents.

Ellen's foot had kept beating time to the melody, and Ronald remarked that if she kept time so well he was sure she could sing, and that hers truly was the land of song.

She obeyed the call, and sang that exquisitely plaintive melody called "Limerick's Lamentation," which touched the heart of every hearer; and when it was concluded, Ronald made her promise she would teach it to him, as it was one of the loveliest airs he had ever heard. "But it is *so* sad," he added.

"And well it may be," said Ellen. "It was written to commemorate the expatriation of us poor Irish after the violation of the treaty of Limerick, and hence its name."

"I will learn it," said Ronald. And so he did, and the air became afterwards a great favourite in Scotland, where it is now known under the name of "Farewell to Lochaber," for the beauty of the strain caught the ear and waked the genius of Burns.

Ned was now called on to contribute to the harmony of the party, and said he would attempt a variety in the style of the song he should give. The others treated of war and exile; he should deal with a softer subject, which was the unfailing contrast to war in the hands of the poets.

"Aye—love!" said Ronald: "you lowlanders are always thinking of sighing and whining after your lady's apron string. Oh! the mountains for me, which brace a man's nerves to bolder strains!"

"Softly," said Ned: "in the first place I am not a lowlander, —I came from the region of mountain and lake as well as yourself, and I never heard it objected to a warrior that he could play the lover also. Nay, my love-song even shall not treat of the valley, but hold forth the fitness of the mountain for tender recollections as well as warlike achievments. Why should we not

'Come thro' the heather'

at the behest of a lady as well as of a king?" and he bowed low to Ellen as he spoke, and then began:—

The Mountain Dew.

I.

By yon mountain, tipp'd with cloud,
By the torrent foaming loud,
By the dingle where the purple bells of heather grew,
Where the Alpine flow'rs are hid,
And where bounds the nimble kid—
There we've wander'd both together through the mountain dew!
With what delight in summer's night we trod the twilight gloom,
The air so full of fragrance from the flow'rs so full of bloom,
And our hearts so full of joy—for aught else there was no room,
As we wander'd both together through the mountain dew!

II.

"Those sparkling gems that rest
      On the mountain's flow'ry breast,
Are like the joys we number—they are bright and few,
      For a while to earth are given,
      And are call'd again to heaven,
When the spirit of the morning steals the mountain dew.
But memory, angelic, makes a heaven on earth for men,
Here rosy light recalleth bright the dew-drops back again;
The warmth of love exhales them from that well-remember'd glen,
      Where we wander'd both together through the mountain dew."

Even the fiery Ronald admitted that a song not unworthy of the mountain might be sung to a softer theme than war, and one after another of the party gave some snatch of—

"Music wedded to immortal verse,"

and right pleasantly passed the day, until the shadows warned them it was time to return and join the evening feast, which the Prince was to hold again in Glenfinnin. As they descended to the valley, Ned seized many an opportunity of tendering his services to Ellen, whose beautiful hand was often within his, as he steadied her footstep round some precipitous ledge, or afforded her support as she sprang from some overhanging rock, too high to dare a leap from, without such aid. Happy, happy Ned!—he would have wished the descent to be interminable, but such sweet moments must come to an end, and he found himself too soon at the mountain-foot, where preparation for festivity was in active progression.

It was not long till the feast was spread, and the Prince and his adherents (much increased in number by fresh arrivals) re-enacted the scene of the former evening. Again to the King's health did Glenfinnin resound; again shrieked the pipes in wild music; again the fantastic dance beat the ground—but there was no jig. Ellen, pleading fatigue, had retired early, so the jealous glances of the rivals were spared, as well as their moonlight walk and meeting of the preceding night; and if Kirwan did not sleep soundly, Ned certainly did.

CHAPTER XXVII.

THE following morning, at an early hour, the forces of Charles Edward started on their southern route, and the house of the "gentle Lochiel" was their next appointed halting-place.

Now, while the Highlanders are on their march, it may be as well for the author to beckon his kind companion, the reader, into a by-path, and have a few confidential words with him about the march of his story. Let him (the reader) not be afraid that he is about to be dragged through the high road of history, with which he is as well, if not better acquainted than the author himself. The story of the adventurous Prince is too well known by the world in general, to afford rational hope to an author that any fresh research or "new dresses, scenery, and decorations," of his, could invest that romantic drama with a fresh interest. Therefore, once for all, let it be understood, that no more of the history of this period will be touched upon than properly belongs to the affairs of the persons connected with our story. In touching on the immediate time and place of such startling historic events, it cannot be forgotten that the greatest novelist of any age or country has made the theme his own, and that while the course of the present tale lies through such beaten ground, the author feels like a trespasser, pursuing his game over a manor that must be ever well preserved in the grateful memories of admiring millions. Therefore, with what speed he may, he will hasten his course, nor venture one step he can avoid in a region it were literary sacrilege to profane.

And now, so much being said, let us join the general march, and halt with the Highlanders and the "gentle Lochiel."

The gathering of the clans was increased at the home of the gallant chieftain. Mac Donald of Glenco, Stuart of Appin, and the younger Glengarry, joined their forces to those already assembled; and though despite the Arms bill, they were wonderfully provided with offensive weapons, nevertheless, some hundreds were wanting in that essential point of war, and a council was held to deliberate on the best mode of remedying the deficiency.

After the council had broken up, the theme of its deliberation continued to be the subject of conversation among the leaders, and repeatedly regret was expressed that the Prince had come so ill provided with arms. Tullibardine, Lynch, and others of the Prince's immediate followers, reminded the chieftains that it was not from lack of foresight such a want was experienced, but that the fortune of war had interrupted that most necessary supply—the ship bearing the military stores having been intercepted.

Kirwan could not resist this opportunity of saying something to annoy Ned, and though his better nature pointed out to him at the instant he spoke, the unkindness and injustice of his words, the demon of jealousy would not let him be silent, but goaded him on to wound in any way he could.

"Yes," said he, "if those on board the *Elizabeth* had only done their duty, and fought their ship becomingly, we should now have plenty of arms and ammunition."

Ned, in the peculiar relation he stood with Kirwan, was quite as ready to take, as the other to give, offence, and instantly retorted, "If the *Doutelle* had not deserted the *Elizabeth*—"

"Deserted!" interrupted Kirwan, captiously; "you forget his Highness was on board—too precious a freight to endanger; besides, what could a light-armed brig do against a fifty-gun ship? while the *Elizabeth*, carrying sixty-seven, should have been able to beat an inferior adversary."

"The *Elizabeth*," said Ned, "was an old and inefficient ship, while the *Lion* was perfect in all respects; and I feel myself bound to bear testimony to the gallantry of the captain and crew of the Frenchman. No ship could be better fought."

"Very possibly," said Kirwan, superciliously, "I only mean to say it was a pity she was beaten."

"She was not beaten," replied Ned, warmly. "It was a drawn battle, and a bitter and bloody one too; there was not a stick left standing in either ship."

"We have lost our arms, however," returned Kirwan.

"If the *Doutelle* had used her guns," said Ned, "we should not want arms; not only the *Elizabeth*, but the *Lion* too, as our prize, would have been here."

"Oh," said Kirwan, "it's easy to talk of what would have been. I speak of what happened. *Your* ship was driven back."

"If you talk of *my* ship," said Ned, "I must talk of *yours* —and I should rather be on board the ship that fought, than the ship that ran away."

"Ran away!" echoed Kirwan, furiously. "What do you mean?" and he laid his hand on his sword.

"Peace! peace!" cried Lynch, authoritatively, and restraining Kirwan's arm. "Gentlemen, this is an unseemly and uncalled-for altercation. We are too few to quarrel among ourselves—let our swords be drawn on our enemies, not on each other. I make it a personal request to each that not a word further pass between you.—I am sure no offence was meant on either side."

A general exclamation of "certainly not," arose among the chieftains, though some suspected there might have been; and Lynch was quite sure that there was, and grieved to think upon the cause, and not wishing to trust the men longer in each other's company, passed his arm through Kirwan's, and withdrew from the group, which by common consent dispersed immediately afterwards.

Ned's temper, though ruffled, soon recovered its tone, from the consciousness that he had repelled any affront that was meant, and maintained his position; and during the evening, in the house of the Highland chief, he renewed his opportunities of speaking with Ellen, undeterred by Kirwan's lowering brow, which, despite his efforts to the contrary, betrayed his inward feelings.

The next day, too, while pursuing their route to Blair Castle, the seat of old Lord Tullibardine, he often walked by Ellen's bridle-rein, as she sat her rough highland pony, down the steep declivities of the mountain road; and though often obliged to give place to Kirwan, equally arduous in his attention, yet Ned made a good fight for the place of honour, and lost no opportunity of being near the lady of his heart.

This struggle for the post of "groom in waiting" between the rivals, was not unobserved by Lynch, who would gladly have prevented it by assuming the place himself, but that his presence was demanded in front, beside the Prince, who was in close converse with him on the subject of the expected share Ireland would take in the insurrectionary movements, while Tullibardine was called on for his counsel.

The old lord, who had been actively engaged in the conference, soon became abstracted, and seemed scarcely to hear a word that was addressed to him. This absence of mind was accounted for to the Prince, by one of the chieftains, who told him they were approaching Blair Athol, and that Tullibardine's heart was full at the thought of nearing his old halls after so long an absence. It was even so. Thirty years had elapsed since the heroic old man had been in his native land, whence the same cause had procured his exile that now induced his return, and his countenance betrayed the varying emotions that stirred his soul, as he drew near the castle.

As they topped an acclivity, the turn of a sharp angle in the

road revealed to the old lord his ancestral towers; first clear
and distinct, but soon dim and uncertain, for he saw them
through the mist of affection which his heart sent up before his
eyes, as he looked on the home of his childhood. Other emotions
there were, too, as well as those of affection. This staunch
adherent of his king had received the father of the present
prince in those very halls; then, on an enterprise like the
present, had proved his fidelity, and forfeited his estates; and
now was returned, after more than a quarter of a century of
exile, to risk all he had remaining—his life—in the same
desperate cause.

Ashamed to have witnesses to his emotion, the old man
hastened onward, upon the pretence of being ready to receive
the Prince at the castle. When he reached the portal there was
a reception awaiting himself. Some old adherents of the house
who yet survived the ravages of time, and the still more actively
depopulating measures of the law, after "the fifteen" were ready
to receive him at the gate, and hailed him as the "Duke of
Athol," the title held by his Whig brother, (or the "fau'se
laird," as the people called him,) by way of reward for his
adhesion to the Guelphic interest.

One fine old man, in particular, whose white hairs proclaimed
age, and on whose face a scar indicated warlike service, was
foremost in welcome : calling down blessings on the head of the
old lord, he ran before him into the castle, shouting, "It's a
your ain again !—a' your ain !"

But Tullibardine did not follow. His prince being close at
hand, he awaited his arrival at the portal, where he received
him with loyal welcome as he alighted, and prayed him to enter
his castle, which he considered less his own than his king's.
He stood uncovered as he spoke, and when he had finished his
short but devoted speech, he threw his bonnet in the air, as a
signal to the surrounding retainers, whose answering shouts
made the walls of Blair Athol ring again, as the Prince entered
its gates.

Much confusion was apparent in the interior appointments,
owing to the sudden departure of its recent occupant; the open
doors of closets and cupboards with emptied shelves, papers
scattered about, and remnants of valueless utensils, showed that
documents of any value and all the plate had been removed.
Old Tullibardine, after ransacking every corner of his castle,
came back laughing to the Prince, swearing "the loon had not
left as much as a silver spoon in the house." Rejoicing, however, that the cellar could not be emptied at a short notice, the
brave old gentleman set about getting up a feast directly, and all

16

the resources the neighbourhood could furnish were put in requisition for the purpose. In the meanwhile the Prince was conducted by his host through the castle, much of which had been modernised, to the great grief of Tullibardine, who regretted each innovation, which made his castle look less like what it was when he had left it. On entering the garden his surprise was still greater, to find additions to a considerable extent had been made in this department, even to the luxury of green and hothouses, and the culture of foreign fruits. It was at Blair Athol Charles Edward first tasted pine-apples, which the banquet of that festal day furnished. A wild and singular banquet it was—the dishes were of a sufficiently substantial character for the old baronial times; the exigencies of the hour precluded the possibility of carefully cooking anything; while the produce of the gardens and the cellars bespoke modern refinement, and were fit for the board of a king; but even here the absence of all suitable accessories was ludicrous. The commonest ware, and not much of that, bore costly delicacies; and the choicest wines were quaffed from horn cups. But still right joyous was that wild banquet, and the ancient hall of Blair Athol rang through the night with loud merriment, till dawn surprised some of the carousers at their potations, and the hoarse exhausted song of the reveller was but a prelude to the clear, outgushing melody of the lark.

That morning melody had wakened Ellen from her slumbers which had been deep and refreshing, far removed from the riot of the hall; and she arose to enjoy the early fragrance of the gardens she saw sparkling in dew beneath her window. To rove through a garden was at all times to Ellen an exquisite pleasure, and she found in that of Blair Athol much to admire It seemed as if great care had been bestowed on this department of the establishment, and in her walk among its flowers the morning passed swiftly away. As the day advanced, stragglers running to and fro indicated the stir of life again about the castle, and the old lord himself was soon after seen making his appearance upon a grassy slope, that led from the house to the garden. As in this neighbourhood there was a beautiful bed of flowers, Ellen hastened thither, doubting not she should find him, but on reaching the spot she stood alone amidst its bloom and its fragrance; she raised her voice and called on him by name, but no answer was returned, and then, stepping into one of the neighbouring walks, she commenced a search. At length she caught a glimpse of him through an opening in an old hedge, whose antiquity showed it to be an original boundary of the garden, and she followed to keep him company. As she approached, she observed him looking attentively upon the trunk of an ancient tree, beside which an old but flourishing bush of white rose was growing, and he had just taken a knife from his pocket as if to cut some memento on the bark, which already bore the rough scams of some former carving.

On being addressed by Ellen, the old gentleman turned round and saluted her courteously, while she inquired how he could choose to ramble in that grass-grown and neglected place, while so beautiful a garden lay so near, ·

" My dear child," he said, "this *was* the garden. Yonder is the doing of my Whig brother, who loves new kings and new fashions better than I. *This* is the place where I stole apples as a boy, and I would not give this neglected, grass-grown spot, for ten times the 'beautifications' that have been made at the other side of that hedge. Do you see that old tree ? I have climbed it when it and I were younger, to the terror of my poor mother. It bears a memento, too, of my hand in manhood— look here!" and he pointed out to her, as he spoke, the initials of his name, and the date, 1715, carved in the bark.

" In that year," he said, " I fought for the royal house which now I fight for. In that year I planted that white rose, the emblem of our cause, beside that tree ; and now I return, after thirty years of exile, and the tree still stands, and the rose still flourishes ; good omen of success ! And do you wonder I love this old garden better than the new one ? No! I see you don't, by your glistening eyes! And now I am going to carve my name and 1745, on that same old tree, whose bark shall bear the record that Tullibardine was ever loyal to his king. Yes! that tree and I are older and weaker than we were when I played among its branches. I am too old to climb, and it too weak to bear; but still, though shaken by time, we are un- changed in nature. As well might that tree assume another foliage as I become a Whig. As well might it desert its roots, as I desert the cause of Charles Stuart." Ellen's heart swelled at the enthusiasm of the old man, who began carving his memorial on the tree, while she commenced a careful selection of the choicest neighbouring roses, as a welcome tribute to the Prince, saying she was certain the flowers would be doubly welcome when he heard the history of the tree from which they had been gathered.

Having culled her bunch of roses, Ellen sauntered up and down the old garden, waiting till Tullibardine had finished his carving on the tree, that he might bear her company ; and as she approached the hedge, she fancied her name was spoken at the other side of it. She paused and listened, and distinctly heard her name repeated, and by a voice which she recognised for Kirwan's. A reply was returned, but the intervention of the fence prevented her from hearing sufficiently well to know who spoke, though she rather imagined it was Ned. She caught the sound of Kirwan's voice again, and in a higher tone, which seemed to produce a louder reply than before, at once identifying Edward as the speaker. There was a peculiar tone in the conversation, indistinct as it was, that could not be mistaken for friendliness, and a suspicion flashed across Ellen's mind as to its nature, which, while it made her heart tremble, also piqued her curiosity, and approaching still closer to the hedge, she listened breathlessly for the next word.

Now Ellen, though the soul of honour, and the last in the world who would wilfully play the eavesdropper, could not resist this temptation. But who could blame a woman for listening under such circumstances? Hearing her own name mentioned, and that in an angry tone, between two persons whom she knew were her admirers, and trembling for what the result might be,—perhaps a deadly quarrel, which it would be her duty to prevent. She stood in a state of perfect fascination, as the conversation proceeded, and the speakers having drawn nearer, she could gather much of what was said. Kirwan's tone was haughty and intemperate; Edward's, though indignant, more under restraint. She heard Kirwan calling Edward to account for his over assiduous manner to herself, which Edward defended as being perfectly within the limit of homage which any gentleman may offer to a lady. This Kirwan denied, and a good deal of what followed was lost; but it seemed a hurried discussion of how far attentions might go without being construed into meaning anything, and Kirwan seemed to assume to himself the right of questioning any approaches to Miss Lynch, an intervention which Ned did not seem at all inclined to give way to. Something offensive followed, implying that Edward was not entitled to look so high. This was followed by an enthusiastic outbreak on Edward's part, not in assertion of his own deserts, but asking Kirwan who *was* worthy of so "divine a creature." Words ran higher every moment, and, at last, in a very violent tone, Kirwan called upon his rival to abandon all pretensions to Miss Lynch's notice, and desist from further "intrusion upon that lady." Ned replied with excellent temper, that when that lady's manner made him feel his attentions were intrusive, he should retire, but that he would not receive dismissal from other hands. Kirwan, in still stronger language, insisted on his renouncing all pretension to her society, on the spot. Ned very shortly and indignantly gave a plump refusal, and Ellen heard some enthusiastic expression about laying down his life a thousand times for her. She then heard Kirwan say, with terrible distinctness, "One of the thousand will do for me, sir—draw!"

The next instant she heard the clink of swords, and, uttering a piercing scream, she sprang to the entrance through the fence, and ran into the garden, where she beheld the two young men engaged in deadly encounter, and rushed between them. At her presence they dropped the points of their swords, while Tullibardine made his appearance suddenly, startled by Ellen's cries, and following her footsteps rapidly. She, pale as death, looked silently at the combatants, who stood mute and abashed before her, while the old lord, with stern dignity, reproved them for the outrage they had committed, reminding them that while the Prince honoured the castle with his presence, it became a palace, within whose precincts to draw a sword was punishable with death.

"Surrender your swords to me, sirs," said Tullibardine.

The young men obeyed.

"You are both under arrest, sirs; and I desire you instantly to walk before me to the castle, where you shall be confined till a court-martial be called."

"My lord," said Ned, "I only beg to assure you that I was ignorant of the law it seems I have broken."

"Then, sir, 'tis well if you do not learn an over-dear lesson," answered Tullibardine, sternly. "Go before me, gentlemen," he added.

"Oh, my lord!" exclaimed Ellen, whose heart sank at the name of a court-martial, "for Heaven's sake pardon the thoughtlessness of these gentlemen, who, I am sure, quite forgot the neighbourhood of the Prince, and are therefore unintentional offenders."

"It is quite clear they *did* forget, Miss Lynch, and so do you seem to forget what is due to your Prince, in interceding for such bold offenders."

Ellen had never heard the old man speak so harshly before, and hung her head to conceal the tears which his reproof had caused, and with a heavy heart followed him to the castle, whither he advanced, marching his prisoners before him. On reaching the hall he sent for two armed Highlanders, and giving directions to a servant to place Kirwan and Ned within the strong rooms of the old turret, desired the Highlanders to keep watch at the door of each chamber.

The prisoners were marched off immediately, and Tullibardine returned to the garden, whither Ellen followed, notwithstanding the rebuff she had already received, to endeavour to soften the anger of the punctilious old nobleman : but she found him inexorable ; all the arguments she urged in favour of the prisoners were in vain. Most fitly she suggested the wisdom of not weakening their small force by the bad example of letting a quarrel in their own little band be a subject of inquiry and punishment, while there was a common enemy to be fought ;— that at such a moment, unanimity among themselves was of more consequence than the observance of court etiquette ;—and that the probable ignorance of both, certainly of one of the party, of the nature of the offence they committed, ought to be mercifully taken into consideration. But to all these sensible observations the old courtier was deaf. In his view everything was less important than the respect due to royalty, and the argument advanced, of the Prince standing in need of friends at the immediate moment, only made him more indignant with the offenders.

" When our Prince is here," he said, " almost at the mercy of his lieges to restore him to power, it more behoves us that he shall not have his royal dignity despised nor abated one jot ; his very weakness, in this case, makes his strength ; for what is wanting to him in real power must be made up to him by the homage of loyal and true hearts ; and though he might not, at the present moment, be able or willing to assert his dignity and privileges to the fullest, it is the duty of his servants to see that they be not infringed ; and in my eyes, Miss Lynch, an offence against our ill-provided Prince, our royal Master's *alter ego*, in this humble Highland dwelling, is as great an offence as if committed against the potent Louis in the *Tuileries*."

Ellen assured him she was not insensible to the loyal spirit in which he spoke ; it was only in a prudential point of view she urged him to be merciful and say nothing about it ; and that if the secret lay with the parties already in possession of it, there was no fear of the affair reaching the Prince's ears ; " and then, my lord," said she, enforcing her argument with one of her sweetest smiles, " you remember how truly and beautifully the poet says,

> ' He that is robbed, not wanting what is stolen,
> Let him not know it, and he's not robbed at all.' "

But Ellen's smiles and quotations were in vain. She might have smiled her life out, and exhausted a whole library without moving Tullibardine. He returned a stern look in exchange for Ellen's smile, and said,

" Miss Lynch ; the poet there speaks of a purse ; and would you place money on a level with the dignity of the crown ?"

" At least, my dear sir," answered Ellen, still trying to force him out of his severity by playfulness, "you will acknowledge they are both gold."

"Or silver," Miss Lynch, returned my lord, with chilling severity, "as the case may be. Miss Lynch, the subject is not one to treat with levity, and in one devoted to your King, as I know you are, I am surprised to observe the temper in which you discuss this subject. An offence punishable with death—death, Miss Lynch, is committed in my garden, and I am not to see the offender punished, forsooth, because you can quote poetry!"

"This is unjust, my lord. In devotion to my king I will yield to no one, and I only appealed to your prudence and mercy to induce you to overlook what is, after all, but a breach of etiquette, too heavily punishable to make it Christian-like to prosecute.'

"Ho, ho!" exclaimed Tullibardine, getting very angry. "So, Mademoiselle, you first spout poetry and then preach Christianity to me, to make me forget the honour of my Prince; but you shall learn, Mademoiselle, that old men are not to be moved from their duty by love-sick young ladies."

Ellen felt the phrase "love-sick" severely, and replied with spirit to Tullibardine: "My lord, since you so mistake my motives, I shall take my leave;" and, making a low curtsey, retired with dignity; but when she was sheltered from the stern old man's view, tears sprang to her eyes, and she cried with pure vexation that the state of her heart should be suspected.

Of this, I believe, a woman is more jealous than a miser of his gold.

CHAPTER XXVIII.

THE parting words of the old lord presented to Ellen a new aspect of the affairs of the morning. Hitherto her views and motives regarded the interests of others: now they assumed a selfish form—a rare occurrence with her. The sternness of Tullibardine's manner left no doubt on her mind that he would bring the offenders to punishment, and the stinging phrasfi "love-sick" conjured up a host of hateful imaginings as to the facts that would come out in the course of the examination. The cause of quarrel would naturally become a matter oe question, and therefore her name would inevitably be mixed up in the transaction, and in a way of all others most grievous to a lady; for where is the woman of right feeling who would not shudder at being supposed the cause of a duel? Such were her thoughts as she wended her way to the castle, and sought her chamber; her pretty notion of presenting the roses to the Prince being abandoned in the serious considerations of the hour. She began to hope that perhaps neither of the gentlemen engaged would confess what was the cause of their quarrel, but that hope was abandoned in the speedily-following belief, that on so serious a matter they must waive all delicacy, and answer every question asked. Nay, as she was present, perhaps she herself might be called on to declare all she knew about the matter, and then, "what *would* become of her?" To stand the gaze of a court of inquiry, and be forced by her own word of mouth to declare how important a share she had in the transaction—it was too dreadful, and she wrung her hands in very bitterness of grief, pacing up and down the chamber, exclaiming in an under breath, "What is to be done!" Poor Ellen! she was in sad perturbation, and was long undecided what steps to pursue:—whether to let things take their course, or speak to her father, and telling him all she knew about it, seek his counsel. Yes—she *would* tell her father, and her hand was on the lock of the door to open it, and go forth to seek him, when the project was abandoned on second thoughts.

She had serious objection to speak to Lynch on the subject, for she dreaded his blame. He had made it sufficiently ntelligible to Ellen, that a union with Kirwan would please him, shd he might, perchance, say, that had she thought more of his wishes, and accepted one so worthy in every way, this could not ave occurred. Then again, the quarrel implied that the advances of some one else must have been sufficiently apparent to arouse the anger of her former suitor, and therefore there must be a long talk about love affairs, which to Ellen Lynch was the most hateful thing in the world, and that determined her to say nothing to her father. Such a dislike ever belongs to minds of refinement and imagination. Those of grosser clay may discourse in common of such engagements, and see nothing more in treating of them than of others. To love, (if ever they do—and to marry, which they do if they can,) is nothing more in their eyes than a worldly concern, which they would as soon iscuss as any other matter; but to a sensitive nature there is omething beyond earthliness in all that belongs to love. It is held too sacred a theme to be the common talk of the world— too precious to be approached by everybody—the very hoard of the heart, guarded with a miser's care, and bolts and bars are put upon it that none may pass but the one who is lawful partner in it. So strongly does this feeling imbue sensitive natures, that they have a repugnance even to the imputation of a love which they bear not. Its very name touches a chord in their souls, which the finger of the jester may not approach. It is then—

> " Like sweet bells jangled out of tune."

To produce harmony, one chosen hand alone can wake it, **and** then it doth

> " Discourse most eloquent music."

When Ellen had abandoned the thought of speaking to her father, she next entertained the idea of seeking the Prince, and interceding for the prisoners at his feet; but here again she dreaded her motive might be questioned, and shrank from the attempt. What, then, was to be done? She saw nothing could free her from her embarrassment but the liberation and flight of the prisoners; and this idea took final and firm possession of her mind, and towards its achievement all the resources of her invention were called into action.

To reconnoitre the turret where they were confined was her first object, and this she undertook on the instant. She thought it likely the prisoners would be looking towards the window, if window there was in their place of durance; and she had not the east doubt that if she made her appearance before them, the

gentlemen would not be unlikely to approach the casement to
look at her. She put her scheme in practice, and it answered
admirably ; both her admirers rushed to the windows, as she
paced the grass plat in its vicinity, and she was glad to find that
those casements lay on different angles of the turret, so that
communications might be held with one without being under the
observation of the other. Satisfied of this fact, she summoned
Phaidrig to her presence, determining to make him her confident,
and seek strength in his advice.

All the objections she entertained to speak to others on the
subject vanished as regarded Phaidrig; he was an attached
adherent of her family, loved her to devotion, and, as an inferior,
would feel the confidence reposed in him an honour, binding him
to respect and silence, which an equal might not observe.

"Phaidrig," said Ellen, as he entered her presence, "I have
sent for you to have a confidential word with you about something."

"Oh yis, Miss,—I guessed you'd be throubled about it."

"You know, then, what I allude to ?"

"To be sure I do," said Phaidrig, who wished, with that
delicate address belonging to the Irish people, to spare her the
awkwardness of opening the subject, therefore dashed into
it himself; his natural perception leading him at once to the
right conclusion as to what that subject was :—"you mane the
scrimage in the garden, this morning ?"

"Yes, Phaidrig."

"I thought so. Indeed it is a crooked turn the thing has
taken, Miss Ellen."

"'Tis most painful, Phaidrig."

"Sure, then, it's a quare counthry," said the piper, "where
they wouldn't let gentlemen have their quarrel out their own
way."

"'Tis not for their quarrelling, Phaidrig,—it is for drawing
their swords so near the presence of the king."

"Musha then, but the ways o' the world is quare! Here's
half the swoords in Scotland goin' to be dhrawn in the king's
cause, and out o' them all you mustn't draw one in your own."

"Not just _that_, Phaidrig : it is drawing the sword within the
forbidden limit, is the offence—so near the king's presence, you
understand."

"Arrah, Miss Ellen, you have too much _sense_ not to see that
is _nonsense_. Sure you may flourish your swoord undher a
king's nose, so near that you've a chance of cuttin' it off, as long
as it's in a battle—and you're a hero for that. But if you are
some perches out of his sight, and stone walls betune you and

him, you must keep your blade in good behaviour. Isn't that rank nonsense, Miss Ellen?"

"You must remember the respect due to the prince, Phaidrig.'

"Faix, the man who wouldn't respect himself first, and back his own quarrel, would have but little respect for a prince, or be little likely to stand up for his cause. But, to come back to the story, as I said afore—it's a crooked turn, and how can we make it sthraiter?—for that's the matther."

"Could we not help them to escape from confinement?"

"I dar say," said Phaidrig, "with a little head-work. But is the danger so great as to require it?"

"The offence is punishable with death."

"Death!—oh murther!—Tut, tut, Miss Ellen, they wouldn't kill them for that—don't think it."

"The old lord is desperate about it."

"Yes—I dar say—he's a bitther owld pill. But the Prince himself, Miss, wouldn't hear of it? he'd just maybe give them a reprimand when he made an inquiry into the thing—and—"

"That," interrupted Ellen, "is the thing of all others I wish to avoid—inquiry. I would not, for the world, have the cause of this quarrel made a talk of. You are an old, an attached follower, Phaidrig—faithful and kind; and I don't hesitate to tell *you*, that—" But she did hesitate. "In short," she continued, to be candid with you—I mean that sometimes gentlemen will—will—"

"Will fight about a lady," said Phaidrig, slily.

The words called a blush to Ellen's cheek, but its pain was spared by the blindness of her companion. "You are right, Phaidrig," she said; but though *you* know that, I would not wish the world to know it."

"Faix then they'll make a sharp guess at it, Miss."

"Do you think so?"

"Sartinly."

"Why, gentlemen may fight about many things."

"Yes, Miss Ellen, after dinner. When the wine is in and the wit is out, a hot word will sometime breed a quarrel; but when gentlemen, in the cool o' the morning, go seriously to work, it's mostly a lady is at the bottom of it."

"Do you know, then, the people here are aware of the cause of the duel this morning?"

"No—I don't know it—but I suppose they are not fools, and have their eyes and ears as well as other people : so, as far as that goes, take no throuble about it, for I'll go bail they are up to it."

"Well, let them!" said Ellen, pettishly. "Let them suspect what they like, so long as there is no examination—no words about it."

"Ah!—there it is!" said Phaidrig, "that's the way o' the world all over. It's not the *thing* we care so much for, as the *thing being talked of.* But why would you care, Miss Nelly, *alanna*; sure what's the shame of your being beloved by two brave gentlemen?—for indeed they are brave. The one loves the flowers you tread on, and the other the ground they grow out of; the one is an old friend, the growth of family connexion; the other a newer one, turned up by chance in an hour of trial—and well he behaved in it, and since that same, I hear, was near you in throuble again. Kierawaun is good owld Galway blood, and Fitzgarl is a good name, no denying it, though he may not know just the branch he belongs to—but I'd be book-sworn the good dhrop is in him, for he gives his money, and keeps his word like a gentleman; Misther Kierawaun will have a purty little estate one o' these days, and Misther Fitzgarl has a rich uncle at his back; throth, I couldn't make a pin's choice between them; it's only yourself could do it, Miss Nelly; and indeed I would, if I was you, and settle the dispute out of hand."

"Ah, as cunning as you are, Phaidrig," said Ellen, laughing, (for confidences with inferiors in rank are made easier by mirth,)— "cunning as you think yourself, you shan't find me out. Besides, my good Phaidrig, remember these are not times for wedding— the king's cause before ours."

"*Lanna machree!*" said Phaidrig, tenderly, "the cause of Nature is before the cause of kings,—there is no jewel in the king's crown worth the pure love of a pure heart."

Ellen was touched with the truth of the saying, but still, trying to laugh, told Phaidrig he was getting poetical.

"Miss Ellen, I can't help it, sometimes. Sure, when the truth is strong in us it will come up, like a spring, bright and bursting, and flow out of us, whether we will or no."

"Well, Phaidrig, all the poetry in the world won't get our friends out of their confinement—we must consider how that is to be done."

"Then you are still for their escape?"

"I would prefer it."

"Then your will is my pleasure, Miss, and I'll do all I can for you."

Ellen told the piper how the prisoners were situated; upon which he said a rope was all they wanted for their purpose, by which the prisoners could lower themselves from their windows.

Ellen questioned the danger of such a mode of descent from such a height.

"Tut!" exclaimed Phaidrig, "you forget Misther Fitzgarl is used to the sea, and a rope is as good as a flight o' stairs to him."

"True," said Ellen, quite satisfied with the remark, and made no further observation. But this incident, slight as it was, furnished the acuteness of the blind man with a clue to her feelings.

To give notice to the prisoners of the intended efforts in their favour was the next object, and this, Phaidrig promised to effect by means of his pipes. Led by Ellen to the part of the turret which fortunately for them lay at a remote angle of the building, she desired the piper to play the "Cuckoo's Nest," as that, she knew, would attract Edward's attention. Phaidrig wanted to know why that air would produce that effect, to which Ellen replied, that much as he knew, he must be content not to be in all her secrets, and cunning as he was, she defied him to find that out. The fact was, the "Cuckoo's Nest" was the melody to which Ned had sung his song at Glenfinnin, and the moment Phaidrig played it, Ned appeared at the window. What was his delight to see Ellen wave her hand to him, and point to Phaidrig's pipes, as much as to say, "observe what he plays." She waited no longer than to tell Phaidrig Ned was listening, but her momentary presence was enough to enchant the captive. The signal she had chosen to give him, too, was the air of the song he had sung to her, and his heart beat with transport. Phaidrig next played "*The Twisting of the Rope;*" next in succession, "*The Foggy Dew,*" and then "*Yourself along with Me,*" after which he retired.

This language of music Ned thus translated—"by the assistance of a rope he was to effect his escape in the evening, when Phaidrig should call him." He was watchful now for every passing circumstance; no light or sound escaped him, as he held careful watch at the window. It was some hours, however, before anything worthy of observation occurred; but then he saw he had rightly read Phaidrig's warning, for a rope was lowered opposite his window, and he lost not a moment in drawing it rapidly into his room. He coiled it up, sailor fashion, and was looking about the chamber, which was very bare of furniture, to see where he might stow it away to escape observation in case his room might be visited, when he heard a foot outside the door, and the key turned in the lock.

CHAPTER XXIX.

How the rope was lowered to Ned, lest it might be a mystery to the reader, or supposed to be the work of some "sweet little cherub" that was "sitting aloft" on the roof of the castle, we shall explain; for all supernatural agencies we beg to disclaim in this our truest of histories, which treats but of human affairs throughout. Phaidrig having promised to supply the rope "somehow or other," Ellen carefully reconnoitred the turret, and found, by reckoning its battlements, exactly the points where the windows lay; and as she had ascended that very turret the day before, in company with Tullibardine, who wished to show her a fine view from the platform on its top, there was no difficulty in her ascending the tower again for the same supposed reason, and under the folds of a cloak it was easy to conceal the coil of rope, and thus, without the slightest suspicion attaching to her act, she was enabled to supply the necessary means of flight to her captive friend, though it must be confessed fortune presented an embarrassment in the time of its arrival, which was most inopportune.

In a castle under regular "watch and ward," all these plottings and schemes of deliverance would not have been so easy of design and execution; but, with the irregular nature of the armed forces about it, it was no such difficult matter. The superiors in command were engaged in council most of the day contriving their campaign; and as for the Highlanders, they were straggling idly about the hills, or enjoying the rest the halt afforded, or cooking their dinners, or, in short, doing anything but taking care of the castle; which, after all, there was no necessity for guarding, save for the two prisoners, who were too unimportant to excite a care; for the Prince was in the midst of devoted followers, no enemy was within scores of miles, and why should the Highlanders "fash" themselves about regular military order?

Ellen had kept close to her chamber all day, save at such times as she stole abroad in furtherance of her own peculiar plans. This she did to avoid the chance of encountering any question, or being engaged in any conversation on the business of the morning, and it was not until late in the day she had a visit from her father, whose services had been in constant requisition for some previous hours in the council. She feared he would make some mention of the morning's adventure, but in this she happily deceived herself. Lynch was equally annoyed at the circumstance as his daughter, and knowing besides how painful it would be to her, abstained from any allusion to the subject. It had already given him sufficient pain; he had endeavoured to dissuade Tullibardine from following the matter up in the spirit of indignation which he first evinced on the subject, but in vain. The old punctilious courtier was resolute on punishment, therefore Lynch dropped the subject as soon as he could with him, and depended on the graciousness of the Prince for a more sensible and merciful termination of the business. After a brief visit, Lynch left Ellen to the solitude of her chamber, while he went to join the feast in the hall.

CHAPTER XXX.

In the meantime how fared it with Ned in his prison-chamber? We left him rather in a dilemma. Fortune is a capricious sort of dame, often behaving like the ill-natured cow, who when she has given plenty of milk, kicks down the pail, and Ned trembled for the fate of his rope which the slippery lady had sent him. By "slippery lady," we by no means intend Ellen. Heaven forfend we should give so ungracious a title to a heroine. Oh, no!—we mean to indicate Fortune by that epithet, and as no one has ever accused her of being over steady, our conscience is free from reproach; we have not been the first to take away her character, and we call her slippery without remorse; whereas a young lady to be so, particularly when she was on the roof of a house, where a slip would be a serious matter, would endanger not only her good name but her neck.

But to return to Ned and his rope. When he heard the key turned in the door, and he standing with the aforesaid rope in his hand, whereon depended his hope of liberty, he thought all was lost; but, as in desperate emergencies, thought, stimulated by the spur of necessity or danger, sometimes suggests a sudden measure of escape, so, on the present occasion, she stood Ned's friend. In an instant he laid down the coil of rope close to the

hinged side of the door, which, on being opened, screened the
object it was so important to hide, thus making the means of
discovery also the means of concealment.   A servant entered,
bearing some refreshment, which having deposited on a little
rickety table, the only one in the room, he asked, civilly, if there
was anything else Ned required; and Ned, only wanting his
absence, got rid of him as fast as he could, and the door being
once again closed, and the rope safe, it was crammed immediately
up the chimney, until its services should be required at the time
of "the foggy dew."

The long-wished-for hour at length arrived, and when the
evening shades began to gather on the hills, and the revel without
and within the castle had unfitted all for guardianship, Ellen
and Phaidrig stole forth, and at the turret's base gave the pipe-
signal.   Ellen watched the window anxiously, which soon was
opened,—she perceived Edward emerging from the casement and
prepare to descend—she trembled with anxiety as she looked at
the fearful height, and was forced to lean on Phaidrig for
support.   It was too dusky to distinguish the rope, and when
Edward's hand let go the window-sill where he had steadied his
weight before he had committed himself to the rope, to avoid
oscillation as much as possible, and that Ellen saw him swinging
in middle air, she shut her eyes and held them closed until
Edward's voice close beside her assured her of his safety.

"Dear Miss Lynch!" he said, "how shall I thank you
for this kind interest in my fortunes?"

"I do not forget," said Ellen, "how much I owe to you.   On
the score of obligation I am still in your debt."

"No, no!" returned Edward, "the pleasure of serving you
is sufficient reward for the service;—but this present escape of
mine—to what is it to lead?"

"To freedom, of course," said Ellen.   "You must fly this
place immediately, and escape the consequences of this morning's
rashness."

"To me it seems," returned Ned, "that to break my arrest
is a greater offence than the one for which I was confined.   I
have no desire to fly from trial;—but perhaps my kind friend
Phaidrig here can explain the matter?"

"Not a bit," said Phaidrig; "it's all her own ordhering, and
so let her explain it herself.   Just walk off a bit there with the
young misthriss, Masther Ned, out of my hearing, and you can
say what you like to each other."

The obvious hint in the piper's speech did not escape Ned,
who lost not an instant in seizing Ellen's hand and pressing it
tenderly, at the same moment leading her away; but she

resisted gently, and said, in a flurried manner, to Phaidrig, that she had no secrets to communicate.

"Tut, tut, tut, Miss Nelly, don't vex me," exclaimed Phaidrig; "go off there and talk your little talk together, or by this and that I'll make a screech on the pipes that will bring the whole castle about your ears, I will!"

"Phaidrig?" exclaimed Ellen, in a tone expressive of wonder, and implying command.

"I'm in airnest, Miss Nelly, and you know I'm wicked when I'm in airnest. Go off and talk, I tell you."

"You surprise me, Phaidrig."

"Faix then I'll *astonish* you if you don't go." Filling the air-bag of his pipes with some rapid strokes of the bellows as he spoke, he laid his hand upon the chanter, and raised it in menace. "Be off, Miss Nelly, you little stubborn thing, or I'll blow—I will, by St. Patrick!"

Ned, adding his entreaties to Phaidrig's menaces, and enforcing his request by drawing Ellen's arm within his own and pressing it gently to his heart, whispered low in her ear, "Pray come."

He then led her, unresistingly and in silence, some twenty paces apart. Both their hearts were beating rapidly, for Phaidrig's words had prepared Ned to speak and Ellen to hear what neither had contemplated in this meeting.

Edward was the first to find his tongue; he prayed her to tell him her reasons for wishing his flight.

She answered her fears for his safety, and assured him Lord Tullibardine was bent on the extreme punishment.

"Fear not for my life," said Ned; "even if the severe discipline of the old lord urged him to the uttermost, the affair must ultimately rest at the Prince's option, and I will never believe he would, under present circumstances, permit matters to be carried to extremity; and I am so blameless in the occurrence of this morning, that I have no dread of standing my trial for it."

"No, no!—No trial," said Ellen, "for my sake, no trial!"

"I see, by your objection, you know the cause of the quarrel, and can feel your motives for suppressing all question about it; but let me assure you, I am guiltless of involving a lady's name so unpleasantly."

"I believe you," said Ellen.

"I was called upon at the sword's point to renounce all claim to you—you, who are all my hope in this world. Yes, Miss Lynch, yes; let me once for all avow, that without you, this life is valueless, and I am careless how soon I lose it, unless

17

it may be dedicated to your service—service is a cold word—Oh, Ellen! you are my worship, my adoration!"

It was the first time he had ever called her Ellen, and he was startled at the sound himself. "Pardon me," he exclaimed, "for the liberty my tongue has taken with your sweet name!"

"Oh, don't talk of ceremony with me," said Ellen. "So tried a friend as you is more than deserving of so small a familiarity."

"Bless you!" exclaimed Ned, venturing to raise her hand to his lips, and imprinting on it a devoted kiss.

Ellen withdrew her hand suddenly.

"Be not offended, Ellen. This night must make me hope or despair for the future. In the first place, let me tell you, your father is aware of my love for you."

"Indeed!"

"Yes, on leaving Nantes, my uncle avowed it to him, and offered to make all his fortune ours if he would consent to our union. Your father did not refuse—he only made me promise not to address you as a lover until this expedition was over, and candidly avowed he had intended another union for you.—I guessed it was Mr. Kirwan. Think then with what heavy heart I saw you leave France in his company—led to the boat by his very hand—his companion on board the same ship. Think what bitterness was added to defeat, when, after the furious action we had sustained, *my* ship was driven back, while *his* proceeded in safety, bearing off all I prized in the world, giving to my rival the advantage of such fearful odds, that the chance was he should rob me of that treasure for whose sake I had engaged in the desperate fortunes of Prince Charles. Oh! did you but know the risks, and trials, and difficulties, I encountered to get back from France to England;—the additional dangers that beset me there in holding communication with the disaffected in the midst of jealous and watchful guardians of the law. Did you but know the obstacles which had to be overcome in following here with speed—the sleepless nights I gave to travelling, that I might once more be near you. Oh! when I tell you all this,—done for your sake,—and that you remember I kept my promise to your father, and did not plead my love, you must give me credit for forbearance. But now forbearance were folly. The time absolves me—I may—I must speak, and I ask you at once to be mine!—Yes, adored one, if I am to fly, be you the partner of my flight; my uncle will receive us with open arms—fortune is before us—leave these scenes of danger and coming war, for peace, and security, and love!"

"Your ardour hurries you strangely away," said Ellen, laughing; " you must think women made of very yielding materials, to suppose that the moment a man names marriage, they are ready to jump into his proposal, and a post-chaise at the same time. Oh, Mister Fitzgerald! is that your opinion of the sex? —those divinities you so much adore!"

Ned felt very foolish at this sudden parry of Ellen, which left him open to her ridicule, and even through the gloom he could perceive the mirthful malice which twinkled in her eye, as she thus suddenly cut him off in his heroics.

Ned was all penitence in a moment for his presumption, begged her to consider the urgent circumstances which betrayed him; prayed her not to laugh at his folly; protested that no one could have a higher opinion of the sex, but as for their being all divinities, he vowed he never said any such thing, and swore she was the only divinity of them all.

" Of course," said Ellen, " of course!" laughing heartily, while poor Ned stamped with downright vexation, and prayed her not to laugh at him.

" One comfort the poor women have," added Ellen, " is, that each one is a divinity to somebody, for a little while, at all events. Grecian, Roman, and Snub have their various worshippers. But now, to be serious, and return to the business of the night ——you must fly."

" Suppose I cannot reconcile it to my sense of duty," said Ned.

" Or suppose that you refuse *me* so small a request," returned Ellen reproachfully—

" No, no!" exclaimed Edward passionately, "I can refuse you nothing;—for your sake I would—"

" Well, then," said Ellen, with peculiar sweetness, " for *my* sake."

There was an expression in that one little word " my," which went to Ned's very heart, and dropped balm there; it had that peculiar eloquence especially belonging to women, which may be called *the eloquence of tone*, in which they are so excelling, that the ear must be dull indeed which cannot interpret the melodious meaning.

" You will go now," continued Ellen, " now that I desire it."

" To do your bidding in all things is the dearest pleasure of my life," said Ned; " your first bidding I will obey, but before I go, let your second bidding be, to bid me hope."

" Have you no cause, then, to hope already?" said Ellen, with mingled sweetness and reproachfulness.

" Yes, yes, I have indeed!" said Ned; but pardon, if, before I leave you, I would wish to hear——"

Ere he could finish the sentence, the alarum bell of the castle rang out fiercely, startling the soft silence through which their own whispers were audible, and Ellen, uttering a faint cry of terror, exclaimed they were discovered, and besought Edward to instant flight.

"Say you love me, then!" he cried, "before I go."

The sudden alarm, added to her previous excitement, had so overcome Ellen that, breathing a faint sigh, she sank into Edward's arms. He pressed her to his heart, and kissed her, but found she was quite insensible—she had fainted. He bore her hastily in his arms to where Phaidrig had been left waiting, and, followed by the piper, sought for the present, a shelter from discovery in one of the shadiest spots of the garden, while the alarum bell still kept up its discordant clangour, calling the inmates of the castle to be "up and doing." It was a sound to make the hearts of fugitives tremble.

CHAPTER XXXI.

Ellen, on recovering her consciousness, found herself lying on a grassy slope, her head resting on Phaidrig's lap, and Edward kneeling beside her, bathing her temples—a handkerchief swept across the dewy grass supplying the cooling drops. The alarum bell was still ringing, and instantly recalled her to a sense of passing events.

"*You* still here?" she exclaimed, clasping Edward's hand; "for heaven's sake fly!"

"Let me see you quite recovered first," he answered.

"I am, now," she said, springing to her feet with surprising energy—"fly, I beseech you!"

"Do, Masther Ned," said Phaidrig, "I will take care of Miss Nelly."

"Will you not say, then, before I go," said Edward, in a lower tone to Ellen—

"Hush!" she said, enforcing her word by laying her hand on Edward's breast, and unwilling he should pursue his question within the hearing of a third person.

"I know the question you would ask, and to save time, now

so precious, will answer it without your speaking further. I say
yes—I *do*—I *will !*"

"Bless you!" cried Edward, raising her hand unresistingly
to his lips.

"Go now!" she said, "I tremble for your safety!—and see,
what light is that flickering about the castle?—they have lit
torches, and are coming to search the garden, perhaps.—Fly, fly!"

"Farewell, then!" said Edward, relinquishing her hand,
"we must trust to chance for our next meeting."

"You shall hear of us soon," said Phaidrig, "we are to
march to Perth to-morrow, and on the main bridge of that town
you'll find me at night-fall ;—off with you, now!"

Edward obeyed; and, as he passed by the old hedge, recognised the scene of his encounter in the morning. So far
from regretting it, he blessed the incident whose consequences
had revealed to him the precious secret that to him was worth
all the world. He cleared the fence at one bound, and commenced his night-march to the southward cheerily. Nor staff,
nor scrip, nor guide, had he ; but love supplied the place of all.
He faltered not—he hungered not—he found his path with
readiness : for he was loved. This delicious consciousness gave
him a might, unknown before, to conquer all difficulties, to live
through all dangers, for the sake of the bright reward before
him : for now he knew that Ellen should one day be his own.

All through that live-long night did Edward pursue his
journey. It was long and toilsome ; and when the next day he
reached the town of Perth, he gladly entered the first inn which
presented itself, and sought the rest and refreshment he so much
needed. The table was soon spread with substantial viands, and
Ned, after his long last, fell to with a hearty will, that did ample
justice to the good things of "mine host." While thus engaged,
he had a word now and then with the bare-footed "hizzie," who
was running in and out of the room ever and anon, and he
found the fame of "Bonnie Prince Charlie's" gathering had
gone abroad—that the government authorities were already
alarmed at his approach—while the people, if he might judge
from the *eye* of the attendant girl, were ready to receive him
with open arms, though her Scotch prudence kept her tongue
under proper control ; and her expressions were, at the most,
but ambiguous, though sufficient to satisfy Ned that he had not
fallen into the enemy's camp ; so, having despatched his hearty
meal, he thought the best thing he could do was to keep quiet
within his hostel until his friends should arrive ; and as the
quietest place therein was bed, and the welcomest also, Ned
desired to be accommodated with a sleeping-room, and leaving

orders to be called in the evening, gave himself up to the luxury
of a sound sleep.

He was, therefore, quite refreshed by sunset, when a hearty
shake from the "hizzie" warned him it was time to rise.

His waking glance met the broad grin of the lass, who told
him, with evident glee, that the Prince, and his Highland forces,
were in the town, and that she thought the folk were "a' gane
clean wud wi' joy!"

If in the morning it behoved Ned to keep out of sight of the
Prince's enemies, in the evening it was equally necessary not to
be recognised by his friends; therefore, he waited till darkness
rendered his appearance in the streets less dangerous, and inquiring his way to the main bridge, he hastened to seek Phaidrig.

The faithful piper, true to his appointment, was already
there, and met Ned with hearty welcome, desiring a boy, who
had been his guide, to remain on the bridge till he returned.
He took Ned's arm, and retiring to a less frequented place, told
him how all fared at the castle since he had left it.

"After all," said Phaidrig, "the alarm wasn't about your
escape at all, but some sheds, nigh hand the castle, wor set a-fire
by some o' them drunken thieves o' Highlanders, in their wild
faisting and divilment, and a purty bonfire they made, in throth.
And, as it happens, it would have been betther if you had staid
where you wor, for the young misthriss, you see—"

"I hope no unpleasant consequence has ensued to her," interrupted Ned.

"Aisy, aisy," said Phaidrig, "how you fly off at the sound of
her name, agra; I was only going to tell you that the young
misthriss was out in her guess about the throuble you wor in; and
your life was'nt in danger all the time, as big and bowld as the
ould lord talked about it."

"Indeed!" exclaimed Ned, in delight; "then I need not fly
—I may still remain near her."

"Ow! ow!" cried Phaidrig, "not so fast, Masther Ned;
don't hurry me, and you'll hear all in good time. You see, the
Prince would'nt hear at all, at all, about two gentlemen being
killed on his account, and so he towld the masther—Captain
Lynch, I mane; but the owld lord was in such a fume and a
flusther, that he was let to plaze himself with the bit of imprisonment, and all that; and it was not until the next mornin' that
the Prince sends for him, and tells him he makes a particular request of him to say no more about it, and just to be contint with
the confinement of the gentlemen, and a bit of a reprimand. So,
when old Tully-bo goes to let them out, you may suppose, Masther
Ned, one o' them was missin; and I lave you to guess who that

was; and, my jewel, cart-ropes would'nt howld owld Tully-bully, he was in such a rage at his arrest being held in contimpt, and the prison broke!—and off he goes to his highness, and says, that as he bowed to the Prince's pleasure in allowing such offenders to get off so aisy, he hopes the prince will stand by him, in turn, and not see an owld and faithful servant so abused and held in contimpt, as for a prisoner to *dar* for to go out of his power ; and so, the end of it was, to patch up the owld fool's honour, it was agreed, that if misther Kierawaun was to be pardoned, misther Fitzjarl must be punished if ever he is coteh for breaking his arrest; and there it is just for you, the length and the breadth of it."

"How unfortunate!" said Ned.

"Thrue for you!" said Phaidrig, "you know I always re-marked you had a great knack for gettin' into throuble."

"So, all Miss Lynch's care for me has only exiled me from her presence!"

"Just what she says herself," said Phaidrig—"throth, she's in sore throuble, and blames herself for not having spoken to her father about it, for he was in the Prince's confidence all the time, and could have towld her how 'twould be ; and she is angry with herself for her breach of confidence to the father, and thinks this is a sort of punishment on her for it."

"Poor dear young lady!" exclaimed Ned ; "and is the captain conscious of her share in this adventure?"

"Not a word has passed about it, but the masther is too cute not to see how it is."

"And do you think he is angry?"

"Not a bit.—Of the two, I think he's rather plazed."

"Why?" said Ned.

"Because it puts you out o' the way, and leaves the field open—"

"To Kirwan!" interrupted Ned, anxiously. "True ; true; he will be near her."

"The divil a much good that will do him, I think," said Phaidrig.

"Do you think so, my kind, good Phaidrig?" exclaimed Ned, eagerly.

"To be sure I think so. Don't you think so yourself?"

"Oh, Phaidrig, to be absent, and know that a rival is near the woman you adore."

"But if you know the woman cares more for you than him," said Phaidrig.

"May not his presence enable him to turn the scale?" answered Ned,

"Yes," said Phaidrig; "but it is to turn it more in your favour. I tell you, Masther Ned, if a woman has once got the real liking in her heart for a man, I'm thinking absence is often the best friend he has; for he is always remembered in the best colours, while the one that is thrying to throw him over is showing himself up, maybe, in the worst. When lovers are together they sometimes will have a little scrimage now and then; when they are absent there is no unkindness between them. I hear them say, how soft and inviting the mountains look far away; while I know myself how rugged and rocky they are when you are upon them. And is'nt it so with the best of friends? they sometimes break their shins over each other when they are together. When we like people, we like in the lump; just as the mountain can only be seen in the distance, the little faults, like rough places, are not persaived far off, it is only when we are near we find them out."

"Perhaps it is so," said Ned. "At least you are a kind fellow, Phaidrig, to endeavour to make me think so, in the absence to which I am doomed: though when a blind man talks of the visual beauties of nature, to illustrate his argument, it might shake one's faith in the soundness of his judgment."

"Isn't love blind?" said Phaidrig, with a chuckle; "and who so good as a blind man to know his ways? Remember the owld saying, 'Set a thief to catch a thief.' I tell you, Masther Ned, the lover remembered at a distance is seen, like the distant mountain, to advantage; for what is memory but the *sight of the heart?*"

"True, Phaidrig; 'tis a good name for it."

"And in that sight I am as sthrong as any man," said the piper. "Oh, don't I see my darlin' dog, my bowld Turlough, as plain as if he was here, while I miss him sore."

"Your dog!" exclaimed Ned, astonished and half indignant that a brute should be named as a subject for fond memories at the same time as his mistress.

"Ay, my dog; and why not? as trusty a friend as ever man had, bowld and faithful, and as knowledgable as a Christian a'most; all he wants is the speech to make him far above many a score, ay, hundreds of men I have known in my time: and when them divils o' sailors took me away, poor Turlough was on shore and it's less for my own want of him I grieve, than for the fret that will be on himself while I'm away—poor fellow, he'll pine afther me, I'm afeard."

Notwithstanding Phaidrig's affectionate consideration of Turlough, Ned still disrelished the juxta-position of a dog and a lady, and assuring Phaidrig that he had every confidence in the merits of his canine friend, still he would rather he'd change the subject, and return to Miss Lynch.

"To be sure," said Phaidrig. "Every one for his own; you're for Miss Nelly, and I'm for Turlough. Though, let me tell you, I love Miss Nelly as well as ever you did, though afther a different fashion, and would lay down my life for her, or the masther either. Don't I know all about them as well as they know it themselves? and she, when she was a *dawnshee* thing, afther losing the mother—ah, that was the sad day for the masther, and he was a different man ever since; and she, the darlin', as good as goold ever and always, and, of late times, goin' here and there, through hardship and danger, with the Captain at home and abroad. Oh, there's not the like of her in a million!"

"Now, Phaidrig, there is one question I would ask you," said Ned, "since you talk of knowing the Captain so well. When first I saw him at Galway I thought he was a foreigner, and——"

"Yis, yis," said Phaidrig, quickly, "I hear tell he does look foreign: but sure no wondher, his mother was Spanish; besides, he has been abroad so much himself, it might give him the foreign air."

"But what I was going to ask you was about his real rank, for the second time I saw him was in Hamburg, and there he went by the name and title of Count Nellinski."

"Yis, yis," said Phaidrig, "I know he has gone by different names in different places, when engaged in stirring up interest for the Prince; and '*the Count*' passed off well in Jarmany, and gave a high colour to the thing in some places, and made it not so aisy to trace him; though as for *that* name you spake of—Nellinski I mane, sure it's nothing but his own and his daughter's put before it."

"How's that," said Ned.

"Don't you know that the Irish people, in their own tongue, call Lynch, *Linshi?* and put *Nell* before that, and there it's for you, chapther and verse, as plain as A, B, C."

"So it is," said Ned; "that never struck me before. Then he is really only Captain Lynch?'

"Divil a more."

"And not noble?"

"Except in his nature; and not a complater gentleman ever stepped in shoe leather. A little *high* betimes, may be, and given to admire the *owld blood*, and that's one reason he favours Misther Kierawaun; he would like that family connexion."

"But you think that *she* " said Ned.

" Likes him well, as a friend, but the love never was in it ;
though he tried hard for it, and I'm sure loves the ground she
walks on, poor fellow : but it's no use. Och, a woman's heart is
a quare thing !"

" And now, Phaidrig, I am going to ask you another
question ; how comes it that you seem to favour my cause,
though you were a staunch adherent of Mister Kirwan long
before you knew me ? "

" I'll tell you then ; it's not that I value Misther Kierawaun
a *thraneen** less, but that the love I bear Miss Nelly would
make me go through fire and wather to sarve or to plaze her ;
and I have often thought how hard her place is, going about the
world in danger and hardship with the masther, and how much
betther it would be she was married and settled. And that
same the father would like himself,—and threw the Kierawaun
in her way always to bring it about, but it would never do.
For, gentleman as he is, as I said before, the love never was in
it. And I found out the other day, by a sthray word or two of
hers, that you were near her heart ; and do you know, now, I
always had a notion from the first that she liked you."

" Do you mean to say, from our first meeting ? "

" Yes, indeed, that same night in Galway. Oh, faix, you did
good sarvice that night ; without your help that night the
masther would have been taken, and as sure as he was, he'd ha'
been hanged, for it 'went out on him' that he was working hard
in enlisting for 'the Brigade,' and stirring up the counthry for
the ' owld cause,' and they were ' hot on him.'"

" Oh, blessed chance !" exclaimed Ned, "since it won me
her love."

" I don't say 'love' exactly," said Phaidrig ; "but *favour* you
won, no doubt, that night in her eyes ; she liked the bowldness
of you ; the masther, too, praised your spirit, and often I heerd
her afther that night, when we were hiding in the hills of *iar Connaught*, wishing she could know you were safe, and had not got
into trouble on her and her father's account. Somehow I
thought, by the way she spoke, that in the little sight she had of
you, you plazed her eye, or she wouldn't be so busy in thinking
about a young blade getting into a scrape for a sthreet row.
Well ;—then they escaped out of Ireland ; and the next I heerd
of you and her was from yourself, when we travelled up here
together to Scotland ; and it was plain to me, from the way you
spoke, that you wor over head and ears in love with her. So,
the first opportunity she gave me, I thought the best thing I

* A blade of grass.

could do was to make you both undherstand one another, for, as I said before, the darling girl is in a sore position, and the sooner she is out of it the betther."

"Oh, Phaidrig," said Ned, "as you have done so much for me, could you not urge her to fly with me at once, and end all difficulties?"

"I know she would not hear of it," said Phaidrig. "She is too fond of her father to leave him, and nothing will make him desert the King's cause. No; your plan is to help the cause as much as you can, either down in England or over in France, and that will find you fresh favour in her eyes, and win over the father to you—for there is where the difficulty lies. I towld you he is very high betimes, and given to the owld families and big names."

"Well," said Ned, "Fitzgerald is a good name."

"*Wow, ow, ow*, Masther Ned," said Phaidrig, slily, "that won't do for me."

"What do you mean?" said Ned, startled unexpectedly by the form and manner of Phaidrig's answer; for he had borne his adopted name unquestioned so long, that he began to think it his own, and he repeated to the piper, "What do you mean?"

"Oh, Masther Ned, Fitzjarl is a good name—but you know—"

"What?" said Ned, anxiously.

"That it's not your own."

Ned felt confoundedly puzzled; but wishing to make as good a fight as he could on such tender ground, he retreated from assertion by turning querist, and demanded of the piper if Fitzgerald was not his name, what other name was.

Phaidrig at once replied by returning the hated patronymic —"Corkery."

Ned felt terribly abashed, and, on recovering himself sufficiently from his surprise and chagrin, asked, with an exclamation of wonder at Phaidrig's sagacity, how the deuce he found that out.

"Aisy enough, faith," said the piper.

"You're a deep fellow, Phaidrig."

"Pheugh!" ejaculated the blind man, "there's no depth in that."

"Then how, in Heaven's name, did you discover it?"

"Do you forget the fisherman in the Cladagh?"

"Ah! now I see!" exclaimed Ned, "he carried a letter to my father."

"The very thing," said Phaidrig.

"What a fool I was to forget that!" said Ned, stamping with vexation,

"Aisy, aisy," said Phaidrig, "don't put yourself in a passion; and mind, Masther Ned, you're as good in my estimation as if you came from the earls of Kildare or the knights of Kerry, for you have the *rale* right feeling and behaviour of a bowld brave gentleman, and a king could have no more."

"Does *she* know this?" asked Ned, careless of the piper's concluding laudatory words.

"Not a taste of it," said Phaidrig.

"Nor her father?"

"No.—They went out of Ireland soon afther that night; and it was not until I went back to the Claddagh I knew it. And, as I tell you, you are as good in my eyes as if you were Fitzjarl in airnest; only, if you go to talk with the captain about the *blood*, you see, Fitzjarl is too good a name not to be able to tell something about where it came from."

"What a fool I have been!" said Ned, despondingly.

"Don't fret," said Phaidrig; I know very well what put you on this. You have a feeling above your station, masther Ned, and that's always troublesome; and you didn't like the name of Corkery—'twasn't *ginteel*—no offence, masther Ned."

"No, no, Phaidrig, you're a good kind fellow, and a clever fellow—you know me as well as I know myself."

"Betther, maybe," said Phaidrig; "for I know those you come from. Your mother came of a good family; reduced they wor, like many a good family in poor Ireland, but her blood was gentle, I tell you; and the 'good dhrop' was in her from both father's and mother's side."

"Indeed!" said Ned, delighted. "Then I have good blood in my veins;—how do you know this?"

"Oh, by a way of my own," said Phaidrig; "but we have no time to talk about that now. Only remember, the less you get into a 'tangle' with the masther about the *name*, the betther; and Miss Nelly advises, and I think she's right, that you should do some special sarvice in the good cause, and make yourself stand so high as a servant of the Prince, that you may come back here soon and defy owld Tully-bully."

"Does she suggest any such service?" said Ned. "I will gladly do anything at her bidding."

"Fairly spoken, Masther Ned; and now a last word more with you. Meet me here to-morrow night again. Keep close in the manetime, though; for, by the powers, if Tully-bully lays hands on you, he'll mark you. Meet me here, I say again, to-morrow night, and I'll have more news for you."

"Remember," said Ned, "there is nothing too difficult or desperate for me to undertake."

"I know it," said Phaidrig—"good night."

"Phaidrig," said Ned, hesitating—"before we part, tell me truly—are you certain she does not know my name is Corkery?"

Phaidrig burst into a fit of laughter, which he could not repress for some time, while Ned besought him to desist, strongly deprecating his merriment.

"Oh, its grate fun!" said Phaidrig, when he recovered his breath; "sure poor human pride is a quare thing. Here's a brave fellow, that all the dangers in the world couldn't dant, and he thrimbles at the sound of a name! But don't be afeard, I'll not sell the pass on you—good night—good night."

Ned having reconducted Phaidrig to the bridge, where the boy was waiting, shook his hand heartily, and they separated until the following evening, when Ned, at the appointed hour, was there again, and soon joined by the piper. He, desiring the boy, who was his guide, to "go to *where he knew*," seized Ned's arm, and followed, whispering to him that he was taking him to "Miss Nelly;" on hearing which, Ned started off at such a pace, that the blind man nearly lost his footing in attempting to keep up with him, remarking, that if "a spur in the head was worth two in the heel," a spur in the heart was still better. After threading some narrow streets, the boy stopped before a door, which was opened without knocking, on Phaidrig's whistling a few bars of the air called "Open the door softly."

Softly and quietly they entered, too, a gleam from an open apartment at the end of the hall giving sufficient light to indicate the passage, and, in another instant, Ned stood in the presence of Ellen, seated at a table whereon were materials for writing. She laid down her pen as he entered, and extended her hand, which he pressed fondly, and continued to hold, as he gazed on her face, which was paler and more thoughtful than ordinary. They were silent for some time; at length, Ellen, with hesitation, said—

"I fear you will think my conduct of last night deficient in proper reserve; but—"

"For Heaven's sake!" exclaimed Ned, "do not attribute to me so unworthy a thought of you—you, who are my—"

"No more!" said Ellen; "a truce to all high-flown speech."

Ned still held her hand, and said, "Do you remember you presented this little hand to me the first night I met you?"

"Did I?" said Ellen, casting down her eyes, while something like a smile of consciousness played on her lip.

"Yes," said Ned. "To remember the touch of that fairy hand was my greatest pleasure for many and many a day, till chance threw in my way a more tangible remembrancer. Do you know what that is?" he said, laying down before her on the

table a shrivelled up shapeless thing, impossible to recognise—
"That," said Ned, "once bore in its delicate shapeliness a faint
resemblance of this fair hand—for it was your glove."

"And where could you get my glove?" said Ellen, in surprise.

"In Hamburg."

"I never saw you in Hamburg!"

"No, but I saw you; you were stopping at the *Kaiser-hoff*
there."

"Yes."

"I went to see you there—you were gone. I asked to see
even the room which you inhabited, and there I found this
glove, and made a prize of it; and it was often the companion
of many a meditative and hopeless hour. It was the only thing
I saved when I was shipwrecked. Amidst the horrors of the
fiercest tempest I ever witnessed, I thought of that little glove,
and could not bear to lose it. I secured it next my heart before
I jumped into the sea; and the death-struggling swim for my
life has made it what you see, shrunk and shapeless, but still
precious to me;" and he kissed, and replaced it in his bosom.
"Do you not remember, at the farewell supper of the Prince at
Nantes, when the song of 'The hand and glove' was sung,
I told you I had got the glove *already!*"

"I remember," said Ellen, "though I could not understand
it then."

"The song," said Edward, "prophesied, that he who won the
glove, should win the hand—and here it is!" he said fervently,
as he raised it to his lips, "it is—at least, it *will be* mine!"

Ellen looked at him thoughtfully, and said, "Dark days, and
dangers, and difficulties, are yet before us. Be it enough to
know that you are esteemed—and now, no word more of
romance, but listen. That sealed packet on the table is to
be entrusted to your care; it is from our Prince to Louis of
France. It behoves us that the King should know how far,
beyond all hope, our cause already prospers, and that he should
be urged to lend a helping hand in good time to raise a brother
monarch to a rightful throne. When I found that you must
absent yourself for a time, it struck me you could not better
employ yourself than in being the messenger to render such
good service—service that will win you honour, and for which
your former pursuits peculiarly fit you; and I, therefore, undertook to promise the Prince that I would procure a messenger on
whom he could depend. He did me the honour to confide in my
judgment and prudence in the selection of that messenger, and,
without further question, entrusted me with this packet. I found
I did not count myself higher in the Prince's confidence than

I stood; and I'm sure I did not make an empty boast when I promised to find the messenger." She smiled sweetly on Edward, as she spoke; and he was profuse in assurances that, to do her behest, was the dearest pleasure of his life, and in thanks for the honour she had procured him.

But while he was talking about " devotion," and " honour," it suddenly occurred to him that he was quite without the proper means of prosecuting so important and difficult a service. He had neither horse, nor arms, nor money; for, by this time, Ned's purse had run low, and an oppressive feeling of shame-facedness came over him, to confess this to his " ladye love."

" This letter," she said, as she folded and sealed what she had been writing as Ned came into her presence, " is to one you already know, the good father Flaherty, who will give you his aid in Paris. And these," she added, as she put some documents into an unsealed envelope, " will give you facility wherever you land in the French dominions; and now the last word is *speed*."

Ned wished to tell how he was circumstanced, but could not get out a word.

" You must start early to-morrow," said Ellen.

" Certainly," answered Ned; though he did not know how.

" As for the means——"

" Are you already provided then?"

" I can't exactly say I am, but——"

" But what?" said Ellen.

" Oh, to talk to a lady about money is so horrid!" said Ned, growing quite scarlet.

" To be sure, the *bashfulness* of an Irishman is the strangest thing in the world!" said Ellen, smiling. " He could not ask a lady for some few gold pieces, though he has little hesitation in asking for her heart. Is it less valuable I wonder!" said Ellen, mischievously.

Ned gave a groan of denial, and said she must admit talking about money matters to a lady was awkward.

" Not when it concerns a commission which she herself originates," said Ellen. " But make yourself easy on that point—I have provided all; thanks to the Prince."

" The Prince!" said Ned in wonder; " I heard he had not a *Louis d'or* left."

" Not yesterday," said Ellen; " but the public money of Perth was seized to-day, and here is some of it." She laid a tolerably well-stocked purse on the table as she spoke; and going to an old cabinet in the corner of the chamber, produced a handsome pair of pistols, and a sword, telling Edward, at the same time, a horse should be at his service in the morning. " And now," said she, in a voice somewhat low and tremulous, "fare-well—and Heaven speed you!"

Edward having secured his packets, buckled on the rapier, and placed the pistols in his belt, pressed to his heart the fairy hand which was presented to him, and would have spoken; but words were difficult, where so many thoughts were struggling for utterance. When and where might they meet again, when both were involved in adventures so doubtful and perilous! At such a time the deeper emotions of the heart are better looked than spoken; and after gazing steadfastly upon Ellen for some seconds, he suddenly drew her to his heart, and after a fervent and silent embrace, hurried from her presence.

———

CHAPTER XXXII.

WHEN the rumour first went abroad that the young Pretender had landed, travelling was sufficiently dangerous to those who were interested in his cause; but now that it was known he was advancing on the capital of Scotland, the authorities were doubly vigilant, and kept a still sharper eye on all suspicious persons; and all those whom government influence could induce to play the spy, or entrap the friends of the Jacobite cause, were on the alert to get the promised reward for securing and giving up the disaffected. In numerous instances innocent persons at this time were involved in trouble, and sometimes in danger; how much more, then, did hazard attend the movements of the real adherents of the Stuarts, the moment they got beyond the circle which the Prince's armed power rendered secure, or while they were yet beyond and sought to join his ranks. To cut off all communication of aid from the Lowlands to the insurgents, or of intelligence from the Highlands of the northern successes already achieved, was of importance to the government, and hence the Forth and all the roads leading to it were sharply watched, and bribery employed in some of the small houses of accommodation by the way side, to engage their owners against the Jacobite cause.

Thus circumstanced was the house where Ned stopped

bait his horse after a hard ride.   It was in a neighbourhood where certain flying reports had aroused the suspicions of government touching the intentions of the Drummonds, and a sharp look-out was kept there, so that, as fate would have it, it was the most unlucky place Ned could have put his head into; but, as Phaidrig always said, " he had a knack for getting into scrapes."   A rough, short, shock-headed fellow, in a kilt, who was landlord, answered to the summons of our traveller, and took his horse to lead to the stable, while Ned entered the house and ordered a mouthful for himself while the nag should be feeding, for he had left Perth at an early hour, and had tasted nothing since. The larder of this roadside hostel was not particularly extensive, as, indeed, one might infer from its outward appearance, and the homely fare Ned was promised was not of a nature to require much cooking, therefore was Ned rather surprised at the length of time he was allowed to fast, and to every inquiry he made, the assurance was so often given, it would be "ready immediately," that he began to suppose he should not get anything, and had made up his mind to take the road without tasting the delicacies of "mine host," when his horse had been accommodated : for Ned was one of those good tempered fellows who took things pretty much as they came, and, on the present occasion, as "getting on" was his principal object, he cared less for his own comfort than that of the beast, on whose good service so much depended.   When, on asking again, he received the same answer of "ready immediately," he said he would not take anything, but proceed the moment his horse was fed, and that they need not take any further trouble about his repast."

To this the host replied, he was sure Ned was too much of a gentleman to order a dinner and not stay to eat it—it would be using a host hard to do the like.   He was sure "his honour would stay."

There seemed to Ned something more in this than what lay on the surface.   It struck him there was an intention existing here to delay him, and, this suspicion once aroused, he regarded all that passed since he had alighted through that medium, and felt a sudden distrust of the people about him.   He determined to leave the house at once, and with this view went to the stable to mount directly ; but what was his surprise and increased uneasiness, to be unable to find his horse any where.

He called the host, who, in answer to Ned's inquiry after his horse, answered that he had sent off a boy with him to a neighbouring " burn" to drink.

Ned saw the landlord was telling a falsehood as he spoke, but, feigning credence, he returned to the house with affected

18

indifference, though filled with serious alarm. **After a few** minutes' consideration, his resolve was taken to leave the place at once on foot, and take chance for his escape, rather than remain among enemies. But to do this he must revisit the stable, for there, in the panel of his saddle, his despatches for France were concealed, for greater security.

Having seen the landlord re-enter the house, Ned returned to the shed, by complaisance called a stable, and soon had his knife at work in ripping his papers from his saddle; but quick and cunning as he was, the astute Scot was a match for him; for, before he had completed his work, in ran the landlord after him, and just caught him in the act of pulling the papers from their place of concealment.

" Hegh!" he exclaimed, "that's a rare pouch ye ha' got for yer honour's letters. I doubt they're unco precious or ye wad na hide them i' your saddle.

" What is it to you where I have my letters?" said Ned, very angry.

" Dinna fash, mon, dinna fash, I dinna want to read them! I can mak a guess o' the contents!" said the fellow with a grin.

" Can you make a guess of the contents of this?" said Ned fiercely, as he drew a pistol from his pocket, and springing between the landlord and the door, presented it at his over-curious host.

" Hegh! ye wad na commit murder," he shouted, in alarm, as he held his hands between his head and the levelled weapon.

" I would think very little of shooting a treacherous rascal like you," said Ned. "Tell me where you have concealed my horse, scoundrel!"

He swore it was gone to be watered, and swore so loudly, that Ned saw it was to attract attention from the house. " Don't talk so loud," said Ned, in a very significant under tone, "I am not deaf. If you want the house to be *really* alarmed, the report of my pistol will do it most effectually; and if you make any more noise, that report is the next thing—*and the last thing* —you shall hear."

There was a certain earnestness in the way this was said that carried belief with it, and reduced the landlord to obedience. Ned taking a piece of rope that hung from a ring in the wall, made a running noose in a moment, and desired his prisoner to put it over his shoulders. There was a refusal to comply at first, but the levelled pistol again procured submission, and when compliance was made, Ned, by a sudden jerk, had the landlord's arms pinioned to his side, in another instant he sprang behind him, and his nautical experience had made him so conversant with knots and nooses of all kinds, that the treacherous landlord was bound hand and foot and laid on his back, in little more than the time it has taken to relate it. A small wisp of straw, placed across his mouth and tied down with a handkerchief, prevented his making any outcry, and Ned was about leaving the shed and making the best of his way from so inauspicious a spot, when the clatter of horses' feet startled him ; and as he saw four horsemen trot into the yard he gave himself up for lost, supposing them to be the authorities to whom it was intended he should fall a victim. Nevertheless, he determined to present a bold front, and, if the worst came to the worst, sell his life dearly. Notwithstanding the desperate circumstances in which he supposed himself to be placed, he was perfectly collected; for his was that determined courage which bestows self-possession in the hour of danger; therefore he calmly, though intently, observed the motions of the horsemen. Three of them alighted, giving their nags to the care of the fourth, who, though not in livery, seemed to be a servant. The dismounted men entered the house, and as the face of the attendant was turned towards Edward, he had an opportunity of observing it carefully, and it struck him he had seen it somewhere before. Memory suddenly came to his aid. It was on the race course of Galway he had met him, on that eventful day when his heart became enslaved by the fair unknown one. It was in attendance on her and her father this very man had been riding; it was not likely, therefore, he was in connection with the enemies of the Stuart cause. Ned at once approached the servant, and addressed him, noticing the great beauty of the horse he held.

To this the servant returned a brief assent, but did not seem inclined to enter into conversation.

" I think I have seen your face before," said Ned.

" You could not very well see it behind, sir," he answered; Ned recognising, in the quibble as well as the accent, a countryman.

" Were you ever at the Galway races ?"

" It would be hard for me to remember all the races I have been at." said the other, evasively.

" If I don't very much mistake," said Ned, " ' of all the birds in the air, and all the fish in the sea,' you love the *blackbird.*"

The man made no answer, but returned a searching look.

" If so," pursued Ned, " ' war hawk !' don't be afraid of me. You were riding behind Captain Lynch, at Galway."

" Are the Captain and you *great** sir ?"

* Very intimate.

" Fast friends," said Ned, " and in the same cause."

" He's very great with my master," said the servant.

" May I beg the favour of his name?"

" Colonel Kelly, sir."

" Of Rosconimon?"

" The same, sir."

" Then I must speak with him," said Ned, entering the house, and proceeding at once to the little parlour where the Colonel was seated in company with Drummond, afterwards created duke of Perth by James, but contemptuously characterised by the bitter Horace Walpole, as the " horse-racing boy," which title sufficiently accounts for the gallant steed Ned noticed.

Apologising for his apparent intrusion, Ned told the gentlemen the suspicions he entertained of the house, relating the manner in which he had been served, and the measures he adopted respecting the landlord ; " and, as I have reason to believe," said he, " that your political opinions are the same as mine, I thought it my duty to warn you."

" Then we had better mount and be off at once," said a third party, whose name was unknown to Ned.

" You forget," said Kelly, " this gentleman has lost his horse and cannot go, and 'twould be ungenerous to leave him in jeopardy, after his friendly warning to us."

" Perhaps a good horse-whipping to the landlord would procure speedy restitution of the nag," said Drummond—" we'll see." He left the room as he spoke, followed by the whole party; but, as he emerged from the house, he suddenly paused, and cast a quick glance down the road, as if some object in the distance attracted his attention. Shading his eyes with his hand, he looked keenly for a few seconds, and exclaimed, " There are the red-coats!"

All now looked in the direction he indicated ; and, winding down a path that led to a hollow, about a mile distant, a party of dragoons was visible.

" We must fly instantly," said the nameless gentleman, putting his foot in the stirrup at the words.

Drummond uttered a strong negative to this, and laid his hand on the shoulder of his precipitate friend.

" If we fly now," said he, " the loons will see us going up the next hill, and our apparent flight will encourage them to follow; and though we might outstrip them, and effect an immediate escape, it would not be safe to ride through the next town with dragoons at our heels—no; we must beat them."

" Desperate odds," replied the other.

" Not with such as those," said Drummond; " Gardiner gives

them more prayers than drill; and you'll see how ill they can take cold steel and lead."

"Lead?" returned Kelly, "you forget they are used to Gardiner's sermons"—the devil-may-care Colonel joking in the moment of danger.

"We'll preach to **them** after another fashion," said Drummond.

"Then we had better lose no time in getting our text ready," replied Kelly.

Their arrangements were soon made. A hole was knocked through the shutter of a window which flanked the door; all the shutters were then barred, and all the pistols of the party given to Kelly's servant, to be fired in rapid succession, when the house should be summoned, so that the dragoons might entertain the belief that several were within to make defence, while the gentlemen should remain mounted, with drawn swords, concealed behind the shed and a peat-stack, and make a charge on the troopers at a proper time. The landlord was dragged into the inn, bound as he was, lest the entrance of the soldiers into the shed might put them on their guard, while the women were taken from the house that they should not unbind him, and join in overpowering the solitary man within, who, as his master told him, was to be " an entire garrison in his own person."

Mick (the servant) having barricaded the door, the gentlemen mounted, and took their post behind the peat-stack, where the women were also concealed under their surveillance. They were barely ready in these their preparations, when the distant tramp and clatter of the troopers were heard, and soon they wheeled into the yard, and the word "halt," brought them to a stand before the inn.

The officer in command called " house!" but no reply was returned. He repeated the summons with as little effect; whereupon he ordered a couple of dragoons to dismount, and force the door open with the butt end of their carbines.

This was the signal for the " garrison" to commence hostilities.—Mick delivered two shots, so well directed, that a couple of saddles were emptied, and three more galling fires flashing from the loop-hole in rapid succession, simulated a well-armed force more than prepared for the favour of this military visit.—At the same moment Drummond, pointing to the women, exclaimed with an oath, " Now we'll cut these jades' throats!" and affected to put his menace into execution. The women set up a terrific screech, which was all Drummond wanted, and which he knew the dragoons would mistake for the shrill shout of an onslaught of Highlanders. The four men joined a wild "halloo!" to the women's yell, and rushing sword in hand on the rear of the dragoons, filled them with such terror, that they fled, panic stricken, and never drew rein till they reached the next town, filling it with alarm at the awful account they gave of a numerous detachment they encountered—of being betrayed into an ambuscade by a rascally landlord, who had been bribed into their interest, as was believed, but who had thus sold them to their enemies; and the aforesaid "rascally landlord" afterwards suffered severely for the consequences of this occurrence; for nothing could clear him in the opinion of those whose gold he had taken. It may seem incredible that a troop of horse should thus be beaten by five men; but the subsequent events of 1745 exhibited still more glaring instances of the miserable cowardice of Gardiner's dragoons.*

The field being won, "the garrison" was ordered to open the gates, and out walked Mick with a cocked pistol, demanding from the dismounted dragoons, who could not run away, their carbines, which they gave up.

Mick then marched them before him into the house, and shut them up in durance.

He then gratified himself by a little exercise with a stirrup-leather on the landlord, between every three or four whacks giving him moral advice as to his future conduct respecting what Mick called "tricks upon travellers."

"This is a good day's work," said Ned, "four horses, accoutrements and arms—articles the Prince stands most in need of. One of the horses, however, I must take in default of my own lost one."

"Better take mine," said Drummond. "You need a sound steed on the enterprise you tell me you have undertaken; and here is one that will never fail you."

He dismounted and handed the rein to Ned, who hesitated for a moment to accept so valuable a gift. "Tut, man," said Drummond, "but for you all our lives might have been lost—this is but a small return; besides, 'tis for the good of the noble cause in which we are all engaged. Take him—if pursued, there

* At Frew they permitted Charles' force to pass the ford without the slightest opposition, the first splash of the Highlanders in the Forth being the signal for their headlong flight. At Colt bridge they ran again, the affair being jocularly known to this day as "the canter of Colt Brigg" At Prestonpans their disgrace was completed. Their Colonel could not induce them to charge. He died on the field, while they fled without striking a blow, and, with General Cope at their head, never cried stop until they reached Coldstream that very night—a distance of upwards of fifty miles—a pretty good run.

is not a horse in Scotland can catch him, and there is no leap you can turn him to he will refuse. And now one word more before you go. It will be about evening when you reach Stirling, and I would counsel you to let the sun be well down before you cross the bridge, for it is right under the castle, and 'the Lion,' as the old keep is called, has sharp eyes, and claws too—so keep clear of them. Cross the bridge in the dark, and get through the city as soon as may be, and leave the strong-hold some miles behind you before you sleep."

Ned promised to attend to the caution, and having got back his pistols, reloaded them, mounted his mettled horse and was about to leave, when he paused and requested Colonel Kelly, when he should see Captain Lynch, to tell him he had met his daughter's messenger, and that he was so far well on his way.

"Is there anything more *I* can do for you?" said Drummond. "Favour me with your name, and for your good service this day call upon me at any time, and I will not fail you."

"Sir," said Ned, "since you think so well of my poor services, perhaps you will tell the Prince that Captain Fitzgerald, of his Highness' first regiment, had it in his power to be useful."

"I will," said Drummond, "and more than *that*."

"I fear, Sir, you are inclined to overrate my doings," said Ned modestly; "but if ever you chance to speak of me to Lord Tullibardine," he added, while a waggish expression played across his face—"I don't care how highly you praise me."

"Ho, ho," returned Drummond, smiling. "Some fun I see—well, let me alone for helping a joke. I will play your trumpeter to the skies the first time old Tullibardine falls in my way."

"Do ; and you'll see how fond he is of me!" said Ned, laughing, and putting spurs to his steed, which answered the summons something in the way an arrow responds to the twang of the bowstring.

"That's a mettlesome, sporting fellow," said Drummond, ooking down the road after him; "how well he sits his horse!"

At such a pace Ned was soon out of sight, when his friends at the inn set about completing their work. The landlord, for the treacherous part he played Ned, was threatened with hanging, a punishment only remitted at the prayers of the women, who were then set at liberty, and told they might release their master, which they had some trouble in doing, not understanding the mysteries of the scientific knots in which Ned had bound him.

It was at first intended to leave the dragoons at the inn; but as the horses were an object, and it might look suspicious to see them led by gentlemen, it was determined to make the dragoons mount and accompany them, while O'Kelly's servant could ride one of the beasts and lead the other.

The charges of the carbines being drawn, the inoffensive weapons were returned to the troopers, who were made to appear like a guard of honour to the gentlemen. They, making a *detour* to avoid a neighbouring town, where they apprehended the presence of the military, soon struck into a road which lay towards their friends, and thus the dragoons, seemingly protectors, were led captives into Perth by the dashing Drummond, who made a creditable entry into the Jacobite lines, not only bringing the service of his own sword to the cause, but horses, arms, and prisoners.

It was evening when Ned approached Stirling Castle, that most beautiful of embattled structures. The golden tints of sunset lit up its sculptured richness into bright relief; moulding, dripstone, corbelle and mullion caught the glowing light; the fretted windows flashed back the red rays, till old Stirling glittered more like a castle of fairy tale than a creation of this world. If all the beauty of its interior structure could not be seen by Ned from the road below, still there was enough to charm his eye; the very cliff whereon it is seated spires up so nobly, the guardian castle crowns its heights so fitly, and when, as at that hour, its embattled wall and every "coign of vantage" glows in the flattering light of an autumnal sunset, where is the traveller who would not pause to gaze on Stirling Castle?

Thus paused Ned, according to order; but without such order, thus would he have paused to feast his eye with the picturesque enchantment of the scene. He waited till the glowing towers had faded into grey, and shadow and mist were spreading below, before he dared to pass the Forth. When assured the keenest eye of "the Lion" could not detect him, he dashed across the long and narrow bridge, and the stony streets of the royal city rang to the hoofs of his mettled charger, which soon bore him beyond the "strong hold," as Drummond recommended, and he passed on many a mile before he slept. The next morning, at an early hour, he was on the road, and travelled that live-long day; the gallant horse behaved well, and enabled his rider to sleep at the foot of the Cheviots that night. The next day he pushed on for Tynemouth, where, in his smuggling days, he had made an acquaintance who could serve his turn on the present occasion. His friend was propitious. The horse was sold, and Ned's purse considerably strengthened in consequence, which enabled him all the sooner to get a cast over the herring-pond, by the good price he offered for that friendly office. In fine, Ned used such diligence in the prosecution of his journey, that in ten days after his quitting Perth he arrived at Paris.

CHAPTER XXXIII.

ON Ned's arrival, he repaired to the quarters of the worthy Father Flaherty, to whose good offices, being already indebted for getting him out of Bruges, he was to depend for getting him on in Paris.   The Father was not at home, but, as Ned was given to understand, attending a sick call.—Ned said he would wait his return.

Though we should be sorry to intrude upon our readers an account of all the sick calls of Father Flaherty, yet we think he they have a right to know something of this. It was not to one of his regular communicants the priest was summoned to administer the last consolations of religion ; he did not even know her name ; the messenger said a carriage was in waiting to bear him to the lady who besought his offices, and the priest hastened to fulfil the request.

A beautiful woman lay within the chamber he was invited to enter : sickness had not wasted her noble form, for the attack under which she was sinking was sudden, and the approach of death did not mar the fine cast of her countenance, whose paleness only indicated retreating life ; and what the eye had lost in fire, was more than compensated by the shadowy thoughtfulness which filled it, and became the pallor better than a brighter look.   With a low, sweet voice she addressed the priest, and giving him an open letter, asked him, "Did he recognise the handwriting ? "

The Father knew it at once for Ellen Lynch's.

" You see to whom it is written," said the lady.

He referred to the address, and found the direction was to " *Mademoiselle Le Couvreur;*" and then turned his eyes at once from the letter to the lady.

She told him she was at her last hour, and besought his sacred offices ere she should depart—that she knew her profession excluded her from the benefit of holy rites, but now **the** tragic scene of fiction, and sadder tragedy of real life, being both over with her, she hoped his gentle heart would have pity on a dying woman and repentant sinner, and that he would not refuse her the last rites of the church.

The Father knew of the guardianship Adrienne had thrown over Ellen, and the remembrance of that goodness inclined his heart more readily to melt at the prayer addressed to him ; and not being of the regular clergy of Paris, and hence, free from diocesan authority, he was free to obey the dictates of his benevolent nature, and conceded the dying Adrienne's request.

She expressed a fervent gratitude, and asked him to give her back the letter : on receiving it, she said it was a consolation to her in these her last moments, for it contained thanks from that " angelic girl," as she called her, for being preserved from ruin, and as being thus an evidence of the best act of her life, was therefore a comfort to her in death ; and with these words she held the letter to her heart.

" And now, Father," said Adrienne, " for thy office—brief and imperfect as it must be, for I cannot do all the laws of the Church require.   You will ask me to repent, and with contrite heart promise to lead a regenerate life for the future.   I *do* acknowledge my sinfulness—and with contrite heart ; but as for the regenerate life, it would be a mockery," said the noble-hearted woman, " to affect a good intention and talk of a future that I know exists not for me in this life.   It is to the next alone I can look, and for that next, oh, Father, prepare and cheer me with the holy words of promise."

The kind-hearted Irishman, deeply touched by her words, with as little of form as might be, was content to receive a " general confession," which therefore needed not privacy, and her weeping attendant stood by while she was shrived.

A brighter and more composed expression beamed on the face of Adrienne ; and, as the priest knelt and prayed beside her, and administered the last office, her fading eye was raised devotionally to heaven, while she still held Ellen's letter to her heart, together with the rose she plucked and divided with her at parting.   The sacred duty of the priest being ended, he rose from his knees, and sat beside the bed, and spoke of comfort to her.

" Father," she said, " I die happy ; and when your own spirit shall be passing away, the remembrance of this goodness you have shown an erring woman, perhaps, will be a comfort to you as this letter is to me.   Marguerite," she said to her attendant, who wept silently beside the bed, " let this letter, and this flower, be buried with me—place them over my heart :—it will soon cease to beat."

The attendant, struggling with her sobs, besought the priest to obtain permission for her mistress to lie in consecrated ground; but her mistress interrupted her by saying, she knew that was impossible.

"But it matters not," said Adrienne, "there is a spot I would rather rest in than in *Notre Dame;* it is the parterre before my country house—there, on the spot I parted from *her* —by the rose-tree, Marguerite—there it was I felt and said, as her sweet eyes beamed with gratitude, that I could fancy a seraph had for once looked kindly on me; and there let me lie. I think I see her angelic look now—now.——Marguerite—your hand—I am dying—farewell. Father—God bless you for your charity——I die happy!"

She spoke no more; the voice of Adrienne was silent for ever, and in a few minutes her noble heart was pulseless; yet the lifeless hand still held the rose—that treasured memento of her happiest hour.

The Father knelt beside her bed, and prayed for her passing spirit. His oraison concluded, he arose, and stepped, with silent tread, from the chamber.——Why do we step so softly near the dead? We need not fear to break their sleep. Alas! we cannot wake them!

CHAPTER XXXIV.

THE task is wearisome to wait on men in office, and seek the favours of a government for a foreign state. Edward found this to his cost. With what weariness of body and vexation of spirit did he lie down, night after night, fatigued with profitless days of labour. There was an eternity of promises on the part of the French executive; they dealt largely in the future tense, but it was impossible to screw them to the present. It was always " We will."

The first account of Charles Edward's success was received with considerable distrust, as liable to the high colouring of interested partisans; but soon after Ned's arrival the news of the battle of Prestonpans was received on undoubted authority, and then the friends of the Stuarts, in Paris, were loud in exclaiming the time had arrived to strike. But still the French government was in no hurry. If, in the former case, it would be imprudent to build hopes of success upon such questionable information, in the latter they were inclined to trust the Prince would be the architect of his own fortune without their aid; the secret motive in both instances being their own, rather than the Stuart interest. Whatever embarrassed England was gain to them; or, to use a phrase then in fashion, and which continued so down to the time of Buonaparte, " whatever made a diversion in favour of France " was enough. Later accounts brought intelligence of Edinburgh being in quiet occupation of the Prince—next came news of his advance into England—the French cabinet pleased to consider the game won. Some trifling aid was now given; a few troops, and many officers of the Irish brigade, were allowed to volunteer in the cause, and scramble over to Scotland in wretched transports; but nothing like effective assistance arrived at the right moment. Ten thousand men from France would have settled the question in the first instance. But no—they dallied—George had withdrawn his English troops and several thousands of his allies from the Low Countries, to defend his throne at home, and left France to reap her military harvest of success in the Netherlands,—and this was enough for France—the " diversion " was made, and Charles Edward was left to do as best he might

All through this time how earnestly did Ned exert himself—but in vain. He lived in one continued fever of excitement; he was scarcely sane.

But now a change came over the fortunes of the Prince—the untoward retreat from Derby was heard of, and then France thought it necessary to keep up "the diversion" a little longer, and some money and arms were forwarded; but still the cry of the Stuart's friends was for men—"Send an army," they said.

At length something like such a movement was intimated, and Father Flaherty and Ned were in the beginning, middle, and end of all sorts of machinations; and finally an order was given to Edward to start for the Low Countries, where he was commissioned to communicate with the chiefs of brigade in all matters of information or assistance they should claim at his hands in connection with an expedition to Scotland; and Ned, in a dilirium of joy, set out on his mission, accompanied by Father Flaherty, than whom a stauncher adherent of the Stuarts did not exist. They travelled day and night, until they found themselves in Flanders, where they undertook immediate communication with the military chiefs, who questioned much, and referred again and again to the capital for fresh instructions: but still no active measures were taken.

And now, news of the battle of Falkirk had arrived;—still the Prince, weakened as he was, had beaten his enemies, and Ned besought a timely aid—but it was not granted, and the chill of delay was working discouragement to the cause in all quarters. And now the Duke of Cumberland, and his foreign brigades, had advanced on Scotland. The Prince could no longer hold Edinburgh—he fell back on the Highlands.—The star of Charles Edward had set!

A fever had been in Ned's blood for months. Excitement on excitement had prevented it from being manifested in the shape of downright malady. It might be said one fever had driven another out, and preserved him from disease. As long as the chance of achieving good by his exertions was before him, he kept up; but when he could do no more, the poison which had found vent in action became malignant, and a fierce fever set in.

Fortunately the worthy Father Flaherty was in his company when it first made its appearance, and he hastened to have him conveyed to Bruges, where he got him put to bed; but not till he was in a state of high delirium.

For weeks poor Ned lay in fever, quite despaired of. He raved alternately of love and war. Now he was boarding a ship; anon he was calling on Ellen, in plaintive terms, to come

and release him from prison.   Sometimes he fancied he was
travelling with speed to Paris, would grasp the pillow suddenly and
feel it, and saying " all was right," put it under his head with
much care.   One day, however, when the nurse who attended
him left the room for a moment, as he sank exhausted into a
doze, he suddenly started up, and getting out of bed laid hold
of a knife, and on the nurse's return she found he had ripped
open the pillow, the feathers were flying about the room, and
he chasing them up and down, swearing all the time his letters
had been stolen, and that he would shoot the landlord.   Father
Flaherty entering at the moment to inquire how the patient got
on, Ned fell on him, accusing him of being the villain who had
stolen his letters, beating him with the pillow-case, and feathering the Father's black garments in a most absurd manner.   The
priest ran out and shut the door, and "raised the house" to
help him to restore himself to a respectable appearance.

" I darn't show myself in the street in this fashion," says the
Father, " sure man, woman, and child would be afther me ; and
I with a sick call on me, and can't go out in this figure.   Maybe,
nurse, you could get another brush—the divil sweep him—with
his pillow.   God forgi' me ! the poor mannyac ! Lord, look down
on me !—down, indeed ; faith I'm as downy as a swan, or rather
a goose, I may say.   Hurry, hurry ! pick me, brush away ! musha,
I'll never be clane.   I darn't appear in this figure in the streets, they
are so fond of scandal here ; and, indeed, I could not blame them
if they said it.   Sure if I was rowl'd in a bed I couldn't be worse."

Thus went on the Father for half an hour, while half a dozen
people were trying to restore him to his sable state, which, by
dint of great labour they did at last, and then the Father was
hastening on his mission—his " sick call."   But here, after all his
annoyance, the gentle spirit of the worthy man, displayed itself.

" Stop," he said, " I forgot, the poor boy is raving about letters ; we must try and soothe him."

He got some papers, and made up a packet, which he sealed,
and was returning to the chamber to give it to Ned, when, as he
reached the door, he paused, and exclaimed, " By the powers,
maybe he'd feather me again—ow, ow ! that would never do.—
Here jewel," said he, handing the paper to the nurse, "take it to
the crayture, and comfort him ;" and away went the simple and
benevolent priest.

The nurse on re-entering the chamber found her patient still
greatly excited on the subject of his lost letters ; but when she
handed the packet to him, he became calm at once, returned to
bed, placed the packet carefully under his head, and fell into a
profound sleep.

Perhaps that little thoughtful act of kindness which the priest exercised was the saving of Ned's life; it may have been the means of procuring immediate repose at the critical moment. Ned slept for eight-and-forty hours, and awoke free from fever.

As it usually happens in such cases, he was quite unconscious of all that had occurred. The bed and room were strange to him—the view from the window was not familiar—where was he? As this question was suggested in his mind, he heard a peal of bells, and the well-remembered strain gave him the answer. He knew he was in Bruges; that sweet chime—

"Most musical—most melancholy"—

recalled the memory of Ellen, and, with her, link by link, the chain of circumstances was remembered, until the hour he fell sick. Here the chain was broken—what had brought him there? He stretched forth his hand to draw the curtain of his bed, and the trifling action seemed an exertion. His hand, too, was emaciated—the truth dawned upon him—he had been ill.

His nurse now entered the room softly, but finding him awake, went briskly up to the bed smiling, and congratulated him on his recovery. It was Ernestine, Ned's friend on a former occasion; he recognised her, and asked many questions, but she told him he must be quiet, and giving him a drink, which he took eagerly, left him. He soon fell into that soft, momentary slumber which convalescents enjoy, during which he dreamt of Ellen. He fancied they were in the Highlands, that he was helping her to climb the heather-crowned cliffs; his arm was round her waist to support her, until they gained the summit; then they sat down together, saying sweet things. He lay at her feet, admiring the graceful outline of her reclining figure. She looked so kindly on him, and so lovely—oh, so *very* lovely! He opened his eyes, and, instead of the form his vision pictured, there was fat Madame Ghabbelkramme, squatted beside the bed.

He shut his eyes again, with a feeling of disgust.

"Ha—you be goot agen now!" said she, "bote you foss ferra bat."

Ned made no answer.

"Me elat for dis; fen youn bien goot, me bin clat; and fen youn bin gooter, me bin clatter, clatter, clatter!"

"Clatter, clatter, with a vengeance!" said Father Flaherty, who entered in good time to save Ned from the old harridan's persecution; "Madame, what brought you here at all?"

"Min come to 'muse him."

"Pretty amusement you are," said the priest.

"Ya Vader Flart, you know me ver grabble," (agreeable she would have said.)

"D—l grabble you," said Father Flaherty, losing all patience, "go out o' this, and don't be disturbing the boy."

"Vader Flart, you bin alfays but mans to me."

"Go down stairs, and don't make any more noise here," said the father, disregarding her displeasure; "you'd bother a rookery, so you would." With these words he made her leave the room, she almost crying with vexation, ejaculating all the way down stairs, "bat mans—Vader Flart—bat mans!"

"What did you let that old bother up here for?" said the Father to Ernestine, who came running up stairs.

Ernestine said the old woman had taken advantage of her back being turned, and made her way to the young gentleman.

"Ay, indeed—the young gentleman," echoed the priest—"you just said it, The young gentleman—bad luck to her, the ugly fat old divil! she is as great a fool about the young gentleman as if she was eighteen years instead of eighteen stone—my heavy hathred to her!—And now, Ned, my poor fellow, how goes it with you—you're wake, I suppose?"

Ned gave a faint smile, as an answer to the question.

"Never mind that," said the priest, "now that you're well, we'll soon get up the strength; we'll give you the jelly, and the fish, and the soup, and the nice white mate, and the dhrop o' claret. Whoo!—by the powers, we'll make you live like a fighting-cock!"

CHAPTER XXXV.

FATHER FLAHERTY's prophecy was fulfilled. Ned gathered strength fast, even against the depressing influence of the evil tidings that soon came pouring in from Scotland. At last the tragic drama was brought to a conclusion on the fatal field of Culloden, and all that could now be done was to let friendly ships hover about the Scottish coast to pick up any stragglers who might escape the vengeance of the savage soldiery, stimulated to the most sanguinary and revolting excesses by the "butcher"* who commanded them—the atrocious Duke of Cumberland,—whose memory is still execrated in the hills and valleys he drenched with blood—not the hot blood of battle, but the cold blood shed in ravening vengeance afterwards. Not even the blood of men would satisfy: women and children were given up to carnage and to indignities still worse than death. Nor age, nor sex, nor rank, was regarded. Every excess that could shock humanity was in open practice every day;—a licentious soldiery, foreign and domestic, was let loose to do their worst—and not only to do it with impunity, but to win favour for their atrocities in the eyes of their merciless leader.

The instant his strength permitted, Ned embarked in a French vessel employed in the charitable act of hovering about Scotland, and affording refuge to the fugitives who could escape their hunters. In this duty, as he heard from time to time, from the lips of eye-witnesses, the recitals of blood and depravity in course of constant commission, how his heart was torn—how his imagination heaped horror on horror that might have befallen those who were so dear to him! Had Lynch fallen a victim to the cold-blooded carnage? Or was Ellen?——Oh, horror!—to think of her was to be driven to the verge of madness. The exertions he made to get off fugitives from the land were prodigious. There was no risk he did not run with the

* "He left behind him in Scotland the name of *the Butcher*, and the people of England, disgusted sooner than any other with cruelty, confirmed this title to the hero of Culloden."—*Pict. Hist. Eng.*

"It was lately proposed in the city to present him with the freedom some company; one of the alderman said aloud, 'then let it be of butchers.'"—*Horace Walpole.*

19

boats, whenever tidings were heard of parties hanging about
the shore for escape, in the hope that Ellen might be among
them, but in vain : refugees crowded to the vessel, yet still had
Ned to endure the agonies of suspense. The captain, finding
his ship so full, proposed running to the Flemish coast, landing
the unfortunates, and returning again to the service of humanity;
but Ned prevailed on him to wait another day; intelligence was
had of some fugitives who proposed attempting their escape on
board the Frenchman the next night, and as a lady was reported
to be amongst them, Ned would not give up the chance of
finding in her his beloved Ellen.

The point being ascertained where the attempt would be
made, the vessel ran in under the land when it was dark, and
Ned, with a boat well armed, pushed off. The signal-light was
seen to glimmer on the shore ; with muffled oars they pulled
silently into an inlet, and the hunted adherents of the ill-fated
Stuarts came from their hiding-places among the rocks. Foremost of the party was a wounded man, supported by two companions towards the boat, and passed along by the assistance of
the sailors to the stern sheets, where Ned had charge of the
helm ; but how was he startled, when, in extending his hand to
the wounded stranger, and placing him beside him, he recognised
in his pale and haggard face the features of Kirwan !

Ned's heart bounded with expectancy ! From Kirwan's
presence he was certain the reported lady of the party would
turn out to be Ellen; but as yet no lady appeared, though
several persons had entered the boat.

"Push off now," said the last who embarked.

"Avast !" said Ned, who turned to Kirwan, and asked in a
voice which quivered with anxiety, "is not Miss Lynch of your
party ?

"Yesterday," replied Kirwan, faintly, and manifestly speaking with difficulty, "yesterday she was—but—but—"

"But what ?" cried Ned, "answer—for God's sake, answer!"

The answer was, the heavy fall of Kirwan's lifeless corse
upon Edward's breast.

Oh ! fearful break that death hath made in the sentence !
"yesterday she was—but—"

An apalling array of possibilities respecting Ellen, rushed
through Ned's brain, and he sank backwards, insensible as the
corse under which he fell.

Immediate assistance was offered; but the kindly offices were
suddenly disturbed by the approaching clatter of horses' feet
and the clank of arms, showing too plainly, that the dragoons were
upon them, and no time was lost in shoving the boat from the

shore and pulling vigourously out to sea; not, however, before the troop had time to send a volley after the fugitives: but darkness favouring their retreat, the fire was ineffective, while, the flash of the guns from the beach betraying the position of the pursuers, the arms of the boat were employed with more effect in returning the compliment, while the soldiers' fire could not produce the same fatal result to them, as the boat was shifting her position every moment. The well-plied oars, however, soon placed the enemies out of each other's range, and the speed, urged by danger in the first instance, was now continued for humanity's sake, as they wished to reach the vessel as soon as possible, to obtain the needful assistance for Ned, who still lay insensible in the bottom of the boat, a faint breathing being the only indication of life he retained. Consciousness soon returned, however, under the restoratives employed when he was placed aboard, and he began to gaze wildly round the cabin, whither he had been borne. After asking a few incoherent questions, he became fully sensible of all that had taken place, and inquired if Kirwan were dead or had only fainted from loss of blood. On being answered that he was dead, he exclaimed, "Then I shall never know her fate," and hid his face in his hands. It was with much persuasion he was prevailed on to go to his berth; but he could not sleep. All through the night he thought of nothing but scenes of outrage, and when, towards morning, exhausted with mental anguish, he sank into a doze, it was only to dream of darker horrors. He rose, with haggard cheek and sunken eye, and ascended to the deck, where, at so early an hour none but those doing the duty of the ship were present, therefore he might pursue his melancholy train of thought undisturbed. On casting a look astern, the Scottish shore was no longer visible, and a glance at the compass showed him they were running down for the Flemish coast. On exchanging a few words with the officer of the watch, he learned that the body of Kirwan had been committed to the deep at midnight; and it just flashed upon Ned's memory that two years before, in that very sea, he had snatched him from the watery grave to which he was now consigned: and there seemed to him a singular fatality in this coincidence. "He has been strangely mixed up," thought Ned, "in all that has influenced my destiny. He was with *her* the first night we met, and he died with her name upon his lips. He was my rival through life—in death, his broken answer is agony. The rivalry I have outlived,—but does the prize for which we contended still exist?" He groaned in mental anguish at the question, and turned from the lieutenant to pursue his walk in silence. The Captain soon after came on deck, and handed some papers, found on Kirwan's person, to Ned, as he seemed the one who knew most of the deceased. Ned anxiously opened them, hoping he might discover some clue to Kirwan's recent movements, and thence be more able to infer something of Ellen's fate ; as, from his last words, it was clear he had borne her company but the day before he died. The first document was a commission in the Irish brigade ; but, on the fold of a letter within it, Edward recognised Ellen's handwriting, and eagerly opened the paper. He paused for an instant, the internal monitor—honour— suggesting the question if he were justified in reading it; but the circumstances of uncertainty in which he was placed, satis- fied his conscience that he committed no violation of propriety by the act, and he read.

"You complain of my recent coldness, and appeal to our long friendship in your behalf, claiming, on that score, a gentler consideration at my hands.—Had you been content with me as a friend, you should have ever found me the same—unchanged and unchangeable. Even when taking the extreme advantage of the position in which my father's favour placed you, you urged me by a question always painful to both of us ; I never denied you the friendship beyond which I could not go ; nay, I pardoned even importunity, and abated not my regard : but when you assumed the right to question others on the subject of their esteem for me, you committed an offence which you cannot wonder I feel deeply.

"To tell you all the pain I have endured at my name being made the subject of a brawl, would be to tire you with a repetition of my own daily suffering. The circumstances under which it occurred, and the high personage offended by it, have made it a matter of provoking notoriety ; such affairs as these tend to lessen the respect which the unobtrusiveness, properly belonging to maidenhood, is sure to maintain, and which, till now, I have never forfeited. I fancy I hear myself pointed out for observation, as '*the girl the two fellows fought about*,' and shrink at the impertinent glances of the hot-headed mad-caps who are about us. Oh! how could you respect me so little as to reduce me to this?

"Nevertheless, I forgive you,—for my father's sake, and the sake of old friendship; but, remember, it is friendship *only*. Ask me no more questions of *any sort*,—if you do, even the friend- ship which I still bear you must cease. For the future, let there be kindness, but, also, silence between us on one point. You understand me, and ought to know me well enough to be certain

I will hold to my resolution. Once and for all, remember—we are *friends;* how long we remain so depends upon yourself.

"ELLEN."

Oh! woman, woman, how tyrannous is the dominion of a deep love for thee, over the heart of man!—we see it here in the case even of a rejected lover.—Poor fellow—these lines of the loved one, though they condemned him to despair, he could not part with.

Ned now opened the second paper; let the reader judge how his heart sank when he read it.

"DEAR KIRWAN,

"We will meet you at the pass to-morrow, and run the risk of reaching the coast; better anything than this uncertainty of concealment. One thought alone oppresses me, too painful to speak of, even to you—almost too terrible to think of myself—therefore I write my wish before we meet. In case of attack from the military, our party will fight to the death, of course, and Ellen must be under your especial care. For this purpose, I enjoin you to keep where there is least of danger during the fight. If we prosper, (which God grant!) it is well; if not, (and the Divine will be done!) my lovely girl must not survive defeat. To your hand, then, I entrust this last and dreadful act of friendship; as I would have given her to you for life, so do I for death, if needful—the more difficult trust to discharge. But I enjoin you, by every tie of honour and humanity, set her pure spirit free. Were there no other hand to do it, I would emulate Virginius; but you will spare me so fearful a task: I know you will. God help us, we live in fearful times, when a father thinks it virtue to contemplate the death of his own beloved child—and, oh, how I love her!——I cannot venture to write another word.

"Remember—I depend on you.

"MARTIN LYNCH."

These dreadful lines scarcely left a hope. The father's terrible injunction to Kirwan, in case of disaster, stood fearfully prominent to the coldest conjecture: what must the heated imagination of a lover have conjured up? Defeat was the signal for Ellen's death—and that defeat had ensued, Kirwan's wounds were but too palpable evidence. Ned burst forth into a passion of grief, which he found it impossible to control, and gave himself up to utter despair.

In the meantime the vessel neared Ostend; the fugitives who

had escaped the slaughter debarked, and the ship prepared to return to the Scottish coast, further to pursue the work of charity
in which she had been engaged. The Captain proposed to
Edward to continue in this service, suggesting, that he might yet
recover his apparently lost friends, and that, even in case of
failure, the mere occupation would be beneficial to him; but
Edward refused ever again to approach the land which had
proved so fatal to his hopes, (for he had given himself up to the
conviction that Ellen had perished); and, taking a sad farewell of
the ship and his companions, he returned to Bruges, and sought
his old friend, Father Flaherty.

CHAPTER XXXVI.

DISASTER having so scattered the principal personages of our
tale, the reader must pardon a scrambling chapter or two in which
the loose threads of the story will be caught up, rather than any
attempt made to perfect the web of our history: the detail which
that would lead to, both as to the persons concerned and the
times and places in which the events befel, would be painful, and
the painful is an ingredient which the novelist should use
sparingly, as a good cook should use pepper.

First, as to our hero. The meeting between him and Father
Flaherty was full of sadness—not merely of commiseration on
the Father's part; for he loved Ellen earnestly, so there was communion of sorrow between them. But the good priest's sense of
humble submission to the Divine will, gave strength to his words
as he taught Edward to submit. His consciousness of an overruling Providence to guard, and mercy to spare, made him
eloquent to induce his young friend to trust. And Edward derived such consolation from his words that his grief, though not
less, became more tolerable.

But while the father exhorted his young friend to hope, his
manner showed that the reed on which he would have another
lean was too slender to support himself:—poor Father Flaherty!
he was too simple to impose upon a child. It was too plain
he thought all hope was past; and Ned, when alone, would repeat to himself, " Though he bids me hope, he thinks she is

dead." Then would he fall into a reverie, and ask, " Could it so be ? Was she indeed no more ? The beautiful and bright, in an instant snatched away—the object and motive of his life— that for which he had dared, and hoped, and struggled, and achieved so much—vanished like a dream ? Could he be doomed to so wretched a fate ?" His soul shrunk from the bitter belief, and the faintest glimmer of hope would be welcome to his darkness :—*she might yet live.* Then would he pursue *that* phantom, created of his wishes, till his exhausted heart sank in the fruitless chase, and his reverie would end, as it had begun, with the melancholy phrase " She is dead !"

In a short time, however, tidings reached the Netherlands that revivified hope even in poor Ned's heart. It was reported that many fugitives had escaped to Ireland, and he determined at once to go there and endeavour to solve the uncertainty that was sapping the sources of his life. He informed his kind friend the priest of his intention, who pronounced in favour of the movement, declaring Ned " should leave no stone unturned until he rooted out the mysthery :"—be it known, all this time, that Father Flaherty thought less of the chance than even Ned, but he kept that to himself; for, as he thought, if it would do no other good, it would "give the poor boy something to do," and thus conduce to that special cure for melancholy known in Ireland under the expressive title of " divarting the grief."

So Ned went to Ireland, and of course he found very strange things going on there :—there must be something in the air of Ireland to make everybody, even the sensible English, cut strange capers in that land of unrest.

It may be received as an axiom, that if a nation be tranquil under its rulers, that is all the rulers might require. Well— Ireland was so quiet under the rule of Lord Chesterfield's vice-royalty, that he spared all the army out of Ireland to quell the rebellion in Scotland. But the moment the rebellion in Scotland was quelled, England withdrew the pacific Chesterfield and sent back the army to Ireland.

Now, the existence of a standing army in a country would naturally be considered to imply the existence also of some important object that could not be achieved without it—some point of statesmanship that could only be carried at the point of the bayonet. But no such object then existed in Ireland ; the power thus given was wielded by a few unwise people in the support of some cruel practices, and many silly ones.

Among the former was the amusement of priest-hunting, which, in a country abounding with hares, seems rather a mistake. Among the latter, one may suffice as a specimen. It was not permitted in Galway that a Roman Catholic merchant should wear his hat on 'Change. Only fancy a standing army for the mighty purpose of enforcing the cry of "Hats off!" We can only laugh at the absurdity now, but the matter turned out to be more than a joke for Ned. It fell out thus :—

He went to Ireland in search of his beloved Ellen ; he knew that she and her father, if in Ireland, would be sheltering in the mountain wilds of Iar Connaught, and as his road lay near Galway, he thought he might as well go and see his old father, of whom he had taken such sudden and disrespectful leave, and ask his forgiveness; for when we are smitten hard by trouble ourselves, we are more inclined to think of the trouble we have given to others. Misfortune is the mother of repentance.

It was in this spirit Ned entered the walls of his native town, some years after he had fled from it, in consequence of the memorable night adventure that was the beginning of his romantic fortunes ; and his subsequent life of independence and daring, and intercourse with the wide world, was not calculated to increase his respect for the small magnates of the secluded spot he returned to ; in fact, Ned never thought of the matter at all, and had utterly forgotten all about the wonderful dignity of such little great people; and the incident we are about to record, instead of awakening his memory and his respect, only roused his indignation.

As he was going to his father's house, who should cross the street by the corner Ned was approaching, but old Dennis himself. Ned's first impulse was to follow, and at once speak to him ; but on second thoughts he paused. "I cannot, nor ought not, embrace him until I have asked his pardon," said Ned to himself; "and as the street will not do for that, I had better wait till I see him at home." He followed, however, at a distance, and watched the old man as he plodded onwards towards the Exchange. He was a good deal altered since his son had seen him last. His hair had grown grey, and he had become more bent; his step, too, was slower, and less steady, and his whole aspect had a subdued air about it, which spoke of suffering. The unpleasant question suggested itself to Ned, "If he had any part in producing this;" and his heart smote him, and an inward promise was made that he would endeavour to make amends in the future for the past.

Just then a burly, swaggering person, with a large gold-headed cane and a laced coat, going the same road as old Corkery, brushed rudely by him, and made the old man stagger against the wall.

"What an insolent ruffian," thought Ned, "to shove against an old man in that manner. I'd like to kick him."

The old man against whom the offence was committed seemed to take the affair as a matter of course, and plodded on as if nothing had happened. Indeed, so lost was he in some melancholy musings respecting the sad condition in which old age had overtaken him, without one of his own blood to aid him, that he forgot even the business of the Exchange, whither he was proceeding; and this state of absence continued even after he had entered that place

"Where merchants most do congregate;"

for he had forgotten to take off his hat.

He did not wait long, however, without some one "refreshing his memory;" for the identical swaggering gentleman with the gold-headed cane came up to him, and, with a fanciful flourish of the aforesaid cane, knocked off old Corkery's hat.

Ned, who had followed his father, arrived just in time to witness the act. The same bully who had shoved the old man against the wall had committed a fresh and grosser offence; and instantly the indignant son rushed upon him, and, shouting forth the words, "Insolent scoundrel!" he struck his clenched fist into the face of the offender, and upset laced coat, hat, wig, and dignitary (for he was one of the great men of the corporation), and the uproar that arose on his fall baffles description.

Several ran to the assistance of the fallen corporator, while others attempted to lay hold of Ned, amidst cries of "Down with him!" "Seize him!" but he, whose thews and sinews were braced by hardy service, knocked down the lumbering merchants "like nine-pins," and strewed the pavement of the Exchange with wigs and cocked hats; but, observing the approach of some liveried gentlemen, carrying long poles of office, Ned saw further fight was impossible, so he turned to the right about and showed them a fast pair of heels for it. The hue and cry was raised after him—a regular "Phillilew!" but, intimate as he was with every lane and alley of the town, he left his pursuers far behind him, and soon had perfect choice to go unobserved whither he would. At first he thought of his father's house; but it was likely that would be searched: for Ned by this time remembered where he was, and the consequences attendant on his act. He turned in an opposite direction, therefore, and walked smartly into the fish-market, where, by the quay side, he could find some boat to take him over to the *Cladagh*, that sure sanctuary for any gentleman in his circumstances.

After Ned's disappearance, the question of "Who is he?"

ran round the Exchange, but nobody knew—nobody but one—
and he, of course, would not. This was his father, who, in the
first glance he caught of him, knew his boy, improved in appearance though he was, almost beyond recognition. The blusterers
crowded round old Corkery, and desired him to tell who the
scoundrel was who dared to raise his hand against a Protestant
gentleman, but the father pleaded ignorance.

"You're a lying old crawthumper!" cried one.

"Not a one o' me knows, indeed, gentlemen," said Corkery.

"I'd make him tell!" cried another; "I'd give him some holy
water under the pump."

"Sure, you are all witness I made no complaint when my hat
was knocked off."

"Curse your impudence!" exclaimed a third speaker.
"Complaint indeed! What right have you to complain? Of
course it was knocked off, when you dared to show your face
here with your hat on."

"I beg your pardon, gentlemen—I quite forgot—my poor
owld head was thinking of one thing or another, and it was a
forget, and nothing else, that kept the hat on me."

The affair at last came to a conclusion by the arrival of the
mayor, who reprimanded Corkery bitterly for his "outrageous
conduct," as he was pleased to call it, in causing a riot and
breach of the peace on the high 'Change of the ancient and loyal
town of Galway, by a gross and daring violation of its laws and
privileges.

Poor old Dennis took his bullying quietly, and got off
'Change as fast as he could, amidst scowls and growls, and sought
his home, trembling for the fate of Ned, in case he should be
taken.

CHAPTER XXXVII.

NED, in the meantime, had made his way over the river, and went to the cottage of the fisherman, where Lynch had sheltered on that eventful night which witnessed the initiatory step of Ned into the regions of romance. The fisherman was not at home; but his wife, who was mending a net at the door, told Edward she soon expected his return, and, Ned proposing to wait for him, the woman rose, and inviting our hero to enter, dusted a rude chair with her apron, and requested him to be seated. A fine little boy was tying a piece of rag on a skewer, which he had stuck into a flat piece of wood, the whole representing boat, mast, and sail to his juvenile fancy; the toy of the child indicating the future occupation of the man. The little fisherman in embryo paused in his work on the entrance of the stranger, whom he eyed with a furtive sidelong glance under his little brow.

The mother resumed her work at the door, but soon laid it down and went away. She turned into a neighbour's cottage and asked her,—would she "just run up to the corner, and watch for her husband coming home, and give him the 'hard word' that there was a strange gentleman waiting for him at home; for sure there was no knowing whether he would like to see him or not—because they were *quare* times, and *hard* times." After this precaution she returned to the door and resumed her work. In a few minutes one neighbour after another came up to where she sat, and looked keenly into the house at Ned while they spoke to the mistress, and having reconnoitred, passed on. Ned knew too much of the habits of the people not to see he was an object of observation, if not of suspicion; but, aware that to betray such a knowledge on his part would be to confirm their bad opinion of him, he waited his opportunity for letting them understand him. This occurred ere long, for a large-boned, dark-browed man soon came up to the door, and, after giving the civil word to the woman of the house, strode into it, with the words, "God save all here!"

Ned frankly returned the accustomed response of "God save you kindly!" at which the aspect of the man became softened, and, after exchanging a few words with Ned, he walked out again.

At last the man of the house himself returned and Ned rose

to meet him. The fisherman did not recognise him, but a few
words from Ned recalled him to his memory. On the mention
of Lynch's name, the fisherman cast a searching look at his
unbidden guest, and said, in an under tone, "Arrah, then, do
you know where the Captain is?"

"No," said Ned, eagerly; "do you?"

"Me!" said the man, as if he wondered how any one could
ask him the question. "Musha! how would I know?"

Ned made no observation; but it struck him there was something in the fisherman's manner that indicated the knowledge
he disclaimed. Eager as he was for knowledge on that point,
however, he wisely forbore to urge it, well knowing it would be
of no use, and fearing it might damage what little interest he
might have in that quarter, and which he needed to employ.
Leaving, therefore, the matter as it stood, he related his adventure on the Exchange, and for the second time requested the
fisherman's good offices in going to his father, and telling him
where he was; adding, that, as it might be unwise for Ned to go
into the town, he hoped his father would come over to the
Cladagh.

The message was carried, as Ned wished; and an hour did
not elapse until he had the satisfaction of receiving the old man's
welcome and blessing. As for all the pardon he expected he
should have to ask, his father cut it short. He admitted Ned
had behaved like an "undutiful young blackguard," but he
hoped he knew better now; and "'pon his soul, he was mighty
well grown, so he was." The fact was, old Corkery felt proud
of the handsome person of his son; and, though he was rather
uneasy as to the consequences of the affair of the Exchange, yet
in his heart he could not help liking Ned the better for knocking
down the bully who had insulted him.

The fisherman and his wife had the politeness to make a clear
house of it; and father and son being left together, an account of
Ned's adventures since he quitted Galway filled old Corkery with
immeasurable wonder; but most of all he wondered how Ned
could have the assurance to make love to a *rale lady*. At this
brightest and darkest portion of the story, Ned was much excited, and candidly told his father that the chance of finding
her, in case she had escaped the Highland massacre, was his chief
business in Galway.

"Faix, then, she has as great a chance of being massacray'd
in Galway, I can tell you, as in Scotland; for they are hot afther
any one they suspect of having anything to do with the rising;
and the divil a much they scruple doing anything. As for you,
Ned, what with your smuggling, and privateering, and having to

do with the rebels, there's as much on your head as would
hang fifty, and I advise you to lave Galway ' while your shoes
is good.'"

" Not until I have sought for her?"

"Very well,—you'll have your own way I see. But, if I was
you I'd make off to Spain as hard as I could to the uncle.—Wow
—ow!—and there's more of the wondher!—Who'd think of
brother Jerry turning out a great Spanish lord?—Faix, I'd like
to go to Spain myself and see him, only maybe he would'nt speak
to a body now that he's so grate a man."

" Ah, sir, you little know my uncle!"

" To be sure I do, when I never see him since he was a boy."

"He has a noble heart."

" And plenty of money, you say. Faix, that's where I'd go,
Ned."

"Surely, Sir," said Ned, somewhat excited, "you would not
have me desert——"

"Oh, the young lady, you mane. 'Pon my word, Ned—not
that I wish to make you onaisy, or wound your feelin's, but I
think that your lady is in ' kingdom come.'"

Ned buried his face in his hands, and sighed heavily. His
father's bluntness was revolting, and the conversation after this
slackened considerably. The little there was of it treated of
immediate affairs; for Ned seemed to shut himself up, as it were,
respecting the past, and his father urged him to remove, for the
present, from the neighbourhood of the town, however he might
be determined to remain in the country ; for he assured him the
affair of the Exchange had produced a strong sensation in the
high places of Galway, and that if he should fall into the hands
of those in power, it might be as much as his life was worth.

" My life?" returned Ned, with an incredulous smile. " What!
—for knocking a man down? No, no,—there's no law for that."

" Who said there was?—that is, no regular law. But, God
help your head! it is little they care for any law but what they
have power to do themselves."

"Come, come, father. I know they are arbitrary enough,
but I cannot believe my life is in danger."

" Can't you, indeed?—Oh,—your sarvant, sir,—maybe not.
See now, Ned.—You have come back from furrin parts, and may
know a grate dale more nor me about imperors, and sultans, an l
the kings o' Bohaymi, and all to that—and about ginteel manners,
and counts, and countisses,—and indeed I hope the young woman's
alive,—but in the regard to a knowledge of the town o' Galway
I'll give in to no man; and I tell you my owld heart would
grieve to see you in the power o' the high people o' Galway this

night. God help your head! its little you know of it. It was
bad enough when you left it, but it was a paradise on earth compared to what it is now. We could go to mass then, in a sly way
with a little care,—but now—oh jewel!—by me sowl it's dangerous to tell your beads beside your own bed for fear the bedpost
would inform on you. It's little you know what Galway is
come to. The wind of a word is enough to condemn a man,
much less knocking down one o' *themselves*. Your life is not
worth a sthraw, my buck, inside Galway gates, and that's a
thruth. They'd hang you as soon as look at you, and no one to
call them to account for it afther."

Thus went on old Corkery, giving, in his own quaint, dis-
jointed way, a melancholy account of the times. Edward listened
heedlessly, as far as he himself was concerned, but grieved to
hear that the place of refuge, where he fancied his darling Ellen
might have escaped, was scarcely less dangerous than the den of
murder in Scotland. But the recital rather stimulated than de-
pressed him; he *would* remain, and seek for tidings of his beloved
one, in defiance of danger. But it was clear, from what his
father said, that he must quit the neighbourhood of Galway, and
the fisherman was then summoned to take part in their council.
He suggested that the readiest mode of putting a good distance
between Ned and the town, suddenly and safely, would be to row
up the river and cross Lough Corrib, on whose opposite shore he
would be perfectly beyond the chance of recognition or reach of
capture. For this manœuvre the fisherman prepared by going
above bridge, and from a friend on the wood quay borrowing a
small boat, which he rowed to a convenient spot beyond the
reach of observation from any of the ramparts or batteries; and
securing the boat to the bank, under the shelter of some flaggers,
he returned to the cottage, whence, at nightfall, Ned and he left
the *Claddagh*, and making a detour to escape all chance of observation from any of the guards of the gates, the boat was reached
in safety, and they embarked. Lustily they pulled at their oars,
and headed well against the rapid stream; the towers of Menlo
and the castle of the Red Earl were passed, looming darkly over
the waters. Soon after, as the stream widened, they lost sight
gradually of the banks, and the broad waters of the lonely Corrib
opened before them. The ripple on the boat's side and the measured
stroke of the oar were the only sounds that broke the silence,
save when a brief question and answer were exchanged between
Ned and his companion. After pulling vigorously for about an
hour, they approached the eastern shore, and crept along it towards the northward until a small creek offered a landing-place,
and they jumped to the bank, and made fast the boat. The ruins

of a small castle were on one side of the creek, and of an ancient church on the other. To the former the fisherman led the way, and said he supposed Ned knew where he was now.

"No," said Ned; "I have never been on this side of the lake before. What castle is this?"

"Aughnadoon, your honour. It's right a gentleman should know the house he sleeps in, for it's here you must sleep to-night, barrin' you know the road to some village or town nigh hand."

"That I don't," said Ned.

"Then you had betther wait till morning will give you the use of your eyes; so shut them up in the mane time here, till you want them." He entered the castle as he spoke, followed by Ned, who groped his way after him. The fisherman threw down a couple of large boat coats, telling Ned these were the only feather-beds the castle could boast of; "for you persaive," added he, with a chuckle, "that they keep open house here for want of a hall door." Ned assured him he knew what it was to lie hard betimes, and he would not find him a discontented guest in the halls of Aughnadoon.

"If you're particular," said the fellow, "you can put a lump of a stone undher your head for a pillow."

"Thank you," said Ned, "I am not fond of luxury."

"Long life to you!" said the fisherman; "you have got what is betther than beds and pillows and all the luxuries of the world—you have a merry heart."

"Not very merry, if you knew but all," said Ned.

"Well, you're not afraid to look danger, or hardship, or sorrow in the face, and that's the right sort," said the fisherman. "I hope you'll sleep, sir. Good night, and God be with you." He lay down, and soon his heavy breathing told Ned he was fast asleep; and ere long *he* slumbered as soundly.

CHAPTER XXXVIII.

MORNING had not long dawned on the Castle of Aughnadoon when Ned and the friendly fisherman woke from their slumbers, the nature of their beds not being calculated to induce over sleeping. The fisherman remarked that he feared, from Ned's appearance, his resting-place had not agreed with him; the fact was, that the influence of painful dreams produced a mental depression upon Ned, against which he could not contend. The visions of the night had conjured up forms and words fearfully real and of woful import; and though he endeavoured to account for this nightly visiting of fancy as the consequence of the conversation held with his father on the preceding evening, still he could not shake off the influence which dreams, despite the best efforts of waking reason, will sometimes impose upon us. He thought that Ellen had appeared to him, telling him she was dead, that she had lovingly remembered him in the hour of death, and visited him thus to relieve him from the rack of uncertainty in which he lived—that she was at rest and happy, and therefore he should grieve no more. The dream was so vivid that he started from his sleep, and, even when wide awake, was still calling upon her name.

It was under this strong mental impression that his brow was saddened, and his cheek so pale, as to induce the remark of his companion, who, immediately after rising, busied himself in preparing breakfast. Unfolding a piece of sailcloth, he drew forth some dried fish, a loaf of coarse bread, and a mug. Spreading the sailcloth over a large stone, it served for a table-cloth, and having laid the bread and fish upon it he went to the lake and filled his mug, and called upon Ned, on his return, to partake of the fare, for whose humbleness he apologised. Ned thanked him for his kind thoughtfulness in providing any refreshment whatsoever, and partook of it rather to gratify the fisherman than his own hunger, for, in truth, he felt little inclined to the meal, and ate so sparingly, that his host said he feared such hard fare was unwelcome to a young gentleman.

The repast being ended, Ned inquired the "lie of the country," and what were the neighbouring towns, and his guide pointed out to him all he required. "Right before you," said he,

" is Headford—Shrule a little on the left of it. Tuam you can go to by crossing the country over there; and up to the north lies Cong—or you can make over by Ross Abbey, towards Lough Mask, and so on to Ballinrobe."

"Well, you have given me choice enough," said Ned, "so I may as well start at once, and let you go back to Galway. And now, my friend, here's a trifle in return for the service you have done me."

"Tut, tut, sir,—do you think I'd take money from you?"

"And why not? I have taken you from your occupation, and you should be paid for it."

"Why if you came to me a pleasuring, sir, and wanted my boat on the lough, or my hooker on the bay, then, well and good, you might pay me; but when a gentleman in trouble comes to my house and puts his trust in me, then all must be done in honour, and the stain of lucre mustn't be on it."

"I will not offend you then," said Ned returning the money into his purse, well knowing the high spirit of the humbler classes of his countrymen, "and I hope you pardon me for the offer; and since what you have done for me is not to be a paid service, but one of friendship, give me your hand before I say good bye."

He shook the outstretched palm of the gratified fisherman heartily, and, leaving the castle, they walked down to the boat, which soon was bearing the honest fellow of the *Claddagh* back to Galway. Ned stood on the beach looking after him, and thought how rare, in any other country, is the noble spirit found among the Irish people, whom poverty cannot teach to be mean or sordid, nor oppression grind into brutality. No!—despite all their sufferings, there is a generous blood amongst them that remains untainted.

Ned, as the boat lessened into distance, turned from the shore, and struck across the country. He had not made up his mind whither he would go, but the day was before him, and he had time enough to choose; so pushing over towards the blue line of hills that bound Lough Mask, he wended his way, filled with melancholy thoughts, which the stillness and desolation through which he passed were not calculated to dispel. He did not meet a human being, and, save the cry of wild birds that sometimes swept above his head towards the long waste of Corrib's waters, stretching far away to the dark high mountains in the north-west, he did not hear a sound. A more lonely walk could not be taken, and the unbroken monotony of the stony flats over which he passed was wearisome. It was a relief to his eye, when, after some hours, he saw the ruins of an abbey rising in the

20

distance, and to this point he bent his steps. On reaching it he could not help noticing much of architectural beauty that was attached to the spot; and he wandered about the ruins for some time, insensibly attracted by their picturesqueness. Many tombs were within, as well as without; some whose elaborate sculpture showed the place had once been of importance. Many of these bore inscriptions, and he employed himself in that occupation, so common under such circumstances, of reading these records of the dead. The scene, and his immediate occupation, were in singular accordance with his frame of mind and the spirit of his last night's dream. He was amongst graves, and he sat down and mused, and his musings were very sad. His eye rested on a mural tablet of black marble, richly ornamented, whose ancient letters still bore, in their antique cutting, remains of former gilding.

After a curiously scrolled Orate, followed the name of her to whose memory the tablet was inscribed, with an elaborate statement of whose wife she had been, his titles and possessions; next, of her own family descent; and, lastly, her beauties and virtues were recorded in these quaint words—

> Well faboureð of Boðpe butte more beautifulle of
> Soule . pe ͨaskette of pe Flesƿe hath bpne
> Stole bp Deiƿe . pe brpghte Jewelle pt
> Contapneð haiƿe bpne couetteðe bpe pe
> Lorðe of Hostes for pe Tresoirie of Heabpn.

The description was one that suited Ellen Lynch—" well favoured of body, but more beautiful of soul;" and Edward thought of her as he read it, and then he pursued the thought " had death stolen the casket of *that* bright jewel, too?" His eyes were yet fixed on the tablet while thus he thought, and as he saw its mouldings fallen away; its emblazonry defaced, its gilding tarnished, and the very sanctuary, where it had been placed, open to the rude visitings of the elements, a sickening feeling of the nothingness of all human things came over him. In truth, the scene was a sad one; the tomb, with its broken tracery and faded gilding, was a mockery to the words it bore. This lady of beauty and worth—this rare piece of mortality, " coveted by Heaven," was utterly forgotten, as if she had never existed. He who loved her and raised this tomb, all that cared for her memory, had passed away; the consecrated temple, where her remains were laid with honour, was a ruin; and the very faith in which she died, then in its " pride and power," was trampled in the dust—dared not show its head in the land covered with its fanes; and which, having preached life eternal to others, it was now present death to avow.

Edward quitted his seat before the tomb, and paced slowly across the chancel, thoroughly saddened in spirit, subdued to the lowest key-note of melancholy, when, as he was about to pass through a shattered porch, he saw a figure, darkly draped, slowly rising from a tomb, and stood riveted to the ground, struck with amazement, his eyes fixed on the apparition, and almost doubting the evidence of his own senses, thinking an overheated imagination might deceive him. But no—it moved —it rose still higher from the grave—he staggered among some rubbish against the archway which he grasped for support—the apparition turned its head—and, oh Heavens! what words could tell his sensations, when he saw the pale features of Ellen Lynch! —A wild, half-suffocated, exclamation escaped his lips, and he sank senseless to the earth.

It was some time before returning consciousness restored Ned to action. When he awoke from his trance all was lone and silent; nor sight nor sound was there to startle his living senses, as, awe-struck, he cast timid glances around, and listened with painful eagerness. His own embarrassed breathing was all he heard, and that almost frightened him. After some effort he was enabled to gain his feet, but his knees trembled, and it was by an extraordinary effort he succeeded in getting clear of the abbey walls, and, without once looking behind him, he made what speed he might from the precincts of a spot where he witnessed a sight so appalling; and, when his strength permitted, (and it increased with increasing distance from the point of terror,) he ran till he gained a road, and the sight of a beaten track was most welcome, as associating ideas of human beings and things of this world. He pushed on rapidly, the body keeping pace with the wild rush of strange thoughts that coursed through his brain. How he would have welcomed the sight of a fellow-creature to bear him company, were he the poorest beggar in Galway! but miles were passed without his seeing any one, a chilling loneliness was the characteristic of the entire country he passed through. On gaining a slight elevation, on whose summit he perceived that from the road, descending immediately at the other side, he should be shut out from the view of the country he had passed, he could not resist looking back towards the abbey—the first time he had dared to do so. He saw it standing, in stern solitude, in the dreary flat he had crossed; it seemed the very place to be haunted by mysterious terrors, and he shuddered to remember what he had witnessed within its walls. He turned and descended the acclivity, and pursued the road before him, a prey to superstitious wonder and sad thoughts; and, after journeying for a couple of hours, it was a relief to him to see a town in the distance before him.   He supposed it to be Tuam, and on reaching it, found his conjecture to be right, as he inquired from a woman the way to the nearest inn.

"Faix, there's not so many o' them, but you may find out when you turn into the High sthreet," said the woman, pointing the way, which Ned pursuing, a large sign, swinging from a scrolled iron bracket in front of a straggling whitewashed building, indicated where the traveller might find accommodation.   As Ned was approaching the house, a man alighted at the door and entered, and, from the glimpse he caught, he fancied he should know him.   He hurried to the inn, followed the horseman to the parlour, and exclaimed on seeing him, "Finch, by all that's wonderful!"

CHAPTER XXXIX.

THE surprise of Ned and Finch was mutual at this unexpected rencontre ; and rapid inquiries passed between them touching the why and wherefore of their meeting in that remote spot.

"I am right glad to see you, Ned, my lad," said Finch, "not only for the regard I bear you, but for my own especial good ; for of all the men in the world you are the one for my purpose at this moment.   I say how's the lady ?"

Ned grew ghastly pale at the question.

"Hillo, how ill you look,—nothing wrong I hope.   Ned, my lad, pardon me if I have asked an awkward question ; women are queer creatures, but I thought that was all right."

Ned still continued silent and looking miserable.

"Come, come!" said Finch, slapping him on the shoulder; "don't be so downhearted about it.   There's as good fish in the sea as ever was caught, if she has proved false."

"False!" said Ned, reproachfully.   "No, no, Finch ; there was no falsehood in her nature,—she was an angel!"

"Then what the deuce is the matter?" returned Finch.

"She's dead," replied Edward.

"Dead!" exclaimed Finch, in utter amazement.   "Then that confounded piper told me a lie!"

"What piper?" said Ned, eagerly.

"That Phaidrig fellow."

"What!—Phaidrig-na-pib?"

"Yes."

"When?"

"Yesterday."

"Then she *is* alive!" exclaimed Ned, nearly convulsed with emotion.

"Why, Ned, what's all this?—first dead, and then alive. Are you in your senses, lad?"

"Scarcely, indeed, Finch. I'm half mad, and no wonder. I have been on the rack of uncertainty so long that my poor head is bewildered, my brain is Bedlam."

"Softly, Ned, softly," said Finch, kindly.

"But of Phaidrig,—tell me, Finch, where did you see him?—Whatever *he* says is true,—*he* must know."

"I saw him in Athlone, two days ago."

"I would give the world to find him!—Was he stopping in Athlone?"

"That's more than I can tell. I saw him in the street, and spoke to him. Asked after you first, and he said you were in France; then after the lady, and he said she was well. I inquired were you married yet—he shook his head; and on my attempting some further questions, said, in his own significant way, 'the less was said about people in these times the better;' and altogether felt disinclined to pursue conversation when he found *I* knew nothing about *you*."

"But he said *she* was well?"

"Decidedly."

"Thank God!" said Ned, fervently.

"But wherefore did you imagine she was dead?"

"It would take too long to tell you now. Strong presumptive evidence and my own terrible imaginings convinced me: but Phaidrig must know the truth, and I will seek him."

"Remember, it is two days since I saw him in Athlone; and it will cost you two days to reach it; and after that space of time is it likely you will find one of so erratic a life?"

"A piper is a traceable person," said Ned.

"Yes, if they would let you trace him," said Finch: "but all I can say is, that since I have come into the country I never was in a place where you can get so little information. I have heard much of the intelligence of the Irish, but in my experience everybody seems anxious to impress you with the belief that he knows nothing."

"Oppression has taught them the use of equivocation," said Ned. "I can imagine their not giving a straight answer to an Englishman; but *I* would get the truth out of them."

"Well, you know your own countrymen best. Perhaps it *is* oppression has done it. On *that* score, I, as an Englishman, can bear witness that so wretched a state of things I never saw. If you have not some one to stand godfather for you as to who you are and what you are doing, and where you are going, you are suspected and bullied by the upper ranks,—as badly off as a man without a passport abroad ; while among the lower, there seems so wide-spread a distrust, that it is difficult to get an answer on any subject."

"You are certain Phaidrig said *she* was alive," interrupted Ned, heedless of Finch's observations.

"Certain."

"Then I don't care about anything else," said Ned. "I'll start for Athlone at once, and get on Phaidrig's track."

"And I must bear you company, lad ; for I am engaged on a venture in which I will secure your co-operation, now that I have you ; and though a trip to Athlone will turn my back on the point I want to reach, yet your object is a more pressing one than mine, and I will wait your convenience."

"You may assist me, too, perhaps," said Ned. "At all events your company will be most welcome. A lively fellow like you is a treasure to a poor devil like me, who has been grieved nearly to death."

"I have had my own share of grievances, too, I can tell you," replied Finch. "I have been in troubled waters since I saw you."

"I notice you don't look quite so smooth and spruce as usual."

"No, i' faith. The world has used me scurvily o' late, Ned, as you shall hear ;" and Finch thus commenced a recital of his adventures since his separation from his friend.

"You left me in London, Ned, full of joy for past luck, and high in hope of more. While I was waiting for our prizes being turned into cash and ready for delivery by the prize-agent, I dashed away in pursuit of town pleasure, as you know is my wont, and ran my purse pretty low. Well, I went to the agent for a supply of rhino for immediate use, but the scurvy rascal said it was irregular until the accounts were made out, at which time I should have all my money at once. I stormed and swore at the rascal, but it was no use ; he stuck to his text that it was irregular, and he would not do it."

"Why, he advanced me a hundred pieces." said Ned, "at your request."

"Yes, and glad I am you had the luck to get them, for 'tis more than any body else got out of him."

" What!—no return from your prize ?"

" Not a rap, except the coined treasure, which had been at once divided amongst ourselves ; but the cobs of gold, and silver bars, and the chests of the plate from the Spaniard, and the price of the brig and her cargo, which we picked up coming home, all were swallowed by that land shark prize-agent. I went the day after he refused me, to remonstrate, and to threaten I would certainly expose this unusual shabbiness on his part, and take good care it should be known wherever I could trumpet it, and that he might find his agencies not so plenty if that was the way he used the free-hearted lads of the ocean. In short, I had made up a fine speech on the occasion, Ned, fit for a member of parliament in the opposition, when, judge of my astonishment on walking up to his house to find it shut."

" Had he failed then ?"

" Smashed, Ned; scuttled, filled, and went down : sunk with all our treasure aboard, lad. The rascal had been insolvent for a long while, but contrived to keep his head above water until such time as he could make a good haul, and be off with it ; and we had the luck of it, Ned. Yes, the rascal pouched the bulk of our prizes, and made a clean start of it, and we never could trace his retreat."

" This was hard, indeed, Finch."

" The shabby scoundrel, to leave me on the flags of London, without even a rouleau in my pocket ; if he had even given the hundred I asked him for—but without a guinea—'twas hard, Master Ned. Lord, how I cursed him! Well, sir, when the thing got wind, a mob of sailors, toward the end of the day, got round the house, and the wicked speeches they passed one through the other acted like fire on gunpowder, and a pretty explosion it made at last. They determined to gut the house, and to it they set, and were not long about it either. Smash went the windows, which, though well barricaded, were no more than cobwebs before the Jacks. Bang! scramble they went through them, just as if they were boarding a ship—such boarding was never seen in that lodging before—and, in two minutes after they were in, out came—flying—tables and chairs, beds, sofas, looking-glasses, and lustres. ' Heavo-o!' was the word from above; ' Take care of your hats,' they cried to the crowd below, which, at a respectful distance, cheered the work of destruction, and raised shout upon shout as the pile of demolished furniture increased in the street. At last they began to pull the house to pieces ; the sashes were demolished, window-shutters and doors dragged from their hinges, and smashed into splinters; and, when all had been demolished that was breakable, they came marching out with bed-posts in their hands, waving the curtains, like so many banners, in triumph, and shouting like thunder. Just then the authorities arrived, in time to see they were too late, and attempted to arrest the rioters; but you may suppose what a chance they had against the tars armed with bed-posts. They soon cleared the street of the constables, to the infinite delight, and amidst the acclamations, of the populace. Well, that was small satisfaction to me, with all my money gone. I must set to work and make more, and a wild thing I did, Ned, very soon. Somehow, talking with you, and seeing the cursed illiberal things they were doing at head quarters, gave me a great disgust to those Hanoverian rats, and, by Jove! I thought I would make some money for myself, and do the young Pretender a good turn too—and what do you think I did, Ned?"

"How should I know?"

"I'll tell you then. You know there were many seizures of arms made by government, and these cases and casks of arms were stowed away in some old warehouses on the river-side. Now what did I do, think you, but compass the getting hold of these arms, and shipping them off to Scotland, where I knew the insurgents would be right glad to buy them up—a good speculation—eh, Ned?"

"But a dangerous trick."

"Not at all. Never dreaming of such an attempt, the authorities took no particular care of these stores, so I started the plan to some wild dogs I knew down on the river, and a small craft was got ready for the venture, and lay just below Greenwich, in a quiet part of the stream. We then got a lighter barge, and having prepared ourselves with ladders and boring materials fit for effecting an entrance to the store, chose a dark night and a favouring tide for our feat; and with most perfect ease, and free from interruption, we transferred a large quantity of arms from the store to the lighter, and dropped down with the tide to our cutter below Greenwich, where we shipped our dangerous cargo; and then it was slip cable, up gaff, and away. At dawn we were passing Gravesend, and we were at sea before the trick we played ashore was discovered. An English craft, and under our own colours, we held our course uninterrupted without the smallest suspicion from the cruisers and privateers that swarmed in the channel, and got on right well until we approached the Scottish coast; but there our movements were suspected, and we were chased by a king's ship, and run ashore. We had barely time to avoid being nabbed by his majesty's blue jackets, who got into their boats and seized the cutter, and most likely would have pursued us, but that it was nightfall, and a chase would have been nopeless. In half an hour after we saw our cutter blazing away at a furious rate, and that was the result of our adventure so far."

"A bad ending, Finch."

"Not ended yet.—The cutter being seized, and her name known, would lead to a discovery of the persons engaged in this affair, so London was no place to go back to, and Scotland was not a handy place to stay in neither, as we could not give a good account of ourselves, and 'look sharp' was the word among King George's friends; so, hearing that they were fitting out some privateers in Dublin, we thought it best to make our way to Ireland, and volunteer for a fighting ship again."

"I wonder you left it off, when your first cruise had been so successful."

"'Twas all very well at first, Ned, but there were soon too many privateers; besides which, the king's ships were thicker on the sea, and left less for privateers to take. Well, to return to my story. To Dublin I repaired, and there—"

"Hold, Finch!" said Ned, abruptly arresting the narrative.

"Wha; now?"

"Did not Phaidrig's manner imply that Lynch was in trouble?"

"Most decidedly—it looked very like as if the captain was playing least in sight."

"Then it was *herself* I saw!" exclaimed Ned, starting up and pacing the room. "Oh, what a fool I have been through superstitious terror!"

"How is that?"

"Finch, I am ashamed of myself, and you will laugh at me. But indeed the circumstances were so appalling—the time—my frame of mind—that—"

"Hollo!" cried Finch; "what *is* it you're talking of?"

"In short," cried Ned, "I thought I saw her ghost."

"Her ghost?" echoed Finch, in amazement.

"Yes," said Ned, who then related his adventure in the abbey.

"I own it was enough to shake one's nerves," said his friend.

"Oh, to what miserable straits they have been reduced," cried Ned, "when a noisome vault under a ruin is their hiding-place. She who had graced a court, forced to shelter in a grave-yard.—Oh, horrible!"

"Is it not strange she did not recognise you?"

"I know I uttered an exclamation of terror when I saw her, and she, most likely, at the sound of human voice so near their hiding-place, was influenced by fear, more justifiable than mine, and retreated."

"Then, when you recovered from your swoon, you did not attempt to solve the mystery."

"No; I confess I fled in horror. But now I will not lose a moment in returning to the place. Heaven grant I may find her!"

"That is not likely, my friend. They would scarcely remain after what you tell me."

"True," said Ned, sadly. "Oh, what a coward idiot I have been! When I might have clasped her to my heart! When I might have joined her, never to be separated! But I waste time in words. To horse—to horse, Finch!"

They were both soon mounted, and rode at a rapid pace to the abbey. Ned was hastening to the spot where he had seen Ellen appear, when Finch warned him not to enter too suddenly. "You may produce alarm," said he; "or, maybe, get a pistol-shot. Give some signal of a friend being here."

Edward called upon her name, at the mouth of the tomb, but no answer was returned. Finch and he then descended, and, through what had once been a charnel vault, an opening was made to a sort of crypt, beneath the abbey. It was dimly lighted from narrow loop-holes a little above the ground; some rude seat, and a plank resting on stones, by way of table, indicated that it had served for a habitation, and the yet warm ashes of a turf fire showed it had not been long deserted.

CHAPTER XL.

THE evidence which the vault afforded of being recently inhabited, coupled with the few words which Finch had exchanged with Phaidrig, having satisfied Ned that Ellen was living—that it was herself, and not a spectral appearance he had witnessed—his mind was relieved from the harassing doubt which so long had preyed upon it; but with that craving of the human heart for the possession of its whole enjoyment, never contented with an instalment, he now was beset with a desire to see the living object of his wishes, almost as distracting as his former uncertainty. In the morning he would have been content if any one could have assured him Ellen was in existence; but having, in the course of pursuit, satisfied himself she was so, the spirit of the chase was still warm, and he felt disappointment at being checked at the point so near the completion of his happiness. He examined every crevice and cranny of the vault with vexatious impatience; repeatedly he placed his hand over the decaying embers of the fire, and ventured to calculate by the heat how long it was since it had been fed. He stood·in the midst of the vault, and looked around him as if he would have questioned the very stones, to tell him of those whom they had lately sheltered; and, thrown hopelessly back upon his disappointed desires, he turned to Finch a dejected look and asked what was to be done.

Finch, whose tact and experience told him there was no use in trying to persuade a lover to be reasonable, had looked on patiently at all Ned had been doing in the vault, and had not made one word of comment; but, when he was appealed to for his opinion, he said he did not see any use in staying there, and recommended a return to the town.

Ned, after some little more lingering in the place where his beloved one had been, complied; and as they retraced their road to their inn, nothing was spoken of but the possibility of discovering her retreat, and plan after plan was suggested by both for putting in train a likely course of inquiry. Ned reverted, after all, to his first suggestion of finding Phaidrig, who would certainly be possessed of any secret connected with Lynch and his daughter; and Finch, not seeing anything better to be

done, agreed to go back as far as Athlone, where the piper had
last been seen, and try to get on his trail, and hunt him up.

The day was now far spent; it was evening when they re-
gained their inn at Tuam and they retired early to rest, that they
might be the better prepared for an early start and a long journey on the morrow. At dawn they were mounted, and nothing
of particular interest occurred for two days, during which they
made what haste they might for the shore of the Shannon. On
the evening of the second, they crossed the long bridge which
leads over the ample river to that old town of so much historic
interest, and the scene of many a well-fought day; and having
secured a lodging for the night in their hostel, they sallied forth,
before they retired to rest, to commence the inquiry for which
they had travelled so many weary miles; and success so far
crowned Ned's efforts, that he ascertained the road Phaidrig took
on leaving the town, and Finch rejoiced it was to the west, for
in that direction he wished to journey. So far both were pleased,
and sat down to their supper with more contentment than hitherto; and once fairly put on the track of the piper, Ned's spirits
rallied, and then, for the first time, he inquired of Finch the
particulars of the circumstance which had made him a traveller
in these western wilds, and which led to a meeting in which he
so much rejoiced.

"The case was this," said Finch. "When I had cut and run
from Scotland, and made my way to Dublin, one day, as I was
strolling about, looking at whatever was to be seen in the city,
I saw, lying beside the Custom-house, a knowing-looking craft
that I thought I should not be unacquainted with. On inquiry,
I found it was a smuggler, which had been recently seized, whose
crew were thrown into prison until their trial should come on;
and, as I calculated the commander of the craft was an old acquaintance, I could not resist the temptation of paying him a
visit in prison."

"Under your peculiar circumstances, that was not over
wise," said Ned.

"True," said Finch;—"and yet, when you say 'not over
wise,' it is not *that* exactly, either. You and I, Ned, and those
who, like us, have known adventure, often do rash things, not
from want of wisdom but from carelessness of consequences,
which becomes, at last, so habitual, that we do with our eyes open
things that people in ordinary might fairly set down to want of
perception rather than want of fear. And, after all, I don't
know if we are much worse off, in the long run, than the most
cautious. Your cautious fellow is nibbling away, bit by bit his
enjoyment, in calculating how far he may go, while your bold-

face attempts whatever comes in his way by assault, and takes his chance for success or defeat. They say a ' brave man dies but once; the coward dies every day;' and so it is possible your cautious gentleman endures more mental torment in imagining the many predicaments he is to avoid, than the headlong fellow who falls into his one scrape, and pays the penalty of it."

"It is not impossible," said Ned; "at least, you have made out a very plausible case for rashness, and, unlike many, your practice coincides with your preaching. But now to your fact. You visited your friend in prison ?"

"I did, and, as he was suffering from a wound, he was in the sick ward. As I passed along between the rows of beds with which it was crowded, a pair of dark and anxious eyes were cast upon me from beneath the coverlid of one of those couches of double misery—the bondage of a prison, and the thraldom of sickness. Oh, what a wretchedness to be reduced to!—though perhaps, after all, it may be a relief. The poor devil has a chance of release,—death may become head-turnkey, and set him free!"

"You are getting too discursive and eloquent, Finch," said Ned, smiling.

"Ah, Ned, by Jove you would not smile had you witnessed what I saw. That sick ward,—Lord, I shall never forget it!— I think, were I its inmate, I should go mad. But those eyes I was telling you of——"

"Well."

"I passed on, and went to the upper end, where my respectable acquaintance, the smuggler, lay; and after I had a few words with him, an attendant of the ward addressed me, saying one of the patients wished to speak with me. I followed him, and he led me to that bed whence those anxious eyes had gleamed out upon me. The sick man was a Spaniard, one whom I had met in a foreign port; he recognised me as I passed his bed, and in his dying need was fain to entrust to me, a casual acquaintance, a secret of which it required a trusty friend to be the depository. To the end of my life I shall never forget the anxious look of that haggard face, as he confided to me his tale, and enjoined me, by hopes of the blessings, or fears of the curses of a dying man, to be true to my trust."

"What was it?" said Ned, grown anxious by the romantic nature of Finch's preamble.

"Briefly this," said Finch. "His ship was wrecked on the western coast; a large amount of treasure was saved, and, to preserve it, was buried close to the shore, after which the survivors of the crew gave themselves up as prisoners, the Spanish captain

intending, whenever peace should procure him his liberty, to
raise his treasure, and return to Spain. As prisoners of war,
they were forwarded to Dublin, where he fell sick from injuries
sustained in the wreck, of which he was dying when he spoke to
me. It was the fear this money should be lost to his family
which gave that painfully-anxious look to his countenance. As
soon as I promised to undertake the trust he became calmer,
and I had the satisfaction of smoothing that dying stranger's
pillow. He was liberal, too, in the condition he made with me,
giving me one-third of the treasure as the price of conveying the
remainder to his family in Spain."

"That was but fair," said Ned; "for it is a task of difficulty,
danger, and anxiety."

"Greater than I thought, Ned; for I did not know the state
Ireland is in, and without the aid of an Irishman, I am certain I
could never achieve it; and of all Irishmen, you are the man
for my turn, and I thank Heaven for having thrown you in my
way."

"I will do my best for you.'

"For though I am not superstitious in my nature, I confess I should not like to be under the fearful vengeance with
which that dying man vowed his spirit would pursue me were I
false to, or neglectful of, my trust. 'Pon my soul, Ned, I almost
shudder when I remember that man's dying bed:—the anxious
thoughts of his far-distant home and wife and children, and his
only hope of their being placed beyond want resting on a com-
parative stranger, whom he sought to bind by alternate hopes
and fears to the interests of those who were so near to his heart
when its last pulses were beating. Oh! 'twas a fearful scene."

"One I should not like to have been engaged in," said Ned.

"And which I regret," said Finch. "But I could not resist
those dying entreaties."

"Which, with all your good intentions, you may not be able
to fulfil. Fancy the difficulty of finding a given spot such as
you seek, however accurately described."

"So far, I am as well provided as any man but he who buried
it could be. The place is laid down for me by the points of the
compass, and with bearings that can scarcely fail to discover it."

"But, on such a coast, how difficult, abounding as it does with
bay, creek, and inlet, so similar in detail, however varied in their
general form; cliffs and rocks are hard to be distinguished from
each other, and the sea in one night might alter the features of
the place so as to render it untraceable."

"All true, Ned; but I have a landmark more distinguishable
than any you have named,—a castle, on the shores of a bay, and

in the neighbourhood of mountains and headlands that furnish such bearings as the storms of centuries could not destroy."

"If buried in a castle, take care some one is not before you in lifting your treasure, for the peasantry here have such a general faith that the ruins of antiquity are full of hidden money, they are everlastingly digging in such places."

"Well, 'tis not *in*—but outside the castle mine is buried; so the fears you would waken may slumber, and you shan't frighten me, Ned. But come, we have talked enough of this,—let's to bed. We will take the road together for the west to-morrow, each in search of his treasure."

"Ah, what's your treasure to mine," said Ned, with a lover's enthusiasm.

"There's great similarity between them," returned Finch.

"How?"

"Mine is buried; so was yours:—wasn't she in a tomb?"

"Yes, but, thank Heaven, though entombed, alive."

"Not a ghost *yet*, Ned,—eh?" said Finch, laughing at him.

"Don't be too sure you wouldn't have been frightened your-self, Finch."

"Then there's another point of resemblance. I have to take my treasure to Spain: I fancy you would like to bear your's to the same place?"

"That I would," said Ned, "safe out of this unhappy country!"

"Then go a-head, lad! To-morrow we'll make sail together in chace, and good luck to us!"

CHAPTER XLI.

THE country through which the road of our travellers lay on
the following morning, is, perhaps, the most unpicturesque in all
Ireland.   Except the Shannon, which is, throughout its long
course, always fine, there is little even now, for many a weary
mile, but dead uncultivated flats, presenting nothing to interest
the wayfarer in his daily toil, and making the road seem twice
its real length, not to speak of our longer Irish miles.   There
is little to indicate, as you look across the Shannon, that anything in the shape of temptation lies beyond the monotonous
level before you : no one could suppose that such charms as
those which abound in the Western Highlands of Ireland lie
beyond these forbidding flats, which, duenna-like, scowl upon
you but to scare you away from beauty.   Over this road had
Finch to travel, retracing two days' journey, at no time a
pleasant thing unless you have a very charming companion, but
particularly objectionable when the road is such as we have
described.   It is nearly as bad as eating one's words, to swallow
such miles over again.   So Finch thought, and could not forbear
telling Ned it was unfortunate they did not know, the day
before, the course Phaidrig had taken, which would have spared
them such annoyance ; but Ned, who knew the scenery of the
west, told his friend to be patient, and a few days would reward
him in the display of natural beauty, in which the Atlantic side
of Ireland abounds.

For some days they pursued the road to the westward,
picking up intelligence here and there about Phaidrig, whom
they traced farther and farther in the same direction at each
remove.   They crossed the borders of Galway and entered
Mayo, and found themselves, the succeeding evening, in Ballinrobe, where the piper had been the day before, and left, still
pursuing, however, a westerly course.   Ned and Finch pushed
onward on his trail, and soon Finch admitted the truth of all his
friend said respecting the beauty of the country, when the bold
yet graceful forms of the mountains which bound Lough Mask
burst on his view, with the fair expanse of waters they embrace,
its woods sweeping down to the indented shore, and its picturesque old castle crowning a commanding height above the

lake. It was a truly lovely scene, and Finch paid it the tribute of the warmest admiration.

"What a lovely country!" exclaimed he.

"Yet how wretched!" returned the native, who knew it. "Its natural resources are great, yet it is poor and powerless under a fearful misrule. When will it end?"

"Not in our time," returned Finch. "But I feel I am prophetic in saying that half a century will produce a mighty change over the face of all Europe, and in the general emancipation of mankind from despotism, Ireland must have a share."

We will not pursue the political discussion that ensued between the two friends as they rode along, but thus they continued to converse of the miserable condition of the fine country through which they passed, until another charming view opened upon them. A large mass of picturesque ruins appeared, seated on the banks of an exquisitely beautiful river, whose clear and rapid waters swept round the base of the mouldering walls, reflecting arch and gable and pointed window on its limpid surface, and gushing over an ancient weir, which had been constructed close beside the abbey, that its original inmates might not have far to go for their salmon. Of a verity the fast days of Cong in the olden time must have been the feasts of the year, with such fish as its river could furnish; but as our travellers saw it, there were neither feasts nor fasts; its walls were desolate, and its beautiful sculpture falling to decay. A few miserable hovels were scattered up and down, the best amongst them being a small inn—here, while our travellers paused to bait their horses, they strolled into the ruins, having the proprietor of the little hostelry for their *cicerone*, who pointed out the objects most worthy of attention, and dwelt with considerable pride on the fact that Roderick O'Connor, Ireland's last king, was interred there. Having touched on this, he launched forth enthusiastically in praise of the ill-fated Roderick, enumerating his heroic deeds in the gallant stand he made against the invader, cursing the treachery that betrayed him, and mourning his untimely fall. But still there was more of triumph than mourning in the tone of the peasant; and while his eye gleamed as he spoke of the glories of the past, Finch looked on with a quiet smile.

Ned, observing it, addressed him. "You think it odd," he said, " that this poor fellow, in the midst of want, and in a land of wretchedness, bowed down by oppression, talks of bygone glories as familiar things."

"By no means," replied Finch. "It is because the present

is so wretched that these people refer to the past, and under the pressure of reality fly to whatever flatters the imagination."

But, quitting the affairs of Ireland, they turned to the consideration of their own; and after consulting with their host on the point they wished to reach, he recommended them to leave their horses with him, and push across Lough Corrib, whereby the pass of Mam Turc would be reached with more ease and speed. Acting on his advice, they procured a boat of very rough construction, and a boatman to match, and Ned was once more on the waters of Corrib. As they stretched away towards the head of the lake a small island lay upon their left; as they passed the boatman bowed his head reverentially.

Finch, noticing the action, inquired the cause.

" Sure an isn't that *Inch a Guila*, your honour, where there is the remains of a church that St. Patrick built himself, and called afther his own name, *Tempul Phaidrig*, and no one hereabouts ever passes that blessed spot without bowin' the head to it."

Finch drew from his pocket a small telescope, and directing his view to the island, observed some ruins; the only ascertainable form amongst them being a little Roman arch, which stood out in distinct relief against the sky.

As they passed along, the boatman had legend and tradition of many a spot in the neighbourhood, and bid them " just wait a bit till they came to the upper lake, where *Caistla na Kirka*, or the Hen's Castle, stood; and it was called the Hen's Castle because a mother, in the ould times, built that same in the middle of the lake, to keep her boy beyant the grab of a wicked uncle that wanted to lay howlt of him."

" Like the children in the wood," said Finch.

" Not a bit like it," said the man; " for the divil a bit o' wood is on that same rock, only stone, and not much of that same."

" You give but a poor account of the lady's territory."

" And great territory she was in, sure enough; and no wondher she was frekened, with that thievin' uncle afther the babby."

The lake now began to narrow, bounded on each side by hills of considerable height and beautiful form, increasing in Alpine character as the boat advanced; while farther still in the distance the water seemed bounded by a mass of mountains, forming a perfect labyrinth of beautiful forms, as their outlines interlaced one with another, and peak after peak spired into the clouds.

The scene was of that surpassing beauty which imposes silence on the beholder, and mutely Finch and Ned cast their eyes around them, the exclamation only of " How beautiful!" escaping at intervals; for Ned had never seen this portion of the

lake before, and was in no less admiring wonder than his friend
From time to time they asked the boatman to rest on his oar
that they might dwell on some fresh-opened point of view, which
became more and more lovely as they advanced.   The autumn
had shed her varied tints on the scene ; and the long wild grass,
the ferns, and the heather, which clad the hills on either side,
were enriched by the contrast of grand masses of limestone rock,
which seemed to form the frame-work of the structure whereon
all this enrichment had been wrought ; and the blue tint of that
labyrinth of hills, still in the distance, made the golden hues of
the foreground more vivid.   Finch thought nothing could sur-
pass in beauty what he had already seen, but there was a crowning
loveliness yet in store.   Where the lake seemed to terminate,
up rose from its tranquil bosom a conical hill of considerable
height, crowned at its summit, and fringed to its very edge, with
clustering woods of oaks, whose sturdier forms and thicker foliage
were occasionally relieved by the graceful line and silvery glitter,
and waving sprays of the bright-barked birch.
    It was a view to surfeit one with loveliness—to make one gaze

"Till the sense aches ;"—

and it was with such a feeling Finch declared it the most beautiful scene he had ever beheld.   And now they approached the
base of the wood-crowned hill, whose leafy beauty was multiplied
by reflection in the calm waters at its feet—and here a fresh
surprise was in reserve.   A narrow passage between this wooded
hill and an adjacent overhanging height formed an inlet to the
upper lake, whose stern grandeur was startling—in such sudden
contrast to the softness of the recent view.   The inlet was
passed, and a region of desolate loneliness struck a chill to the
heart.   Stark sterility was there, and a silence that was oppressive ; the scene would have been repellant but for the noble
outline of the overhanging mountains, which blended beauty with
awe in a singular degree ; but awe predominated.   A vast sheet of
dark deep water lay imprisoned within these giant hills ; and,
standing in the midst, was a small castle perched on a rock
barely above the water's edge, and merely affording foundation
for the building.   It was *Caistla na Kirha*.   The thought was
painful, that any one could have been so driven by fear as to

"Dwell in that desolate place ;"

for, truly, to continue the poet's words, who so dwelt might have
said,

"I am out of humanity's reach."

The only living thing, whose dwelling it might legitimately be, was the eagle, that solitary lord of mountain wilds, who, in the true spirit of a marauder, seeks the valley tand he plain but for plunder, and makes his home in the hills.

The place might be deemed the very sanctuary of Silence; so much so, that it appeared a sort of sacrilege to disturb its waters with the oar. The very boatman, the uncultured hind, relaxed his vigour, and pulled more gently.

While thus they glided over the dark waters, a boat suddenly shot out from the castellated rock, and pulled up the lake in advance of our travellers. The circumstance attracted the attention of all, and it seemed the boat ahead was urged with considerable speed, so much so, as to suggest the notion of escape. Finch at once made use of his telescope, and the fugitives seemed to be a male and female peasant; but, as he observed more intently, it struck him that, in these apparent peasants, he discovered the features of Lynch and Ellen.

"What do you make them out?" said Ned.

"Look," replied Finch, handing him the glass.

In an instant, there was a shout of surprise from Ned, who exclaimed, "'Tis she! 'tis she!—Give way there!—pull for your life!" He stood up in the boat, waved his hat, and shouted at the top of his voice, but this only seemed to urge the headmost boat to greater speed.

"Let us take the oars, Finch!" exclaimed Ned, suiting the action to the word, and seizing one of them. Finch followed his example, and the boatman was relieved of his toil by the powerful hands that now made the frail boat tremble under their strokes, and bound through the water. The effort on board the chase seemed also to increase; fast flashed the water around her, but still the rearward boat was gaining. Ned was in a state of painful excitement. "They fear us, manifestly," he said; "but if we could only gain upon them sufficiently to let them see us, what happiness it would be for all parties! Pull, Finch!—pull for your life, man!"

"By dad, you'll pull the side out of her betune you, if you pull any sthronger!" said the boatman; and indeed the crazy craft strained and shook under each stroke of the oars, and seemed likely to fulfil the boatman's prophecy—but still the rowers relaxed not.

Thus, for about half an hour, the chace continued, when the boat of the fugitives suddenly doubled round some rocks at the upper end of the lake, and disappeared. Ned's excitement increased at losing sight of her, and he employed greater exertion himself, and urged his friend to the same, amidst exclamations of disappointment, fear, and hope. The lapse of time was short between the doubling of the boats round the point. That in pursuit came rushing to the shore, and ran high upon it with her own force. Out jumped Ned—but the poor fellow had the mortification of seeing, a few paces further on, pulled ashore, under the shelter of an overhanging rock, the boat that had contained his treasure, lying empty. Ned was almost frantic, and enacted those absurdities which men will be guilty of under great excitement; he stamped, and ground his teeth, and tore his hair; and, clenching his uplifted hand, and casting a look of bitter vexation upon the deserted boat, swore, **in no very** measured terms, that— "it was too bad!"

CHAPTER XLII.

WHILE Ned was lamenting his hard fate, Lynch and his daughter were making their utmost endeavours to ascend the mountain side by a steep and rugged path, known but to few, leading to a deep and not very perceptible ravine, where a small crevice in the cliff afforded temporary concealment; which, having reached, they sat down to recover breath after their toilsome and rapid run. Neither could speak for some minutes; Lynch was the first to break the silence.

"Nell," he said—and the affection which beamed in his eye was the more touching from the sadness with which it was blended—"this is a hard life for you, my girl; would to God you were anywhere else!"

"Thank God, I am here!" was the answer, as she grasped his hand, and pressed it to her heart. "Do you think I could be happy away from you?—the anxiety and uncertainty I should then endure would be worse than the toil and privation we sometimes are forced to undergo together."

"You are a brave girl, Nell, and Heaven will reward you some day, I trust, for all your heroic and tender devotion; but if this lasts much longer I fear you will sink under it—and then what should I do without you?"

"Indeed, father, I never felt better in health in all my life; I often remember that beautiful phrase—' The Lord tempereth

the wind to the shorn lamb,"—and I feel as if I had preter-
natural power bestowed upon me to sustain me through our
trials, which, with God's help, will soon be over, I trust."

"Amen! But I am so beset, my girl—watched so narrowly,
and hunted so closely, that it is hard indeed to avoid the toils.
Driven the other day from the abbey, and now, when I thought
we might reckon on quiet for a few days in that lonely lake,
again disturbed. I may soon be driven to sword and pistol for
personal defence, and in that case your presence would but em-
barrass me. Would to Heaven you were in a place of safety!"

"Think of anything, dear father, but a separation! Even if
you commanded, I think, in that case, I should be disobedient,
and would not leave you—I say, would not—I had better say,
could not!" And she wound her arm gently round the soldier's
neck.

A slight quivering of his lip was the only evidence of Lynch's
emotion, which was deep nevertheless.

"Darling Nell, you must lie down and sleep; you need to
be fresh for the long walk we must take to-night."

"Indeed, father, I need it not."

"Nell, this is not *separation;* you must obey me. I insist on
your sleeping."

"I have taken that walk before, father, and think nothing of
it."

"Nell, you'll make me angry!"

There was a tone in his voice, which Ellen understood so
well, that she made no further remonstrance. The truth was,
she did want rest, but liked not the idea of her father being left
to his own gloomy thoughts; for her principal object in being
with him was to endeavour to divert the melancholy which began
to settle on him. Now, however, in obedience to his will, she
went forth, and plucked the long, seared grass, and fern, and
heather, which grew at the entrance of their rocky hiding-place,
and, spreading this simple provision at the inmost corner of the
narrow nook, she drew the large blue cloak of the peasant garb,
in which she was disguised, around her—and she who had been
used to the downy couches of Paris, lay down patiently on this
humble bed. She could not sleep for some time, but, to please
her father, pretended to do so. This feigning, made for so
amiable a purpose, soon induced the reality; and the father found
alleviation of his troubles in kneeling beside his sleeping girl, in
prayer.

CHAPTER XLIII.

NED, after looking up and down in the neighbourhood of the boat, was fain to give up the chase as lost, and yielded, perforce, to the advice of Finch, to continue their course to the landing, which would place them on the path to the pass of Mam Turc. Once more they pushed off on the lake, and half an hour brought them to the end of their water journey, where, after ample directions were given by the boatman for pursuing the right road, he assured them the natural formation of the pass would sufficiently "direct them without any direction at all;" and after losing full ten minutes on this profitless harangue, Ned and his friend started on the double pursuit of the piper, if he should fall in their way, or the treasure, if they got nearer to that before they met with Phaidrig. After they had toiled over a precipitous mountain, for three or four hours, and the shadows of evening were overtaking them without any visible shelter for the night within view, though they had already achieved more than the distance at which the boatmen promised them some shepherd's huts; when, in fact, they began to feel rather uncomfortable at the prospect of passing the night in an unknown mountain region, with nothing over their heads but the "canopy of heaven," (which, though beautifully spangled, is none of the warmest in the nights of autumn,) just then their attention was attracted by the approach of a dog, which came running towards them at speed, and made a circuit round them, sniffing in that peculiar manner by which the animal makes his acquaintances, and retains a recollection of them. He sniffed first at Finch, and then at Ned; but, in the latter case, one sniff was not enough—he repeated the action again and again, and uttered an impatient whine, which spoke as plainly as dog could speak— "Bless my heart, where have I met you before?"

"The dog knows you," said Finch.

"It seems so," said Ned; "and yet I do not remember him."

A louder yelp escaped the animal.

"You see, he takes no notice of me," said Finch. "You are his object of recognition: if his master be near, you are closer to a friend than you think."

"It might be an enemy," said Ned. "How are we to know he is the dog of a friend?"

"Like master, like dog," said Finch; "and that dog entertains amity."

The dog gave two or three snorts, as if to clear his ducts of scent of all impression they had already imbibed, took a fresh sniff at Ned, and a short bark followed.

"By Jove!" exclaimed Ned, on sudden recollection,— "Could it be the piper's dog?"

"That would be luck indeed!" said Finch.

"I'll ascertain in a moment," said Ned. "I remember his name was ———. Confound it!—why can't I remember? His name was ——— What the deuce is this he was called?"

Finch came to his aid, and ran through a bead-roll of dog's names, to which Ned as constantly returned "No."

"Cæsar?"

"No."

"Buffer?"

"No."

"Pompey?"

"No."

"Prince?"

"No—none of those common names—and yet it was the name of an Irish Prince, too, I remember—one of the O'Connors!"

"Paddy?" said Finch, with a smile

"Confound you!" returned Ned; though he could not help joining in the laugh; "what a name for a prince!—Paddy O'Connor—Stop—I have it!" cried Ned, clapping his hands— "'Turlough!'—that's the name!"

The moment the word escaped his lips the dog bounded towards him, and testified extreme joy; while Ned, still calling him by his name, with all the usual praises of "good fellow," and so forth, almost hugged him with delight. "Yes, Finch!" he exclaimed, "Phaidrig cannot be far off." Then, turning to the dog, he ran through several sporting phrases, such as, "Where is he, boy?—To him, lad!—Phaidrig, Phaidrig!— Where is he?—Find him out, boy!"

The intelligent brute seemed to understand his meaning perfectly, answering his calls by expressive looks and short barks—bounding forward in advance, then turning round, wagging his tail, and barking, as much as to say—"Follow me!" The travellers accepted his invitation; and, while they followed, Ned expatiated on the extraordinary intelligence of this animal. "He only saw me once before," said he; "and that some years ago; but the occasion was a remarkable one, certainly."

"And yet you did not remember him," said Finch.

"That may be readily accounted for," replied Ned, "by its having been night when we met; and sight fails in the dark, though scent does not."

"Showing the superior power of that faculty, in some cases," returned Finch; "though we speak so contemptuously of people being led by the nose."

While thus they conversed, lauding *Turlough's* intelligence, he, like a modest dog, held his tongue; for the moment he found himself followed he went on silently. Suddenly they lost sight of him, but pushed on nevertheless, fancying he had passed some turn in advance. At this moment they were engaged in a narrow defile, with a wall-like barrier of rock on each side, so perfectly inaccessible as to call forth the notice of the travellers upon its qualities for defence. They turned an angle in the path, but they could not see the dog before them; at that moment, however, they heard his voice, and the next instant he came running after, headed them, and barked, as if to turn them back. They paused, and *Turlough* retraced his road, and stopping before a large mass of rock, shivered as if with lightning, he entered one of the crevices, whence a small rill was trickling. They followed, and soon began to ascend a little water-course, and ere long the sound of a large stream was heard. Still onward plashed *Turlough* through the water, which it soon appeared was but a small escapement from a mountain stream, which the dog soon after crossed, clambered up the opposite side, and stood on the summit, barking his invitation to his friends below. They were obliged to strip off their shoes and stockings before they could follow; and wading the stream, whose slippery bottom of smooth round stones needed careful treading, they got safely over, clambered the opposite bank, and continued to ascend a sharp acclivity, partly morass, or, where the ground was firm, covered with long grass, so slippery, from the constant drainage of the hill, as to render ascent a work of labour. At length a small table land was gained, crowned by a noble group of rocks, which bore a fortress-like aspect, and to this place the dog ran at his utmost speed, sprang up its side, and disappeared, though his bark could be heard when he was no longer visible. Ned and Finch continued their course towards the rocks, but before they had reached their base they perceived two figures on the summit, one of whom was Phaidrig. Ned shouted with delight at sight of him, and called on his name blithely; the piper clapped his hands for joy, *Turlough*, barking, rushed down the rocks and jumped round Ned, while Phaidrig was hastening towards him, assisted by his companion, and, when within reach of Ned, the warm-hearted piper could not resist, in

the impulse of his joy, hugging Ned to his heart, while he poured
out blessings on the happy minute that brought him back, mingling his pious ejaculations with a wild "*hurroo*," and a fantastic
caper now and then.

"Musha, but you're welkim!—hurroo!—What the divil kep'
you so long away?—the Lord be praised for his mercies,—sure
I knew you'd turn up some day;—and won't *she* be glad of it,
the darlin' Oh, murther, Masther Ned, but I'm the happy
blackguard this minit!—hurroo! Only it's too late, I'd be off
and bring you there; but wait till to-morrow;—we'll rise with
the lark, go as sthrait as the crow, take the wather like a duck,
see the fair swan, and then you may coo like the dove. Hurroo!
—Where's my pipes? By Jakers, I'll play this night till I
split the bag! And how are you, Captain Finch?"

"How do you know I'm here?"

"Don't I hear you laughing at me?—Laugh away—my
heart is as full as a barn with joy, and by the powers we'll
thrash it out to night. Come in wid you,—I suppose you are
tired and hungry,—come in. And how did you find me out?"

"We've been tracing you from place to place for many days,"
said Ned, "but at last had the good fortune to meet *Turlough*,
and he remembered me, and led us here."

"Signs on him!" said Phaidrig. "*Turlough, ma bouchal*, come
to me!" The dog sprang to him, and Phaidrig, stooping, patted
his head, while the dog licked his face. Don't be shocked,
ladies, at the coarseness of this fact; it is an author's business
to tell truth. "*Turlough*, my jewel, you've more gumption than
a counsellor, and a better heart than most o' them. Hurroo!—
Come in, and have something to ate, and make haste, or there
will be none left," and he dragged Ned along.

"But how came *Turlough* to be so far away from you?" inquired Ned.

"For the rayson I want you to come in,—because we're
short of ateables, though the dhrink is plenty; and so I towld
Turlough to go and pick up a bit for himself, and it was marau-
din' about he was, lookin' for a rabbit or a hare when he seen
you; but the sinsible craythur, he knew betther than go huntin'
and lave his friends on the road. Where is he?"

"He's gone off now," said Phaidrig's comrade of the rock.

"See that!" said Phaidrig. "Now that he has done his
duty to others he thinks of himself. Oh, I wish all the Christians
was like him! Come in,—come in now, Masther Ned,—and
you, too, Captain Finch, are heartily welcome."

With these words Finch and Ned were conducted up the
pile of rocks, and when near the summit an ample opening,

downwards, appeared, into which they descended; this natural chasm, spanned across with boughs of birch and thatched with heather, forming a rude but not uncomfortable habitation.

It was a wildly picturesque retreat. In the recesses of the cave arms were piled, which the flickering light of a turf fire brought out in bright touches, sparkling through the shadowy depth with a Rembrandtish piquancy. Trophies and implements of the chase were suspended from the roof, or rested here and there along the sides of the cavern. Feathers and skins of bird and beast made a motley sort of tapestry, which hung fantastically around, and gave a barbaric air to the place, which some of the costumes of the inmates tended to increase. The fur of the hare contributed caps and waistcoats to not a few, and other cuts and materials of costume would have astonished a fashionable tailor.

Some eight or ten persons were just beginning a meal, in a remarkably unceremonious fashion. A jutting rock of tabular form served for about five of them to "cut their mutton" on, while the remainder sat where they could, and rested their trenchers on their knees. The former rejoiced in the lofty title of the "board of green cloth," being covered with a rude matting of fresh rushes, while the stragglers were named "the boys of the side table." One in a faded uniform was called "cook," and was engaged in serving out broth from an iron pot, his ladle being formed of a large scallop shell, tied on the end of a peeled hazel twig.

The party who conducted the new comers called a halt to those within. "I say, lads, here are two hungry recruits come to join our mess, and, as the commons are short, start fair."

Finch and Ned were received with a merry welcome, and seats at the board of green cloth were given up to the visitors, with an expression of regret that they chanced to call when the larder was so ill provided.

Ned requested they would make no apologies, and reminded them it was Friday, on which day it was fit to fast.

"And pretty catholics you find us here," said one of the party, "eating meat nevertheless."

"Hold your tongue, Donovan!" replied the cook, helping the broth. "I'll swear this is fasting fare; for whatever comes out of a scallop shell must be fish. Isn't that good theology?"

"The doctors of the *Sorbonne* could not make better," said one of the boys of the side table.

"Couldn't make better?" repeated the cook. "Is it the theology or the broth you mean?"

"Both," replied the other.

"Good boy, Dillon!" said the cook. "Hold out your pannikin, and I'll help you for that.'

Dillon obeyed; and as the cook ladled him his portion, he said, "There's some theology for you!"

"I wish there was a little more meat in it," said Dillon.

"That would be divinity," returned the cook,—"you confuse your terms, Master Dillon,—Allow me, sir," he said, addressing Finch, "to help you to some of this infusion; I think I can fish you up a bit of solid,—observe, I said *fish*."

"Thank you, sir," replied Finch, "but I have no scruple of conscience on the subject, as I happen to be a protestant."

"A protestant!" exclaimed the cook. "Oh, then, sir," said he, with an air of burlesque politeness, "pray take the ladle and *help yourself*, for that's the protestant fashion in Ireland."

Finch heartily joined in the laugh which the comicality of the rejoinder excited, while he admired the address of the man who could utter so bitter a sarcasm without giving offence; for the tact and good humour with which it was done rendered it innoxious,—the point only tickled, it did not sting.

"I think it is time you stopped your mouth," said one of his comrades, when the laughter subsided.

"Faith, I think so too, " replied he, helping himself. "I'll stop my mouth like the rest o'ye."

Thus they went on, cracking their jokes about the slenderness of their meal and poverty of their accommodation. Many a sumptuous board had not such mirth and wit about it; and all this occurring in a wild mountain hiding-place, amongst a set of men whose lives were in daily jeopardy, struck Finch with surprise and admiration. They talked of such and such a hunt; reminiscences were made, such as "The time I was living at the hall,"—"The night of Lady Lucy's rout,"—"When the Prince went to the opera,"—"The day we dined with the Marshal,"— all these things were remembered in their present privation without an apparent regret: they seemed to be just as merry, as light, and bold-hearted, as if their hunts and halls, and Lady Lucies and Marshals, were theirs as much as ever. They took their present condition as a part of life's drama they must go through, with as much *nonchalance* as an actor assumes the character of a king or an outcast on the stage, and leaves it off when the curtain is down. Just so these daring fellows looked forward to getting their own again, and resuming their proper place in society; but in the meantime were just as jolly as ever. Many of them were fugitives from Scotland, after the fatal day of Culloden; but though the cause they loved was at a low ebb for the present, they hoped for fresh aid from France and Spain, and were willing to "bide their time" in their present difficulties.

The cook's functions having ceased, another comrade, under the title of "cellerman," was called upon; and his department was in a more palmy state than that of his brother officer. A keg of whiskey—the right "mountain-dew"—was placed in the midst; the brotherhood gathered round, and, basking in the blaze of a turf fire, which gave, at once, light and warmth to the cave, the theological cook recommended a dram after their fish.

The cellarman requested he would confine himself to his own business, and not interfere with his department; and indulged in some sportive exposition of the intimate relation between soul and spirit as he served a dram to each of the party.

"By the bye," said Finch, "I am surprised that there should be any want for fish, in reality, here. I should have expected there was salmon in plenty."

"Oh, the salmon is plenty enough, sir," replied the cook; "the matter is, to catch it; and we have only one fisherman amongst us—Master Blake over there is our Izaak Walton, and he came home empty handed."

"I had but little luck to day, I own," said Blake.

"Little luck!" repeated he of the ladle; "your fisherman's language always needs translation—and 'little luck' means 'no fish!'"

"They would not rise!" said Blake.

"As for rising—they are waiting for the Spaniards, maybe, to do *that*, like ourselves :—try a Spanish fly next time, Blake."

"That would be a blister!" said the fisherman.

"Well, a blister rises—maybe 'twould rise the salmon—and that's more than you can do."

A laugh rewarded the cook for this successful hit at the angler, who took it most good-humouredly, and only threw back a sportive "Bad luck to you!"—with wishing him "a blister on his tongue."

"Tongues are only blistered when people tell lies—and that's truth I told now."

"He has you again, Blake!" was the cry.

"Come Ffrench!" said Blake—for Ffrench was the name of the temporary head of the culinary department—"if I can't always rise a salmon, you can always raise the song; and, better than the fish, your songs are always in season."

"Songs are not unlike fishes," replied Ffrench. "A song is the spawn of a poet; and, when healthy, a thing of life and feeling, that should increase and multiply, and become food for the world! Here is one, that all Ireland, at least, will heartily digest."

Fag an Bealach.[*]

I.

Fill the cup, my brothers,
  To pledge a toast,
Which, beyond all others,
  We prize the most:
As yet 'tis but a notion
  We dare not name;
But soon o'er land and ocean
  'Twill fly with fame!
Then give the game before us
  One view holla,
Hip! hurra! in chorus,
  Fag an Bealach!

II.

We our hearts can fling, boys,
  O'er this notion,
As the sea-bird's wing, boys,
  Dips the ocean.
'Tis too deep for words, boys,
  The thought we know—
So, like the ocean-bird, boys,
  We touch and go:
For dangers deep, surrounding
  Our hopes might swallow;
So, through the tempest bounding,
  Fag an Bealach!

III.

This thought with glory rife, boys,
  Did brooding dwell,
Till time did give it life, boys,
  To break the shell:
'Tis in our hearts yet lying,
  An unfledg'd thing;
But soon, an eaglet flying,
  'Twill take the wing!
For 'tis no timeling frail, boys—
  No summer swallow—
'Twill live through winter's gale, boys,
  Fag an Bealach!

Pronounced, *Faug a Bolla*, meaning, "leave the road," or "clear way."

IV.

Lawyers may indict us
  By crooked laws,
Soldiers strive to fright us
  From country's cause;
But we will sustain it
  Living—dying—
Point of law or bay'net
  Still defying!
Let their parchment rattle—
  Drums are hollow:
So is lawyer's prattle—
  𝔉ag an 𝔅ealach!

V.

Better early graves, boys—
  Dark locks gory,
Than bow the head as slaves, boys,
  When they're hoary.
Fight it out we must, boys,
  Hit or miss it—
Better *bite* the dust, boys,
  Than to *kiss* it!
For, dust to dust, at last boys,
  Death *will* swallow—
Hark!—the trumpet's blast, boys,
  𝔉ag an 𝔅ealach!

The song was received with rapture, and the chorus went with a shout. The inuendo of the early verses pleased every man, who translated it to his own taste ;—the very cause why inuendo is always so successful in pleasing or annoying;—the individual imagination of every hearer does more than the most elaborate endeavours of the poet could achieve.

Even after the song was ended, the men were humming snatches of it, and the refrain of *" Fag an Bealach"* was echoed from mouth to mouth. The theme stirred their blood, and Phaidrig was called on to play the "Blackbird" in his tip-top style.

It was an unusual thing for Phaidrig to be left so long idle; one cause of it, perhaps, was that he kept in the back-ground, engaged with Ned in earnest discourse about Ellen, while the rest were employed on more stormy subjects; but, once being enlisted in the business of the evening (and after *Fag an Bealach*), he knew they would make a roaring night of it, so giving Ned a hint " to take care of his head," which Ned took occasion to repeat to Finch, Phaidrig "yoked" his pipes, and there was no patriotic strain on record which was left uncalled for.

Meanwhile the cellarman's keg was getting lighter every moment, and, along with it, the heads of the company, till at last there was such an exuberance of patriotism, that several gentlemen were singing different songs at the same time; while Phaidrig, under the especial patronage of Ffrench, was lilting particularly wicked tunes above them all.

At last, the noise, by degrees, died off; the dry lairs of fern and heather, which surrounded the cave, were occupied by those who were able to find their way to them, and the silence of sleep succeeded the loud wassail which had startled the night wind as it swept the summit of that lonely mountain.

CHAPTER XLIV

The next morning the guests of the mountain retreat bade adieu to their entertainers, and started under Phaidrig's guidance. On the road the piper had been put into possession of the business which brought Finch to the west, and arranged, in consequence, a double plan of action. He promised Finch a guide, who should lead him to a certain point in the neighbourhood where his venture lay, promising that he and Ned would join him after having seen Ellen. Their mountain track was beguiled of its length and toil by the interchange of intelligence between Ned and the piper respecting the various fortunes which had befallen Lynch and his daughter in Scotland, and Ned in his pursuit of them. Those of the former were of painful interest; their numerous hair-breadth escapes—their wanderings, concealments, privations, and final escape from Scotland, formed a romance of more terrible reality than was ever conjured up by fiction; and their subsequent sufferings in Ireland were not less deplorable, though of a more monotonous character;—it was an unbroken series of anxious watchings and hidings to escape detection; for Lynch had rendered himself so obnoxious to the authorities, by the extent and frequency of his former enlistments in Ireland, and subsequent endeavours to foment a rising in the young Pretender's favour, that a large reward was offered for his apprehension; but the cupidity of meaner enemies, thus excited, he had less cause to dread than the personal rancour entertained by some, high in power, who were straining every nerve to discover and arrest him.

"Why does he not fly the country?" said Ned, "instead of living within this circle of entrapment you describe."

"That's no such aisy matter," said Phaidrig. "All the passes out o' Galway are watched; and as for getting off by the coast, it is so lined with cruisers, that it would be madness to attempt it, unless one had some fast boat that could go like the wind; and you know we could get nothing here but a heavy fishing boat."

"Wait till I have a talk with the captain," said Ned. "I think I see a way of stealing a march on the enemy."

"Musha, how?"

"If we could get him further down to the south, where he does not enjoy so dangerous a celebrity, an escape might be managed thence."

"Ay, there's the matther!—but how to get out of Galway is the murther—for every pass in it is watched!"

"My plan is this," said Ned: "let a boat be in readiness on the west bank of the Shannon at a given place; we must get a first-rate horse for the captain; in one night he could cross the county, get on board, and drop down the river to Limerick, where an embarkation on board some ship bound to an English port could be effected; and, once safe in England, I'll engage to manage a flitting to France—that's a road I know well. What think you, Finch?"

"It looks well; but I don't know the nature of the country on the river."

"It is admirably suited to the purpose—sufficiently wide to give the opportunity, in case of being threatened from the shore, to take the choice of either bank for a landing; and pursuit by water need not be dreaded, for boats are far from plenty on the river."

"I think you hit it off well," said Phaidrig. "We'll talk to the masther about it; and now, Captain Finch, we must soon part company; you ought to be seeing some huts soon, forninst you, high up a little to the right."

Ned and Finch on looking in the direction indicated, saw some smoke rising from a little dingle in the hill-side; and there Phaidrig told them lived the guide to whose care he intended to confide the captain. Half an hour brought them to the hut; the goat-herd undertook the trust requested; a place was appointed for their reunion in a few days, and the friends separated.

As Ned and Phaidrig now pursued their journey, they could talk uninterruptedly of Ellen, and she, therefore, formed the theme of their discourse for some hours, as they bent their way back again towards Corrib's upper lake. Ned inquired of the piper how he could tell where Lynch had retreated after leaving the castle. Phaidrig, with a chuckle, answered, "By a way of my own—aisy enough when you see it."

"But you are going back now direct for the place you have left?"

"Ay, I must first go there, before I can tell where they are. You'll see all about it soon."

As Phaidrig said, the means were simple enough whereby he ascertained the course the fugitives had pursued. On reaching the spot where Lynch and Ellen landed, the boat was still laying there; on hearing this, Phaidrig said Lynch must have considered himself closely pressed, or he would have placed the boat in its regular secret haven. "But now to find out where they are gone!" Saying which, he groped for a fissure in the rock, and putting in his arm to its utmost length, drew forth a little twig of birch. Phaidrig held out the branch in a theatrical manner before him, and assuming an air of great importance, uttered, in a measured, pompous manner, the following words, which he addressed to the stick :—

"I command you, upon the vartue of your oath, to tell me where thim you know is gone!" He then applied the stick to his ear, and gave a nod of satisfaction, and told Ned it was all right; that Lynch and Ellen were about five hours' journey out of that spot.

Ned laughed at this piece of mock magic, in which the piper's sportive humour had indulged, acknowledging his trick was a good one, and the means of communication simple indeed.

"Simple enough," said Phaidrig, presenting the twig to Ned; "look at that—do you see anything on it?"

"Yes, several small nicks."

"Count them."

"Seven."

"That's the whole art and mystery of it," said Phaidrig. "You persaive that manes they are gone to No. 7. There are many hiding-places throughout these mountains, such as you saw last night, where some hundreds of people are concealed, and they are all numbered. The numbers are got off by heart, like A, B, C, by these gentlemen in throuble and their followers. The principal leaders have each some sign of their own to distinguish them. This twig, you see, has a forked end to it,—that's Lynch's sign. There are other signals in there." He pulled forth a straight stick, notched as the other; a twig twisted into a ring, and marked; a bunch of five twigs, tied together with a piece of grass. "Now all these show that certain men have been hiding in the castle yondher, and have gone to each of these different coverts. That twisted twig is O'Kelly,—the straight one Burke,— the bunch is D'Arcy.—So I could tell where all o' them went after leaving this, and so from place to place follow them."

"But suppose," inquired Ned, "that Lynch had landed on the other side of the lake, how could he have made his signal?"

"There is another signal rock at the other side."

"But how can you tell if they have left long ago or lately?"

"By the freshness of the cut. You see the sticks are all cut at the end. Now Lynch's is fresh, O'Kelly's is lying here some time, Burke's is an owld date,—quite dry, you see." He handed them to Ned as he spoke, he himself telling by touch and smell what Ned's eyes convinced him to be true.

"Cleverly contrived," he said.

"And so simple," said the piper. "A notch on a stick is as readable to a blind man as to them who see : and up and down through these mountains there are signal rocks appointed to each hiding-place, for putting the sticks in. We call them our post-offices."

"A good name, Phaidrig."

"But stop,—we mustn't rob the mail," said the piper ; and he restored all the sticks to the crevice in the rock, after which they left the place, and pushed on for number seven.

"You'll see one of the quarest divils you ever see," said Phaidrig, "to-night. He's a sturdy owld chap, that always lives in the saycret place the masther is gone to, and there's but one tune in the world he cares for, and my heart is broke playing it to him whenever he lays howld o' me."

"It is to be hoped the tune is a pretty one."

"Not it, in troth,—its only that quare thing, *Ree Raw* I suppose you know it?"

"I do. It is a sort of half drony, half lilting, monotonous thing," and Ned commenced whistling.

"That's it," said Phaidrig. "That's a nice thing to play for hours together."

"For hours!" echoed Ned.

"Ay, faith. He would not let me eat, drink, nor sleep, if he could help it, but keep me evermore blowing away at that *Ree Raw*."

They had been walking for about three hours, when they

reached some very broken ground, where the blind man's footing seemed more insecure than usual. "I wish I could get on faster, for your sake, Masther Ned. I know you are burning with impatience to see the darlin' lady; and no wondher, and right glad she'll be to see you, and here you are hampered with the tardiness of a blind man." He had hardly uttered the words when he made a false step, tripped, and fell down an abrupt bank. Ned ran to his assistance, and attempted to lift him, but a sharp cry from Phaidrig made him desist.

"Don't stir me—don't stir me, Masther Ned—my leg is broke."

"Oh, my dear Phaidrig, I hope not," said Ned, kneeling down beside him, and supporting him in his arms, while *Turlough* ran up, as if he understood something untoward had happened, and began to whine.

"This is a cross thing to happen at this present," said the piper.

"At any time it is dreadful, Phaidrig. Are you in much pain?"

"Yes; when you stirred me I got a sharp twinge. Straighten the leg for me, Masther Ned, and lay me quiet, with my back to the bank—that's it: now I have a plan to enable you to make your road good to Miss Nelly."

"I will not leave you, Phaidrig."

"Sure you must leave me, if it was for nothing but to get me help. See now,—I hope *Turlough* will undherstand me, and if he does, all will be right;—just untie the pipes, and take them out and yoke them to me, and I'll thry a plan.—*Turlough! Turlough!*—here boy!" He began to talk to the dog in his own peculiar style, telling him he should "go and find him;" then he would point to Ned, and tell the dog to "take him to him." After this he began to play *Ree Raw* at a most tremendous rate, and cheer on the dog with the cry of "To him, boy—fetch him there!"

The sagacious creature became much excited, looked up eagerly to his master, as if endeavouring to catch his meaning, and Ned regarded with admiration the heroic disregard to his own suffering the blind man displayed, while struck with surprise at his readiness of invention to supply, through the intelligence of his dog, the guidance his mishap interrupted.

His opinion of the dog's intelligence was not overrated; the animal uttered a few low short barks, as if to express understanding of his meaning, and, first fixing his eyes on Ned, ran forward some twenty yards, and looked back, as if waiting for him.

"He's off," said Phaidrig—

The dog barked.

"He's calling you," said the piper: "I know every bark in him; he undherstands my meaning, and will lade you clever and clane to the place."

"I am loth to leave you, Phaidrig."

"Sure you must lave me to get help for me, if for nothing else; and, as it happens, the owld fellow I towld you of where you are going is the best bone-setter* in the counthry; and some o' the boys in the hiding-place will come over and bring a door with them to carry me. There, now, be off—put your tender-heartedness in your pocket, and start, for the sooner you go the sooner I will have help. There,—*Turlough* is barking again;—go, and God speed you."

"My dear Phaidrig, for your sake I will urge my utmost speed. You are satisfied the dog understands?"

"Depend your life on *Turlough*, I tell you—good-bye!"

"Farewell!" said Ned, running after the dog, which dashed on in advance, while the wild lilt of *Ree Raw* from Phaidrig's pipes pursued them as long as they were within hearing.

The ground which it would have taken the sightless Phaidrig two hours to traverse, from the difficulty of progress its roughness presented, was crossed by the hawk-eyed and swift-footed Ned in half the time. The dog led the way to a rocky rift in the side of a steep mountain, where some goats were feeding. At the upper end of this dell a hut was reared against the face of the cliff, which formed its back wall; its roof was of fern and heather, and its chimney of sods, held together by rude wattles woven through them. More care seemed to be bestowed on this portion of the structure than is generally the case in such a hovel, where a hole in the roof mostly answers the purpose of chimney and window—letting the light in and smoke out; but in this case not only the outward but inward contrivance of the fire-place seemed to have been attended to, for a wide-mouthed flue stood out from the rock inside the hut, and carried up the blue smoke merrily, which, curling along the side of the cliff as it escaped, was scarcely perceptible at a distance, from the similarity of its colour to the heights which towered above.

So elaborate a description of a chimney would be unnecessary but that it was the most important part of this hut,—in fact, the hut was for no other purpose than a screen to an opening in the cliff, which led to an extensive cave, to which

* The name for a rural mender of fractured limbs among the peasantry.

this wide flue formed the entrance, while it also concealed it;
and the chimney-top outside served to carry off smoke from the
principal fire within the cave, as well as from the bit of fuel
burnt for deception without. The thing was altogether so well
masked that an ordinary observer would never have suspected
the trick.

The door was shut when the dog approached the hut; he
scraped for admittance without being attended to, and on Ned's
arrival his tapping was equally disregarded, therefore he raised
the latch and made his entrance. *Turlough* rushed in after him,
and Ned's amazement may be guessed when he saw him run up
the chimney. Much as his doings had previously surprised him,
this last touch appeared the strangest of all; and after a short
pause, which the oddity of the feat produced, Ned looked up
the chimney after his friend, but he was gone. He then went
outside, expecting to see him on the roof—but he was not there
either. He looked up and down, and whistled for him, and at
length called lustily on his name—but in vain. *Turlough* was
nowhere to be seen. While thinking this looked very like
witchcraft, a man issued from the house, which Ned had found
empty, and he became still more puzzled. Where the deuce
could *he* have come from? While he was *thinking* this, the
mysterious person asked him the same question in so many
words, giving a sort of grunt at the end of the sentence, which
was his habit; and Ned replied, he had come from Phaidrig-
na-pib.

" And why did not Phaidrig-*na-pib* come himself?—hegh!"

" Because his leg is broken,"

" Humph!—What broke it?"

" Accident."

" I didn't think it was intinshin!—hegh! And is it intinshin
or ax'dent brings you?—humph!"

" Intention," said Ned, who, amused with the fellows gruff
peculiarity, gave answers as short as the questions.

" There's bad and good intinshins—hegh!"

" Well—mine are good," said Ned; " and with such intentions I come to see Captain Lynch."

" Faix, then, you won't see him here—humph!"

" I must!" returned Ned, anxiously. "I am his trusty
friend!"

" I dunna sitch a person."

" Yes, you do—he came here last night. You need not fear
me!"

" Fear you?" returned he, with a surly look, that scanned
Ned from top to toe, before he gave his grunt.

" I mean, you may trust me. I wish Phaidrig was here to vouch for me, and to play you *Ree Raw*."

The fellow gave a very interrogatory growl, and a searching look at the words.

" You see I know something about you. Let me see the captain."

" I don't know him, I tell you—hegh !"

While he was in the act of denial, Lynch emerged from the hut, and hurried up to Ned, holding forth his hand. A hearty grasp, and a few words of warm welcome followed.

" Miss Lynch ?" said Ned, inquiringly.

" Is well, and here. You shall see her in a moment. Where's Phaidrig ?"

Ned briefly related the accident; and Lynch, turning to the gruff old Cerberus, said no time should be lost in hurrying to his assistance.

The fellow thrust his fingers into his mouth, and gave a piercing whistle, and in a few seconds after, several men came from the hut.

" Come with me," said Lynch, addressing Ned. " You will make all right about Phaidrig," he added—turning to the old warder.

A grunt of assent followed.

" Let me see Miss Lynch for a few minutes," said Ned, "and I will return with them, and show the way."

" You needn't mind," replied the growler; " them that brought you here will lead us back—go in wid you—I *towld* you I didn't know the captain—hegh !"

" Come," said Lynch, leading Ned into the hut, and showing him the mode of ascent to the cave within the chimney—a strange road to a love-meeting—though, after all, it is most appropriate—Cupid is a climbing boy.

Such a meeting between friends, after so long an absence and intervening anxiety, as that which followed between Ellen, her father, and Ned, can better be imagined than described. Hours passed by unheeded, in their varied and affectionate communion; there was so much to tell and so much to inquire, of the past so full of painful interest, and the present so fraught with danger.

Ned ventured, however, to prophesy hopefully of the future, holding out, in their flight to Spain, a prospect of security and repose. Lynch here, with an enthusiasm in the Stuart cause which all his suffering could not tame, declared he would remain in Ireland as long as there was a chance of a blow being struck in their favour. " But you," he said, addressing Ned,—"you,

must not attach yourself to my desperate fortunes—for desperate
they are, though I am determined to dare them."

"I will never desert you," exclaimed Ned, fervently.

A look, beaming with affection, from Ellen's sweet eyes—
looking sweeter for the sadness which partly shaded their lustre—
was Ned's reward for this expression of hearty devotion to her
father. He, grasping the young man's hand, said—

"I know you are attached to me—and I know the cause.
You have often served my daughter and myself at need——
and—"

He was suddenly interrupted by a loud tapping at the outside
door, and he rose and left the cave. In a few minutes he
returned supporting a wounded man ; on beholding whom, Ellen
rushed forward, exclaiming, "Father Flaherty !—Oh—dear father—you bleed !"

"I do, my child—but 'tis only a flesh wound. Lynch, prepare
for defence ;—they have hunted me close, and are not far off."

"Are there many ?"

"More than I could wish. Where are the rest of our companions ?"

"They are absent."

A look of agony passed across the priest's features as he
exclaimed, "Then God have mercy on us !"

"Are you still able to fight?"

"Yes,"

"Here is one who will give us brave help," said Lynch,
pointing to Ned.

"What, you here !" said the father ; "I wish we had happier
times for our meeting, Ned ; but I am glad to see you—make
haste—let us stand by the door and defend it."

"Ellen, go into your hiding place in case of the worst," said
Lynch, as he took from her hands several weapons that she had
brought from a recess in the cave, and distributed them to Ned
and the priest.

Thus armed, they descended from the cave to the hut, and
piling several logs against the door, rendering it capable of resistance, they stood in wait for the approach of the priest-hunters,
in case they had tracked him to the retreat. They soon heard
the tramp of horsemen, and looking out through the loops with
which the place was provided, awaited their coming with deadly
determination to sell their lives dearly.

"Hold your fire till they are closer," said Lynch; "we can't
throw away a shot'tis well our powder and ball are in car-
tridges ; we canload in the dark."

The hunters were now so close as to be visible, and surrounded the hut, swearing violent oaths, and calling for the priest with a profanity of expression unfit to be recorded. The answer was a well-directed fire from the hut, which caused other yells than those of triumph from the assailants.

"Force the door!" was the cry from without. Some men descended from their saddles at the command, while others came down at the leaden invitation sent out to them from the hut. A rush was made at the door—the logs inside resisted those without, while Lynch, as they pressed close to the entrance, plunged the bayonet with which his gun was armed through a chink in the door, and a shriek of agony succeeded, with a heavy fall.

"He has it!" exclaimed the captain, with savage exultation.

A fresh shout was raised outside. "Burn the vermin in their nest," was the cry.

It was scarcely uttered, when several flambeaux, with which such hunting parties were provided, were lighted, and thrown on the thatch of the hut, after which, the assailants rode swiftly out of reach of gunshot, to which the light exposed them with more certainty—a result not thrown away on those inside, who sent telling shots after the incendiaries. When quite out of range, the merciless party turned round to enjoy the sight of the blazing hut, which they barbarously imagined was the fiery tomb of their victims; little dreaming of the safe retreat the cave afforded those whom they would have sacrificed to the flames. Their shouts rose high in proportion to the height of the blaze, as in fiery tongue-like form it licked the grey cliff which stood out in ghastly relief against the dark sky.

The glare soon passed—and as the fire was nearly out, the hunters rode off; but they had not paid the full reckoning of their adventure. The party who had gone for Phaidrig, was a strong one and well armed, and was entering the dingle as the first flash of the blazing hut told them what had taken place. Laying the piper in a place of security, they distributed themselves at the mouth of the pass, in the most advantageous order, awaiting the exit of their enemies, who, as they were retiring in high glee after their supposed triumph, received a murderous fire along their whole line. Taken thus by surprise, they were panic stricken,—they fancied they were entrapped into an ambuscade, and "*sauve qui peut*" was the cry, while dropping shots after the fugitives, lent additional vigour to their spurs.

CHAPTER XLV

WHEN Phaidrig heard the hut was fired, and the glen in possession of enemies, he forgot all bodily pain in the agony of mind he endured, lest the few left behind in the hiding-place had fallen victims to the attack; and when, after the flight of the priest-hunters, his friends came to carry him to the cave, he besought some of them to run forward and ascertain the truth.

"Shout, if they're safe," said he, "for my heart is on the rack till I know,—run, boys, run, if you love me!"

Several complied with his request, and dashed onward, while Phaidrig was slowly borne along by the rest. The nature of their burden, the darkness, and roughness of the ground, retarded their progress, so that they had not half reached the end of the glen before their companions in front had ascertained the safety of the inmates of the cave, and gave the signal shout. It was returned by those who were advancing, and by none more vigourously than the disabled piper, who mingled thanks to Heaven with his transport.

As it was impossible to remove Phaidrig into the cave without running the risk of disturbing the setting of his leg, which had been effected by the old growler before he was shifted from the spot where the accident occurred; a shelter was made near the warm embers of the burnt hut, where, under care of one of the brotherhood, he remained while the rest entered the cave, and were soon engaged in active council as to the course most fitting to pursue, under existing circumstances. It was to be looked forward to that the discomfited hunters would return in greater strength to recover their dead, whom they were forced to abandon; in which case the present post would be untenable, and the sooner it was deserted the better. Some advocated an immediate removal to another of their haunts, but the majority seemed to consider morning would be sufficiently early for their flitting. While such matters were discussed within the cave, Ned and Ellen visited the piper, who found comfort in the gentle pitying voice of his "darling Miss Nelly;" and when she had retired for the night to an innermost nook of the retreat, which formed a perfectly separate apartment, Ned insisted on remaining without to keep company with his friend Phaidrig, whose requests to the contrary were in vain; and thus passed the night.

At the earliest peep of dawn the inmates of the cave were in motion. Packing up the few conveniences the retreat could boast of, they prepared for a march; but before they started, endeavoured, by rolling some large stones, and placing a quantity of heather, naturally disposed, in front of the entrance to the cavern, to conceal from their enemies, who might return to the spot, the existence of so safe a hiding-place, to which, after the lapse of some time, they might again resort with security. To be certain of this asylum remaining undiscovered, it was agreed that one scout should remain behind and watch from an over-hanging eminence the proceedings of the party which should return for their dead. Lots were cast for the fulfilment of this duty; he on whom it fell took it merrily, and having obtained three day's rations for his subsistence, and an extra supply of ball-cartridge, he bade his friends good-bye, and mounted to his eyrie, while they commenced their descent. The sentinel of the cliff tracked his departing companions with his eyes as long as they remained in sight, and when left in sole possession of the mountain solitude, he occupied himself in selecting the best and safest point for the fulfilment of his duty, and then engaged in making it as comfortable as mountain-bivouac might be, and, when completed, he threw himself down within his lair, close and watchful as a hare in her form.

Meanwhile his companions were pursuing their route to another of their hill hiding-places; the burden of bearing Phai-drig being changed every half-hour among the party, while the wounded priest leaned on Lynch, Ned having the more precious charge of Ellen. It was the most delightful day they had known for a long and weary time; even thus surrounded with difficul-ties, flying from persecution, the presence of the lovers to each other had a charm superior to external dangers. What dark or dismal thought could be entertained by him who now looked into the gladdened eyes of the lovely girl he supported over crag and torrent; more lovely, he thought, even in her simple peasant guise, than in the fashionable frippery of courts, in which he had adored her; besides, he now looked upon her more securely as his own—there was that in Lynch's manner which implied consent, and for some hours of their journey Ned had uninterrupted care of Ellen. At length a halt was called. A small defile was approached, in which, should they be attacked, the party must have engaged to disadvantage, therefore scouts were thrown out to the right and left, who, ascending the heights on either side, reconnoitred the pass, and ascertained its safety before the main body ventured on passing. This having been achieved, Ned and Ellen were again permitted to lag in the rear, and enjoy distinct companionship; and not the least of their plea-sure was the communion of admiration produced by the grandeur of the scenery through which they passed. The lonely labyrinths of the wilds they traversed presented eternal changes of the most picturesque form; that noble group of mountains, known as the "Twelve Pins of Bunabola," whose lofty peaks are among the first landmarks seen by the Atlantic navigators. rose right before them; and the intricate interlacing of their bold yet graceful lines, called forth fresh admiration as each advance of the travellers presented them in some novel combination. Lake after lake, too, they passed, tranquilly slumbering in their mountain-cradles, but at length one burst upon their view of surpassing beauty—its waters, reflecting the dark rich tones of the hills above, gave more brilliant effect to an uninterrupted belt of lilies that lay upon, or rather round its bosom, girdling it with floral loveliness. Ellen and Edward paused; they thought they had never seen anything half so beautiful in all their lives, they gazed and gazed upon it in silence for some minutes, and looked rather than spoke their admiration. He stole his arm round her waist, and whispered, "Here, darling one, here—could not we dwell for ever, and wish no happiness beyond?"   He seemed to feel by anticipation all that the bard of his country, then unborn, so beautifully expresses of some place—

"————————enchanting
Where all is flowery, wild, and sweet,
And nought but love is wanting;
We think how blest had been our lot,
If Heaven had but assign'd us,
To live and die in that sweet spot."

But no—they might not live, whatever chance there was of dying there; and Ned, as he held his beloved one to his heart, sighed to think that in their native land there was no safety for them, and that liberty and security were only to be found in exile.

A shout from the party in advance recalled them from their fond reverie, and they hastened to follow their friends; but as they were losing sight of the lily-girdled lake,

"They cast a longing, lingering look behind.

Their course now tended upwards towards the innermost recesses of "the pins," within whose labyrinths lay the retreat to which their steps were directed, and the scene of loveliness they had just quitted rendered the savage nature of the region they began to ascend more startling. Rugged and precipitous were the paths, often intersected by deep gullies, through which the mountain-torrents foamed and roared, overhung by toppling cliffs whose projecting crags seemed almost poised in air—so delicately balanced, that fancy might suggest the touch of a child sufficient to cast them from their misty heights. Sometimes the echoes were challenged by the "bark" of the eagle, himself so unused to visitors in this, his own domain, that the presence of man startled him not, insomuch that the party in many cases approached within twenty yards of the royal bird ere he quitted his perch upon the rock; and even then he spread his ample wing so leisurely as to give assurance his flight was not one of fear, but rather of a haughty retirement from unwelcome intrusion. What an idea of solitude was conveyed by this absence of fear on the part of a wild creature : had it known more of man it would have felt more alarm at his approach !

How finely this fact is touched by Cowper, in the expressions he attributes to Selkirk on the desert isle :—

> " The beasts that roam over the plain,
> My form with indifference see ;
> They are so unacquainted with man,
> Their tameness is shocking to me."

But in the case of our fugitives, the tameness was not shocking : it was the evidence of a remoteness from the haunts of man most welcome. The ascent now became more difficult as they advanced, painfully so, indeed, to those carrying poor Phaidrig, who, in his disabled state, where rest was so necessary, had borne the rough journey, not only with patience, but even mirthfulness, often interchanging a joke with his friends on the way. Now the bearers were obliged to be often changed, and great care and ingenuity employed to get him up some of the sharp acclivities, where, often the strength and activity of an able man were required to achieve his own passage. In all those "delicate cases," the gruff bone-setter was intendant of the process, and growled his instructions to the operatives under him how to proceed, swearing occasionally, if they were awkward or precipitate, that they would " spoil his work " if they did not take care. By dint of toil and skill, however, Phaidrig was safely brought to the topmost step of this mountain ladder, which the rest of the party had already achieved, one of their

number having been forwarded to give the requisite signals to those in possession of the retreat, that friends were
coming. Those friends were heartily welcomed, and one difficulty
alone presented itself—it was, that there was scarcely accommodation for so many, even if they were all men; but the case was
rendered still more awkward by a lady being of the party.
This was soon obviated, however. All set to work vigorously to
prepare a temporary shelter for her. A heap of stones was
collected close beside the cave—of these, rude walls were
rapidly formed, roofed over with the same material, the crevices
were stopped with grass, mosses, and heather, and the interior
furnished from the cave with goat and sheep skins, which with
the addition of a couple of military cloaks, formed no bad
sleeping place. A rougher shelter, by way of guard-house, was
raised beside it, to be occupied by Lynch and Ned; and these
preliminary preparations for the night being made, the party
entered the principal retreat, which in its general features
resembled those already described, and where the same rude
fare and careless conviviality were to be found. The splints and
bandages on Phaidrig's leg being looked to by the bone-setter,
who pronounced all safe, and Father Flaherty's wound having a
fresh dressing, the work of the day was over, and the evening
was given up to such enjoyment as the circumstances of the
time and place could afford.

CHAPTER XLVI.

The earliest act of the succeeding morning was the united devotion of the mountain refugees, as they knelt at the sacrifice of the mass, performed by the wounded priest. To many of those present, the religious exercise was the more welcome, as it was long since they had enjoyed it—more welcome, because in the minister who officiated they beheld a human being elevated by spiritual influence above the first law of his moral nature, which prompts to self-preservation, and who, in the commission of this act, rendered his life forfeit to the cruel customs of the times—more dear, because as they knelt in the faith of their fathers, their tenderest sympathies and affections were engaged; but, dearest of all, from that principle of resistance to injustice so deeply rooted in the human heart, which exhibits increase of fortitude in proportion to the violence of aggression; that principle which has made patriots and martyrs. Without a Gesler we should not have had a Tell, and piety has ever been increased by persecution. It matters not in what cause, or in what faith, this undying principle of human nature is exercised! as it was, so it is, and ever will be. The unmolested English, who for centuries have walked quietly to church, with their prayer-books and bibles under their arms, and who have heard smooth sermons from velvet-cushioned pulpits, cannot know that desperate earnestness of faith which possessed the Covenanter of Scotland and the Catholic of Ireland, who worshipped in mountain dells and secret caves, whose prayers might have for their response a volley of musketry, instead of the peaceful "Amen;" whose religion *indeed* might make them think of eternity, for in its exercise they stared death in the face.

Ned, it may be remembered, was first impressed with a love of his religion at Bruges, where he saw it in its pomp; but now, his heart, expanding to higher emotions with his increasing age, stirred to deeper sympathies than the Galway *boy* could entertain, and kneeling beside the woman he adored in the proscribed faith of his nation, he felt the holiest aspirations he had ever experienced. What were the lofty columns of the gorgeous cathedral compared to the towering cliffs, whose pinnacles hung above them!—what the fretted roof to God's own heaven!—what splendour of sacerdotal robes so impressive as the blood stained bandage of that wounded priest!

The morning sacrifice over, the morning meal succeeded after which a dispersion of the party took place among the hills some to the waters, towards their base, in search of fish ; others amidst their coverts, to find game ; some to collect fuel. Lynch, Ellen, and Ned, with the wounded priest and disabled piper, were left in possession of the retreat. A portion of the day was spent in making the accommodation, so hastily undertaken the evening before, more comfortable, and then a long consultation ensued between the three gentlemen as to future movements. In the course of this discussion, Lynch declared himself fully as a consenting party to the union of Edward with his daughter, and even expressed a desire she could be prevailed upon to quit her present life of danger, and, under the protection of a husband, retire to Spain. Ned strove to influence the father to accompany them, urging, as an inducement, the unlikelihood of Ellen's consenting to leave him ; but he was immoveable on this point, until all hope of a movement in the Pretender's cause should cease.

"The reverend father here," he said, "has brought over encouraging news; we may confidently look for aid from France, where the Prince has arrived."

" He has escaped then from Scotland ?" said Ned.

" Yes," said the *padre*, "all Paris was alive about him—nothing was talked of but his romantic adventures and wonderful escape ; and the first night he went to the opera, the whole house rang with admiring welcome."

A shade crossed Lynch's brow, as he repeated in a tone of vexation, "The opera!—the opera!—Oh, Charles Edward, while you are enjoying sweet strains at the opera, the wailing of widows and orphans in your cause rings throughout these isles!"

"A good many thought the same thing in Paris, I can tell you," said the father, "though the senseless mob shouted."

"With all my devotion to him and his house, I cannot shut my eyes to such frivolity," said Lynch.—"The opera!—good Heaven!—to plunge into the luxurious dissipation of Paris, while the heads of brave men are brought daily to the block in England—'tis monstrous!"

" And yet you *will* stay here, sir, for his cause," said Ned.

"For *the* cause," returned Lynch, impressively—"It is not alone for him we fight—'tis for our homes and faith as well."

" As for the homes of Ireland," said Father Flaherty, sadly, "few of them are safe—many of them have passed to the hands of the stranger; and of all places on the earth, Ireland is the saddest for a true Irishman."

"But our faith stands fast!" returned the enthusiast, "they cannot rob us of that."

"As for the faith, my dear Captain," answered the priest, "you could enjoy that unmolested in Spain; and I am inclined to be of the same opinion with my friend Ned, that you might as well make a start of it along with the young people, and be off, particularly as you are so marked a man."

"If the promised aid from France should not arrive *this* time," said Lynch, "why then, perhaps——"

"You will fly with us," said Ned, joyously.

"Let us wait till the hour arrives," said Lynch, "'twill be time enough to speak then—for the present, we will say no more; let us seek Ellen."

He rose and entered the cave, where his daughter was sitting beside the couch of Phaidrig, whiling away the tedium of his confinement by her companionship. The piper's gaiety was unimpaired, he was as mirthful as ever, and Ellen was laughing at one of his little pleasantries as her father entered.

"Instead of Phaidrig's being downhearted over his misfortune, father, he has been making me laugh," said she.

"What's the fun, Phaidrig?" inquired Lynch.

"Oh, I was tellin' Miss Nelly, your honour, that instead of being worse, I'd be the betther o' my accident."

"How?"

"Because I'll soon be able to do with my leg what I can't do with my hands."

"What is that?"

"Ulick, the bone-setter, says my leg will begin to knit in a few days."

Lynch smiled at the oddity of the conceit, and said, however much his leg might knit, he feared it would never make him a pair of stockings.

"Oh, that would be too much to expect," replied Phaidrig; "one leg to work for the other; 'twould be enough if it worked for itself, it's then I'd have a pet leg, like the mayor of Londonderry."

"I never heard of him," said Ellen; "what an odd conceit—a pet leg! I have heard of a pet lamb, or a pet kid—but a pet leg!—"

"What is that but a pet calf?" said Phaidrig. "Well, this fellow was a little mad, and used to dress up his pet calf in all sorts of finery, while his other poor shin of beef had all sorts of

ill-usage. One was decked out in silk, while ragged worsted
was good enough for the other. One had a fine footstool
to rest on, while the other was knocked about against chairs and
tables; and the pet leg he called his protestant leg, while the
other he called his papist leg; and sure, if he was walkin' the
road, he picked out the clane places for his protestant leg, and
popped the poor papist leg into the dirtiest puddles he could
see.”

“ That's one of your own queer inventions, Phaidrig,” said
Ellen, laughing.

“ Thruth every word of it, Miss ;—but wait till you hear the
end of it. He wanted to put his poor papist leg into such a
deep dirty ditch one day, that he fell down and broke it. Well,
he was taken home, and the docthor was sent for, and the leg
set and bandaged up, and he was put to bed; but, my dear,
what does he do in the night, when the nurse is asleep, but take
the bandages off his papist leg, which he thought had no right to
so much attention, and put them on his protestant leg. The
next morning, when the docthor came, he asked to see the leg,
and out the pet leg was popped, with the bandages on it; and
sure the docthor forgot which leg it was was broke; and feeling
the leg straight and right, said that would do, and went away;
but, my jewel, a mortification set in in the poor ill-used limb
before the mad thrick of the Londonderry mayor was discovered,
and then there was nothing for it but to cut it off—and the poor
fool sunk undher the operation; so that the end of it was, he
lost his catholic limb first, and lost his life next, for overpetting
the protestant leg.”

Ellen's quiet smile at the sarcastic drift of Phaidrig's story
was in singular contrast to the knitted brow of her father, as he
shook his head, and remarked, how much bitter truth was often
to be found under the guise of a fable.

“ But, to leave fables, Phaidrig, and come to facts,—what is
the rendezvous you have appointed with Mr. Fitzgerald's friend,
this Mr. Finch, whom you have sent down to the coast somewhere; for I understand it will be time to start to-morrow, according to agreement made at parting? Can you instruct a
guide to lead our young friend ?”

“ Aisy enough. It's a snug little place in the hills, not far
from the Killery harbour; many of our friends here can find the
way ready. It will be only a pleasant day's walk.”

“ Then to-morrow you must start,” said Lynch to Ned.
“ And now, Ellen, come out and take a ramble with us in the
hills; I will show Fitzgerald a splendid scene from a neighbouring point, commanding a view of Glen Hohen and Lough Ina.

Besides, I think Phaidrig has been talking rather too much; the quieter he can keep the better, for some days."

With these words the party sallied forth on their excursion, and, after a delightful ramble, reached the point of view Lynch had promised, which more than realised all he had said. As they topped the acclivity that opened to them the long-stretching Ina and its wooded islands, some red deer, startled by their approach, bounded before them down the heathery steep, giving life and additional beauty to the scene. Resting in this beautiful spot, the party enjoyed a pleasant conversation for awhile. Ellen delighted to see the sternness and sadness of her father unbent and softened, as he emerged from his habitual gravity to share in the interchange of livelier thoughts than of late he had indulged in. After a while he arose, and seating himself apart at some distance, took a small book from his pocket and began to read intently.

" That is a breviary he is engaged upon," said Ellen, in an under tone to Ned. " My father, ever strict in his religious duties, is now more so than ever; he says he knows not the hour his life may be forfeited, and he tries not to be overtaken unprepared. It makes me tremble to hear him talk sometimes so certainly of such terrible things as may happen."

Ned here took occasion to urge his suit respecting her retiring with him to Spain, as in accordance with her father's wishes; but she silenced him at once with a resolute " Never."

" No, Edward—I will not desert him: I will join you in urgent entreaty to induce him to fly the country *with* us—but without him I will never go."

There was an earnestness in her manner which showed that to shake her resolution would be impossible, therefore Ned tried it no longer; but they consulted on the most likely means of inducing Lynch to abandon the Stuart cause for the present in Ireland; and sweet moments were passed in inventing arguments in which their own future hopes formed a principal part.

" Perhaps, dearest Ellen," said Ned, softly, and slily coaxing her hand within his,—" perhaps, darling one, if we were married at once it might induce him ? "

Ellen bent her eyes archly upon him, and with a significant shake of the head, and a smile full of meaning, asked him how, in their present circumstances, he could venture to make such a proposal to any woman whom he thought possessed three grains of sense. " But, perhaps, you think all women are fools on this subject ? "

Ned protested he entertained the highest opinion of the capacity of female intellect in general, and of hers in particular,

"Could I think otherwise of you, my darling!—my angel! —my——"

Ned's raptures were cut short by the tiny hand being raised with a forbidding action, and a whispered recommendation being given not to talk nonsense, more particularly as her father was approaching them.

Lynch suggested it was time to go back to the retreat, where, on their return, they found their companion, who had been left behind to watch their last asylum, already arrived, and with the good news which he was dealing round to his friends, that their enemies had not found out the secret of the cave when they came to remove their dead. That so safe a hiding-place remained undiscovered was welcome intelligence indeed; for not only would it have been the loss of a choice asylum, but would have given a hint to their enemies of the nature of the places they selected for their abodes, which might have led to further evil consequences. The arrival of the sentinel amongst his companions, after fulfilling his dangerous duties unscathed, was rejoiced at, and the cave was rather the merrier for the event.

CHAPTER XLVII.

Next day Ned, after a gentle farewell from Ellen, was on his way to the Killery harbour, under guidance of one of the brotherhood of mountain-refugees; and, as evening was closing, after a delightful walk through scenery of the same class already described, he reached the point where he might expect to find Finch. The expectation was realised: he found his friend enjoying an autumnal sunset which shed its glory over the Atlantic, as glowing under the golden light, it was seen through the majestic frame of a mountain-pass, with all the beauty of Claude, and more of grandeur.

Warm was the greeting of the friends; and, ere they slept that night, many an important move regarding their future proceedings was planned,—and when Finch was of the council, a thing planned was nearly as good as executed. But, in this case, one of those trivial circumstances which sometimes tend to mar the best laid schemes, interfered with the working out of the present. It was agreed that the sooner a remove from Ireland was made the better, particularly as regarded Lynch; and, as Finch had previously offered, he again said the treasure he sought, if found, was heartily at Ned's service, to get himself and his friends out of trouble. In search of the point laid down in Finch's instructions, he and Ned started the day following. The place, near which the treasure lay, was only a few miles distant; and a ramble along the shore of a beautiful bay towards a rocky point, which formed its southern extremity, placed them in view of a small castle,—one of those early structures for defence, a square sturdy-built tower, machicolated at its angles. As they drew near, they perceived a great number of people actively engaged in the neighbourhood in the formation of large heaps of some material obtained from the sea. On a nearer approach it was perceptibly sea-weed, which, on inquiry, they found was burnt in large quantities at this season for the production of kelp. After the customary exchanges of civility between the peasants and the strangers, Finch and Ned commenced their observations to ascertain the true bearings of the important spot which contained the treasure. This they were not long in finding, for the peaks of the mountains in the background, and the markings of the shore, gave points easily recognisable. Having ascertained these, the next point was to measure the distance from a certain angle of the castle, and when this was done, (and it was obliged to be done slily, for the peasants were numerous and close beside them,) they found, to their great discomfiture, that a very large heap of the kelp-weed lay directly on the spot.

Here was what huntsmen call "a check." In any case, to have an occupation in progress which congregated the peasants about the castle would have been awkward; but here was the very spot they wanted for the exercise of their own peculiar practice in possession of kelp-burners, and, to make the matter worse, many more days were yet to be employed in the collection of the weed, and afterwards a period required for drying and burning. Had they been a fortnight earlier, they would have found the same spot in utter loneliness; but as the weed was found in great abundance on the shore bordering on the castle, a gathering of the neighbouring people always took place at the fitting season to collect and prepare their kelp, and the old castle made a sort of general head-quarters during the process.

While this state of things lasted, it was manifest that any attempt to raise the treasure would have been dangerous, and there seemed nothing for it but to wait until the kelp-burning was over, and, in the meantime, Ned proposed to Finch to join the party in the hills.

"You know they are outlaws," said Ned, "and of course their company is dangerous; and as it seems some six weeks must pass before you can revisit the castle with safety, perhaps you might as well return to some neighbouring town, where you and I can meet occasionally; for, of course, my dear Finch, wherever a 'certain person' is, there will I continue; and nothing can induce her to leave her father."

"And do you think," returned Finch, "that I would desire to be in any better place than where a beautiful girl, inspired with the noblest feelings, chooses to harbour in the face of all dangers?"

"I know, my dear fellow," said Ned, "you are as dauntless of danger, when necessary, as any human being, and under such circumstances it is I have seen you; but when it is *not* necessary to expose yourself——"

"Pooh! pooh!" interposed Finch. "A handful of danger, more or less, in the course of a man's life is nothing; besides, here I have something new to see. I have witnessed adventure enough by sea and shore; but this mountain life, of which you have given such a romantic description, will be new to me, if you think your friends will not object to my sojourn among them."

"You know how you were welcomed the other day at the 'board of green cloth!'"

"True," said Finch, smiling at the recollection. "But there is a difference between a casual courtesy like that and a permanent residence."

"As long as their own residence is tenable anywhere, I will ensure you a hearty welcome, and perhaps something above the ordinary temperature of Hibernian warmth, from the proof you give of contempt of danger."

The next day proved how justly Ned had estimated the feelings of his companions; for nothing could exceed the warmth of Finch's reception at the cave. Here for many days the novelty of their mode of life, and the splendour of the scenery, were enough to amuse him, after which, the intimacy which arose between him and Lynch held his attention engaged. They found in each other a congenial spirit of enterprise,—the invention to engender plans, resources to meet the difficulties of execution, and hearts to dare every obstacle. Thus it would happen, that they would sometimes ramble into the hills together, while others of the party were engaged in the daily routine of procuring supplies, as already described, and, ensconced in some mountain dingle, or stretched on some hill side among the heather, hours upon hours were passed in dreams of possible adventure, so that, at last, it became a usual thing for Lynch and the guest to set out in the morning, remain together all day, and not return till the evening.

At the same time, another couple of persons were wont to pair off for a ramble together through the hills; and Ned and Ellen, thus engaged, were, in nursery-tale parlance, "as happy as the day was long." Among many haunts, the most favourite was a small river, which, having its origin in the hills, bounded wildly from crag to crag, and made its precipitous road to the sea by a succession of picturesque falls, one more beautiful than another. This stream was remarkable for abounding in a species of mussel, frequently containing pearls, which, though inferior in lustre to the oriental, were still of great beauty, and in search of these Ned and Ellen passed much of their time. He, as well as his "ladye love," had assumed the peasant guise, (a practice rather common to the refugees,) as thus they might appear with less chance of observation from evil eyes when they ventured from the security of their mountain retreats, and trusted themselves towards the plains. In these loose habiliments, Ned was more free to wade and search in the shoals of the pearl river for the shelly treasures which were destined for a necklace for his loved one, who, seated on some jutting rock, smiled on the labours of her lover, as she received from his hand the produce of his search. How many happy days were thus spent; happy, in spite of all their doubts, difficulties, and dangers!

By good luck, however, the retreat remained unsuspected by " the authorities;" and in the unmolested security of the hills the refugees got on gaily. Phaidrig's leg, under the growling orders of Ulick, was mending fast, so much so, that he could sit up a little, and give his friends a lilt on the pipes. Lynch found more repose than he had done for months; and Ellen, freed from pressing anxiety on her father's account, and rejoicing in her new-found companionship, recovered all her good looks, and was never seen in more beauty. It might be that the delicacy of tint which is esteemed in a courtly ball-room (which rouge, perforce, is sometimes called to light up,) was somewhat invaded by the mountain air; but that same bracing atmosphere brought with it health; and if the cheek bore a glow beyond the standard of *haut ton,* the clear bright beaming of the eye sustained it, and might have shamed the languid glance of a court belle; while the elastic tread of the mountain heroine displayed in finer action her symmetrical form than could the dropping of the conventional curtsey, or the gliding of the stately minuet. To Ned she seemed more charming than ever; and in truth she was so; for not only had the girlish beauty, which first enslaved him, become ripened, but the eventfulness of her life had called her mental energies into action, and thus a more intellectual character was given to her countenance. How often had her lover gazed upon it in all its fitful changes, whether it beamed with mirthfulness to the passing jest, or glowed with indignation at some instance of wrong; or if the eye was raised in hopeful appeal to Heaven, or glistened with the tear some tale of pity drew from the deep fountain of sympathy which lay within her noble heart; or, dearest of all, if it met his own enraptured gaze, and exchanged that glance of mutual endearment, confidence, and devotion, which true and earnest love alone can waken!

When people happen to be in the aforesaid condition of our young friends, it is proverbial how swiftly time passes, and Ned could scarcely believe, when he was told that six weeks had elapsed since his visit with Finch to the castle, and was called upon to join the skipper in a second exploration of that spot. They set out forthwith on their adventure, and found a scene of utter loneliness where before so many busy people were congregated, and, free from all observation, were able to carry on their operations in uninterrupted safety. Those operations were perfectly successful. A considerable sum in doubloons and pistoles was raised, and our adventurers, having provided themselves with haversacks on quitting the cave, were enabled to sling the cases of treasure therein over their shoulders, and in three days from the time of their departure they returned to their friends rejoicingly, and were received with the applause due to prosperous enterprise.

An extra jollification was held that night in honour of the event, and the following day a consultation of Lynch and his more immediate friends took place, to consider the safest mode of getting out of Ireland; for the Captain, at last, on the arrival of some disheartening intelligence from abroad, had consented to fly the kingdom. Finally, Ned's plan of reaching Limerick by the Shannon was adopted, with such additional stratagems as Finch and the Captain himself could bring to strengthen it.

A fleet horse being indispensable for the transit of Lynch across the closely-beset county of Galway to the Shannon shore, a trusty emissary from the hills was despatched to a friend in the lowlands, naming a time and place where the steed should be in waiting. Now, seeing that in those days it was against the laws for a Catholic in Ireland to possess a horse above the value of five pounds, it was not such an easy matter to procure what Lynch wanted; but as Protestant masters could not do without Catholic servants, the good offices of an underling who kept the stud-farm of a gentleman who bred his own racers and hunters served the turn, and Darby Linch (for that was the care-taker's name), for so high and distinguished a member of his tribe as the Captain, would have gone through fire and water for him, and, of course, would make any horse under his command do the same thing, though it should cost the same Darby his place the next day.

This being arranged, the next point was to make a movement of the principals towards Corrib, whose waters were to be recrossed to Augh-na-doon, as the safest point to progress from; and when the hour of parting came, it was not without pain and many a heart-tugging grasp of daring hands that Lynch could part from his outlawed friends, in whose wanderings, and perils, and privations he had been for months a partaker.

As for Ellen, she wept bitterly, for she knew that some hearts were left to ache in those mountain-wilds, pining for wife, or child, or true love, from whom their desperate fortunes cut them off; and in the rejoicing at her own release and the prospect of happiness to herself, the contrast of the fate of the less fortunate, touched her gentle soul.

As Phaidrig was allowed to follow the fortunes of "the masther," as he constantly called Lynch, a chosen few from the retreat set out with the party to carry the piper over the mountain-passes; for, though he could manage with the assistance of a stick to get on pretty well on level ground, too great an exertion of the restored limb might be dangerous.

By dint of an early start and a long march, *Caistla-na Kirka* in the upper Corrib, was reached the evening of the first day, and made their resting-place. They continued on the rocky islet till the evening of the second, when they re-embarked for the lower lake. The narrows, through all that exquisite scenery which had so charmed Finch on his first entrance to the hills, were passed during twilight; when the open lake was reached, where greater danger might be apprehended, night had settled over the waters, and under its protecting shadows a safe passage was effected to Augh-na-doon, where the emissary who had been despatched from the hills was waiting, provided with refreshments and good news for the fugitives. Here, after a hasty meal, a general scattering of the party took place. The refugees of the mountains took their oars, and went back to their protecting hills. Finch, Ned, and Ellen, took Phaidrig under their charge, to commence at once their journey towards the appointed place of embarkation on the Shannon, where, by preconcerted arrangements, a boat was at their service, while Lynch was to retire to his old hiding-place in the abbey for three days, by which time the "advanced-guard," as he called it, could reach the river, and have all in readiness to receive him after his midnight gallop. Ellen fondly embraced her father again and again ere she parted from him, even then loth to leave him for so short a time; but he strove to soothe her fears, exhorted her to dependence on Heaven's mercy, and, with mutual blessings, at last they parted.

Lynch pursued his way alone to the vault, where the mountain *gilly* was to rejoin him after he had guided the others to a neighbouring friendly hut, where a common car and horse were ready for their use, as it was still in peasant-fashion they proposed to pursue their journey, certain that such a mode afforded more security. Travelling thus, they could stop at the humblest carrier's inn on the outskirts of each town they had to pass, where, even if they were suspected, they might rely on finding humble friends willing to facilitate their movements; while, had they gone as gentlefolk, the region of the first-class hostelry might not have been quite so safe, where, if they had even escaped suspicion and betrayal from its owners, they ran the chance of meeting some straggling emissary of power.

Having reached the hut, the horse and car were put at once into requisition, and the *gilly* having waited until he saw the party fairly started, returned to Lynch, while the others pushed on that night as far as Headfort.

CHAPTER XLVIII.

THE road was pursued in safety the following morning by our travellers, and the third day placed them under the shelter of a fisherman's hut by Lough Ree. Earnest were Ellen's prayers for the safety of her father that night, as she knelt in deep and prolonged devotion ere she slept; for that night was one of toil and peril to him. He was even now on his dangerous transit across the country, and the storm that was raging as she prayed, she trusted would prove but an additional safeguard to him, as fewer wayfarers would be abroad. She awoke often in the night, and ever as she woke the storm was louder and her prayers more fervent. As it approached morning she could sleep no longer, and arose and called the fisherman, that he might be on the look-out upon the high road to guide the horseman through the by-path which led to the hut. He lit a fire before he departed, and Ellen during his absence piled up the turf sods upon it, that a comfortable blaze might meet the weather-beaten traveller on his arrival.

Finch, Ned, and Phaidrig, still slept, and Ellen sat companionless by the fire, in that state of anxious thoughtfulness which ever possesses the mind when the hours are pregnant with adventure. Ever and anon, amidst the heavy gusts of wind, she would start from her reverie, and listen for the wished-for tramp of a horse. No,—it was but fancy,—he comes not yet. Twice thus had she been deceived, but the charmed third time deceived her not,—it *was* the foot stroke of a steed; she hurried to the door through whose chinks glimmered the first glimpse of dawn She threw it open, and stood abroad amid the beating of the thick rain that came dashing heavily in her face in the rude gusts of the blast; but, oh! more pleasant than the brightest sunshine she ever saw was that dim and stormy dawn, for through its mist she beheld her father speeding onward,—the last turn of the rough path is passed,—his panting horse is reined up,—he springs from the saddle, and is locked in the close embrace of his beloved and loving child. They neither could speak from excess of emotion, and stood in the storm, heedless, perhaps unconscious, of its fury. At length the sweet girl spoke,—"Come in, dear father; you are wayworn, and want rest."

" The horse, Nell—the horse must be cared for ;—as gallant a beast as ever carried a soldier !" and he patted the panting beast on his arched neck, that was white with foam, notwithstanding the heavy drenching of the rain.

" He must share the house with us, then," said Ellen, "for there is not any other shelter."

" And well he deserves such Arab courtesy," said Lynch, leading him at once into the hut.

The sleeping men were roused from their lairs, and the beds they had reposed on were scattered into a larger "shake down" for the horse by Lynch's own hands, before he would think of any comfort for himself. Then, amidst the gratulations of his friends, he took some slight refreshment before the welcome blaze of the turf fire; and having cast his drenched garments, and obtained some dry ones, he threw himself on the rough couch of the fisherman, and was soon sunk in the profoundest slumber.

Lynch slept long, for the weather continued too boisterous to attempt the lake, and his friends did not wake him until it moderated towards evening, and was time to embark. An unnecessary moment was not lost; the boat was shoved from the shore, whence they glided under a favouring wind, with a hearty "God speed you" from the trusty fisherman. They passed Athlone in the night, a point of danger, and then for many a mile there was perfect security before them. The air became piercing cold upon the water, and Ellen felt it so bitterly that, on reaching Clonmacnoise, they ran their boat ashore, and sought shelter in the little chapel of the lesser round tower that stands on that long-sacred and still-venerated spot—the second Christian foundation in Ireland. At dawn they were again on the waters, and were favoured with a lovely day for the time of year, and without let or hindrance of any sort they made good way down the stream, and by night were not far from Bannagher. Here again they stopped for the night, close under the bank, making a sort of awning of their sail for the protection of Ellen, while the men kept watch and watch about, anxiously awaiting the light which was necessary for their next day's navigation, as the river became narrower, more winding, and dividing into different channels ere opening again into the ample space of Lough Derg. The welcome dawn arrived at length, and the favourable nature of the weather rendered the beauties of the surrounding scenery more vivid. The sun came brightly out, and cheered the spirits of the voyagers. Another successful day's sail, and much of their danger would be over; the prospect of escape was now so near, it might almost be said they were happy.

The lovely aspect of nature had something to do with this state of feeling; the beauty of the river increased at every fresh turn in its tortuous course; sloping green banks lay on each side, small tufted islets, crowned with beautiful trees, occasionally rising from the centre of the stream; the trailing branches of the pendant trees rippling the calm course of the waters with streaks of light, which sparkled over the surface until they became gently lost in the widening waters, which gradually spread as they opened into Lough Derg, whose hilly boundaries were becoming visible over the crests of some wooded heights on their left, beneath whose shelter rose the remains of an ancient castle, whose walls had suffered from war as well as time—indeed, less from the latter than the former, which, under the guidance of the merciless Cromwell, left but few specimens of castellated architecture unscathed in all Ireland.

Portumna Castle, the ancient hold of the Earls of Clanricarde, lay on the opposite shore, and as the present earl was one active in authority, and whose power might be feared, the boat was laid close to the bank which bore the ruined towers, whence no danger might be apprehended; and a favouring breeze just then springing up, they hoisted their sail, and hoped to win the wide waste of Derg's dark waters unperceived, after which all apprehension might be set at rest. They now laid by their oars, the wind giving them sufficient speed, and they scudded merrily along, when their apprehensions were aroused by observing a flag suddenly displayed from the top of the ruin as they came abreast of it, and a shot fired, which seemed to indicate a demand from that quarter that account should be rendered by the voyagers ere they cleared that pass of the river.

"Keep never minding," said Ned; "'tis our only plan, and the boat has good way upon her now. We shall be soon out of harm's way."

"They have hoisted the flag again," said Finch, "as if they were signalising."

"Perhaps exchanging signals with Portumna Castle, on the opposite shore."

Finch instinctively looked in the direction.

"You cannot see it," said Lynch; "'tis hidden by the woods, but must be perfectly visible from yonder towers."

They now saw several armed men run down from the castle to a small inlet that ran up towards it from the river, and, disengaging a boat from the bank, embark with the apparent intention of pursuit.

The moment this was perceived by the fugitives, they instantly seized their oars, which they plied with vigour, to gain additional speed. Their pursuers were not long in following, and when they cleared the inlet and gained the open water, they hoisted a sail as well, so that there was no mistaking their desire to overtake the foremost boat, which seemed to gain, however, on the pursuers, and was making a good lead into the lough, which stretched far and wide away, dark and rough, and crested with spray under the influence of the breeze, which increased every minute. In this the fugitives rejoiced, for their boat was stiff, and standing well to her canvass, would be sure to outstrip the lighter one that followed in the rough water; but their joy was short-lived, for just as they cleared the extreme point of the right bank of the river, and that the whole lough was open, they saw a larger boat than theirs under sail, and stretching across, apparently with the intention to intercept them.

Not a word was said, but all gazed anxiously at this strange sail, and then at each other, and the anxious looks that met too plainly revealed that evil forebodings possessed the minds of all.— Ned was the first to speak.

"What think you, Finch?" said he, appealing to him as the highest authority in aquatic matters.

Finch, clenching his teeth hard, strongly aspirated, and half growled between them, the characteristic reply of a sailor—it was merely—"*d—n these lakes!*"

"But what's to be done?"

"I say, d—n them again!—If it was the honest sea we were in, lying well to win'ard, as we are, we might beat them blind; but with that wall of hills on our weather-bow, we're done.— Curse it—we're like rats in a corner."

"Let us run for it, however, while we can," said Ned; "there's no knowing what luck may do for us yet."

As he spoke a gun was fired from the larger boat.

"There's no mistaking that," said Finch. "We must lower our canvass, or determine to fight it out."

"No fighting," said Lynch, in a calm steady voice. "Against such odds it were but waste of life. Let them overhaul us—perhaps we may be unmolested; but, at all events, I am the only one on whom their vengeance can fall, and if my time is come, so be it.— God's will be done!"

Ellen grew deadly pale as he spoke, and clung to him.

"Nell, my girl, this is no time for quailing. I expect from you all your firmness.—As you love me, be calm and resolute."

With wonderful self-control, the noble girl relaxed her fond hold, and assumed an aspect of composure, though her cheek and lips, in their abated colour, betrayed the agitation of her heart.

"Let us strike our sail at once," said Lynch, "and wait for our pursuers."

Ned obeyed the orders; and then, when he had no further duty to perform, he seated himself beside Ellen, and, gently taking her hand, whispered such words of encouragement as his ingenuity could suggest at the moment.

Phaidrig, who had been listening all this time, and had not spoken a word, got his pipes ready, and began to play.

"What the deuce are you lilting for now?" said Finch, who was beginning to feel rather savage at the turn affairs were taking.

"It will look aisy and careless," answered Phaidrig, "to be playing when they come up to us."

Finch, though he made no answer, admired the address of this little manœuvre, and took it as a lesson to clear his own brow, which was rather severe at the moment.

The boat in pursuit was soon alongside, containing some soldiers, and an officer, who questioned those on board the chase who they were, whence they came, and whither going.

To these questions answers were returned in accordance with a previously prepared-story the parties had agreed upon; but, as it may be supposed, no answer could satisfy the officer, who only made his inquiries as a matter of course, and ordered the voyagers to put about, and go back to the castle until they should be examined.

"What offence, sir, have we committed," inquired Finch; "that we should be stopped on our way?"

"You're an Englishman I judge, from your accent," was the inconsequent reply.

"I am, sir," said Finch; "and, from your very Irish answer, I guess you are a native.—I ask again, what offence have we committed?"

"That's what we want to find out, and therefore turn you back for examination."

"According to that practice, sir, you presuppose every one guilty?"

"And a pretty near guess too, in this d——d rebelly place," said the puppyish fellow, with an insulting laugh.

"I'd have you remember I am an Englishman, sir!—We Englishmen are jealous of our liberties, and take care what you're about."

The impudent coxcomb gave a long whistle, and exclaimed, "Liberties indeed!—very fine to be sure.—Why didn't you stay at home with your liberties, and not come here?—We'll give you a touch of our law-practice that will enlighten you perhaps, so lose no time in improving yourself—turn back to the castle. I'm d——d sorry to disoblige so pretty a girl; but don't be afraid, my dear," he said to Ellen, with a disgusting leer, "we are particularly kind to the fair sex."

At this insolent speech Ned's eyes flashed fire, whereupon the puppy became more saucy. "Ho, ho!" he said,—"one fellow is jealous of his liberties, and the other jealous of his girl,—we'll do justice to both."

The orders to go back to the castle were obeyed, and no more was said, though the boats continued abreast of each other; but a succession of impudent leers at Ellen were continued by the insolent soldier, while looks of indignant defiance were returned by Ned. Finch, in the meantime, observed the larger boat in the offing had gone about, and bore away to the point whence she came, as soon as the armed boat in pursuit had taken charge of the chase, which now, under guard, was fast approaching the castle, many of whose military inmates had strolled down to the water's edge to await her arrival, and seek in this little event some variety in the dull monotony of their lives in so remote a spot.

On entering the inlet which led from the river to the castle, the guard-boat shot ahead, and the insolent coxcomb in command stepped ashore, and was ready on the bank, when the boat of our voyagers touched it, to hand Ellen out, having previously "tipped a wink" to his idle brother officers in waiting, as much as to say, "You shall see some fun."

Lynch was the first to land, and waited to assist Ellen, but the coxcomb said to the sergeant of his party, "Pass him on!"

"I wish to hand my daughter from the boat," said Lynch, laying particular stress on the word daughter, in hopes the presence of a father might tend to procure that respect for his child which he saw there was not sufficient of true manliness to insure her at the hands of this insufferable puppy.

"Pass him on!" was the repeated order; and Lynch, making an effort to control his feelings, made no further objection.

Ned was now about to debark, but Ellen, in a whisper, besought him to "be calm," and let her go first. Then, with a dignified self-possession that so often disarms impertinence, she gave her hand to the fellow she loathed, to hand her from the boat, but he rudely seized her as she jumped to the shore, and forcibly kissed her.

Ned had been choking with rage up to this moment, and with difficulty had obeyed Ellen's command to let her pass him, but when he saw the indignity put upon her he sprang like a tiger upon the offender, seized him by the throat, and flung him to the earth with the foulest epithets.

The wretch, thus justly punished, after recovering from the stunning effects of his fall, scrambled to his feet, and, with a hellish expression in his eye, grasped his sword ; but, before it was out of the sheath, Ned, with the quickness of lightning, snatched the blade from the scabbard of the sergeant who stood near him, and met the murderously-intended thrust of the infuriated soldier with an able parry. Stung by the personal indignity he had suffered in the presence of his brother officers, the coxcomb, in a state of revengeful frenzy, pushed desperately at Ned, whose fiercest passions being roused by the insult inflicted before his face on the woman he adored, could have sacrificed at the moment a score of lives to his vengeance, and, therefore, used his weapon with the deadliest intention. The officers by-standing drew their swords, and rushed forward to beat down the blades of the antagonists, but before their assistance could avail, Ned had driven his weapon to the very hilt through the body of the aggressor, who, uttering a yell of agony, staggered back—fell to the earth, and, with one convulsive struggle, turned over on his face, and literally bit the ground. 'Twas a sudden, terrible retribution—the hot libertine lip that had violated the sanctity of a maiden's cheek now kissed the dust.

There was a pause and a silence of some moments, all seemingly paralysed by the suddenness of the catastrophe. At length the senior officer present spoke, and ordered Ned to be taken in charge.

Ned, as he gave up the sword, said, "I appeal to you all, as soldiers and men of honour, to remember the act was in self-defence."

"You struck him," said one of the younger officers, angrily; "you—a prisoner at the time—struck him."

"And would repeat the act under the same provocation," cried Ned boldly. "A prisoner, forsooth!—For what am I a prisoner? We are dragged here, interrupted on our peaceful way, and a woman grossly insulted—what law is there for that?"

"You'll know more about the law before you're done with it," said the officer, with a menacing nod.

"I must beg you to be silent, lieutenant," said the senior officer, who, turning to Ned, told him he should have fair play. He then desired the dead body to be carried to the castle, and ordered the prisoners to proceed there also.

While all this was going on, Ellen clung to Lynch, while her eyes were turned on Ned ; and when he joined the party she gave him her hand, and walked on silently between her father and her lover, for she could not speak. Finch and Phaidrig were in the rear, the Sergeant walking beside them The Sergeant,

24

judging from his weather-stained face, which bore a scar also, had seen service, and, as far as manner could imply, thought Ned had done no more than he ought.

"I think I have seen the elder of those prisoners before," said he to Finch in an undertone.

"Indeed!"

"I'm sure of it."

"Where, do you think?"

Phaidrig's ears were all alive for the answer.

"Abroad," said the Sergeant.

"You're mistaken," said Phaidrig; "he never was abroad in his life."

"Don't talk so loud," said the Sergeant. "I mean him no harm; I would rather stand his friend if I could."

Finch looked him in the face as he spoke, and there was an honest expression in it that never belonged to treachery.

"You are an Englishman," said Finch.

"Yes."

"So am I. Britons do not like tyranny and oppression."

"No."

"You would help us if you could.'

"As far as I dare; but do not speak any more now. When you are locked up I will see you."

The party now progressed silently to the castle, on reaching which the prisoners were conducted up a narrow stone spiral stair to the summit of one of the towers, where they were placed in a small strong room, and a heavy door fastened upon them. After the lapse of about an hour the bolts outside were gently drawn, and the Sergeant made his appearance.

"You're as good as your word," said Finch.

"Hope I always will be."

"I hear you have seen me before," said Lynch.

"I have, sir."

"I do not remember you."

"It was a crowded and busy place we met in; but I cannot forget you, sir—for you saved my life."

"Where?"

"At Fontenoy, your honour. You were an officer of the Irish brigade that hot day."

"Well?"

"When the Duke of Cumberland's centre was broken by your charge, and we were routed, some French regiments came bowling down to take vengeance for the mangling they got in the morning; but the Irish lads got between and would not allow slaughter, and your own hand, sir, turned aside a blow that would have finished me as I lay on the ground; and I will say, all the Irish lads were kind friends to the wounded English that we left on the field that day*—and I never forgot it—and never will.   You, sir, were amongst the foremost in showing us kindness in hospital, and if, without a heavy breach of duty, I can do you a good turn, I am ready."

"You are a true-hearted fellow, and I thank you," said Lynch.   "Is it long since you have been in Ireland?"

"Not long, sir—and I wish I was out of it.   I don't like their cruel goings on here."

"Did you escape from Flanders, or were you exchanged?"

"Exchanged, your honour."

"I don't know, my kind fellow, how you can help me," said Lynch, musing for a moment.   "One thing alone I beg to remind you of—that the less you say of the brigade the better."

"Mum's the word, your honour—too old a sojer for that."

"If your honour can't say anything," said Phaidrig, "may I put in a word?"

"Certainly, Phaidrig."

"Do you think now," said the piper to the Sergeant, "that there would be any use in asking lave of that elderly officer, who seems a dacent sort of a body, to let me go on a little bit of a message?"

"Certainly not; you are a prisoner."

"I know that; but I mane to go undher guard."

"I fear not; the officer would not like to do it without authority from Mister Nevil."

"Nevil?" exclaimed Lynch, anxiously—"Jones Nevil?"

"The same, sir."

A shade passed across Lynch's countenance; it was noticed by Finch.

"That seems bad news," said he.

Lynch did not answer; but in the clasped hands and upraised eyes of Ellen, Finch could read woful tidings.

"Well, if I can't go, maybe you could slip a smart lad across the river, and bid him run to Portumna for the bare life; and if the lord is at home, tell him there's one here may die soon, who has a secret for him that he is behowlden above all things to hear; and that when he hears it, he wouldn't for half his estate not have known it: and if the lord isn't at home, let the messenger go through fire and wather till he finds him."

* This often happened. On one occasion, in particular, though I cannot remember the name of the action, the Irish brigade, after a victory, went through the field, seeking the wounded English who suffered in the adverse ranks, and showed them the tenderest care.

"That shall be done," said the Sergeant.   "Anything else?—make haste, for I must not venture to stay here longer."

"Do that, and 'tis plenty—but do it soon."

The Sergeant pointed through a window in their prison, that looked upon the waters, and said, "You shall see a messenger cross the stream in five minutes." He then withdrew, and bolted the door on the outside.

According to the soldier's promise, the anxious watchers from the tower saw the boat unmoored from the bank, and two men embark. The boat was pulled across the river; one of the men went ashore, and started at a good pace up the opposite hill; he was followed by eager eyes until he had gained the summit, and was lost in the woods that crowned its crest, while the friendly boat returned to her moorings.

Lynch asked Phaidrig what hope he could entertain of any benefit from the presence of the Earl of Clanricarde, for whom he had sent, he being a staunch adherent of government, and rather severe in the authority he was appointed to exercise over the province, and further expressed a belief that Clanricarde was now aware of his (Lynch's) presence in Ireland, and would be amongst the readiest to arrest him, though he confessed they might all be careless of anything that might happen now, being already in Nevil's hands, which were the most unsparing into which they could fall.

"But still I cannot see the drift of this mysterious message to the Earl, Phaidrig," added Lynch.

"Masther! masther!" said Phaidrig, "don't be asking me any questions about it; only God send the Earl may be here soon, and I've a way of my own that will melt his heart to all of us."

The confident assurance of Phaidrig in his scheme turned the minds of the prisoners with painful interest to the success of the messenger; and many an anxious eye was cast on the spot in the distant wood where he had disappeared, in the hope of catching the first welcome glimpse of his return.

CHAPTER XLIX

As the presence of regular troops stationed in a ruined castle may appear strange to the reader, it may be as well to give a few words in the explanation of the subject. Under the wise administration of Chesterfield, a confidence in the laws that governed them, and the honesty of the men who administered those laws, arose in the people of Ireland, and a tranquillity, rare in that disturbed land. was the consequence, and the statesmanlike Earl was enabled to spare troops out of the country. But, on the suppression of the Scottish rising, when means of coercion were again plenty, the spirit of justice and lenity which influenced Lord Chesterfield's government, became distasteful to those who had been used to trample on the nation. The amiable Earl was recalled, when justice, lately rendered as a measure of necessity, might be once more dispensed with, and a more iron sway than ever resumed. In consequence of this, an increase in the army was required in Ireland; for, though the people had been held in a state of slavery one wonders at, still, once having emerged from their bondage, it was no easy matter to push them back into it again. For the thousands of additional bayonets thus become requisite in the island there was not sufficient accommodation, and barracks were ordered to be built in various parts of the country. This job—for it was a job—was given to one Nevil,* that he might plunder the national purse as a reward for his outrage of national rights. A member of the House of Commons—his vote was ever at the service of the government. His malignant propensities against the people found him favour in the eyes of Lord George Sackville, and his general profligacy endeared him to the Primate. In working out his contract in the erection of barracks, he frequently converted some old building, or portion of a castle, into a tenement for the military, at a small expense, while he pocketed large sums from the treasury as though fresh barracks had been erected; and, in going his round of provinces, in this prominent position of a government agent, he had frequent opportunities, and he never lost one, of indulging in priest-hunting, or any other species of cruelty he could exercise. His well-known influence at court gave him a

* Alluded to by Lynch in his interview with the Earl of Kildare.

power which few dared, and none wished, to call into hostility,
and thus, in many instances, men were made the instruments of
his vile passions who regretted the obedience they feared to
refuse.

It was thus the old castle on the Shannon became occupied
with soldiers, and Nevil himself being there for a few days,
many vexatious things were done in the neighbourhood, and he
had a willing agent in the unfortunate young man who was killed,
—a nephew of his own,—and partaking so much of his uncle's
savage and profligate nature as to render him a favourite with
his powerful relative.

Ned's plight was, therefore, one of imminent danger, indeed
the officers and men of the barracks looked upon him as a gone
man, and felt assured that the moment of Nevil's return to the
castle, and knowledge of his nephew's death, would be the
signal for Ned's being hanged; for, in those days, short work
was made with the mere Irish, if a great man willed it so; a
regular trial might be tedious and troublesome, and the judgment of the law too slow a process for the satisfaction of an
impatient loyalist.

The anticipations respecting Nevil's course of action were
proved to be but too true; for, when this unscrupulous man of
power returned, and heard of the circumstances of the case, he
ordered the instant execution of the "rebel scoundrel" who had
"*murdered*" that "noble young man," his nephew, one who
would have proved an honour to his profession, and a support
to his "king and his country," &c. &c.

The senior officer in command of the troops represented, that
as the act of the prisoner was committed in the natural desire of
preserving his own life, it might be as well to give him up
to the laws, which would decide the question how far a
prisoner had a right to defend his own life from his captor
before being proved guilty.

To this an order was returned to "hang the rascal instantly."

The officer, though rebuffed, next ventured to suggest even
a court-martial.

This but sharpened the desire for immediate vengeance, and,
with the overbearing threat of a man who knew his power,
Nevil dared the officer to refuse to obey his commands.

The soldier withdrew, disgusted, but fearing to disobey; and
with a heavy heart, the Sergeant, receiving his fatal orders.
reascended the stair, and re-opening the door of the prison
addressed Ned, saying he wished to speak a few words to him
and beckoning him at the same time from the room; for he
had not the heart to speak his message in presence of a woman

and that the woman by whom, passing circumstances led him to believe, the fated prisoner was held dear. But his caution availed nothing; there was an expression in his face, and voice, and manner, that awaked all Ellen's fears; and with a scream she sprang forward, clung to Edward's neck, and with sobs, and tears, and prayers, besought the soldier not to tear him from her—for mercy's sake to spare him yet for awhile—with many a passionate and wild appeal to human feeling and divine assistance; and during the scene of desperate agony all were paralysed but Ellen, who seemed inspired with superhuman courage.

At length, Phaidrig, roused up suddenly into action, and calling on Finch, desired him to look again over the water, and see if any help were come.

"The large boat that headed us in the lake is rounding the point now," said Finch.

"God be praised!" exclaimed Phaidrig, dropping on his knees.

The voice of Nevil was heard from below, calling in a furious voice to "bring down the prisoner."

Ellen but clung the closer to him; and the kind-hearted Serjeant was so agitated, that he was absolutely incapable of action, and could not have dragged Ned from her embrace if he would.

The tramp of many feet was heard ascending the stair; and when several soldiers appeared at the door of the prison, Ellen, overcome by the intensity of her feelings, swooned in Ned's arms.

The soldiers demanded his immediate presence below. Ned uttered no word; but impressing on the pale lips of his beloved one a fervent caress, he laid her gently in the arms of her father, whose hand he grasped firmly for an instant, and with silent exchanges of the grip of fellowship with Finch and Phaidrig, he walked to the head of the stair, where the soldiers awaited him.

"The boat! the boat!" cried Phaidrig to Finch; "where is it now?"

"Touching the shore, and people are landing."

"Is there a fine looking man among them?"

"Yes, and in rich attire."

"'Tis the Earl!" exclaimed Phaidrig, in delight, laying his hand on the Sergeant. "Take me down with you," he cried urgently,—" take me down, and I will save his life yet."

"'Tis against orders," said the Sergeant, hesitating.

"As you hope for peace to your soul at your own dying hour, don't refuse me!" urged Phaidrig.

"Come, then," said the Sergeant,—suppose I *am* punished; I can't see murder done without trying to stop it, and you say you can."

"I can, if I get speech of the Earl," said the piper. "Hurry!—hurry!—Give me your hand—help me down the stair." The last words were spoken as the prison door was closed; and Lynch, with the yet unconscious Ellen in his arms, gazed upon his child with an expression of mental agony of which Finch had never seen the equal.

When Phaidrig and the Sergeant reached the base of the tower, a rope had been just placed round Ned's neck. Phaidrig, as he laid his hand on Ned's shoulder to whisper him something, felt the hempen instrument of death, and a tremor passed over his whole frame.

"God have mercy on us!" he exclaimed.—"This is hasty work; not only death without trial, but without letting a man say a prayer before he suffers.—Sure, they won't refuse you ten minutes to ask for Heaven's mercy." Then in a whisper to Ned, he said, "Ask for ten minutes."

Nevil's voice was heard without, ordering the prisoner to be brought forth.

The Sergeant advanced and told him the prisoner craved ten minutes to pray.

"Not a second!" said Nevil.—"My nephew died without a prayer, and so shall he.—Bring out the rascal, and hang him up at once. Curse you, you bunglers; what are you fumbling at? —One would think you never hanged a man before.—Bring him out, I say!"

The Earl of Clanricarde reached the entrance of the castle as Ned was led forth for execution.

"What is this about Mr. Nevil?" asked the Earl.

"Murder, my lord."

"It will be murder if this young man is hanged, noble Clanricarde," said Phaidrig, confronting the Earl.

"What brings you here, Phaidrig-na-pib," said Clanricarde.

"The hand of God," said Phaidrig, in a manner so impressive, that even Nevil was struck by it.

"What do you mean?" inquired the Earl.

"Will the noble Clanricarde let the poor piper have a word in his ear to save an innocent life?"

"Willingly."

Phaidrig advanced to the Earl, who permitted him to whisper; the words he said could have been but few, for his lips were but a moment at the ear of the Earl; but those words must have been potent, for Clanricarde's face was suffused by a deep flush, succeeded by an ashy paleness. He gazed at Ned intently, but could not speak.

"Lead on to execution!" cried Nevil, profiting by the pause.

"I forbid it!" cried the Earl.

"He slew my nephew," shouted Nevil, white with rage.

"Had he killed yourself, sir," said the Earl, drawing himself up to his full height, and casting a look of disdain on Nevil, "he shall not die but by the laws of the land."

"Do you forget who I am, my Lord?"

"No, sir—though you seem to forget yourself."

"The Lord-Lieutenant shall hear of this," said Nevil.

"I will take care he shall," retorted the Earl.

"Do you know, sir," continued the arrogant minion of power, "that boxes of Spanish gold have been found in possession of these prisoners, clearly proving their connection with hostile states?"

"That shall be inquired into," said the Earl.

"The inquiry shall be conducted at the Castle of Dublin," said Nevil, with a menacing air; "and I will be the bearer of this traitorous gold myself.—Harness my horses, there!—Goodbye, my Lord!"

"Stay, Mister Nevil," said Clanricarde, with an air of serious authority,—"you seem to forget that I preside in this district.—You shall not be the bearer of that gold, sir."

"I have taken it, my Lord, and I insist upon its guardianship."

"Guardianship!" exclaimed the Earl, with a contemptuous laugh;—"guardianship of gold by Jones Nevil!—Sir," he added with iron severity, "I presume you are yet ignorant of what my courier from Dublin has just brought me intelligence of—that Jones Nevil is denounced by the House of Parliament, to which he is a dishonour, for scandalous embezzlement of the public money."

The words fell like a thunderbolt on the hitherto audacious offender, who, overwhelmed by the suddenness of the terrible charge he knew to be true, slunk away; while the Earl entering the castle, was soon after in secret conference with Phaidrig.

CHAPTER L.

CLANRICARDE retired to a small chamber in the castle, where he remained alone for some time, before he summoned the piper to his presence. He was aware that Phaidrig's words had taken him by surprise, and urged him to precipitancy. The instantaneous favour shown to the prisoner, and the contemptuous treatment of Nevil, were the result of sudden heat, unusual in him, so long used to command, and which he was anxious to recover, ere he held further communion with an inferior, whose words had stirred his heart so strangely ; for none knew better than the Earl how much authority is fortified by impassiveness—that cold and steely armour of the great. Moreover, a secret passage of his early life was laid bare to him, when least expected, and the maturer years of the staid and circumspect Clanricarde would not derive honour from such glimpses of the past. But yet the handsome face of that young prisoner bore such strong—such touching testimony to the truth of the words he had heard, that nature, at last, triumphed over the colder calculations of the politic nobleman, and determining to hear and judge of all the piper had to tell, Phaidrig, at his summons, was brought before him.

Having dismissed his attendants, the Earl bade the blind man approach, and addressed him in that under-tone which we insensibly adopt in speaking of secret things, however secure our place of conference may be.

"This is a strange thing you tell, Phaidrig-na-pib."

"'Tis as true as 'tis strange, my lord."

"Are you sure?"

"I wish I was as sure of heaven."

"Can you tell me how, and wherefore?"

"Aisy enough, my lord, if you'll listen a bit."

"Willingly—proceed."

"It is now nigh hand forty years, or something undher, that a brave young gentleman used to rove by the woods and wathers of the broad Shannon, and none abler, I hear, than he was, with the gun and the rod ; and plenty o' game fell to his share. His eye was quick for the rise on the river, or the bird on the wing— nothing escaped that quick eye ; for, by all accounts, it was very clear and bright, and whatever it marked, was its own—the bird of the wood—the fish of the sthrame——"

"What need to talk so much of salmon and woodcocks?" said the Earl, impatiently.

"Ah! but, my Lord, there was more than woodcocks in the wood," replied Phaidrig, insidiously.

"Well—proceed."

"And where there's woods and woodcocks, there must be wood-rangers—that stands to rayson."

"Go on."

"And when wood-rangers are for evermore doing nothing but roving up and down a wood, sure they get lonely, and want somebody to keep company with them—and so they get marri'd—and then, of coorse, they have childre, and the childre is as likely to be girls as boys; and, when the girls grows up, sure they will be rovin' through the wood, lookin' for the wild strawberries and the like; and the brave young gentleman I was tellin' of used to meet a wood-ranger's daughter, that, I hear, was as purty a crayture as ever bent grass undher her foot, and a power o' grass she bent, I hear, by the long walks she used to take with that same young gentleman who used to discourse her soft."

"What was her name?" said the Earl.

"O'Brien, my lord—her father came out of Clare—Kitty O'Brien was the girl's name."

"You are right—that *was* her name," said the Earl, identifying himself at once with that "brave young gentleman," with whom Phaidrig so delicately, as well as artfully, began his tale.

"Well, my lord, when neighbours began to spake, poor Kitty was obliged to lave the neighbourhood, and, indeed, father and mother and all went off, and settled up away there towards Galway —and there it was that many a year after I first knew that same Kitty's daughter—as sweet a darlin' as ever was reared. Och! but my own poor heart knew love's torment then—I ax your pardon, my lord, for takin' the liberty; but, as you bid me tell the story, I loved the ground she walked on—an' that's the thruth."

"Then, in short, I suppose this young man is your son?" interrupted the Earl.

"No, my lord," said Phaidrig; "though I loved him full as well, from the very minit I found out he was the son of my own first love, my sweet Molly, for she wasn't called afther her mother, for fear 'twouldn't be lucky, and might run in the family; and, indeed, she had a soft corner in her heart for myself. But what good did that do me?—I was only a poor blind piper, and, though the tendher jewel used to give a willing ear to my planxties, the chink of a snug man's silver made sweeter music for her people; * and what chance had I agin the rich thrader of Galway, and a decent man too—I own it—but not fit for Molly—for Molly, I do believe, as far as her own heart was concerned, would rather have shared the lot of poor Phaidrig-na-pib, blind and all, as he was, than be put beyond want in the warm house of Denis Corkery."

"Then this young man, I suppose, you have known from his birth."

"Oh, no, my lord," said Phaidrig, sadly. "The minit that I knew my darling Molly was lost to me, I kept out of sight of her, or any chance of meeting her, and never went inside Galway if I could help it, and, indeed, never cared for any woman afther; for when the love is once thrampled out of a man's heart, it seldom or never grows up again, and the first love has a grip with it it never lets go; and Molly was always in the way if ever I thought of another girl—she stuck as fast as a weed in an owld piece o' ground.—If my heart was ploughed up ever so often, the new crop of love was sure to be overrun with the Molly-weed—God forgi' me for sayin' weed— sure it's the flower she was, and the brightest and the sweetest—"

"Well, well—to the point—to the point!" cried Clanricarde, impatiently.

"Ah, my lord!" said Phaidrig, tenderly, "don't be angry with me for praising your own child——"

There was a sudden pause. Phaidrig's sensibility told him he had been hurried by his warmth beyond the bounds of delicacy in speaking of a piper's love for the offspring of a peer (though that offspring was even unacknowledged) within the hearing of the father, who sighed in bitterness at this incidental wound inflicted on his pride—for we never feel more keenly than when stabbed through our own sins. The Earl felt the silence to be awkward, and was the first to break it, by asking how Phaidrig knew Ned to be the son of the Galway trader's wife.

"By accident my lord; and I'll remind yourself of the time I found it out. Don't you remember, about six years ago, when there was a remarkable day at the Galway races, when there was a cock-fight, and your lordship's bird, of the Sarsfield breed, won a main?"

"I remember well," said the Earl; "and you were over busy that day, master Piper, in playing a certain tune—"

"And there was a row in the town that night, my lord—"

* Relations.

"I remember that too—and the Mayor knocked down."

"Faix, then, the Mayor, I am thinking, would't have been so angry," said Phaidrig, with a smile, "if he had known it was a dash of the noble blood of Clanricarde that helped him into the gutther that night."

"What, this young man?"

"The same, my lord."

"But there was clinking of cold steel that night in the riot; how came he into an affray of such quality?"

"Faith, then, its himself handled a blade; as nate as a fencin' masther."

"Indeed!—How came a Galway apprentice by that accomplishment?"

"That I don't know; I suppose the blood of De Burgo was sthrong in him, and he made it out a way of his own."

Clanricarde was pleased at this proof of daring accomplishment in his descendant, and was silent for some time.

"Silent when glad."

"And what became of him after?" inquired he. "How, I ask you again, did you discover him to be the son of the Galway trader's wife?"

"This was the way of it, my lord.—The town was no place for the youth that night; so we took him over the river with us."

"Oh! that's the way you escaped. What were the sentinels about?"

"As usual, my lord, they wor as idle as a milestone without a number, and the devil a foot they marked our road, and so we got into the *Cladagh*."

"Humph!—as usual—that stronghold and refuge for any lawless roisterer. But you said, 'we.' Now, who were your companions that night?"

"Oh, some friends o' mine, my lord, that did not like lodging in the town, and preferred the wholesome air of the mountains of Iar Connaught."

"I thought as much; take care, Phaidrig-na-pib, you don't come under my notice sometime or other in a way I cannot overlook."

"Oh, you know, minsthrels are held sacred, my lord," replied Phaidrig, laughing.

"Not if they play the 'blackbird' too often. Have a care. Remember the fable of the trumpeter, who when taken prisoner, asked for mercy, because the did not strike with the sword, but only blew a harmless instrument; whereupon the conqueror replied, that the trumpeter did more mischief than any armed man, as he, though he did not fight himself, inspired hundreds to fight; and there lies the mischief."

"Thrue enough, my lord," said Phaidrig boldly, and brightening up, "and sure there must be a deep love lying for evermore in the human heart for such sthrains as can inspire to bowld deeds, for there never was one of the mischievous songs or tunes, as you call them, that ever was lost. They live—ay, and live even in the memory of those who hate them; they are thransmitted through friend and foe from generation to generation; and though the hands and hearts lie cold and forgotten of those the minsthrel inspired, *his* words and *his* strains are imperishable as long as there is man's courage or woman's love left in the world."

"Hillo, Hillo, Phaidrig!" exclaimed the Earl, good humouredly, "you are running 'breast high' now, but I must call you to a check; try back, man, and tell me what I have asked twice before. How did you find out this youth was the son of the Galway trader's wife? The third time is the charm, and now I hope you will answer me?"

"Sure I was answering you, my lord, only that you—"

"There you go again—running to fault—steady, steady! How did you find him out? answer short."

"He sent into the town, my lord, from the fisherman's hut in the Cladagh, to his father's, and when I heerd his name, I knew he was the child of darling Molly, and my heart warmed to him as much a'most as if he was my own son—for, indeed, it was a chance I wasn't his father, myself."

"And what has he been doing ever since?"

"Faith, every thing that was dashing, and daring, and bowld, and like a gentleman—and won a lady's heart into the bargain—kind kith and kin for him, faith; the De Burgos wor all divils among the girls, as your lordship knows betther than me."

"A lady's heart?" said Clanricarde, somewhat curiously, with a strong emphasis on "lady."

"Ay, faith as rale a lady as ever stood in satin. Faix, its a quare story, my lord, and something long, but I will cut it as short as I can for you, and sthrive to insense* you upon it."

He then gave a brief history of Ned's adventures to the Earl, who listened with intense pleasure to the numerous traits of gentle blood and noble daring on the part of his grandson, in-

---

* To give the sense of; to inform.

heriting so strongly the mettle of the De Burgo race, notwithstanding the plebeian contact of poor old Corkery, that the Earl
almost wished he could declare him for his own.   Phaidrig, in
the course of his history, wisely dwelt chiefly on Ned's achievements at sea against the Spaniards, and ingeniously avoided as
much as possible such disclosures as would excite the political
prejudices of the Earl.   Jacobite affairs were glanced at as little
as might be, and, finally, he assured his lordship that it was in the
endeavour to leave Ireland, and never again return to disturb the
Hanoverian possession thereof, that they had been pursued and
taken ; and the stirring account Phaidrig gave of young Nevil's
insult to Ellen, and the terrible retribution with which it was
visited, reconciled Clanricarde much towards the prisoner.

"The lady's father is here, too, you said?" inquired Clanricarde.

" He is my lord."

" But as yet you have not told me his name."

" Then, indeed, my lord, if you'll be led by me, I think it would
be just as well maybe you wouldn't ask his name at all—for,
maybe, you wouldn't like to hear it, seeing that in consideration
of the happiness of the young birds you wouldn't hurt the ould
one ; and there's no knowing what names might be objectionable
to your lordship's ear, as governor of these parts—and so, for
shortness, we'll call him ' the Captain.' "

Clanricarde was silent for a while, and then assented to Phaidrig's suggestion ; trusting the piper's judgment rather than his
own desire in the matter, and guessing that the name was one of
which he had better remain in ignorance, if he wished to pursue
his benign intentions towards the fugitives.

Clanricarde was right in thus trusting to Phaidrig's judgment, which, in this case, as in most others, was sagacious.   He
knew that Lynch's person was unknown to the Earl, though of
his name and the heavy denouncements against it he could not
be ignorant ; and he, therefore, threw out the hint to the Governor of the western district that to " keep never minding," as
Paddy says, was the safest course, or, in more poetic parlance,
that " where ignorance was bliss, 'twas folly to be wise."

Anxious as the Earl was now to get the entire party safe out of
the country, under the assurance that they would never return—
thus at once insuring preservation to those in whom he became
so unexpectedly interested, and accomplishing, without blood-
shed, a beneficial move for the Crown, under whose authority he
acted ; nevertheless, had the too-celebrated name of " Lynch "
reached his ear, he dared not have disregarded the numerous pro-
clamations " the Captain " had provoked, and must have given

up the father-in-law elect of his own grandson. Making use of the piper's hint, therefore, and taking advantage of his present ignorance, his object was to get such combustible materials out of his hands as soon as possible, lest he might burn his fingers; for, though Clanricarde's general measures were sufficiently stern to stamp him a staunch upholder of the government, yet the times were such that a wise and merciful inaction might be construed into treasonable activity.

Full of these thoughts, the Earl desired Phaidrig to hasten to the strong room, and tell its inmates to be of good cheer, for that he himself would convey them from their present durance to his own castle, where they might rely that no violence should be offered. "But, a word with you before you part," said the Earl. "Is the secret of the mother's birth known to her son?"

"No, my lord, I never breathed it to mortal till now—nor would not, only for the necessity."

"Well, you may tell him," replied Clanricarde. "I will be glad to acknowledge so gallant a fellow."

Gladly Phaidrig hurried on the welcome message—blithely he restored them to hope, though the secret of this sudden change in their fortunes was not yet revealed; and while he was yet engaged in dispelling from Ellen's mind the terror which the recent scene had inspired, a summons from the Earl to attend him at once to his boat reached the strong room. The spiral stair of the tower was re-trodden with lighter footsteps than it had been ascended; in a few minutes they were on board the boat which had awakened their well-founded fears, and the same sails that had intercepted their flight, and thrown them into the hands of their enemies, were soon wafting them to a haven of safety.

Phaidrig having whispered Ned that he wished a few words with him, they were stowed away together in the bows of the boat, while Finch, at the Earl's desire, moved astern, and gave a "full and true account" of the manner in which the foreign gold came into his possession—that same gold which seemed destined not to reach the right owner, but which was never in such imminent peril as when it got into the hands of Mr. Nevil, whence it had been so timely rescued. Ellen sat beside her father, retired from the rest, and felt, in the temporary quiet of their smooth sail, a relief to the excited feelings which the rapid and startling succession of events had that day so harrowed up. Clanricarde, from time to time, cast a glance towards her charming face, touched by its beautiful expression, and felt that his descendant had inherited not only the daring of the De Burgo, but their appreciation of female loveliness, yet inherent in that gallant race, as the halls of Portumna can bear witness to this hour, in the person of their noble mistress. From Ellen his eye would wander to Ned, whose glance he met once or twice in counter-gaze, as he seemed to listen intently to the discourse Phaidrig was pouring into his ear. The earl felt it was the secret of his half-noble ancestry the piper was imparting, and that nameless intelli-gence of eye, enkindled by sympathy, passed between them, and seemed already to make them known to each other.

The boat, meanwhile, was gliding swiftly to the western shore of the Lough, on reaching which, Clanricarde was one of the first to land, and when Ellen was about to step ashore, the Earl offered her his hand.

"Permit me, madam," he said in the blandest manner. "You have already experienced so much rudeness to-day, that I would wish to make you believe we are not all savages here."

"Thanks, my lord," said Ellen, as she accepted the nobleman's courtesy with becoming grace, and stept ashore.

"And now, gentle lady," he continued in a lower tone, and withdrawing her from the bank, "at once to set your heart at rest, let me assure you no harm shall fall upon your friends."

"Oh! my lord," exclaimed Ellen, clasping his hand between both of hers, and looking up into his face with the heavenly gleam of gratitude, making her sweet eyes more lovely, "I will for ever bless your name for this!"

"Enough, fair lady, enough—pray take my arm; we have a walk before us to the castle."

"My lord," said Ellen, looking at her humble attire, and speaking with a gracefulness of action that contrasted strongly with her outward seeming; "I am in strange costume to have a nobleman for my *cavalier*."

"No matter," replied he; "the walk is through my own woodlands; we shall have no impertinent lookers-on to make remarks."

As they proceeded he entered into conversation with his com-panion, whom he found so accomplished in this respect, that he entertained a high opinion of her acquirements and good sense before their walk was over; and he was inclined to reckon her one of the most charming girls he had ever met ere they had reached the castle, to whose hospitable halls he bade her welcome as he led her through its massive portal.

CHAPTER LI.

THE revelations Phaidrig had made were calculated to stir the various parties concerned in various ways. Clanricarde, it has been seen, was impressed with feelings of tenderness towards our hero, and he, in his turn, was the sport of contending emotions. The first feeling on Ned's part was that of pleasure at having a dash of noble blood in his veins. This might be expected, from the besetting weakness of his nature; but afterwards came the consideration of that awkward "bar-sinister;"—well, that was an accident he could not help; and the blood of De Burgo was in him, beyond denial, and on *his* birth, at least, there was no blot. But then came the consideration of what Lynch might think of this, jealous of honour as Edward knew him to be. With such thoughts was he busy while approaching the castle; and as Lynch and Phaidrig kept close together, engaged in earnest conversation, Ned had no doubt it related to *his* newly-discovered relationship. In this he was not mistaken; but Lynch had no opportunity as yet to speak to him on the subject, in the midst of the bustle which the arrival of this unexpected party produced The Earl, determined to show them every hospitality his castle could afford, set about furnishing them with more suitable attire than at present they wore, and wardrobe and *armoire* were put in requisition to furnish forth fitting apparel; and it was strange to observe the usually stern Clanricarde interesting himself in the equipment of Ned, whom he endeavoured to fit to the best advantage, and was manifestly pleased to see what a good figure the fellow made in the habit of a gentleman.

On holding a private conference, much as he was prepared to like him, he found him surpassing his expectations. Ned's contact with the world had rubbed down whatever shyness he might once have laboured under, and pushing his own way in it had given him a quiet confidence. And if some scenes in his life had not tended towards refinement, love had supplied the deficiency, and inspired him with the power to be acceptable in gentle company.

The Earl spoke with pleasure of his approaching union with Ellen, and went so far as to suggest their remaining in Ireland, where. under his protection, they might be certain of security; but Edward pointed out the impossibility of Ellen's sepration from her father. and advanced so many other good reasons for his going to Spain, that the noble Earl was satisfied of its being the wisest course, and yielded his wishes to his conviction. Being a man of resolve, when once this was determined upon, he thought it prudent no time should be lost in their abandoning the country, and set about ordering measures for an early movement the next morning.

While the Earl was thus engaged, our hero was summoned by Phaidrig to a conference with " the Captain ;" and Ned had misgivings it would not be as pleasant as the one just concluded.

On coming before Lynch, Ned perceived his brow was clouded, and endeavoured to conciliate him by gentleness of manner; saying, he supposed he was aware of the strange history circumstances had brought to light, and feared he was displeased.

"I had rather it were otherwise," said Lynch. "I would prefer a pure descent from the Galway trader than a stained one from a lord. But there is something displeases me still more."

" May I ask it, sir ?"—though Ned guessed what was coming.

"You have been guilty of deception. You have assumed a name to which you are not entitled."

Ned hung down his head and coloured to the forehead; this error, into which an early weakness betrayed him, had often placed him in awkward predicaments, and caused him some qualms of conscience; but circumstances had so involved him in the temptation to continue the deceit, that he never had courage to declare the truth; but now it seemed the hour was come when his folly was to recoil upon him with serious consequences.

" Though there is a stain in your descent, I would not object to you for that—that was not your own act; but assuming an honourable name to pass yourself off for something you were not, is a false pretence, not punishable by law, but falling under the condemnation of all honourable minds."

Ned made a passionate disclaimer of all dishonourable intentions, spoke of it as a youthful folly which circumstances tended to confirm, and made an appeal to Lynch's ear, if Corkery was not a very horrid name, and one that might almost excuse his fault. This Lynch would not admit, and told Ned he had done quite enough of gallant things to make any name respected.

" Could I have dared to lift my eyes to your daughter, sir, under such a shabby name?"

" Using a false name was more shabby—and that's what vexes me Ned. You. a dashing, noble-spirited fellow, to have been guilty of a trick which belongs to swindlers and pick-pockets!"

"Oh, sir," exclaimed Ned, writhing under the words—"do not use so harsh an expression—and—pray do not think it is in the spirit of retort, I remind you of something which may palliate my offence in your eyes.   Remember, my dear sir, that I first knew you as Count Nellinski."

"I had the authority of my Prince for the title, which was used only in political agencies in the service of my king, when its adoption might be useful to him, not to me; while you, without any aim but the assumption of a title that tickled your ears, passed yourself off under a false one.   Nellin-ski is but a variation of my own name (not that I hold even *that* to be strictly right), while Fitzgerald was rather a bold flight from Corkery."

"The very baseness and hateful sound of that name is my best excuse," said Ned.   "Now, sir, be candid; would you like your daughter to be called Corkery?"

"I would rather she were called the name she had a right to, than go, about, like a daw, decked in feathers not her own —and such would be her opinion, I am sure.—Ellen will be angry at this."

"Oh, sir, if you and she knew how often this has been a pain to me, how frequently I wished to confess all about it, but shrank with a false shame from the avowal, you would rather pity than blame me.   I hope I can persuade her to think no worse of me for it—and you, too, sir."

"Corkery," said Lynch, "a woman will forgive much in the man she loves; and though Fitzgerald is a prettier name than Corkery," and Lynch laid much stress on the name each time— "I say, though Corkery——"

"Oh, that hateful name!" exclaimed Ned in disgust, "must I be called that name?—what shall I do when I meet those who knew me under another?"

"Meet them with a prouder front, Ned; for then there will be no deceit about you.   But come," he added feelingly, for our hero's sense of shame touched him, "Ellen will forgive you, as I forgive you, Ned, for the noble points in your character and conduct which have endeared you to both of us—but remem-ber, my dear fellow, you have no right to take another man's name—it is doubly false—it is wronging him if you do it dis-honour, and it may be putting on inferior mettle the stamp that will make it pass current upon the world."

"You are right, sir," said Edward; "and if to acknowledge

and feel sorrow for a fault is, as I have heard, partly atoning for it, mine is not as heavy as it was; and, in truth, I feel happier for this explanation, though I confess I *do* hate the name I must bear."

"Give me your hand—you have a frank spirit; and now that you are willing to do the right thing, I will try to help you to a pleasanter name."

"How, sir?" said Ned, his eyes sparkling with pleasure.

"In marriage sometimes it is stipulated that a man takes the name of his wife—suppose I make that a condition in your wedding Ellen?"

Ned could scarcely speak; but wrung Lynch's hand with fervour, and endeavoured to say something of the honour of being allowed to take the name.

"Ned, what that is mine would I not give you when I have given you my Ellen! She is to be yours, with my blessing. Heaven knows how long I may be in this world—the laws may demand *me*, though Clanricarde will protect *you*, without doubt. Take, then, the name and arms of our ancient family; you will do honour to both?"

While Ned was expressing hope that the favour of the Earl would be extended beyond *him*, their conversation was interrupted by a summons to the hall, where the board was spread in all the proverbial amplitude of Galway hospitality, and afterwards the wine-cup circled freely. The potations of those times were wont to be deeper than ours, whose modern code of after-dinner laws names half an hour as the measure of vinous indulgence after the ladies have retired; and, it is likely, the rounds of the claret-flask were not limited to so stinted a period in the hall of Portumna that day; but there was no excess, notwithstanding. In a society so much higher than he was used to, Finch forbore an indulgence to which he would have yielded at an humbler board, and Ned, hearing the notes of a harpsichord, and Ellen's voice, when the door was occasionally opened, longed to be of *that* party; so he and his friend paired off to the ladies, and left the Earl and Lynch together.

For this Clanricarde was not sorry; he rather wished a few words in confidence with "the Captain;" and there is much that, in the morning coldness of your private closet would be harsh and difficult to treat, which the genial influence of the hearth and the wine cup render smooth and easy. So felt the Earl, as pushing the bottle to his guest he said—

"I know you will excuse something I am going to say to you, Captain. I am here, you know, in a high trust; and though my authority gives me great latitude in the exercise of enforcing or relaxing the laws, yet if, in the latter case, I stretch a point, I wish to satisfy my conscience that I do no wrong to my King. Now, *Captain,* as that is the only name I am to know you by (though the Earl's smile suggested the idea that he guessed a little more), will you promise me, on your honour, that when you leave Ireland *this time*"—and he laid some emphasis on the words—" will you promise, I say, never to return to it again. and to abstain from disturbing its peace ? and then my conscience will be at rest respecting my duty to his Majesty."

"For the sake of those who are dear to us both, my lord, I do promise."

" Captain, your hand : I am satisfied; and, believe me, 'tis better for yourself, as the cause of 'a certain person' is hopeless. But I will say no more—let us join the ladies in the drawing-room, and exchange the acerbity of politics for the sweetness of music."

CHAPTER LII.

WHILE the evening was pleasurably spent in the castle, arrangements had been looked to for the work of the morning. A boat had been forwarded overnight, by the Earl's order, to Killaloe, where it might be removed overland to the foot of the falls, and be in readiness for the voyagers after they should traverse the lake. That work had been done, the boat had been relaunched below the mighty roar and rush of Derg's wide waters, where the variable Shannon, again confined to its river form, pursues its rapid course to Limerick and the sea; and her crew, after enjoying a hearty meal, were reclining on the river's bank, smoking and telling stories, when the report of a gun above the falls attracted their attention. Springing to their feet, they hurried up the slopes, and saw the Earl's yacht shortening sail, and throwing her grappling ashore. The Earl himself was of the party that landed; and among the removals made from the sailing craft to the barge below the falls, were some small strongly-hooped barrels of unusual weight. When these were safely bestowed, the Earl handed to the boat a young lady, who seemed to engross his particular attention, and the rest of the party following, the barge was pushed off, and the rapid course of the river, under the vigorous pulling of four stout rowers, soon bore them to Limerick.

Clanricarde, wishing to avoid the publicity which the lodging at an inn involves, led the party to the house of a private citizen, where they were received with welcome. Lynch and his daughter remained with the Earl, within doors, but Ned and Finch at once set out to find the quickest and most desirable means of shipment. It has been already mentioned that the Irish coast then swarmed with King's cruisers; therefore, to attempt a passage to France in a small craft (unless of such sailing quality as was not to be obtained by chance) would have been madness; so a passage in any merchantman bound to an English port was what they sought whence the smuggling traffic with which they were conversan would help them to a cast across the channel; and, by good luck a brig for London was to sail the following day. No time was lost in striking a bargain, and Finch and Ned returned to their quarters, rejoiced in having made so speedy an arrangement.

Clanricarde and "the Captain," during their sail that day had much converse, and the Earl was won upon by Lynch, whose quiet, though deep devotion to the cause of his country, found respect in the bosom of one whose ancestors were often banded in the national cause   Some had resisted the tyranny of Strafford; one of the noble maidens of the house had intermarried with Sarsfield; and some gallant scions had fallen on foreign battlefields opposed to the interests which the present Earl supported, though he was unwilling to support them in the unwise and sanguinary spirit of the time. He was glad to have some parting words with the soldier who was about to expatriate himself for ever, and it is more than probable, that his brief intercourse of two days with Lynch, had a mutual influence on both for good: —on the powerful peer to direct his attention to the abatement of the severities of government, and the seeking to procure a more wise and liberal legislation; and on Lynch, in convincing him how utterly hopeless was the cause of the house of Stuart.

On the following morning, the bell of St. Munchin's warned our voyagers it was time to embark. The courteous Clanricarde, to secure their safety, bore them company to the brig, whose sails were already unfurled, and the anchor being weighed.   The Earl took Ned aside, and after some brief, but affectionate words, concluded by saying, that as there was a long journey before him ere he should reach his uncle in Spain, he wished to bestow on him a token of his regard, which might be useful to him on the road, and placed in his hands a pocket-book containing a bill on a London merchant for five hundred pounds.   Then, addressing himself to Ellen, he begged her acceptance of a small gift, which he hoped she would wear on the day of her marriage, and presented her with a Maltese cross set in diamonds.

"Phaidrig," he said, "has refused my offer of becoming the piper of Portumna Castle; he will follow you, I find."

"And the noble Clanricarde won't blame me for that same," said Phaidrig, "though I thank his lordly generosity."

"No, Phaidrig; but, remember, the gate of Portumna is always open to you."

"And never was shut yet to the minstrel," said the piper.

"To you it is open on higher grounds than that of your craft, Phaidrig; for your fidelity and affection, and the service you rendered in saving a life that is dear to me; and though you refused my offer of a home, you must not refuse this,"—and he placed a purse, with no inconsiderable sum of gold, in the piper's hand.— not   a word of refusal, Phaidrig; if you will not use it in the shape of coin, the gold will serve for a handsome mounting to your pipes."

The "heave-o" of the sailors, and the measured stroke of the windlass, had ceased; the anchor was up, and the brig began to drop down the river. The time to part was come; short and few, but affectionate, were the words of farewell. The Earl went over the side into his boat, the sails of the brig were sheeted home, and the bent to the favouring breeze on her seaward course.

The voyage was prosperous, but afforded nothing of incident worth relating; therefore, suffice it to say, that in a few days a safe landing was effected in London. A quiet lodging was soon secured for Lynch, Ellen, and Ned; Finch saying he would be off to his old quarters with his good-hearted landlady, "Mother Banks," as he always called her, and suggested that Phaidrig should join him, and enliven, for the few days they might remain, the tavern of the kind widow. This arrangement was thought excellent; and Finch and the piper, (and the faithful *Turlough* into the bargain,) set off directly. It was between "day and dark" when they reached the snug house of call, so that it was no difficult matter to slip in unperceived. Placing Phaidrig in the room of general reception, Finch told him to have his pipes in readiness, and when he should give him a certain signal, to commence playing.

"We'll surprise the widow," said Finch

"Well and good," answered Phaidrig.

Finch then went into the back parlour, where Mother Banks had just lit a candle, and much was the open-hearted landlady rejoiced to see him. They talked for some time about the thousand and one things that had happened since they had last met; and in the midst of their alternate question and answer, Finch gave the signal agreed upon between him and the piper, who opened his chanter directly, and lilted one of his favourite airs. The moment the widow heard the first sound of the pipes, she uttered a hurried and almost breathless exclamation of pleasure; and Finch, laying hold of her hand, felt her trembling violently, while she said, "Poor fellow—poor dear fellow—he's come back;" and her eyes filled with tears. Finch saw, in an instant, that, as he suspected, the widow had a "sneaking kindness" for Phaidrig; so, hastening into the outer room, he led in the piper, to whom he gave a hint, by the way, to give the widow a hearty kiss for a welcome. He executed Finch's order in excellent style, and the widow seemed nothing loth for the first salute; but when Phaidrig kept "continually going on," Mrs. Banks, half suffocated, contrived to struggle out of his arms, and, when she recovered her breath, said,

" Well, Master Faydrig, for a dark man, it is wonderful how smart you are."

" Sure, my darlin'!" says Phaidrig, " isn't it an owld saying that we can find the way to our mouths in the dark?"

" Not to other people's mouths," said Mrs. Banks, coquettishly.

" You thought so before," said Phaidrig; " but now you know the differ."

" Well, well, but you Irish fellows have an answer for every-thing. I'm sure, Master Faydrig, I never thought you were such a rantipole till now. Dear! but my cap is tossed, and my han'kecher ruffled;" and, as she made these complaints, she was fidgetting about smoothing her feathers, and declaring Captain Finch was " just all as bad for laughing so."

" Why, what harm, mother," said Finch. " There's another old saying, you know, that ' seeing is believing, but——' "

" Hold your tongue," said Mother Banks, " I know you're a going to say impudence, so ha' done. I'll contrive to stop your mouth,—I will. And as Master Phaydrig was talking of finding the way there, the proverb shall be fulfilled in the true meaning, by my serving up to you as nice a veal pasty as ever knife and fork was set in."

" And a bottle of the good old stuff, mother, if there is any left."

" A nice little corner in the bin yet, Captain."

" Right, mother!—' Fulfil and fill full' 's the word for old say-ings and old wine."

Mother Banks bustled off; and the larder, and the cellar, and the kitchen, were visited in her kindliest spirit; and there was a merry supper-party of three in the little back parlour that night. They sat up late, and had much talk afterwards; and, as she had asked many questions of Finch about his doings during his absence, he inquired of her how affairs were moving in London in the mean time. She told him they went on but sadly; that those in power, and all who favoured them, had got so " hoity toity" of late, that no " free-hearted" gentleman dared say a word—they must be all as mute as mice now; and, since they had fears no longer from the north, their high-handed proceedings were past all patience. And then the cruel hangings, and quarterings, and gibbetings, to say nothing of all the lords they were beheading on Tower-hill—oh, 'twas fearful!—London was no more the merry place it was; it was turned quite into a slaughter-house, and, indeed, sometimes she wished herself out of it. Finch ventured to conjecture that, nevertheless, her house went on as well as ever. She said it was not much damaged in the main; but somehow the people didn't seem as merry as they used to be, and she had not half the pleasure in the trade she used to have. Most of their conversation was of a "sad-coloured" character; and the next day Finch told Phaidrig he ought to help to gladden the widow's heart with his good humour, and take up his quarters in the house at once as her husband. Phaidrig admitted the widow was a "nice woman entirely," and that no man she would take could do better than have her. Finch expressed his belief the widow would not say nay to him: whereupon Phaidrig started a fresh objection—"he wouldn't lave the masther." Lynch he was determined to follow for the future. In this state of affairs Finch watched his opportunities whenever they offered, to sound the widow as to how her mind lay towards matrimony, and was not long in bringing her to own that the piper was not objectionable. Phaidrig and she were quick in understanding each other, and the question of the piper leaving Lynch, or the widow quitting England, alone remained to be settled. Phaidrig argued that as she complained of London becoming so sad, and as France was a fine frisky place, the best thing she could do was to go there with him.

"But sure I can't speak French," said the widow.

"Arrah, but can't I spake Irish?" said Phaidrig.

"But what good would that do?" said the widow; "they can't understand either English or Irish."

"Well, sure," said Phaidrig, "there would be no disgrace in our not understhanding French; and as they only spake one language which *we* don't understand, and as we, between us, can spake two that they don't understhand, the balance would be in our favour; doesn't that stand to rayson?"

The widow laughed at Phaidrig's whimsical way of settling that difficulty, and after some few days further pressing on his part, she said "she would think of it." Now, as the "woman who deliberates is lost," it may be conjectured how the matter terminated. It must be acknowledged, however, that the landlady's sympathies were unfairly influenced by Phaidrig reminding her what "beautiful brandy" there was in France.

Of the principal personages of our story we say nothing during their sojourn in London; for no incident worth recording occurred. They lived as quietly as possible, and with as much of secrecy as would not arouse suspicion where they lodged. They frequented no public places, therefore the great city was at once dull as well as dangerous; for danger there certainly was to those who had been so actively engaged in the Pretender's cause, as long as they remained in the British dominions. It was with rejoicing, therefore, they beheld Finch, with a smile on his face, pay them a visit one evening to tell them to be in readiness. He, ever since their arrival, had been casting about in his old haunts by the river, to find out when and how a safe run might be made across the channel, and, at length, heard of a promising venture.

"To-morrow night," said Finch.

"To-morrow night" was echoed in the heart of each anxious listener; "to-morrow night" haunted their dreams; to their feverish impatience the intervening time seemed of unusual duration, but the leaden-footed hours at length brought the appointed moment. That night they were on the waters.

CHAPTER LIII.

FIVE days afterwards the welcome towers and spires of Paris rose on the view of a merry travelling party, who were posting rapidly towards that cheerful capital by the northern road. That party consisted of our friends, who had safely passed the perils of the channel.

The earliest business of the next day was a visit to the Irish College, for, by one of the fathers of that establishment, and within its chapel, did Lynch desire his daughter should be married. He and Ned went together, while Ellen drove to her friend, Madame de Jumillac, to request her presence at the wedding. Much was Madame rejoiced at the sight of her dear young friend, who, after some maiden hesitation, told her what was going to happen. Madame wondered any young lady would be married in such a quiet fashion—a wedding ought to be a gay and handsome affair. Ellen said her father disliked parade, and, as it was an object to her future husband to reach Spain with all speed, it was determined she should be married to-morrow. Madame hoped the "destiny" was a "brilliant" one, worthy one so charming, so admired. Ellen silenced the raptures of her friend by giving a brief sketch of the course of events which led to the forthcoming re-ult, and Madame had the satisfaction of knowing that the match, though not brilliant, was, at least, romantic—the next best thing to the notions of a French woman.

"And now, my love," said Madame, "you need not be afraid of your husband being put into the Bastile, and yourself being run away with; that wicked marshal—he is dead."

"Heaven forgive him his sins!" said Ellen, with unaffected piety.

"Amen, my love. France has lost her greatest general, and decorum her greatest enemy; for, it must be confessed, his vices were fully equal to his military glory. Nevertheless, France may well mourn the loss of the gallant Count de Saxe."

Ellen made inquiry after the unfortunate Prince, whose doings. Madame assured her, were not much calculated to increase his popularity in Paris; where, after the first *furor* of his reception, as a hero of romance, his frivolity and dissipation were debasing him into a person of *mauvais ton*. While thus the day wore away between Ellen and her friend, her father and her lover were enjoying an unlooked for pleasure at the Irish College. Judge of their surprise on finding Father Flaherty safe and sound after a marvellous escape out of Ireland. He had been hiding with some fishermen (the mountain retreats having been desperately hunted up), and was wont to go to sea with them. One night a heavy gale drove them off the coast; and, in the morning, they descried a vessel of war under French colours. So providential a means of escape was eagerly seized. The fishermen made signals of distress, to attract the notice of the ship, which bore down, and took the *padre* on board. Father Flaherty, of course, was the person whose offices were sought for the next morning, and maybe the good father wasn't delighted.

"Faith, luck's on your side, Ned; little I thought when I was nursing you in Bruges, poor boy, that you'd ever see the darling girl again. Oh, indeed, be thankful, night and morning, my dear child, for all the blessings Providence has showered on you, in preserving you through so many dangers, and giving you such an angel for a wife at last!"

Brightly dawned the marriage morning. Simply arrayed in white, with no ornament but the diamond cross of Cianricarde, Ellen, leaning on her friend, Madame de Jumillac, and followed by her father, approached the altar in the little chapel of the Irish College, where Ned, with Finch for his bridesman, awaited her. Phaidrig, of course, was there, and Mrs. Banks *would not* be absent. The ceremony was commenced by the kind-hearted Father Flaherty; and, as Lynch gave the bride away, there was an eloquent appeal in his thoughtful eye, which spoke thus to Ned:—"I give you all that is dear to me in this world; be as fond and gentle a protector to her as I have been;" and in the open and manly countenance of Ned there beamed an assurance which set the father's heart at rest. Ellen and Ned were made one; he clasped her to his heart his wedded wife, and in that blissful consciousness he felt all the trials and perils of his life were a million times overpaid. The priest spread his hands over them in benediction, and then all knelt in prayer to ask Heaven's blessing on the married couple. While others bowed their heads within their hands, the sightless orbs of Phaidrig were raised to heaven, while his handsome features bore an expression of profound devotion, as his lips moved silently in breathing a heart-felt supplication to his God for blessings on his master's daughter and the son of his darling Molly.

As the wedding party left the chapel, they were surprised to see Madame de Jumillac's carriage waiting in the court (for they had driven there in hired coaches). "My love," she said, as she kissed Ellen, " you and your husband must use my carriage while you remain in Paris. My servants know where to drive you to. I have prepared a little surprise for you which I know will be pleasing ;—there, ask no questions—submit to be taken where I have ordered."

Madame was obeyed ; the carriage drove rapidly away and left the city some miles behind. For a while Ellen did not know whither they were going ; but some points in a pretty little road into which they turned at last, recalled to mind the route by which she and her father had escaped from Paris two years before, and ere long the pretty house of poor Adrienne peeped above the hedges, and the carriage stopped at the little wicket through which the sweet smile of the benevolent actress had greeted her. There was a sober pleasure in coming to this spot, and Ellen felt how charming an attention her friend had bestowed in procuring for her this surprise. Some delightful days were spent in this pretty, quiet spot; and as happy Ned and his sweet wife paced the smooth turf of the little parterre, and paused betimes at the resting-place of Ellen's benefactress, they hoped her spirit had found peace, and might then be conscious of their happiness, rejoicing even in the beatitude of eternity over the redeeming good of her faulty, fleeting life.

While Ned and Ellen were thus enjoying the first of their honey-moon. Lynch had reported himself at the War Office, and became again attached to the Irish Brigade, but not on active duty. In consideration of his services and increasing years, he was appointed to a post which made Paris his head-quarters ; and the piper had the satisfaction of fulfilling his desire to be "near the masther," consistently with his interest, as he and his wife (for he married the comely widow) set up a *cabaret* in one of the *fauxbourgs*, under the sign of "The Blackbird," and it became the resort of " the boys of the brigade," and every Irishman who happened to be in Paris, and Phaidrig and his rib did right well

But it was requisite that Ned should hasten to Spain, and Lynch determined to bear the young couple company as far south as *Bordeaux*. Finch, too, started with them; and, as they went over precisely the same ground that Ellen and her father travelled in their flight from Paris, they could not help remarking under what different feelings they prosecuted their journey now.

On approaching *Blois*, a remarkable incident occurred. The report of artillery firing salutes betokened the celebration of some ceremony; and on reaching the town they heard the funeral of Marshal Saxe was approaching. He whose presence they so dreaded at that very spot two years ago was now no more;—he sought them living—they met him dead.

He had lain in state at the Chateau de Chambord, with all honours, during which time guard was mounted with as much regularity as though he lived. But the stands of arms which adorned his halls were broken, and his officers put on mourning. Salvos of artillery were fired every half-hour, and when the time arrived to remove his body to the place of sepulture, it was done by order of the king, with all the pomp that funeral rites could embody.

This was contrary to Saxe's own order. His death was worthy of a better spent life, and his dying words were indicative of a noble spirit. "Let my funeral be private," he said; "place my body in quick lime, that nothing may remain of me in this world but my memory amongst my friends."

The procession had already entered the town, whose streets and windows were thronged with sorrowing spectators; the plaintive wail of the music, the dull roll of the muffled drum, the drooping banners, the trailing pikes of his own regiment of Hulans, who guarded his bier, his favourite war-horse, with empty saddle, following, all tended to impress the mind with sadness. Even Lynch, in that hour, forgot his private wrong; the feelings of the soldier prevailed, and as the plumed hearse passed by, he lifted his hat respectfully from his head in honour of the gallant chief who had so often led him to victory.

When the procession had cleared the town, our travellers proceeded on their journey, and Lynch, at Bordeaux, took a tender adieu of Ellen, who promised to visit him at Paris in the following spring. Ned and his wife, in all the glow of honeymoon happiness, passed the Pyrenees, whose beauties enchanted them, and entered Spain. Finch bore them company all the way, for, as luck would have it, his mission led him to the very place where old Don Jerome resided. They reached the end of their journey in safety, and Ned's uncle was rejoiced to see him, and welcomed, with open arms, his lovely wife, to whose gentle care he owed many an after comfort.—The old Don Jerome was now very rich, for another ship of his had reached Spain, and he was enabled to have a very handsome house and establishment. It was one of those heavy portalled, small-windowed houses peculiar to the country, with projecting, shadow-casting roof, and a long, stretching, open, arcade-like gallery, where one might walk at noon protected from the heat. This connected the dwelling with a sort of airy summer-house, which stood in the garden, and commanded a view of the sea; and often in after-times Ned and Ellen could watch, from its height, a certain little boy who somehow or other had liberty to play about the place, and who very often made an umbrella of Don Jerome's *sombrero,* to the old man's great delight; and it must be confessed, Ned and Nelly used to enjoy the infantine capers of this tiny personage; the little fellow, when he could prattle, said, "he would like another little child to play with him," and his indulgent parents contrived to gratify the affectionate wish.

Finch executed his trust like a man of honour; and as the widow of the shipwrecked Captain had a very pretty daughter, Finch was rewarded with her hand and heart, and a handsome dowry; and, finally, inherited all the treasures he had preserved to the family of his friend.

And now what else is to be said?—Oh—poor old Denis Corkery, I almost forgot him. He could never be prevailed upon to leave Ireland. He said he would die as he had lived amongst his old friends in Galway—and so he did. And now what more?—Why, that a great many more little people were running about Ned's garden, and that he and the exquisite Nelly lived long and prosperously, a blessing to each other, and beloved by all who knew them; that visits to Paris were occasionally made, and that the faithful Phaidrig often had the pleasure of dandling in his arms the children of his " darling Miss Nelly."

LONDON: W. H. SMITH AND SON, PRINTERS, 186, STRAND.

25—5—69.